ACCLAIM FOR KEL

"I found I couldn't turn the pages fast enough in Kelly Irvin's latest novel, *Trust Me*. I promised myself just one more page and I'd stop reading for the night . . . just one more . . . just one more. At times I could barely breathe. What a fabulous story! I loved it!"

—CARRIE STUART PARKS, AWARD-WINNING AUTHOR
OF *RELATIVE JUSTICE* AND *WOMAN IN SHADOW*

"*Trust Me* is an apt title for Irvin's new suspense novel. Kelly Irvin is a master at spinning a complex story web with surprising twists and relatable characters. Highly recommended!"

—COLLEEN COBLE, *USA TODAY* BESTSELLING AUTHOR OF
A STRANGER'S GAME AND THE PELICAN HARBOR SERIES

"Though it includes a slow-burning romance and gripping details of chaotic explosions, the novel is, at its core, a heartwarming exploration of faith and friendship."

—BOOKPAGE ON *HER EVERY MOVE*

"Gripping suspense novel . . . Well-paced plot . . . Irvin consistently entertains."

—*PUBLISHERS WEEKLY* ON *HER EVERY MOVE*

"*Her Every Move* is Kelly Irvin at her best with a gripping story that will have you on the edge of your seat until 'The End.'"

—PATRICIA BRADLEY, AUTHOR OF THE LOGAN
POINT SERIES, MEMPHIS COLD CASE NOVELS, AND
NATCHEZ TRACE PARKWAY RANGERS SERIES

"When a lifelong friendship is literally blown apart, a best friend becomes set on finding the killers behind this high-stakes national tragedy. *Her Every Move* is explosive, tender, and races all the way through!"

—JENNIFER GRAESER DORNBUSH, AUTHOR/
SCREENWRITER/FORENSIC SPECIALIST

"Irvin (Every Amish Season series; Amish of Bee County series) packs a lot into this Christian romantic suspense title . . . but does so in a way that makes Teagan and Max feel like complex human beings with strengths, faults, and doubts. The faith of the main characters guides them and their decisions. It doesn't keep them from harm but gives them strength and hope, resulting in a relatable picture of Christianity."

—*LIBRARY JOURNAL* ON *CLOSER THAN SHE KNOWS*

"This brisk, smoothly written thriller from Irvin (*Tell Her No Lies*) pits court reporter Teagan O'Rourke, a murder mystery lover, against a cunning and vicious serial killer . . . Irvin keeps readers guessing the killer's identity—and motive—to the climax . . . Fans of serial killer fiction with a Christian slant will be satisfied."

—*PUBLISHERS WEEKLY* ON *CLOSER THAN SHE KNOWS*

"This is a fun suspense novel that is very different from Irvin's Amish writings, and will definitely attract a new fanbase. Those who like action and suspense should check this one out."

—*PARKERSBURG NEWS & SENTINEL* ON *OVER THE LINE*

"A compelling and timely story, *Over the Line* is a testament to the courage required to forgive. Irvin paints a vivid picture of life on the border—of loyalty and betrayal, fear and love, hope and despair."

—SIRI MITCHELL, AUTHOR OF *STATE OF LIES*

"*Tell Her No Lies* is true romantic suspense at its best! Kelly Irvin has penned a heart-stopping, adrenaline-pumping romantic suspense with an unlikely heroine that tugs at the heartstrings. Highly recommended!"

—COLLEEN COBLE, *USA TODAY* BESTSELLING AUTHOR

"*Tell Her No Lies* is a fast-paced, well-planned story with a myriad of whiplash-inducing twists wherein the suspense is the main course and the romance a tasty, slow-burning side dish . . . bravo to the author for showcasing the plight of our homeless and not treating them as throwaways but humanizing them by giving them faces, futures, and hopes. *Tell Her No Lies* is a perfect read for fans who like a chilling, puzzling thriller with a mild dose of romance."

—*MYSTERY SCENE MAGAZINE*

"Irvin grips readers' attention page after page . . . Vibrant real-world characters and an unpredictable plot keep the adrenaline level high while gentle nudges guide Nina to truth faith and love."

—HOPE BY THE BOOK ON *TELL HER NO LIES*

"No one is above suspicion in a tale sure to appeal to readers beyond its main Christian audience."

—*PUBLISHERS WEEKLY* ON *TELL HER NO LIES*

"I think I've found a new favorite author! What an exciting read—tense, suspenseful, and masterfully written!"

—CARRIE STUART PARKS, AWARD-WINNING AUTHOR
OF *FORMULA OF DECEPTION* ON *TELL HER NO LIES*

"In *Tell Her No Lies*, Kelly Irvin has crafted a story of wounded characters overcoming and fighting their way to the truth. In a world where so many present one facade externally and another inside their homes, this novel shines a light on the power of truth to cut through the darkness. Wrap that inside a page-turning mystery and some sweet romance and it's a story perfect for readers who love multiple threads. This is a keeper of a story."

—CARA PUTMAN, AUTHOR OF THE HIDDEN JUSTICE SERIES

"With plenty of twists and surprises, this is a story readers will be shocked by."

—PARKERSBURG NEWS & SENTINEL ON TELL HER NO LIES

"Well-established as a writer of Amish romances, Kelly Irvin's romantic suspense novels promote faith after betrayal and encourage readers to learn to love and trust again."

—INGRAM ON TELL HER NO LIES

"Irvin . . . creates a complex web with enough twists and turns to keep even the most savvy romantic suspense readers guessing until the end. Known for her Amish novels, this two-time Christy Award finalist shows that her talents span subgenres from tranquil Amish stories to rapidly paced breathless suspense."

—LIBRARY JOURNAL ON TELL HER NO LIES

Trust Me

OTHER BOOKS BY KELLY IRVIN

ROMANTIC SUSPENSE

Her Every Move

Closer Than She Knows

Over the Line

Tell Her No Lies

AMISH

AMISH BLESSING NOVELS

Love's Dwelling

AMISH OF BIG SKY COUNTRY NOVELS

Mountains of Grace

A Long Bridge Home

Peace in the Valley

EVERY AMISH SEASON NOVELS

Upon a Spring Breeze

Beneath the Summer Sun

Through the Autumn Air

With Winter's First Frost

Trust Me

A Novel

KELLY IRVIN

THOMAS NELSON
Since 1798

Published in Nashville, Tennessee, by Thomas Nelson. Thomas Nelson is a registered trademark of HarperCollins Christian Publishing, Inc.

Thomas Nelson titles may be purchased in bulk for educational, business, fundraising, or sales promotional use. For information, please email SpecialMarkets@ ThomasNelson.com.

Publisher's Note: This novel is a work of fiction. Names, characters, places, and incidents are either products of the author's imagination or used fictitiously. All characters are fictional, and any similarity to people living or dead is purely coincidental.

Library of Congress Cataloging-in-Publication Data

Library of Congress Cataloging-in-Publication Data
Names: Irvin, Kelly, author.
Title: Trust me : a novel / Kelly Irvin.
Description: Nashville, Tennessee : Thomas Nelson, [2022] | Summary: "When Delaney Broward finds her best friend stabbed to death a decade after her brother suffered the same fate, she must confront her painful past in order to unmask a killer who isn't done yet"-- Provided by publisher.
Identifiers: LCCN 2021040698 (print) | LCCN 2021040699 (ebook) | ISBN 9780785231936 (paperback) | ISBN 9780785231943 (epub) | ISBN 9780785231974 (downloadable audio)
Subjects: BISAC: FICTION / Christian / Romance / Suspense | FICTION / Romance / Suspense | GSAFD: Romantic suspense fiction.
Classification: LCC PS3609.R82 T78 2022 (print) | LCC PS3609.R82 (ebook) | DDC 813/.6--dc23
LC record available at https://lccn.loc.gov/2021040698
LC ebook record available at https://lccn.loc.gov/2021040699

Printed in the United States of America

22 23 24 25 26 LSC 10 9 8 7 6 5 4 3 2 1

To my family, love always

CHAPTER 1

The cloying stench of pot told the same old story.

With an irritated sigh Delaney Broward quickened her pace through the warehouse-turned-art-co-op toward her brother's studio at the far end of the cavernous hall. On his best days Corey had little sense of time. Add a joint to the mix and he lost his sense not only of time but of responsibility. It also explained why he didn't answer his phone. When he got high and started painting, he wanted no interruptions. His lime-green VW van was parked cattywampus across two spaces in the lot that faced Alamo Street just south of downtown San Antonio. He might be physically present, but his THC-soaked mind had escaped its cell.

Marijuana served as his muse and taskmaster. Or so he'd said.

The soles of her huarache sandals clacking on the concrete floor sounded loud in Delaney's ears. "Corey? Corey! You were supposed to pick us up at Ellie's. Come on, dude. She's waiting."

No answer.

At this rate Delaney would never get to Night in Old San Antonio,

1

affectionately known to most local folks as NIOSA. Everyone who was anyone knew it was pronounced NI-O-SA, long *I* and long *O*, the best party-slash-fund-raiser during the mother of all parties where her boyfriend would be waiting for her. "Hey, bro, I'm starving. Let's go."

Delaney's phone rang. She slowed and dug it from the pocket of her stonewashed jeans. Speaking of Ellie. "I'm at the co-op now. He's here."

Share as little info as possible.

"He's stoned again, isn't he? I'm sick of this." Ellie's shrill voice rose even higher. "I swear if he stands me up again—"

"*Us*. Stands *us* up."

"Stood us up again. That will be it. I'm done. I'm done waiting around for him. I'm done playing second fiddle to his self-destructive habits. I'm done with his starving-artist, free-spirit, pothead schtick. The man is a walking stereotype. I'm done with him, period."

Delaney mouthed the words along with her friend. She knew the lyrics of this lovesick song by heart. The childish rejoinder "It takes one to know one" stuck in her throat. "We'll be there in twenty. You can tell him yourself."

Ellie would and then Corey would kiss her until she took it all back. With a final huff Ellie hung up.

The door to his studio—the largest and with the best light because the co-op was Corey's dream child—stood open. "Seriously, Corey. Think of someone besides yourself once in a while, please." Delaney strode through the door, ready to ream her brother up one side and down the other. "You are so selfish."

Delaney halted. At first blush it didn't make sense. Twisted and smashed canvases littered the floor. Along with paints, brushes, beer bottles, and Thai food take-out cartons.

Wooden easels were broken like toothpicks and scattered on top of the canvases. Someone had splattered red paint over another finished piece—a woman eating a raspa in front of a vendor's mobile cart, the Alamo in the background.

Delaney's hands went to her throat. The metallic scent of blood mingled with the odor of human waste gagged her. A fiery shiver started at her toes and raced like a lit fuse to her brain. Her mind took in detail after detail. That way she didn't have to face the bigger picture staring her in the face. "Please, God, no."

Even He couldn't fix this.

She shot forward, stumbled, and fell to her knees. Her legs refused to work. She crawled the remainder of the distance to Corey across a floor marred by still-wet oil paint, beer, and other liquids she couldn't bear to identify.

He sat with his back against the wall. His long legs clad in paint-splattered jeans sprawled in front of him. His feet were bare. His hands with those thin, expressive fingers lay in his lap. Deep lacerations scored his palms and fingers.

Her throat aching with the effort not to vomit, Delaney forced her gaze to move upward. His T-shirt, once white, now shone scarlet with blood. His blood. Rips in the shirt left his chest exposed, revealing stab wounds—too many to count.

Delaney opened her mouth. *Scream. Just scream. Let it out.*

No sound emerged.

She crawled alongside her big brother until she could lean her shoulder and head against the wall. "Corey?" she whispered.

His green eyes, fringed by thick, dark lashes that were the envy of every woman he'd ever dated, were open and startled. His skin, always pale and ethereal, had a blue tinge to it.

Delaney drowned in a tsunami of nausea. "Come on, Corey, this isn't funny. I need you."

Her teeth chattered. Hands shaking, she touched his throat. His skin was cold. So cold.

Too late, too late, too late. The words screamed in her head. *Stop it. Just stop it.* "You can't be dead. You're not allowed to die."

Mom and Dad had died in a car wreck a week past her eighth birthday. Nana and Pops had taken their turns the year Delaney turned eighteen. Everybody she cared about died.

Not Corey. Delaney punched in *9–1–1.*

The operator's assurance that help was on the way did nothing to soothe Delaney. She sat cross-legged and dragged Corey's shoulders and head into her lap. She had to warm him up. "Tell them to hurry. Tell them my brother needs help."

"Yes, ma'am. They're en route."

"Tell them he's all I've got."

CHAPTER 2

TEN YEARS LATER

NASH RESIDENCE, SAN ANTONIO

Real men didn't cry. Not even during a reunion with a beloved truck.

Swallowing hard, Hunter Nash wrapped his fingers around the keys, concentrating on the feel of the metal pressing into his skin. He cleared his throat. "Thanks, Mom. For keeping it all these years."

His mom didn't bother to try to hide her tears. She wiped her plump cheeks on a faded dish towel, offered him a tremulous smile, and bustled down the sidewalk that led from the house on San Antonio's near west side where Hunter had grown up to the detached two-car garage in the back. It had housed his truck for the past eight years. Almost ten if he counted the two years it took for his case to go to trial. He had no place to go in those years when he'd allegedly been innocent until proven guilty. His friends no longer friends and his job gone, he had no need for transportation.

The door to the garage was padlocked. Mom handed him the key. "My hands are shaking. You'd better do the honors." She stepped back. "I still can't believe you're here."

"I did my time, Ma." As a model prisoner he'd earned time off for good behavior. It was easy for a guy to behave when he spent his days and nights scared spitless.

"I know. All those nights I've lain in bed worrying about you in that place, whether you were safe, if you were hurt, if you were sick." Her voice broke. "I can't believe it's over."

"Me neither."

It wasn't over. In fact, it was just beginning, but she didn't need to know that. His determination to prove his innocence would only worry her more. A divorced mother of four, she'd raised her kids on a teacher's salary and an occasional child support check from the crud-for-brains ex-husband who showed up once every couple of years in an attempt to make nice with his kids. She deserved a break.

The aging manual garage door squeaked and protested when Hunter yanked on the handle. He needed to do some work around here, starting with applying some WD-40. The smell of mold and old motor oil wafted from the dark interior. Hunter slipped inside and waited for his eyes to adjust. A layer of dust covered the 2002 midnight-blue Dodge RAM 1500, but otherwise it remained in the pristine condition in which he'd left it the night he said goodbye and promised he'd be back. "My baby."

More tears trickling down her face, Mom chuckled softly. "After you finish reintroducing yourself, come back inside. I'm making your favorite chicken-fried steak, mashed potatoes, gravy, pineapple cole-slaw, and creamed corn. Your brother and sisters are coming over after work. Shawna's bringing a carrot cake with cream cheese frosting. Melissa's contribution is three kinds of ice cream, including rocky road. She said it seemed appropriate. I hope you haven't lost your sense of humor. And you know Curtis. He's all about the beer."

The last thing Hunter wanted to do was celebrate with his sibs. Mel and Shawna had visited faithfully at first, but less as the years rolled by. Curtis never showed, even though Fab n Dominguez State Jail was only a few miles down the road from San Antonio.

Nor did Hunter want to explain why he'd sworn off alcohol. The conditions of his parole included monthly pee tests—no alcohol or drugs, but that part of his life was over anyway. It had been easy to comply in prison, obviously. Whether he could maintain his sobriety in the beer drinking capital of the country remained to be seen. He'd do AA if necessary. "Mom—"

"No buts. They're family. They love you. You need to live life, enjoy life, make up for all you've missed. You haven't even met most of your nieces and nephews. Did you know Mel is expecting another baby in August?"

"Yes, I—"

"Today we celebrate your new job and your new life."

His bachelor of fine arts with an emphasis in drawing and painting from Southwest School of Art might once have allowed him to teach art in one of the school districts, but not anymore.

It didn't matter. The prison chaplain had hooked him up with Pastor James. The preacher ran a faith-based community center that served at-risk youth. He'd hired Hunter to teach art to those who'd already had their first brush with the law. He figured Hunter could teach life lessons at the same time he introduced them to art as a way to channel their anger at the hand life had dealt them. Learning what happened when a guy got off track would be the lesson.

Even though Hunter hadn't gotten off the track. He'd been shoved off it. By an eager-beaver, newbie detective; a green-as-a-Granny-Smith-apple public defender; and an assembly-line justice system.

He would get by in this world that had hung him out to dry. Especially knowing Mom had his back. She had that *don't-mess-with-me* teacher look in her burnt-amber eyes. Like her sixth graders, Hunter knew better than to argue. It felt good to know she remained in his corner. When everyone else had hit the ground, scattering in opposite directions, she never budged in her belief that son number two could not be a murderer. She'd brought him up better than that.

"You're right. Give me a few minutes."

She patted his chest and stretched on her tiptoes to plant a kiss on his cheek. Her lips were chapped, and the wrinkles had deepened around her mouth and eyes. Her long hair had gone pure white during his years away. "Take your time, sweetheart."

Hunter gritted his teeth. After years of looking over his shoulder, bobbing and weaving around hard-core convicts who'd as soon shank a guy in the shower as look at him, he didn't know how to cope with nice. With sweet. With love tempered with wisdom and a hard life.

"One day at a time." That's what the prison chaplain had told him. *"Get through the next minute, the next hour, the next day."* That's how he did eight years at Dominguez. This couldn't be any harder. He opened the truck's door and slid into the driver's seat. The faint odor of pine air freshener greeted him. And citrus.

More likely that was his imagination. Delaney's perfume simply could not linger that long. *Move on. She has.* She did. To her credit Delaney held on as long as she could—until the guilty verdict. Then she was forced to move on. She couldn't be blamed for that.

Hunter picked up the sketch pad on the passenger seat. In those days he kept one everywhere. Just in case. The first page. The second. The third. All drawings of Delaney. Sweet Laney eating a slice of watermelon at a Fourth of July celebration. Laney rocking Hunter's newborn nephew in a hickory rocker on the front porch. Laney in a bathing suit sitting on the dock at Medina Lake. Laney with her soulful eyes, long sandy-brown hair, and air of sad vulnerability worn like a pair of old jeans that fit perfectly. That too-big nose, wide mouth, and pointed chin. Corey might have been the angelic beauty—totally unfair—but Delaney's face had character. She had a face Hunter never ceased to want to draw and paint.

And kiss.

He turned the pages slowly, allowing the memories to have their way with him. Meeting at a party Corey had thrown when Delaney was a senior in high school. Their first date, ribs and smoked chicken with heart-stopping creamed corn, potato salad, coleslaw, and jalapeños at Rudy's Country Store and Bar-B-Q followed by dancing at Leon Springs Dance Hall.

She had danced with the abandon of a small child. As if she didn't care who watched. Her face glowed with perspiration. Her green eyes sparkled with happiness. His two left feet couldn't keep up, but she didn't mind. She twirled her peasant skirt as she flew around him, her hands in the air, her curves beckoning.

Hunter closed his eyes. Her softness enveloped him. Her sweetness surrounded him.

He needed to see her again. He needed to talk to her. Somehow he had to prove to her that she was wrong about him. Whatever it took. He laid the sketchbook aside. "Come on, dude, let's take a ride."

He stuck the key in the ignition and turned it.

Nothing. Not even a *tick-tick-tick*. He tried a second time. Nada. "I'm an idiot." He patted the steering wheel. "Not your fault, man."

The truck hadn't been driven in years. The battery was dead. He might be able to jump it, but more likely he'd need a new one. Batteries cost money.

One thing at a time. He'd waited this long.

Hunter slid from the truck and eased the door closed. "I'll be back when I get my act together."

In the kitchen Hunter found his mom peeling potatoes. She

pointed the peeler at him. "You can't imagine how good it feels to have you home."

"You can't imagine how good it feels to be here." He landed a kiss on her soft hair. She smelled of Pond's cold cream. The same old comforting scent. Life had changed but not her. "I'm gonna take a walk. I need to blow the prison stink off."

"Enjoy. They redid the walking trail at the lake and installed new outdoor fitness equipment." She waved the paring knife in the air. "But don't stay too long. You have company coming."

"Yes, ma'am." He pantomimed a mock salute and headed for the front door.

One thing at a time. One step at a time. That's how he'd get his life back.

CHAPTER 3

Good smells meant good sales.

The scents of warm coconut oil, mimosas, and pink grapefruit wafted through the open shop windows. On the doorstep Delaney inhaled and rolled her eyes. Her friend Ellie must be on another spring break–induced beach trip down memory lane. A hint of gardenia but not enough to overpower. Delaney's oversized schnoz—a family heirloom—could detect Ellie's aromatic flights of fancy with little problem. If they couldn't close their neighboring shops in San Antonio's historic La Villita artisan district and road trip to Texas's Gulf Coast, at least they could let the familiar scents soothe their wanderlust.

The Beach Boys crooned "Kokomo" on the radio through an open window. Definitely wishful thinking. A cool March breeze lifted homemade dark-blue-and-white-checked curtains. Everything about the small stucco-covered building that housed Mother Earth Oils and Candles beckoned those seeking a peaceful retreat from a troubled world.

If only it were that simple.

The sign on the door was already turned to CLOSED. Usually Ellie left the door open until Delaney reminded her she now had other responsibilities besides providing soothing oils and fragrant candles to people desperate to quell their stress.

Delaney tugged the door open and stepped into a wonderland of infusers, essential oils, handcrafted candles, and wax chips. "Ellie! Quitting time. All the shoppers are busy drinking margaritas on the River Walk or eating ribs and being insulted at Dick's." She pressed her fingertips to the bridge of her nose. Her acute sense of smell could handle only so much of Ellie's passion for scent. "You can go home, stick your feet in the kids' sandbox, and pretend you're on the beach at South Padre."

No answer. Ellie had to be here. Never in the three years since Delaney had gone to work at the neighboring shop You've Been Framed and then took over the lease had her friend left first. They'd always walked together. Tragedy often tore families apart, but in this case it had woven Delaney and Ellie together in a tight hug. Ellie was like the sister Delaney never had.

"Let's go, girl. You don't want the kids to starve, do you?"

Still no answer.

Another scent—crude, ugly, and painfully familiar—alerted Delaney's nose. She sniffed, took another half step, stumbled, and paused.

No, no, no.

"Ellie? Where are you?" Delaney's voice dropped to a whisper. Memories, buried with hundreds of hours of therapy and a determined mental shovel, crowded her. The cloying metallic odor reared up and choked her. Weak-kneed, she gripped the glass display counter that held the cash register and Ellie's laptop. "Come on, answer me. This isn't funny."

Her legs threatened to bail on her. Heart slamming against her chest like a slugger with a Louisville baseball bat, Delaney pushed forward.

One step, two steps, three steps, four.

She rounded the display case. Red paraffin molds lay scattered across the floor. The day's special, a rose-gold lantern etched with delicate seashells lay on its side, melted wax cooling. An Andy Warhol print leaned against the wall, its black frame mangled. Delaney had matted and framed that print. Chairs were overturned, candles rolled under display tables in a topsy-turvy puzzle that couldn't be put back together.

Anger whooshed through her. Delaney forced her gaze past the destruction. Ellie lay sprawled on the whimsical purple-and-pink balloon-print rug she'd picked out to make the plain wood floor warmer. Her brown eyes were open and startled under dark-black eyebrows still lifted as if questioning her fate.

This is not happening. Not again. "Ellie, oh, Ellie, please, Ellie."

No answer. The stepmother of Skye, soon to be four, and Jacob, six, would not be making their favorite mac-n-cheese casserole for supper tonight—or any night ever again.

Blood soaked her white tube top and frothy African-print skirt. Delaney swallowed vomit in the back of her throat. That grotesque smell sent her hurtling back in time to another body and another death mask. Corey's body had been slumped against the wall in his studio. He, too, looked surprised, but he was young, so young. His beautiful green eyes begged her to do something to change the outcome.

Blood everywhere. His skinny chest exposed. Stab wounds in a nonsensical pattern. His face had been ethereal and angelic in repose. So peaceful. It took years for her to overcome the desire to join him.

Her peripheral vision caught movement. Adrenaline returned for an encore. Delaney crouched and swiveled right. A tall, dark figure shot from behind a display case and lunged at her. She ducked. His right arm swept out and over her head.

Delaney backpedaled. She needed traction. Her self-defense training surfaced. She kicked out hard, aiming for the most vulnerable part of a man's anatomy.

Her attacker, despite his height and boulder size, danced back. The kick missed its target.

More backpedaling.

Her keys. Her pepper spray was attached to the key ring. They were in her purse. Her Taser was in her Trailblazer's glove compartment. *"Always be prepared,"* her instructor had said.

She'd failed miserably.

The attacker's breathing bellowed. The sound mingled with Delaney's.

Time passed in slow motion.

His arm swept out. His fist smashed past her uplifted hands into her throat and sent her reeling.

Arms flailing, Delaney staggered back. She hit the floor. Her head smacked against the solid pine wood.

Fighting for air, she grabbed her throat with both hands. She gagged, coughed, and gasped. Black threatened to close in. Purple dots danced on the edges of her vision.

Dying wouldn't be the end of the world. The well-worn thought pingponged inside of her head.

Everyone died sooner or later.

No. Not yet. I'm not through living. I lied. I do want to love, to marry, to have children.

Who was she telling this? Not God. He had stopped listening to her ten years earlier when He let Corey die and left her all alone.

Her assailant paused for a split second over her.

He was a big man. He wore black sweats, a long-sleeved black T-shirt, and black sneakers. A jogger out for a run. Except for the thick black mesh stocking that covered his face, distorting his features and hiding his identity.

No. You aren't allowed to kill me.

Delaney scooted back on her elbows and heels. She threw her hands out, searching for her backpack-style purse. Her keys. Her pepper spray. Her phone. Anything. "Help, somebody, help!"

The words were barely a scratchy whisper. *Come on, come on.*

Another wave of unadulterated, heart-pounding adrenaline flowed through her. She thrust forward, then rolled to one side.

The killer's fingers wrapped around her bicep in a cruel, unwavering grip. He jerked her up. His dark face came within inches of hers. His other hand was empty. He pointed at her and then made a cut-throat gesture. "Stay out of it or you're next."

The hoarse voice struck no familiar chords.

Stay out of what? Delaney tried to ask but she croaked, the words unintelligible.

He let go. She plummeted to the floor. He whirled, shot through the open door, and left her lying there. Still alive.

Why?

She knew who had killed Corey and why.

Who would kill Ellie? Sweet Mother Earth Ellie who'd reinvented herself after her boyfriend's murder.

Why not kill Delaney?

She rolled over and scrambled on her hands and knees, searching for her purse. There. Next to the counter. She dug her phone from the outside pocket and called 911.

"Help. He's getting away." Her throat was on fire. The croak was worse. "We need your help."

"Ma'am, I can't understand you. Tell me what's happening."

Delaney cleared her throat and tried again. A gravelly whisper proved to be adequate. This time the operator understood. Delaney identified herself and spelled out her location.

"Is your friend breathing?"

"I don't know." Delaney fought for calm. *Don't go to pieces now. Keep it together.* "I don't think so. There's blood everywhere. Should I do CPR?"

"EMS is on the way. We need to know if she has a pulse, ma'am. Stay on the line with me while you check."

Delaney edged closer. She held her breath and leaned over as far as she dared. *Move, Ellie, wake up. Tell me it's all a big joke. It's not Día de los Muertos. We're not kids anymore.*

"Ma'am. Ms. Broward?"

Ellie's skin still felt warm and slightly sticky. South Texas humidity, no doubt. "She doesn't have a pulse." Delaney's voice betrayed her with an acute tremble. She cleared her throat again. "She's dead."

Sirens screamed in the distance.

"Help is on the way, ma'am."

"I know." Delaney eased back until she could sit cross-legged without disturbing the blood that pooled around her friend. "Tell them I'm waiting with my friend."

Tell them I'm keeping her company just like I did my brother ten years ago.

CHAPTER 4

"If I were in labor, I would know it, *mi amor*."

His wife's tart assertion over the phone eased Homicide Detective Andy Ramos's angst. After all, this was baby number three, and Pilar had experienced Braxton Hicks contractions before. This baby wasn't due for a few more weeks. Pilar knew the real thing when she felt it. Surely. Andy hoped.

He squeezed between a Fox 29 Ford Explorer and KSAT 12's live truck parked on Nueva Street meters outside La Villita. The media were all over this dead body, like vultures circling overhead, waiting for the opportunity to descend. "Just call me if you need me. I'm headed to a crime scene, but I can hand it off. Call me. I mean it."

"Just do your job and come home safe." Pilar's tone softened. "Love you."

"That's the plan. Love you too." Andy hung up.

He professed ignorance to the Univision reporter who stuck a mic in his face on the small entryway to the art district with the grandiose moniker King Philip V Street and moved on until he found a park police officer. "Could you back the media up? Tell them to park in the lot on Presa Street. Please. If they question you, tell them the chief's mouthpiece is on his way."

The park police officer grimaced but acquiesced. No one liked media duty.

A homicide during spring break in a popular tourist attraction would be media fodder for weeks. And bring intense pressure on PD from City Hall. Tourism served as the heartbeat of the city's economy.

A crime scene investigator wielding a digital camera blocked Andy's entrance to the essential oils shop. He waited for the guy to get his shot, then headed for his final destination: Gregorio Flores, a detective at least fifteen years Andy's senior and the reason he had made the scene. No one in Andy's memory had ever called Flores by his first name. Just Flores.

"Flores, señor, what am I doing here?"

The detective, who stood near the door watching the CSU folks do their thing, grinned his trademark snaggletoothed grin. "Ramos, welcome to the party."

"So what's the deal? On the phone you said this may have ties back to the Broward case. We caught the guy and put him away ten years ago. How's it related?"

"It's possible. Probable. One scenario. Take a gander at the victim and tell me if you recognize her."

Risking the medical examiner investigator's wrath, Andy edged closer so he could get a better view of the victim sprawled on the floor, her shirt soaked in blood. Fake blonde hair, dark eyebrows, brown eyes, midthirties maybe. He searched the catalog of secondary actors, witnesses, and victims that crowded his brain.

"Her hair was probably dark brown," Flores prompted. "She was ten years younger."

"Ellie . . . Ellie . . . Cruz. Corey Broward's girlfriend."

"You got it." Flores air-fist-bumped Andy. "Only now she's Ellie Hill, married mother of two stepkids and small business owner."

"This place is hers?" Andy glanced around. Smelly candles, essential oils, infusers. Stuff his three younger sisters would love. "Back in the day she was a wannabe painter, if memory serves. She talked the talk, for sure, but I got the impression Corey Broward was the one with the real talent."

Not that Andy knew beans about art.

"The woman who found her called Mrs. Hill an artisan. I guess that's something different from an artiste." Flores shoved his dark-rimmed glasses up his nose with one bony finger. "She said Mrs. Hill opened the store seven years ago and turned a profit within two years. Not bad for a small business selling stinky stuff."

"Robbery gone bad?"

"On the face of it, could be. Cash register was emptied. Her wedding ring—a huge solitaire—is missing and so is her wallet and a laptop. But it's what happened with the witness that makes me want to consider all the possibilities."

"Who's the witness?"

Flores straightened to his full six-foot height. His glasses magnified his brown eyes. He seemed ready to burst into song. "You'll love this. Delaney Broward."

"Corey Broward's sister?"

"What are the chances?"

Indeed. The memories flooded back. His first homicide as a detective. Andy had arrived on the scene pumped and primed for action. Delaney Broward, wearing a blood-spattered UTSA Roadrunners' T-shirt, sat cross-legged with her brother's head and shoulders in her lap. Keening softly, she rocked him on the cement floor in a warehouse on South Alamo Street that had been turned into studios for a bunch of artists. They called it a co-op. The EMT said she was in shock. Efforts to get her to let go of the victim had failed. The medical examiner was chomping at the bit, but the EMT was determined not to traumatize her further.

Talking her down had fallen to Andy's partner, Pilar Narvaez, who had a woman's soft touch going for her. For months afterward hazy dreams filled with a sobbing green-eyed woman wearing bloody clothes had haunted Andy. "It could be totally a coincidence."

"Could be." Flores snorted. "And Elvis is alive and living in Rio de Janeiro."

He was right, but it was never good to go into an investigation with tunnel vision. "So she called it in?"

"Yep. One of the park police officers responded first. He and some of his compadres are canvassing the other shops for witnesses as we speak."

"Cameras?"

"Not in the shop, but outside, yes. I'll see what we can get from them."

"What did Ms. Broward say she was doing here? Shopping?"

"She has a shop next door."

Andy rubbed his forehead. The smells were getting to him. He sneezed into the crook of his elbow. "I thought she was studying to be a social worker."

"She said she bailed—my word not hers—five years ago from her job as a Child Protective Services caseworker. A burnout, apparently. She frames and sells artwork. Her shop is called You've Been Framed. Kinda catchy, no?"

"So she saw the offender? Why didn't he kill her too?"

"She asked me the same question. I don't know. She says he had a black mesh stocking over his face. He wore a long-sleeved shirt, sweats, and gloves. No identifying marks showing. Nothing about him seemed familiar."

Flores's cat-ate-the-canary expression tipped off Andy. "What else?"

"After he punched her in the neck, he threatened her. His exact words, according to Ms. Broward, were, 'Stay out of it or you're next.' He made a motion like he'd slit her throat."

"Is she all right?"

"Physically, she'll be okay. EMTs examined her. She's bruised, sore, shaken."

"She got lucky." If there were such a thing as luck. Andy didn't believe in it, but Flores would understand the sentiment. "Stay out of what?"

"The million-dollar question. She claims to have no idea."

"Did he leave the murder weapon?"

"Nope. She said it was a big knife. Which doesn't narrow it down much. I'm sure the ME will give us more after the autopsy."

Knives were second only to guns for weapons used in robberies. Usually they were intended to coerce the victim into giving up valuables. Many times, if victims cooperated, they remained unharmed. Other times, like this one, they escalated. Had Mrs. Hill refused to give up her wedding ring? A deadly move if she had. "So it might have started as a robbery. Or the perpetrator wanted it to appear like a robbery?"

"Possibly." Flores scratched his forehead below a receding hairline and shrugged. "Still, why threaten Ms. Broward? The pieces don't quite fit together."

They would, eventually. Most investigations began with more questions than answers. "Next of kin?"

Flores glanced at his notebook. "Michael Hill, age forty-four. Owner of his own accounting firm. No priors. Not even a parking ticket. I'm headed to make the notification when I get done here. Want to come?"

21

"Actually I'd like to talk to Ms. Broward, if that's okay."

"Have at it, my friend. LT says I can use you and abuse you for as long as I want since your partner pulled his pin and that snot-nosed newbie partner of mine managed to break his ankle. How's your main squeeze doing anyway?"

Flores's partner had been hit by a car while crossing a busy downtown thoroughfare on a green light and in the crosswalk. Andy's most recent partner had retired and headed to the Gulf Coast where he planned to open a bait shop. Andy's first partner was now his wife. "Pilar's good. She's eating us out of house and home."

When they'd finally been forced to admit they were more than partners, it had taken another two years for Andy and Pilar to have the guts to make the walk down the aisle. Pilar had switched from homicide to cyberterrorism during her first pregnancy for obvious reasons.

"Go talk to Ms. Broward and let me know what you think." Flores and his wife had chosen rescue dogs in lieu of children. "Godspeed. Better you than me."

"What's that supposed to mean?"

"She's bitter. And prickly."

"She's an orphan with not a single family member. Her boyfriend killed her brother. She's allowed."

Flores was already moving to talk to the ME's investigator. He didn't care as long as Andy got her to talk.

CHAPTER 5

Delaney contemplated throwing a rock at the river barge filled with tourists passing through the Arneson River Theater on their way to see the sights on the River Walk. Their raucous laughter and ebullient chatter didn't belong here, so close to the scene of Ellie's violent death. With no rock within reach she chewed off another fingernail instead.

The barge pilot waved and shouted, "Hello." Delaney managed a wave. She couldn't imagine smiling ever again. But then, she'd thought the same thing after Corey died. Life tended to smooth the edge off the pain, little by little, like water dripping on a stone.

The police officer assigned to wait with her while the crime scene unit scoured Ellie's shop for evidence shifted from one foot to the other on the narrow, steep steps that split the aisles of the outdoor theater's grassy seats.

"You could sit down. I promise not to report you." Delaney held her hand over her forehead to block the sun and peered up at the woman. Talking made her throat hurt. The words were a whispered croak. "We could be here a while."

"That's okay—"

"Do you have the witness? Her shop is empty." A tall man in a stylish gray suit and pale-lilac tie bounded down the steps toward them.

The officer cocked her thumb at Delaney. "She said she needed some air."

"Thanks. I've got her from here. You can take off." He moved aside so the officer had room to pass. "Ms. Broward—"

"Delaney." She stared up at him. His face was familiar. Older but just as chiseled and clean-shaven. Ocher eyes just as kind. A shudder ran through her. A blast from the past. How was it possible? "Detective Ramos, right?"

"Good memory."

How could she forget the detective who had played a critical role in ferreting out her brother's killer and putting him in prison?

"Where's your partner? Detective Narvaez?" Detective Narvaez had been the one to gently disengage Delaney's arms from around Corey's body. She hugged Delaney and helped her to her feet. With one arm around her waist to prop her up, the detective moved her out of the medical examiner's way. The entire time murmuring encouraging words. "She was nice."

"We're not partners anymore. She switched to cyberterrorism. The guy I've been working with decided to retire suddenly so I'm at loose ends in the partner department."

Delaney plucked a slender blade of grass and rubbed it between her fingers. The theater smelled like spring. It smelled fresh, like Ellie always smelled. "In what universe is it possible that you're the detective assigned cases that involve two of the worst days of my life?"

"I didn't catch this case. Detective Flores called me when he realized there was a connection between his case and the one Detective Narvaez and I solved involving your brother. Are you okay to talk to me? Your throat sounds raw."

"I'll live. If this was a simple robbery, why threaten me? And if it was meant to seem like a robbery and was more than that, why not kill me too?" All the questions that had swirled around in Delaney's head from that second when she realized she would not die today jockeyed for position. They all wanted to be first and they all wanted to be answered now. "He must've had the murder weapon on him. Why let me live?"

"All good questions. Ones we hope to answer during the investigation. The question of why he let you live may be the key to who did this to you and why."

"I can't believe this is happening again." Delaney stared at the murky ribbon of water that paraded itself as part of the San Antonio River. Making eye contact with Detective Ramos was out of the question. He would see her grief, her anger, and her disbelief. "Wasn't Corey enough? He was all I had."

"He's all I have. He's all I have." Those words had been her refrain the day Corey died. She and Corey had been raised by their grandparents after their parents died in a collision with a semi on the way to celebrate their fifteenth wedding anniversary in Port Aransas. Pops and Nana died one after the other when Delaney was in high school. Then Corey when she was a master's student studying social work.

Now Ellie.

"Why don't you start by walking me through what happened today?"

Apparently Detective Ramos didn't have the answers she needed. His only recourse was to ignore them.

Delaney took a long breath. She swiveled and pulled her knees up on the seat so she could put her arms around them. Her purple Converse sneakers were muddy. One green lace was undone. She took her time tying it and retying the blue lace on the other shoe. Finally she met Detective Ramos's gaze head-on and recounted the day's events.

"Before you went into the shop and found Mrs. Hill—"

"Ellie."

"Before you found Ellie, had you been in the shop earlier in the day? Or spoken with her?"

"She has a part-time employee who opens for her and stays through lunch. Ellie has stepkids she's trying to bond with. She makes them breakfast and takes them to the Montessori school before she comes to the shop."

If Detective Ramos found her use of present tense strange, he didn't let it show. It was too soon to relegate vivacious, crazy, funny Ellie to the past tense.

"So we brought our sack lunches out here and ate around noon. She met me here."

Detective Ramos tugged his notebook from his back pocket and made notes. "Employee's name?"

"Kimberly Martinez. She's an art student at UTSA. A potter."

"How long has she worked for Ellie?"

"Since Ellie married Michael and took over mother duties for her husband's two kids. Since November, I guess." Ellie took her new role as mommy seriously. She wanted the kids to like her. "She wanted to be a family. She'd waited a long time for that. She and Michael were already talking about having more."

Grief wrapped itself around Delaney's neck and choked her. She swallowed again and again. *Breathe.* She swiveled away from the detective and studied the people strolling along the sidewalk below. *Just breathe.*

"What did you talk about?" Detective Ramos's voice was soft, the prompt gentle. "Anything stand out in retrospect?"

"Whether almond yogurt tastes better than regular yogurt. Why I don't eat hummus. Whether gluten-free diets are a fad. How disgusting kale is. If this is a rebuilding year for the Spurs or whether they'll make the play-offs. Why Skye refuses to eat white food." The unimportant stuff two friends who've known each other a long time talked about on a sunny day when all was right with the world. "Stuff. The stuff you talk about when you don't know it's the last time you'll ever talk to someone."

"I'm sorry to drag you through this."

"You're doing your job." Delaney straightened her shoulders. She raised her head. "I want you to find the monster who did this and put him away. You did that for Corey and it helped. It didn't bring him back, but at least Hunter isn't walking around free enjoying life . . ."

This time the sobs threatened to pour over the sandbags in a torrent of sorrow. If she started crying, she would never stop. She couldn't do that to the detective. She put her hand to her mouth, gritted her teeth, and pulled a sodden tissue from her pocket to wipe her nose. "Sorry."

"Don't apologize. Take your time. I know this is hard. When you feel up to it, tell me about the intruder."

He was too nice. It only made it harder. Delaney wrangled the emotions back into their box. "The man was about six two or three. He probably weighed 190 or 200 pounds. He was a big guy. I'm in good shape and I didn't stand a chance against him." All the time spent at the gym working out and the hours she spent pounding the bag at home hadn't made a bit of difference.

"He wore dark clothes, high-end running shoes. His whole body was covered, so I can't tell you anything about identifying marks or even the color of his skin. The only thing I can say is that he sounded relatively young and local."

Detective Ramos scratched his furrowed forehead with his free hand. "What do you mean by sounded local?"

Stay out of it or you're next. She ran the words through her head once again.

"San Antonio has its own sound. It's not the Dallas twang or the East Texas drawl or the border Tex-Mex accent. He was from around here, but that's based on one brief sentence. It's not like we had a conversation."

"Got it. Nothing stood out about him?"

"He moved fast. He was strong. It felt like he crushed my windpipe with one blow. Otherwise, no. He was a stranger."

"Did Ellie seem upset about anything recently?"

"Ellie worked hard to be an optimist. It was part of her therapy. Today the sun broke through the early morning clouds and banished the fog and drizzle. It's spring break. She exuded contentment."

"Enemies? Irate customers? Anyone who would want to do her harm?"

"She sells candles and essential oils. She morphed from a hippie-wannabe-artist to Earth Mother. Peace and joy." No one could be so blithely happy so much of the time. "Sometimes it actually irritated me. I felt guilty for wishing she'd tone it down a little. Corey died and she walked around like the world is full of angels, unicorns, butterflies, rainbows, and hummingbirds. Life is too short for long faces, she always says."

"Any problems at home?"

The image of Ellie and Michael sharing a piece of pink wedding cake after a ceremony on the pristine white sands of Riviera Maya, Mexico, floated through Delaney's mind. Ellie had frosting on her upturned nose and upper lip while Michael's grin stretched from ear to ear. *"Best cake ever,"* he opined. "Does Michael know? Should I tell him? It doesn't seem right to tell him something so awful on the phone. Who'll pick up the kids from school?"

"Detective Flores is on his way to break the news now." His expression pained, Detective Ramos ran his free hand through thick, black hair. No one wanted to break that kind of news. "How long had they been married? Did they get along?"

"Five months. That's what's so incredibly messed up about this. Ellie decided to take the plunge after all these years. To get on with life and now this. It makes no sense." It made no more sense than Corey's murder on the cusp of making it big on the San Antonio art scene. "They were practically still on their honeymoon."

"Wasn't she an artist like your brother?"

Not in her wildest dreams. None of their tight-knit group had Corey's talent or drive. "She eventually realized she was a better businesswoman than she was an artist. Her parents helped her finance the shop. She worked really hard to make it a success. That's tough to do in this economy and this location.

"She met Michael at a Small Business Administration workshop and they struck up a conversation. Michael was smitten." So much so he had sent Ellie a dozen red roses after their first coffee "date." "He pursued her. She resisted, but he can be very charming when he wants to."

"Is that a note of sarcasm in your voice? Are you not a fan?"

He could also be overly anal and controlling. "He's divorced, a numbers guy, has two kids, and he's eleven years older than she is. Everyone thought it was an odd case of opposites attract. Michael's a type A personality. He works hard and expects everyone to do the same. It's not a bad quality for a business owner. But sometimes he came on a little strong. He treated Ellie like an employee sometimes instead of his wife. It was almost like she singled out someone the total opposite of Corey. But she was happy, so I was happy for her."

"You can't think of anyone who would want to hurt her?"

Only one person. Delaney's stomach clenched. "The only person I can think of is in prison where he belongs. Ellie testified against him."

The jury took a mere forty-five minutes to convict Hunter of manslaughter. The prosecution argued that he killed his best friend in an alcohol- and drug-fueled fit of rage.

Even after all these years, it still boggled the mind. Every muscle and sinew in Delaney's body had believed Hunter was innocent. Needed to believe he was innocent. But he admitted to being there that night. He admitted to arguing with his best friend. He admitted to getting into a shoving match with Corey in an argument over money and the co-op's future.

Hunter insisted Corey was mixed up with something nefarious, something he kept from Delaney and Ellie. Corey would never do that. It wasn't his nature. It didn't help that Hunter never produced any evidence of this criminal enterprise. Instead, he went to prison, still proclaiming his innocence. Still sending her letters, asking her to believe in him, to trust him.

How could she?

"Have you had any contact with Nash since his conviction and incarceration?"

"He sent me letters at first, but I never responded."

"He was your boyfriend for several years. You gave up on him fairly quickly."

"He was convicted of killing my brother. You saw the same evidence I did. You believed he did it and this is what you do for a living."

As much as she didn't want to believe Hunter stabbed Corey to death, the justice system said otherwise. She had no choice but to accept the verdict and move on with her life. Erasing Hunter from her life had been like amputating an arm and a leg. Like she needed a heart transplant. It had taken years to recover.

"What about the other members of the co-op your brother started? Have you and Ellie stayed in touch with them?"

They'd been like family until Corey's death and Hunter's trial tore them apart. Pain twisted in Delaney's gut. She sucked in air and blew it out. *Let it go, just let it go.* "Zach and Sandy got married. They're still in town, but we don't talk much. Jess is a lawyer now, in family law. He was really there for me during the trial and afterward. We were both at the courthouse a lot when I was with CPS. He's helped me with legal stuff over the years. Four of us stayed close. Ellie, me, Jess, and Cam." Delaney bit her lip, focusing on the small spurt of pain. *Keep it together.* "I need to call Jess and Cam. They'll be devastated."

She stopped, closed her eyes, and breathed.

"Take your time."

"We don't have time." White-hot anger seared through her. It was so much easier to handle. It felt good. "My friends—old or new—didn't do this. They love Ellie. We all love Ellie."

"You know the way these investigations work—"

"I know. I know. I do," Delaney bit out the words. "Okay, Billy Riggins is still Billy. He lifts weights during the day, works as a bouncer until the club closes at night, then sculpts until morning—that and drinks. I'm pretty sure he hasn't slept since Corey died."

"You mentioned Cam. That would be Camille Nakamura?" A faint smile flitted across Detective Ramos's face. "How does she fit into the picture?"

He obviously remembered her. Most men did. The Filipino beauty couldn't easily be forgotten. "She's Camille Sanchez now. She and her husband, Jaime, double date with Michael and Ellie. She babysits for them when I can't. Why? Do you still have a thing for her?"

Detective Ramos's face turned a deep red. "I was never—"

"Don't lie. There's not a man alive who has met Cam and not been bowled over with one look at her."

"I'm married."

Sure enough. His left ring finger sported a plain silver band. "You married Detective Narvaez."

"You're pretty astute." This time the detective's face lit up with a genuine smile. The guy was movie-star handsome. "I did. We have two little girls and another one on the way."

"Good for you." Lives went on. Good people like Detective Ramos and Detective Narvaez got married and had kids. Only Delaney was stuck in the first act of a three-act tragedy. "I'm glad. I bet you're great parents. The kind of parents kids should have."

"Did you move on—?"

"Cam teaches silversmithing at the Southwest School of Art." Delaney's love life—or lack thereof—played no role in this investigation. "She was in a car accident five years ago. Her mobility was affected."

"I'm sorry to hear that."

"Don't be. She's the same force of nature she always was. We're still close. Occasionally one of the others who subleased studios will come by the shop to get something framed, but otherwise, we've lost touch." Corey had been the glue that held them together. Without him they'd drifted apart. Or in Delaney's case, sprinted in the other direction. "Too many memories. Some good ones, but bad ones too. At least for me. I was always an outsider. Corey's tagalong little sister."

"What happened to the co-op?"

"They let the lease on the warehouse lapse. The owners rented it to some company that stores its product there."

"You were studying social work back then. Detective Flores said you quit to buy the shop here. Can I ask what happened?"

Delaney had answered this question a few dozen times, but it never got easier. She'd worked hard for that master's in social work. Gone into debt for it. The desire came from the need to do good in this world, to help others, to make a difference. The desires of a naive college kid who wanted family any way she could get it—or so she'd thought. "I stuck it out as long as I could. One of the children I supervised, a little boy sixteen months old, was shaken so hard by his mother's boyfriend that he suffered a catastrophic brain injury. That was it for me. I needed an occupation that allowed me to go home at the end of the day knowing my best was good enough. I took a job working as an apprentice to the woman who owned the frame shop. I did that for three years. When she decided to retire, I took over."

No matter how many times she explained, it still came out sounding like an excuse.

"It's a tough gig. Burnout isn't uncommon." Detective Ramos leaned forward, elbows on his knees. His tone was kind. "I'm sure it was a hard decision to make. I'm probably a philistine, but I can't imagine how there's enough business framing artwork to keep a person afloat, especially in an expensive location like this one. Don't most people go to Hobby Lobby?"

"It's not just fine art, although I get work from local galleries and artists preparing for exhibits as well as art restoration companies." If that were just it, she'd be sunk, but Delaney had inherited a good client base and marketing plan from her predecessor. "I do shadow boxes, framing of medal displays for veterans, visual art, and even cross-stitch that women want to frame and hang in their homes. You have to know about interior design, color, carpentry, marketing, and business. Except for an occasional customer who doesn't like the finished product, it's a calm space."

"No angry parents?"

"Nope. I feel guilty sometimes, but I'm willing to live with the guilt if it means not having to look into another child's face and know he's in danger of being murdered by someone who's entrusted with his care and knowing there's nothing I can do about it."

Nodding, Detective Ramos tapped his stubby pencil on the tiny notebook in his hand. Another barge swept its way through the narrow bend in the river, then slowed as its pilot regaled the occupants with details of how the theater was home to an endless variety of performances from Mexican folkloric dance to jazz to Alamo Bowl pep rallies celebrated in a city known for its capacity to party at the drop of the proverbial hat.

"Is that it, Detective?"

"I'm sorry, just collecting my thoughts. One more question. Do you have employees?"

"One. Abigail Simpkins, also an art student at UTSA. She goes by Gail. She staffs the shop so I can have Sundays and Mondays off and when I have appointments or have to meet clients off-site."

Detective Ramos rose and stretched. He had to be at least six-foot-two. Delaney was five nine and he towered over her. She forced herself to get up. "Are we done, then?"

"I'll walk you up to your shop. I imagine Detective Flores told you he'll need you to make a formal statement at PD headquarters."

"He did, but I already knew how these things work."

"I wish you didn't."

He was a good man. "That's kind of you to say."

"I wish it for all the family members and friends I meet as I investigate these crimes." He backed out of the row and waited for her to go first. "Violent death and the sudden loss of a loved one are not things I would wish on my worst enemies."

He was also a better person than Delaney. "I do. I wish them on the person who did this to Ellie." Delaney trudged up the steep stairs. "An eye for an eye seems just to me. Whoever killed Ellie deserves a violent death or worse."

"I'm more of a New Testament guy myself. Turn the other cheek.

Love thy enemies. Let God be the judge." Detective Ramos joined her on the red-brick road that led to her shop. "You're not considering a little old-fashioned revenge, are you?"

Delaney halted in front of her shop. The early Victorian building painted a sunny yellow with white trim appeared so inviting. So safe.

No one was safe anywhere.

She crossed her arms and met his gaze squarely. "You'll find I'm not the same person I was ten years ago. I've grown up. No one pushes me around anymore. The man threatened me. He killed my friend."

"We solved your brother's murder. We'll solve this one." Detective Ramos's posture stiffened. His tone turned steely. "As much as I understand the powerful need to do something, I also hope you're not planning to interfere in our investigation."

"I won't interfere or get in your way."

His frown deepened. "You'll stand down, then?"

"I'll stand my ground."

"Spoken like a true Texan." He extracted his business card from his suit jacket pocket. "If you think of anything else that might be helpful, call me."

Delaney pocketed the card without examining it. "Believe me, I'll be in touch."

"Is that a promise or a threat?"

"Take your pick."

"You've been warned."

Indeed she had. It couldn't be allowed to matter. Corey was dead. Ellie was dead.

Delaney had nothing left to lose.

CHAPTER 6

The Texas justice system at its finest. A guy could kill his best friend and get out of jail after only ten years. So that was the value of Corey Broward's life. Andy had received notice of Hunter Nash's parole hearing, but he couldn't attend parole hearings for every bad guy he helped put away. Nash was out of prison. He'd been sentenced to fifteen years with credit for time served. The two years he'd spent in the Bexar County Jail would get him out in thirteen. He was eligible for parole after six. Eight had been his magic number. He was out just in time to be suspect number one in Ellie Hill's murder.

Nash's file showed his next of kin as his mother. He had no other home address. Mrs. Nash had been her son's staunch supporter during the investigation and trial. A petite woman who taught middle school, she sat in the first row in the courtroom throughout the trial. She hadn't let her dislike for Andy affect her innate sense of fair play. "You're simply doing your job," she'd said.

Her expression when she opened the door now was less kind. "You couldn't give him one day of peace?"

"I'm sorry to bother you, Mrs. Nash." Andy fought the urge to duck his head like a kid in trouble in the principal's office. "Is your son here?"

She opened the door wider. "Yes. Come in, if you must."

Andy wiped his feet on the *Texas Forever* rug and followed her into a living room filled with overflowing bookshelves and comfortable, lived-in furniture.

"Have a seat. My son is in the garage tinkering with his truck." The faintest bit of sarcasm tinged her words. "That's what convicted killers do, I suppose. I'll bring you some iced tea. You must be parched with all your hard work."

"That's not necessary . . ."

But she turned and left the room without waiting for him to finish. Her flats made an angry *clickety-clack* on the Saltillo tile.

Andy had dealt with family members in every imaginable situation. Some wore civility like armor. Mrs. Nash undoubtedly felt she must take the high road, even with the man who'd done everything in his power to put her youngest son in prison.

Her pain aggrieved him. Not enough to keep him from doing his job. Not enough to keep him from sleeping at night. Not when he measured it against the pain in Delaney Broward's eyes that night ten years ago when he had encountered her keening as she tried to warm her dead brother's body in her lap.

He picked up a sketchbook lying on the coffee table. Pencil and charcoal sketches of Delaney filled many of the pages. Nash was a talented artist. No one had disputed that fact. However, the idea that he had spent most of his time in prison drawing pencil and charcoal sketches of Delaney was an issue in Andy's book.

The *clickety-clack* sounded in the hallway. Mrs. Nash entered the room first. She looked even more petite with her son looming behind her.

Nash had changed in prison. He'd used his recreation time to build some brawn on his tall frame. Gone was the rangy body, replaced with solid biceps and pecs. The long ponytail had gone the way of a tight, almost-military haircut. Easier in prison. A ragged, fading scar ran from his left ear along his jawline. His eyes, a pale amber-brown like his mother's, were his most striking feature. At the moment they were wary but not hostile.

Andy had expected hostility. He deserved hostility. He stood.

"Here he is, Detective, as promised." Mrs. Nash set a glass of tea on the coffee table alongside a platter filled with chocolate chip cookies. "Help yourself, please, but don't keep him too long. The whole family is coming over to celebrate. You're welcome to stay for supper. Hunter's favorite, chicken-fried steak with all the trimmings. There will be cake and ice cream."

"Mom. He's working. He's not the welcome committee." Nash squeezed her arm. "Give us a minute."

"Sure thing, son." She returned the squeeze and gave Andy one last look that was a cross between motherly and middle school teacher. "You've lost weight. Have a cookie and take the lot home with you when you go." She patted her apron-covered stomach. "I'm saving room for ice cream and cake."

"Ma."

"I know, I know. I'm just excited."

She left them. Nash eased into the love seat across from the couch. He didn't offer his hand. Andy took a seat without extending his.

"I didn't know it was protocol for police to visit convicts when they returned to their communities." Nash leaned back against a large pillow with the verse John 3:16 embroidered on it. He crossed his ankle over his other knee and let his hands rest on his faded jeans. "It's nice of you to come, but I'm good. I don't plan to go on any drunken, murderous rampages in your town, Sheriff, if that's what you came to warn me about. Prison sucked the murderous rage right out of me."

He delivered the words in the same soft, polite tone used by his mother to invite Andy into the house. Sarcasm came in many forms.

"Good to know. Unfortunately, once again, I'm forced to question your sincerity."

"I've been out of prison . . ." Nash glanced at the genteel grandfather clock on the far wall next to shelves so overflowing with books, Mrs. Nash had begun stacking them on the floor and the coffee table that separated him and his adversary. "Eight hours and you're already harassing me. Surely you have new homicides to worry about."

"We're good at juggling." Andy leaned forward and locked gazes with him. "So, eight hours. That means you walked out of Dominguez at nine o'clock this morning. Did someone pick you up?"

"What's this about?"

"This will go better if you let me ask the questions."

"This isn't an interrogation room and I'm not under arrest . . . at least not yet. How did you know I got out this morning? Is there some sort of warning system they use to notify local police departments when a dangerous felon reenters the community?"

If Nash knew anything about Ellie Hill's death, he was doing a good job of faking his bewilderment. Waiting to drop the bomb on him for as long as possible gave Andy the opportunity to find out more about his movements before he lawyered up. Surely the guy had learned something from his first ride on the legal express. "How tall are you?"

"Six two. Why?"

"You weigh 190, 195?"

"Just 185. Prison food is a great weight-loss program. Why do you want to know?"

"Tell me what you've been doing all day, and I'll get out of your face a lot faster."

"Something happened, didn't it? Something you think I had

something to do with." For the first time fear seeped into Hunter's words. He clasped his hands. His knuckles whitened. "Did something happen to Delaney?"

"You first."

"My mom picked me up. We came straight home. I wanted to shower and change. I needed to get the prison stink off me. She made me bacon and eggs and toast for a late breakfast. I ran to Woodlawn Lake Park and ran the trail there. I worked out on the outdoor fitness equipment for a while. Then I sat on a bench and let the sun beat on my face and the breeze blow away the stench of the last ten years. I sketched ducks hanging out on the lake, kids fishing off the dock, and some guys playing a game of pickup basketball.

"I ran back. I took a nap in my old bedroom. The mattress still sucks so I got up. My mom gave me coffee—the best coffee I've had in ten years with real cream and sugar—and chocolate chip cookies. I took another shower. Then she gave me the keys to my truck. It wouldn't start. You showed up."

The socially inept, airhead artist who had trouble stringing two sentences together had disappeared in the school of hard knocks. Hunter met Andy's gaze head-on. He chose his words carefully. His tone was respectful but firm.

"Have you tried to contact any of your old friends today?"

"I don't have any old friends."

"You didn't contact Ellie Cruz-Hill or Delaney Broward?"

"Not today." His lips twisted in a painful smile. This was his Achilles' heel. "Laney stopped returning my calls after the trial. She never responded to a single letter I'd sent her from prison either. Contrary to popular sentiment, time does not heal all wounds. Just tell me, did something happen to her?"

"Physically, she's fine. Emotionally, she's devastated. You would be, too, if you found your best friend brutally stabbed to death in her shop this afternoon." Andy could handle a verbal stabbing with just as much brutality when he deemed it necessary. "Not as devastated as when she found her brother, but a close second."

"Her best friend . . . Ellie . . . you're talking about Ellie? Ellie's dead?" Nash's mouth dropped open. He rubbed his face. He shook his head. "Mommy Earth. That's what we called her. She loved playing the free spirit. Even though we all knew she was the most uptight of us all. She hated dirty dishes in the communal kitchen at the co-op. She put up a sign that said YOUR MOTHER DOESN'T WORK HERE. CLEAN UP AFTER YOURSELVES. She didn't even like sixties classic rock." His voice cracked.

"Seriously . . . you think I walked out of prison this morning after eight years of being a model prisoner so I could kill a sweet, good person like Ellie? What would be my motive?"

Either Oscar-caliber acting or innocent. Too soon to judge. Taking his time, Andy sipped his tea. He leaned back on the couch. "What time did you take this walk to the lake? How long were you gone?"

"What reason would I have for killing my best friend's girlfriend?"

"You didn't need much of a reason to kill your best friend. Ellie Cruz testified against you eight years ago."

"I may be a slow learner, but I do learn." Nash stood. "Am I under arrest?"

"No. We're just talking."

"Well, good. I don't want to be rude, but it's time for you to go."

Andy tapped the sketchbook. "You did some beautiful drawings of Ms. Broward while you were in prison."

"She makes it easy. You should go now."

"It almost borders on obsession, the number of drawings you did of her."

"I had to remind myself that beauty still exists in the world."

"You never draw the world's ugliness?"

"Sure. All the time." Nash picked up the sketchbook and thumbed through it. He stopped near the end. "Is this more to your taste?"

The scene, drawn with heavy, dark strokes, depicted a man with powerful, muscular shoulders and narrow hips, his face carved with animalistic hate, looming over a smaller man hunched on the floor of a shower. His face filled with pain and fear, the smaller man clutched at his chest. A pool of dark liquid swirled down the floor drain. The scene was so real Andy could smell the blood and the fear.

"Visceral is the word that comes to mind." Like a punch in the gut. "It might be more truthful, more real, than the ones of your former girlfriend."

"Gee, thanks. I drew that from memory after I finally had privileges and could buy art supplies from the commissary. It happened my first week in." Nash's fingers went to the scar on his jawline. "Most of the time I was so scared, I couldn't see straight. Most of the time I was afraid I would pee myself every time one of those Aryan Nations guys or a Mexican Mafia dude crossed my path. If you think I would risk going back there for *any* reason, you're the mental case. Like I said, time for you to go."

"How'd you get the scar?"

"I fell in the shower." Nash's expression hardened. "Or I cut myself shaving. Take your pick."

For some reason Nash didn't want to tell this story. "You're lucky he didn't get you in the neck."

"I don't believe in luck."

That made two of them. "You need to stay away from Ms. Broward."

"I'm a free man, Detective."

"With a record. On parole. You're also officially a person of interest in the murder of Ellie Hill." Andy rose and moved toward the door. "I don't think that will make those wounds you spoke of earlier heal any faster. Are you planning to live here with your mother? We'll need to know where to contact you."

"For the time being, but I also misspoke earlier when I said I have no friends. I have no friends from the old days. Among my new friends is a pastor who is giving me a job with at-risk youth at his community center. As soon as I get a few paychecks under my belt, I'll get my own place. You can always check with my parole officer."

Nash stepped in front of Andy, opened the screen door, and held it. He followed Andy out onto the porch. "Because of his work Pastor James has connections to Legal Aid. He told me if I ever need a good attorney to let him know. I plan to do that."

"Blessings with your new endeavor." Andy dug the keys to his PD unmarked unit from his suit pants' pocket. "I'm glad you were able to find a job so quickly. That's a huge hurdle for many convicted felons when they come out of the system. Your parole officer will be pleased as well."

"I was blessed to meet a prison chaplain who took his duties seriously. He probably saved my life in there." Hunter's gaze traveled toward Woodlawn Lake a few blocks away. The yearning in his face made him seem much older than thirty-five. "In more ways than one."

Andy had heard his share of conversion stories from hardened criminals willing to play the system any way they could to earn an early parole or escape a death sentence. Still, he didn't discount them the way his more cynical colleagues did. "God has been known to put people in our lives when or where we need them."

"It would've been nice if He'd given me a decent public defender as well, but Pastor James says God has a plan and He's working on me through all this. I choose to believe that. It got me through some long days and some even longer nights."

Real or playacting? Andy wanted to believe Nash's faith, born in a cesspool, was real. Some people had to go through hell to find heaven. If it wasn't real, the true Hunter Nash would reveal himself.

Andy would be there when he did.

CHAPTER 7

Ellie was dead. Stabbed to death just like Corey. Nausea formed a knot in the back of Hunter's throat. Sheer will kept him from vomiting in front of Ramos. Once again the detective had decided to zero in on an innocent man while a killer roamed the streets of San Antonio. Fists stuffed in his pockets, Hunter plastered a neutral look on his face. "Next time, call instead of just showing up at my mother's house."

"Do you have a new cell phone number?"

"Not yet. It's on my list of things to do."

A tan Suburban pulled up to the curb behind Ramos's unmarked Challenger.

Naturally, Curtis and his wife couldn't arrive five minutes later. They had to show up for the big family get-together right as Detective Ramos was leaving. Hunter heaved a breath and prepared himself for Curtis's passive-aggressive approach to big brotherhood. "See you around, Detective."

Ramos started down the steps. His path crossed Curtis's halfway. Hunter's brother gave the detective the once-over as he bounded past him with a six-pack of Heineken in each hand. He nodded. Then his smile turned into a scowl. He did remember. The detective nodded in return. No words were exchanged.

Detective Ramos stepped from the sidewalk to make way for Curtis's wife, Jody, who plodded along behind him, carrying a dozen helium-inflated balloons and a large plastic wrap–covered bowl. Their four boys tumbled from the Suburban, pushing and shoving and yelling. The twins had been five when Uncle Hunter "went away."

"What was he doing here?" Curtis tromped up the porch steps and waited for Hunter to hold the screen door for him. "Revisiting past conquests?"

"He got lost on his way to the lake."

"What, seven, eight hours out of the slammer, and you're already on the cops' radar?" He shoved past Hunter into the house. "That has to be a record."

Hunter knew better than to respond. Curtis had slipped into the role of head of the household somewhere in the vicinity of Hunter's freshman year in high school. Thus began the arguments about curfews, jobs, cars, dating, drinking, and life in general. Mom insisted he meant well. That he cared. More like he loved lording it over his younger brother and sisters.

"Welcome home, welcome home." Jody raised her face for a peck on the cheek. Hunter obliged. "We're so happy for you. I brought my Dijon mustard potato salad. You always liked it."

She had a good memory and a good heart. "Thank you. I'm glad to be home."

The twins paused long enough to say an awkward hello to an uncle they didn't remember before they moved inside in search of food. Apparently they were starving. Weren't all fifteen-year-olds? Their younger brothers, who'd never met their uncle Hunter, followed suit.

Hunter didn't move. He was stuck to the porch floor. How could he celebrate while Ellie's cold, bloodied body went under the coroner's knife? Ellie had her faults, but her big heart far exceeded them. Nothing she'd said at the trial had been untrue. It simply gave jurors a skewed picture of what Hunter's relationship with Corey had been. They didn't argue all the time. Just sometimes. They were more like brothers than friends. Corey worried about Hunter hurting Delaney. Hunter chafed at Corey's insistence on playing big-brother-slash-father-figure to her.

They should never have gone into business together. The co-op had been a mistake. One that could never be rectified. It destroyed their friendship and ended Corey's life.

But not at Hunter's hand.

A Chevy Tahoe pulled into the driveway followed by a Jeep Grand Cherokee. The SUVs barely fit side by side. His sisters did everything together, even now as married women with children.

Lots of children. Melissa had three and another one on the way. Shawna had four.

Baby-making machines. Only Hunter had none.

Ignoring the ache in his throat, he hugged and kissed and mouthed all the right words. Shawna whooped and did a Snoopy dance all the way to the door, balancing a Costco-sized carrot cake with cream cheese frosting. "Make way, make way, brother of mine. I come bearing carbs."

Hunter had to smile. They were cut from the same mold as his mother. Unshakable in their faith in him. "I'm all about the carbs today."

Mel handed him a massive H-E-B grocery bag and stepped in for an equally massive hug. She pushed back and gave him a fierce once-over. "What you've been through is awful. I hope you can put it behind you and move on. Today is, like they say, the first day of the rest of your life."

"Me too. How's your husband doing?"

"Counting the days until he comes home from Germany. He rues the day he decided to re-up." She patted her baby belly protruding behind a tight, hot-pink T-shirt that showed off her outie. "He'll be back in time for little Nicholas's birth in August."

"Nicholas?"

"Hubby's best buddy in the Marines."

Both women had married soldiers. They really did do everything together.

Mel linked arms with Hunter. Together they moved through the living room overflowing with kids all talking at once over a movie that appeared to involve cars that turned into gargantuan robots. The noise level was through the roof.

"Mom says you learned welding and auto mechanics!" Mel yelled. She stopped long enough to tap her oldest daughter on the shoulder and put her finger to her lips. "Inside voices please."

Trina giggled and nodded.

No change in volume.

"It was something to do."

The aroma of frying meat greeted them in the kitchen. Hunter's mouth watered. Real food. He'd dreamed about it night after night and woke up starving. Curtis had a bottle opener in one hand and a beer in the other. Jody pulled paper plates from the cabinet while Shawna unboxed the cake and laid it in the center of the breakfast nook table. Family. It was overwhelming. Almost too much after so little for so long. His brain teetered between overload and shutting down. He sucked in a breath and willed his heart to slow down. "I thought I would need a trade, that I wouldn't be able to teach."

Hunter never had any illusions that he could support himself with his art. That had been Corey's dream. He had the talent and the ego it took to dream big dreams. What he didn't have was good business sense, which led to some mistakes.

Nobody wanted to talk about that. Hunter didn't. How could he denigrate the memory of his best friend in order to defend himself?

No one believed him anyway. Not even the pipsqueak PD who got his law degree from an online college.

"What are you talking about? A job?" Curtis held out the beer. Hunter shook his head. Curtis's bushy eyebrows popped up. He shrugged and took a long swig instead. "You'll work for me, of course. I've got a sales position open on the floor."

Curtis owned two car dealerships.

That beer looked better and better. Hunter's throat went dry. He went to the fridge and pulled out a pitcher of fresh-brewed tea. Taking his time, he poured a glass, added some lemon juice and a tablespoon of sugar. It took half a glass to swallow the lump in his throat.

Thank You, God, for graciously giving me a job so I don't have to sell cars for my brother. Or anything else. He turned back to face Curtis. "I already have a job."

His brother rolled his eyes. "Doing what? Selling caricatures on street corners?"

He sounded like their dad. Alleged dad. The last time Hunter had seen him was when he showed up two days late for Hunter's high school graduation. He'd harangued Hunter about his decision to attend art school, urged him to join the military to "become a man," and flown out the next day with a promise of a longer visit "later."

Of course, he never came. Mom called him after Hunter had been arrested. His number was disconnected. Letters came back *not at this address, no forwarding address.*

Dealing with Curtis was like déjà vu. Could attitude be genetic? *Keep it together.*

Hunter gulped down the rest of the tea and poured more. *Deep breaths.* He ran through his plan, which had the approval of his parole officer.

"Mom, do you believe this guy?" Curtis shoved a chip loaded

with chile con queso into his mouth and chewed. Cheese dripped from his lip into the scruffy black five o'clock shadow on his chin. "He thinks they'll let a convicted murderer get close to a bunch of kids. Still living in la-la land even after ten years behind bars."

"No need to be nasty, son." Mom manhandled a chicken-fried steak from a pan of hot oil onto a plate covered with paper towels. "If this Pastor James says he has a job, he has a job. Hunter can be good for these kids. He can tell them his story. He can try to keep them from going down the wrong path."

"What's he going to say? Don't get high, drink booze, and stab your best friend? Or don't get caught?"

"I didn't kill Corey." Hunter kept a tight grip on his anger. "I told you that then and I'm telling you now. The person who killed Corey was never caught or prosecuted."

"You forget I sat through the entire trial, bro. The case against you—"

"Was circumstantial."

"You were there. With your buddy the night he died. You admitted that on the stand. You argued with him. You were drunk and high. Your fingerprints were all over the place. You couldn't remember what you argued about. Even your girlfriend and that chick Ellie said you guys fought all the time. Especially when you drank."

Hunter did remember what the fight was about, but his public defender couldn't find any evidence to support Hunter's theory. A key witness couldn't be found. No one believed Hunter's story. "We practically lived at the co-op. We worked, ate, and slept there most of the time. Naturally my fingerprints were all over his studio. His were all over mine."

"Water under the bridge." Mel stepped in between Hunter and

Curtis. "Tonight's about celebrating the future and putting the past behind us."

"Yeah, here's to the future." Curtis held up his beer in a mock toast. "You and me, working together at the dealership. You like cars. Mom said you got certified in auto repair in the slammer. You'll be able to talk all things cars with the customers. It's a good living. You should see the house we bought in Stone Oak. Five bedroom, three bathroom, three-car garage, pool, hot tub. Huge kitchen."

Sometimes Curtis kept talking to hear himself talk. Even when everyone else stopped listening. He didn't have a clue how much salt he managed to pour into wounds. Not that Hunter ever coveted a five-bedroom house with a pool and a hot tub.

"I need some air, Ma." Hunter whirled and strode toward the door. "I'll be back."

His lungs refused to suck in that air. His throat hurt. Pain radiated from the center of his chest. He picked up speed until he pushed through the screen door and out onto the porch.

"Hunter, come on, ignore him. He's a blowhard. Nobody's listening to him." Mel caught him on the porch steps. "Don't leave. All this is for you."

"Ma will understand. Tell her to save me a plate."

"Where are you going?"

Good question. He had four ten-dollar bills and a dollar's worth of change—what was left in his commissary account—in his wallet. His truck wouldn't start. "Do you have jumper cables?"

"I don't think so." Mel's face creased with concern. "Maybe Curtis does."

"No, don't ask that jerk. Please. It'd just be fuel for the fire. Forget it."

"He offered you a job, Hunter."

"Because it allows him to feel magnanimous and lord it over me at the same time. His little brother, the screwup, the convict, the one everyone is ashamed of."

"It's not like that."

Only it was. Hunter had to prove he was innocent. To his family. To Delaney. The only way to do that was to find the real killer. "Do you still have contacts at SAPD?"

Before becoming a full-time mom, Mel had been a 911 dispatcher. "I stay in touch with some folks, sure." Her forehead puckered. "Why?"

"I didn't kill Corey."

"I know."

"I plan to prove it."

She groaned.

"Thank you for your support, sis."

"You'll only cause yourself more trouble and heartache. Haven't you had your fill of both?"

He had. He shouldn't have said anything. Now she would worry. "Go back inside. Enjoy the food. Save me a piece of cake. The rocky road ice cream is all mine. I'll be back later."

"If there's anything I can do to help, I will." Mel planted herself between Hunter and the sidewalk that led to freedom. "You name it."

"Detective Ramos came to tell me that Ellie Hill was murdered this morning. Reach out to your contacts. Let me know what you hear about the investigation."

"On the day you get out of prison, that's—"

"Exactly. That's why Ramos was here."

Mel's mom persona disappeared, replaced with the one she assumed before going on shift for one of the toughest jobs imaginable. "I'm on it."

"Take it easy. Don't make yourself a pest."

"Me a pest? Ha. My buddies miss me. They keep asking me when I'll be back."

It wouldn't happen, not as long as her husband continued to serve his country overseas and they continued to make babies. Hunter slid his arm around her in a one-arm hug. "Thanks."

"You can always stay with me if Mom gets to be too much for you." Mel returned the hug. "I could use some adult company. The rug rats would love having you around too. They miss manliness."

And then she could keep an eye on him. Leave it to Mel to make him want to bawl. "You're all that and a bag of chips, sis."

"So stay."

"I gotta go. I need air."

He needed open space, unending sky, unfettered movement. He needed to walk, run, lift weights—anything to keep his mind off the bottles of beer calling his name from the kitchen.

"I love you, Bubbas."

The childhood nickname was the last straw. Hunter swallowed a big, fat sob. "Love you too."

"I'll tell Mom you need some time. It was a little too soon, a little much to have us all descend on you so soon." Mel patted his face. "We'll save you a plate. Just don't forget where you live and who the people that love you are."

"I won't," Hunter choked out the words, spun around, and sped down the steps. The last thing he wanted to do was bawl in front of his sister.

He headed toward the lake. Dusk crept in from the horizon. Doors and windows were open in the aged houses that lined the wide streets of a neighborhood that surrounded Woodlawn Lake. Anyone who grew up in San Antonio knew killer summer heat and humidity would come soon enough. These fleeting spring days had to be enjoyed outdoors.

The smell of charcoal barbecue wafted in the air. Ranchera music blared from one house, a Spanish telenovela from the next.

A pack of kids played olly olly oxen free a few houses down. Their raucous laughter soothed his irritation. *Don't grow up. Just don't do it. Stay out here playing for as long as humanly possible.*

The desire to have his own kids, to roll around in the grass rough-housing with them, burned through him. In prison he'd learned to stifle it. Out here, kids were everywhere. Constant reminders. Delaney wanted a house full of kids. She wanted a big family.

It seemed like a lifetime ago.

When a person went to prison he didn't just forfeit his freedom. He also lost human connections. Human touch. Uneasy alliances could be formed, maybe even true friendships in rare cases, but a man quickly learned to search for ulterior motive in every overture, even the smallest one.

How long would it take to overcome that defense mechanism or was it permanent?

Given how quickly his so-called friends had bailed on him, Hunter leaned toward the latter.

The next block over a teenager used a shammy cloth to polish a gorgeous classic black Pontiac Trans Am. A garden hose snaked down the wet concrete drive. The smell of wet earth hung in the air. The kid looked up, saw Hunter, and grinned. "Beautiful, ain't she?"

"Gorgeous."

"My pops gave it to me for my eighteenth birthday. His pops gave it to him way back when."

To have a father like that. The kid had no idea how blessed he was. Lime-green envy slithered through Hunter. He banished it with a mental slingshot. Having a mother who gave Superwoman a run for her money made him blessed as well. "That's amazing. It must mean a lot to you to know it was your grandfather's, then your father's, now yours."

"That's what he said. Plus, I got no payments. Just insurance. And gas."

Insurance would be through the roof for an eighteen-year-old male and his muscle car.

His grin so wide it must hurt, the kid wiped down a side mirror. "Gas ain't cheap."

Hunter studied the gleaming car and the kid. Any kid with a car like that would be itching to drive it all day and all night. "Hey, I'm Hunter Nash, Ms. Nash's son from down the street."

"I had her for sixth-grade English. She's legit."

"Yes, she is. Would you consider giving me a ride? There's twenty bucks in gas money in it for you."

The kid straightened. "Hey, aren't you the dude who went to jail for murder?"

"Yep."

The boy shrugged. "Where you're going?"

"Out Highway 16, west of Helotes."

"That's like thirty miles from here. Make it thirty bucks and it's a deal."

"Are you sure your parents won't mind?"

The teen held up his phone. "I'll send Mom a text, let her know where I'm going. It's all good."

"Thirty it is, then."

"Javier." The kid stuck out his hand. "Javier Santos."

Hunter shook it. "Let's roll."

The first step in righting past wrongs awaited Hunter. Starting right now.

CHAPTER 8

Delaney put the Trailblazer in Park on the street in front of Michael and Ellie's home in the historic Olmos Park neighborhood. At dusk the three-story, red-brick, Georgian-style house shone brightly. The lights were on in every window. She planted both hands at the top of the wheel and laid her forehead on them for a few seconds. Maybe Michael didn't need her after all. Maybe his friends had his back.

Michael had accepted Delaney, Cam, and Jess because he knew how much they meant to Ellie. To his credit he wanted his wife to be happy. If he was ever jealous of their tight-knit relationships, he never let it show. He tolerated the walks down memory lane, the inside jokes, and the sometimes-heated discussions about art. Whether his relationship to Ellie's old friends would survive remained to be seen. They owed it to her to have his back now. Even if he decided to distance himself, the kids would still need their "aunts" Delaney and Cam.

Michael had joint custody of the children. His ex-wife, a flight attendant, didn't want to give up her career—apparently the reason they'd ended up divorced. Ellie had confided in Delaney that Michael wasn't a warm and fuzzy type of dad. He couldn't be trusted to know about Peppa Pig or Daniel Tiger and Dog Man graphic novels. He wasn't the kind of dad who braided hair, made dinosaurs from

Play-Doh, or responded to knock-knock jokes. Which made Ellie, thrust into the role of motherhood, determined to learn everything she could as fast as she could.

She was a good mommy, and she wanted brothers and sisters for Jacob and Skye.

The old Delaney had thought she would have tons of kids. That didn't seem likely now. Instead, she hung out with Jake and Skye and told herself it was enough.

It had to be enough.

Deep breaths. Her therapist's voice sounded in her head. *"Deep, slow breaths. Breathe in through your nose, hold it, one-two-three-four, breathe out through your mouth, one-two-three-four."*

Those moments when the walls closed in and she found herself back in the co-op with Corey's bloody body in her arms, all she had was a breathing exercise and the hope that one day it would get better. One day she'd be able to trust her judgment—trust another human being with her heart. Until then, she worked out seven days a week and practiced something that came naturally to everyone else—breathing.

"You're a survivor," she whispered. She'd survived another interview at the police department headquarters. She would keep putting one foot in front of the other. "You got through it once. You'll do it again."

Her therapist called it positive self-talk.

She would be there for rambunctious Skye and sweet Jacob. She had experience with traumatized children. One more long, slow breath. Resolute, she hopped from the SUV and shut the door. Squaring her shoulders, she turned and—boom—ran smack into a body as solid as Texas's Enchanted Rock.

Not again.

This time Delaney was ready. She shoved her assailant hard.

With a startled grunt he stumbled back, giving her precious seconds to tug her stun gun-slash-Taser from the front pocket of the purse hanging from her shoulder.

Zap. Twenty seconds of fifty thousand volts of electric hell delivered directly to his chest.

Gasping, the man fell to his knees, then flat on his face, his body rigid.

Breathing as if she'd just run a marathon, Delaney held the stun gun at the ready. Her legs felt like mush and her arms shook, but she didn't back off. "Stay down and I'll call the police. Get up and I'll zap you again."

"Good grief, Laney. It's me. Jess." Even muffled, the attorney's deep radio DJ voice was unmistakable. He struggled to roll over but couldn't manage it. "I told you I would meet you here."

Stun gun still ready, Delaney leaned closer. Her attacker was no stranger, no threat. Embarrassment raced through her. She shoved the stun gun back in her purse and squatted next to him. "Jess! Seriously? I'm so sorry. Are you all right? You didn't say you planned to sneak up on me."

"No, I'm not all right. You tased me. That hurt like a son of a gun." His face crimson in the streetlight, he curled into a fetal position. "I didn't sneak. I was standing there waiting for you to get out of the car. You seemed like you were in deep thought—"

"Technically I stunned you. This gun does both but at close range, I can use it to stun. I'm so, so sorry. It's been a horrible day. I'm a mess." Sweat rolled down her forehead into her eyes despite the cool evening breeze. It had started all over again. Jumping at shadows. Walking around with pepper spray in one hand, Taser in the other. She'd been past all of that. "That would've been a good time to say 'Hey, Delaney, it's me, Jess.'"

"Hey, Delaney, it's me, Jess." The lawyer, who had given up making beautiful musical instruments after Corey's murder, tried to sit up. His body rebelled. He shook his head as if trying to shake off the pain. "I knew you had a stun gun, but I never expected you to use it on me."

The idea of carrying a loaded pistol in her purse had scared Delaney too much. A gun was no good if a person was afraid to use it. This was a perfect example of why she shouldn't have a gun. Jess might be dead instead of temporarily stunned. "It works for me. I can defend myself without taking extreme measures."

"Stunning a guy is pretty extreme." Jess rubbed his chest. "I guess I should be thankful you didn't shoot me."

"I certainly am."

"We agreed to go in together."

"I thought you were going to text me."

"I saw your car pull up. At that point it seemed silly to text. I could see you from my car."

Jess's reaction to the news of Ellie's murder had been barely contained sobs. His effort to control his emotions had matched Delaney's, but as always, his first concern had been for Delaney and for Ellie's kids.

"Are you sure you're all right?" Delaney surveyed him in the tepid light. Over the years the stocky man not much taller than she was had gone pudgy. His curly blond locks had given way to a short, neat haircut, but underneath it all he was still the guy who never seemed at home in his own skin or his ill-fitting navy suit. "Should I call 911?"

"I'll live. I'm sorry I snuck up on you. It was my fault."

Vintage Jess. Always apologizing for everything—whether it was his fault or not.

"Let me help you up." Delaney moved to a squat and grabbed his arm. "One, two, three."

Together they maneuvered him into a sitting position. He brushed dead leaves and dirt from his pants. The red had faded from his face, leaving his skin chalky white. "I think I can stand now."

"One, two, three, up you go."

Jess wobbled. Delaney threw her arm around his waist. He put his around her shoulders. She guided him toward the driveway. "I really am sorry."

"I know. You'd never intentionally hurt a person. It's not you."

It didn't used to be. "Have you talked to anyone in the family yet?"

"I called her sister. She was glad I already knew. She's the one making all the calls."

"She must be devastated. Why can't a friend of the family make the calls?"

Hunter had made the calls for Delaney. The irony of it still haunted her on nights when she stared into the dark abyss, too bone weary of life to sleep. He'd hugged and kissed and cuddled her. He tempted her non-existent appetite with dishes he cooked from scratch. He slept on her couch for three nights, keeping her safe. Holding her after the nightmares. Making her chamomile tea with honey and lemon to settle her stomach and help her sleep.

All the way through the trial, she held out hope that the police had made a mistake and arrested the wrong man. She couldn't lose Hunter too. But she did. After that, she learned to keep herself safe. To never trust a man for anything.

"She's an oncologist. She has to be a tough cookie." Jess leaned heavily on Delaney. He smelled of Polo cologne and wintergreen Altoids. "I don't think she intended for everyone to show up here tonight though. She's in Kansas City and can't get here until tomorrow. Michael has to be overwhelmed. Not to mention the kids."

"That's the main reason I'm here. The kids."

Jess stumbled. His grip tightened. "So tell me about the robbery—or whatever it was."

Going over the gory details on the phone had seemed wrong. They would only cause Jess more pain now. "I don't know what I walked into the middle of. It happened so fast."

"You saw her killer. Did you get a good look at him?"

Spoken like an attorney doing cross-examination. Delaney was too tired for another round of questions, but she had stunned the guy, after all. "He was tall and big. He had a black stocking over his face. He wore a long-sleeved shirt and jogging pants. And gloves. His hands were big and strong around my neck."

Jess huffed a long breath. "You could've been killed."

"I'm aware. That's the thing I keep asking, which no one can answer. Why kill Ellie but not me?"

"Maybe he didn't mean to kill Ellie. Maybe she resisted. You know how stubborn she could be."

"You don't think I resisted? I'm not a pushover. Not anymore. He caught me off guard, but that won't happen again."

"Laney!"

"He told me to stay out of it. Stay out of what?"

"We've already lost Corey and Ellie." Jess let go as they approached Michael and Ellie's steps. Just Michael's steps now. "We can't lose you too."

"We didn't lose them. They were taken from us. I know who killed Corey and why. He's in prison. Ellie's death is likely totally unrelated to Corey's. He tried to make it appear like a robbery, but his words don't match up to it. The killer didn't expect me to be there, so he made up a threat to rattle me."

"Could it have been an irate customer who wanted his money back?"

"She sold candles and aromatherapy oils."

"An angry husband?"

Delaney joined Jess in staring at the house. A few more steps and they'd be at the door with its camera and smart doorbell. Not the place to have this discussion.

"He adores her. Adored her."

"Leave it to the police to figure out."

"It's Detective Ramos. He remembers me as this innocent, naive little kid. That's not me anymore."

"You always were the strong one." Jess paused in front of the door. He smoothed back his hair and wiped his face with his sleeve. "Corey never acknowledged that, but you were the one who held things together."

Delaney knew better. Corey worked two part-time jobs to pay the bills while she went to college and worked part-time managing a Smoothie King. He still found time to do his art and run the co-op. His oil paintings of life on San Antonio's streets had just begun to make their mark in the art world when he was stabbed to death next to a half-finished painting of Ellie, her mother, and her sisters making tamales. "Thank you, but you're rewriting history."

"I can't believe she's gone."

"At least she got her wish for romance. She was so in love with Michael."

"Yeah, she did. A case of opposites attract, I guess." Jess rubbed his baby-blue eyes with both hands. "I never understood it."

No one did. Aware of the camera pointed at them both, Delaney raised her hand to ring the doorbell. No need to prolong the inevitable.

CHAPTER 9

A reprieve came after all, in the form of Cam Sanchez. The door opened and their old friend stared out at them, leaning on her carved wooden cane.

"You're a sight for sore eyes." Delaney enveloped her friend in hug that almost bowled over the petite artist. "I can't believe she's gone. I can't believe this is happening again."

Cam's cane fell on the tile with a clatter. Her arms came around Delaney. "Thank goodness you're okay. I'm so sorry you had to go through that again. I'm so glad you're here. Both of you. Michael's been asking for you."

Jess picked up the cane and held it out. "You've got dark circles under your eyes. Why are you the one on door duty?"

"I volunteered." Cam let go of Delaney, took Jess's offering, and hugged him. Cam was an equal-opportunity hugger. She drew back, her expressive face full of concern. "What happened to you? Did you get mugged downtown?"

"I tripped and fell."

Leave it to Jess to take the fall—literally and figuratively—for Delaney's mistake. "I used my stun gun on him."

"Delaney!"

"It was—"

"Never mind. It was an accident." Jess intervened. "Who's here? How's Michael doing? And the kids?"

"Michael's sister is on her way from Wichita Falls. He seems to want us around though. He keeps saying we're the ones who loved Ellie the most."

"What about Michael's parents?"

"They were here earlier, but they went to see if Ellie's parents need anything. They both have to work tomorrow, but his dad said he'd help Michael make the arrangements whenever he's ready."

The Hills were nice working-class folks—a Department of Public Works employee and an office manager who lived on the south side and worked downtown. The Cruzes were both plastic surgeons with a stylish new home built near Cedar Creek Golf Course on the north side, down the road from their practice off 1604 and 1H-10.

They managed to make it work, especially after the Cruzes graciously paid for them to fly to Mexico for the wedding.

Relief washed through Delaney. Guilt trotted in ahead of shame. She wouldn't have to face the rest of the family. Not tonight. "How are the kids?"

"Bewildered. He let them eat pizza, potato chips, and ice cream sundaes for dinner. I'm hoping neither one pukes in bed tonight."

"Where's Charlene?"

"Coming in on a flight from Atlanta tomorrow morning. She's already making noise about changing the custody agreement."

Michael's ex was between a rock and a hard place, like many single or divorced mothers. She loved her kids, but her work took her away from home too often to be their primary caregiver. Delaney didn't envy her.

Ignoring the painful ache in her throat, she followed Cam down the hallway to the living room. Michael sat in an overstuffed chair next to an enormous stone fireplace. He hadn't cleaned it out the last time it was used. The black pit still held half-burnt pieces of wood and ashes that gave the room a strange odor, like someone had just returned from camping.

Michael was built more like a pro basketball player than an accountant. He stood well over six feet; had long, lean legs; and big hands. He ran six miles every morning before work. What little black hair remained on his head he shaved. His dark chocolate eyes could pierce to the bone.

The killer was tall. A shiver ran through Delaney. No, surely she would've recognized Michael's voice. Fleeting impressions suggested the killer had more weight. Michael was solid but lean. Wasn't he? It had happened so fast.

Her head said one thing, but her heart said another. Michael adored his wife. Five months ago he had stood on a beach in Mexico and promised to love, honor, and cherish Ellie. Nothing could've changed that drastically since then.

From light to dark. From artistic to a bean counter. From philosophical to mundane.

Still wearing one of the expensive suits he favored, now rumpled, Michael stared into the dark pit as if the answer to all his questions lay in the ruins. His hands gripped an empty coffee mug. Skye was sprawled on the couch next to Jacob. He read aloud from a Dog Man book.

"Laney, Laney!" Skye rolled off the couch, landed on her feet, and trotted toward Delaney. Her chubby cheeks dimpled. She had Michael's dark hair and eyes, but her skin was fair. The remnants of her supper decorated her face, hands, and Dora the Explorer T-shirt. "I had strawberry ice cream. Daddy said I could. He's sad."

"I had chocolate chip with chocolate syrup." Jacob lowered the book. He was the spitting image of his dad, but then Delaney had never met Charlene. Unlike Skye, he didn't smile. "Ellie's not coming home. Daddy says she's dead."

Michael didn't move. He didn't seem to register his son's words. Cam's fingers tightened on Delaney's arm. Delaney patted her hand and tugged free. Kids knew how to get right to the nitty-gritty. Unadorned truth worked best for them in small, gentle doses. She scooped up Skye and went to sit next to Jacob. Michael could wait.

"I'm sorry, Jacob." She put her arm around him and cuddled both kids close. "It makes me sad. I know it must make you sad too."

Skye sighed. "Ellie reads to me at night. Who will read to me now?"

"Me." Jacob's tone bordered on belligerent. The little boy scowled. He slammed the book shut. "Wasn't I just reading to you?"

"Who will tie my shoes?" Skye's head drooped against Delaney's chest. "Ellie always gives me my bath. She takes me to school. She knows when my birthday is."

That she didn't assume it would be her own mother spoke volumes. "We'll figure it out. I promise. Your daddy will take care of you. Your mom is coming home to be with you. Your nanas and pops will take care of you. Your aunts and uncles. Jess. Me and Cam and Jaime will be here. You don't have to worry. You won't be alone."

"Mom's never here." Jacob threw the book on the floor. "She likes airplanes more than us."

Delaney waited for Michael to contradict him. Michael stared into the fireplace.

She picked up the book and laid it on the table. "Your mom loves you very much. She has to work. I know it's hard to understand now, but someday you will. Maybe for now, Cam and Jaime can help you two get ready for bed. You could both use baths, and it's been a long day."

"I don't want to go to bed." Jacob's face scrunched up. His voice quavered. "I want Ellie. She knows how to do my math problems."

"I know, honey." Delaney did know. Losing every single loved one shattered a person into such small pieces there was no putting her back together. "It doesn't seem like it now, but you'll get through it. We all will."

Because they had no choice. Kids were more resilient than adults, but they shouldn't have to be. She handed Skye to Jaime. The little girl didn't protest. His small, freckled face morose, Jacob slid from the couch and approached his father. "Daddy?"

Michael jumped. The coffee cup slid from his hands and landed with a thump on the rug. Jacob picked it up and set it on the table. "Can you come upstairs with us?"

"I'll be up later. Wash your face and brush your teeth. Be sure to say your prayers."

"I know." Jacob didn't move. "You promise you'll come and say good night?"

Michael's Adam's apple bobbed. Tears rolled down his sunken cheeks. Grief had turned him into an old man in a few scant hours. "I promise."

Jacob hurled himself at his father. Michael's arms wrapped around his son. They huddled there as the seconds ticked by. Finally, Michael disengaged. "Go on, Jakie."

Cam took the boy's hand and they made a solemn procession from the room. Delaney dragged a rocking chair closer to Michael and sat. He had returned to his contemplation of the cold fireplace.

"Michael, I'm so sorry."

His gaze glanced off hers and went back to the fireplace. "You saw him. The man who killed Ellie. You let him get away."

His accusatory tone stung. "I tried to fight him. He hit me."

And I thought I was going to die.

"Your description is all they have to go on."

"I did my best. He was big. At least six feet tall, 190. Strong."

"Did he have an accent?"

"Detective Ramos already asked me these questions. He was local."
Michael slumped in his chair. "That narrows it down."

"They're just getting started in their investigation. They may know more than they're telling us." More than they would tell the spouse until they'd investigated him thoroughly. More than they would tell a witness who claimed to have seen the perpetrator. They wouldn't take either of their statements at face value. "It might have been a robbery gone bad."

"Stay out of it or you're next."

Not the words of a robber.

"Ellie and I talked about what to do if someone tried to rob her. She was smart. She would've handed over the cash and anything else he wanted. Even that rock on her finger. She loved that ring, but not enough to die for it. So why kill her?"

"Did she talk about anyone giving her a hard time recently?"

"You sound like Detective Flores." Michael grimaced and pulled at the tie that already hung loose around his neck. "Nobody gave Ellie a hard time. She handed out free samples. She gave away free cookies and served herbal tea in the shop. She dispensed free advice to anyone she thought needed it. In the end that was her downfall."

He was right. Ellie was a good person. She was also a good businesswoman. She knew how to connect with people.

Michael ran trembling fingers over his shiny, shaved head. His shoulders slumped. "I got her killed. It was my fault."

CHAPTER 10

What had Michael done?

Delaney dropped to her knees on the rug in front of him. She took his hands in hers and rubbed them. They were icy cold. "What are you talking about? You loved her. You took care of her."

Michael tugged free. His head dropped into his hands. Muffled sobs seeped through. "It's my fault."

He was an accountant with a thriving company. They took trips to Maui and drove high-end SUVs. The kids went to an expensive private school. "We all felt safe at La Villita. There's never been a security problem. You had no way of knowing. The police will figure out who did it. They'll catch him."

"That's what I'm afraid of. They can't know." He raised his head and stared at her, his face filled with misery. "I can't tell the police. If I do, he'll have me killed. Or worse, he'll send him after the kids."

"Who will?" Jess crowded them. "What did you do?"

Delaney shook her head. *Back off.*

Jess shrugged and gave her his *trying-to-help* look.

"What's going on, Michael? You can tell me. We'll figure it out."

"I took on the wrong client. He had a number of companies. It was a whole new revenue stream." Michael scrubbed his face with both hands. Lines that hadn't been there the day before marred his chiseled features. "When I realized what I'd gotten myself into, I tried to sever the relationship. It turns out that's not allowed."

In San Antonio many businesses had international ties to Mexico, Latin America, and even Europe. The city had a thriving military, medical, and technology-related economy rivaled only by tourism, with its low-paying service-industry jobs. "Who?"

"The name won't mean anything to you. Gerard Knox. He's a bad guy masquerading as a legitimate businessman."

"That's one possibility, but it may not be the only one." Employing that painful one-leg-dragging gait, Cam entered the room.

Her words gave Delaney a chance to corral her own desire to eviscerate Michael. As an accountant he had to be savvy about the business practices of his clients. Companies this close to the border easily had ties to illicit activities. Money laundering, import-export of guns, the narcotics trade, any number of possibilities reared their illegal and monstrous heads. Michael should have told the police immediately. Now he ran the risk of appearing complicit.

Delaney eased back on her haunches and swiveled to glance back at Cam. That there could be other forces at play simply muddied already turbulent waters. "What do you mean?"

"Are the kids asleep?" Michael broke in before Cam could answer. He tried to stand, wobbled, and fell back into his chair. "I should tuck them in."

"Jaime's reading to them. It'll be a while before either one falls asleep." Cam squeezed past Jess. White lines etched around her mouth spoke of pain that never abated. Dark circles ringed her eyes. She'd never regained her stamina after the accident. "Did Ellie seem flightier than usual lately?"

"She was Ellie." Delaney pulled her legs up and sat cross-legged on the rug. "Sometimes I think she inhaled too much of those essential oils. She called me at midnight last week to ask me for Nana's recipe for banana cream pie. She wanted to make it for her mom's birthday."

Her mom's birthday wasn't until June.

Cam planted herself next to the fireplace. "I came over last Saturday to help her clean out the big room on the third floor she's been using for storage. She suddenly got a wild hair that she was going to start painting again."

That Cam climbed two flights of stairs to help probably didn't even register with Ellie. She lived in her own little world.

"She mentioned painting but not the boxes." Ellie never wanted to talk about her art—or lack thereof—with Delaney. She was afraid it would bring bad memories to the surface. She didn't have Corey's talent, but not many artists did. "She thought it would help her destress. I didn't see how she could fit one more thing into her schedule."

"She kept all the boxes at her parents' house after the co-op closed." A look of distaste on his face, Michael shifted in his chair. "She moved them here before the wedding. When she told me what she planned to do, I thought it was a passing fancy."

"We started going through the boxes. She said the room had great natural light. She needed a room of her own." Sadness filled Cam's face. It only made her warm Polynesian features more beautiful. "We'd been sorting stuff into Goodwill, trash, and keep piles when she suddenly grabbed some books and slammed them back into a box. She closed it up and walked out of the room.

"I thought she was coming back so I kept going." Cam shrugged. "She didn't so finally I went to find her. She was sitting on the deck in back, drinking Dewar's on ice. In the middle of the afternoon."

"Too many memories?"

"That's what she said, but I got the feeling it was something else. Something she found in that box."

"Like what?"

"I don't know. She refused to talk about it. I had to wrestle the bottle of scotch from her and get her to take a nap. I didn't want the kids to see her like that."

"You know, I hate to say this . . ." Forehead wrinkled, Jess steepled his fingers. He'd assumed his attorney persona. "But it kind of gives credence to Nash's insistence there was something going on at the co-op. That Corey got in bed with the wrong people to keep it open."

"No. No!"

The negative response rang from all quarters. Jess held up those hands in surrender. "Okay, okay, but what would be in those boxes that would freak out Ellie? She knew everything about Corey and everything about the co-op."

"I knew she was upset about something. I told Detective Flores that." Michael hunched down in his chair. "I'm sorry, Delaney. I had to give him another direction to go in. I told him to take a deep dive into everyone who had anything to do with the co-op. Hunter Nash and your brother were involved in something so bad Nash killed him over it."

"Hunter was convicted of manslaughter because it was simply a drunken fight." The same old ridiculous desire to bawl hit Delaney. As usual, she ignored it. "You have to tell the detectives the truth. Don't you want Ellie's killer brought to justice?"

"I don't know for a fact that Knox did this. And I have to protect my kids, no matter what."

And himself. Delaney reached for a calm she didn't feel. "Did Ellie say something to you about the co-op . . . or Corey's death?"

"It's not like I wanted to talk about her dead boyfriend." Michael leaned forward, elbows on his knees. His dark eyes had gone hard as agates. "But she seemed to need to talk about it. Like she needed a clean slate when we got married. She told me she loved him. She said his death broke something in her . . ." Michael's voice trailed off.

After the funeral and Hunter's conviction, Ellie had rarely talked about Corey. Neither did Delaney. They both tiptoed around lingering pain so excruciating, it still woke Delaney in the middle of the night. Contrary to popular belief, talking about it didn't help. "That must've been terribly hurtful to you."

"It didn't feel good, but I didn't care. I loved Ellie and I was willing to marry her on her terms." He lowered his head and stared at his tassels on his leather loafers. "The day before we flew to Mexico she insisted on telling me the whole story. She said I needed to know who I was marrying. After I'd heard the story I could back out if I wanted to."

"I don't understand. Ellie never said anything during the investigation or the trial that indicated she knew anything more."

"She said Corey'd been acting weird for weeks." Michael shrugged. "He argued with someone on the phone. He disappeared for hours with no explanation. He was moody and irritable—"

"Corey's mood ran in cycles. He was sweet and crazy and silly one day, moody and irritable the next. That was his MO." Corey had felt paying the bills entitled him to occasionally take his stress out on Delaney. Then he would show up one day with tickets to a concert or her favorite takeout. He'd help her study for tests. Compliment her dioramas. "He had a lot on his plate. He took his responsibilities as big brother and as founder of the co-op seriously."

"I'm just telling you what she told me. He needed to make money or the co-op would fold. He asked her to hit her parents up for a loan. She thought it was a bad idea, but she did it anyway. They said no. She said he took the news badly. He told her to forget about it. He'd find the money some other way."

"This is the first I've heard of any of this." Delaney lowered her head for a moment.

"She said she never told anyone—not even you. She felt responsible for the fight between your brother and Hunter Nash. If she'd convinced her parents to make the loan, they would never have fought. Corey would still be alive."

And Ellie and Michael would never have married. That couldn't have been easy to hear. "She couldn't know that."

"She absorbed everyone's hurts, everyone's problems. She took them to heart." Michael's voice broke. "And now she's dead."

"The kids are asking for you, Michael." Jaime stood at the arched entryway to the living room. "They're in Jacob's room. I put Skye in the other bunk bed. I think they'll sleep better that way."

"We should go." Cam went to Michael and kissed the top of his bald head. "Get some sleep. We'll all think more clearly tomorrow. Call us when you get up. We can help with the kids while you start making arrangements."

It would be days before Ellie's body would be released for burial. Delaney knew this from experience. But Cam was right. Everyone needed sleep and a fresh start in the morning.

Beginning with a call to Detective Ramos.

She took her turn hugging Michael and then headed for the door.

Cam followed. "Delaney, wait. Are you sure you're okay to drive?"

"I'm fine. I just need to get home and try to regroup."

"Come home with me and Jaime. Spend the night with us." Cam rubbed Delaney's back. "You shouldn't be alone all the way out there in the middle of nowhere."

Cam's warm hand felt so comforting. It would've been easy to say yes and let someone else take care of her. Cam and Jaime had a loft apartment downtown a few blocks from her job at Southwest School of Art and his job working for the city's cultural and creative arts department. They considered anything outside Loop 410 the hinterlands. "I need some space."

"Fine. I'll let you get away with that tonight, but if I don't hear from you tomorrow morning, I'm coming out there to get you."

Cam didn't drive anymore, but her stern tone made it obvious she meant business. Delaney managed a smile. "Michael and the kids are the ones who need to be taken care of. I'll meet you here. I'll help you with the kids. They're going to need so much TLC."

"That's a plan."

"And while we're here, we need to convince Michael to talk to Detective Ramos about this Gerard Knox."

"Agreed."

"I also want to go through the stuff from the co-op—the boxes you and Ellie were sorting through."

"I don't like the sound of that." Cam's frowns had been known to scare CEOs and bank presidents. "Why would you want to do that?"

"Something freaked out Ellie. I want to know what it was."

"Why?"

"She knew about the co-op's finances. Maybe she saw something that has a bearing on Corey's murder. Or hers."

"It's doubtful but I understand."

Jess lumbered into the foyer. "Understand what?"

Delaney shook her head. "That we can't tie life up in a perfect bow, but we can try to make sense of it."

Jess's bewildered gaze bounced between Delaney and Cam. "Whatever you say."

CHAPTER 11

How could Ellie have loved two men so totally different? How could Michael do something so stupid? Were all the men in their lives stupid? Corey with his co-op and his drug-addled brain. Hunter with his blind faith in Corey and his love of alcohol and pot that had left Delaney to play third or fourth fiddle in his life. Delaney mulled these questions while attempting to stay alive on her nemesis Highway 16 heading north out of San Antonio, through Helotes. A narrow, winding two-lane highway with no streetlights and a sixty-five-mile-an-hour speed limit.

Her beloved Trailblazer's engine strained and rattled as she pushed it to sixty-five. "Sorry, baby." She patted the dashboard. "If I go any slower, the monster trucks and semis will run over us. We'll be a dirty oil slick on the asphalt."

Her old friend fear clapped Delaney on the back. It had taken two years for her to kick fear to the curb after Corey died. That's how long it took for Hunter's case to finally go to trial. The prosecutors wanted to make a deal. Hunter refused to plead guilty, even when his public defender begged him to take the plea bargain.

He insisted he was innocent.

Security for the nearby city of San Antonio offices had seen his truck in the parking lot. One of the co-op artists who stopped by to pick up artwork for the Fiesta art show crossed paths with him in the darkened hallway about an hour before Delaney arrived.

He did it. She'd had to accept this truth even as every atom of her being fought against it. Her crazy, powder-keg-set-to-blow boyfriend Hunter was a murderer.

Delaney turned up an Adele song on the radio. She tapped to the beat on the wheel. A headache played bongos behind her left ear. Home, ibuprofen, a hot shower, a PB and J on toasted raisin bread, and a good night's sleep. Her prescription for getting through life one day at a time.

She pulled into the driveway and parked next to the ranch-style home that had been her grandpa's pride and joy.

The front porch light was out again. Another item for her honey-do list. She didn't mind. The upkeep on the old house built in the early 1980s kept her occupied. She did it all herself—mowed the three-quarters of an acre of land, refurbished the deck, replaced the wooden fence, and built a new pump house over the well—all using Pops's tools. He would've been proud.

She strode up the sidewalk to the deep-red door. Pops wouldn't approve of it, but Delaney the artist did. She used her fob to turn off the alarm, unlocked the front door, closed it behind her, and leaned against the solid wood. Home sweet, safe home.

A soft squeaking sound, a door closing maybe, broke the silence. Delaney stiffened. The drumbeat in her head thrummed. Maybe she imagined it. A product of a nightmare day.

Every muscle tensed, she waited, straining to hear any sound, any movement.

A scraping sound?

A chair being moved?

Or maybe she'd finally lost her mind.

How could someone be in her house without tripping the alarm?

Corey had insisted on installing the system after Nana and Pops died. He worried because Delaney so often spent the night alone while he worked at the studio. After his death and Hunter's incarceration, she spent every night alone.

Should she step outside and call 911?

The scenario played out in her head. A Bandera County sheriff's deputy would pull up to the house, walk around in his cowboy boots, look her over, remove his cowboy hat, and gently break the news. "No one's here, Ms. Broward. Are you sure you haven't been partaking in alcohol or drugs—prescription or otherwise?"

She was sure. Not in eight years and counting.

Delaney pulled her Taser from her purse and stuck it in her waistband. She squatted and untied her sneakers. She removed them and set them gently by the door. Fighting the urge to hold her breath, she grabbed the baseball bat she kept next to the coatrack and slipped down the hallway toward the kitchen.

Pausing at the arched doorway, back to the wall, she took a batter's stance. One, two, three. She flew around the corner, bat at the ready.

"Delaney! What the—?"

Delaney shrieked. She froze, bat halfway to its target.

Time rewound itself. Each second moved in slow motion, stretching and straining to catch up.

It couldn't be. Not possible.

"You're in prison."

Hands in the air like a man under arrest, Hunter Nash shook his head. "Not anymore."

CHAPTER 12

Maybe he'd broken into the wrong house. Hunter stood his ground. Delaney had changed. She'd lost her round, soft curves. And her innocence. Her body was wiry and lean. The beginning of crow's feet edged her green eyes no longer hidden behind tortoiseshell glasses. Her sandy-brown hair, caught up in a ponytail, was longer. Sun-induced freckles dusted her nose. He'd once told her the nose was what attracted him to her. She never seemed to care about its size or ability to dominate her face. Vanity wasn't her style.

Bat still held high, she advanced on him. He should be fearful, but he wasn't. This was sweet, empathetic, heart-of-honey Laney. She carried spiders outside instead of squashing them. She handed out granola bars and bottled water to homeless folks panhandling on the side of the road. She cried at sappy rom-coms and always took the underdog team's side when she watched football games with him on TV. She could find something to like in everyone. She wanted every child to have a fairy-tale childhood—the one she didn't have. And she wanted a house full of kids of her own.

She said that was a hill she was willing to die on.

She couldn't have changed that much.

He'd spent eight years in prison dreaming of seeing her again. In his dream there had been no bat.

"What are you doing in my house?" Her voice rasped as if she had a bad cold. "How did you get in here?"

"Give me a chance to explain, Laney, please." Hands still high, he backed up until he smacked into the island. Her grandparents' house didn't have an island in the old days. "I needed to talk to you."

"Decent, honorable people call when they need to talk to a person. They don't break into her house. Criminals do that."

She shifted the bat over her shoulder. Delaney had been a standout softball player as an undergraduate in college. Her batting average as a senior at the University of Texas at San Antonio was .375 with eighteen home runs and twenty-three runs batted in. An athletic scholarship had paid part of her college expenses. Hunter remembered because he'd attended every game. Just like she'd come to all his art class exhibits and his first gallery showing and the ones after that.

Not that there had been many for his mediocre work. "Seriously, Laney. Put the bat down. You're not going to hit me. You've never hit anyone in your life."

"You don't know me. Not anymore." She rested the bat on her shoulder and dug her phone from her pocket with her free hand. "I have every right to crack your head open. I'd be defending myself and my property. I could kill you. It's a stand-your-ground state. But I won't because I'm not you. I'll call 911."

"Don't do that." Hunter had no choice. If she called the cops and made a complaint, they could come up with a parole violation and he'd end up back in prison. He lunged at her. Eight years of daily calisthenics and prison yard basketball games had hardened his body too. They grappled. She smacked him in the chin with her elbow. He bit his tongue. "Ouch, hey. Give me the bat."

He ripped it from her hand and held it over his head. Delany rushed him. He dodged right. "I just want to talk to you."

Delaney whirled and marched toward him. "You killed my brother and you want to talk?"

The disdain, the agony, the hate in her words buried him. Hunter backed away. She kept coming. He held her phone up high. "I did not kill your brother."

"Here we go again." Sarcasm married disbelief in her tone and in the way she held her body. "Stop already. Just stop. If you came here to try to convince me of something we both know is not true, you're crazy. Give me my phone. If you don't, I'll run to the neighbor's house down the road to call for help."

"Just sit down for one minute. Just one minute." Hunter backed into the kitchen cabinet, but he kept the phone out of her reach. "Hear me out. I served eight years of a fifteen-year sentence—more than half—for something I didn't do. As God is my witness—"

"Don't bring God into this. Where was God when you bludgeoned your best friend with a utility knife? Where was He when Corey bled to death while you ran away like a coward? Where was He when I was left alone in this house with no brother, the man I . . . the man I . . ." Her voice broke. She halted only a few steps from him. Her eyes bright with tears, she shook her head. "Get out. Please, if you have any shred of human decency left, get out of my house. Leave me alone."

"The man you loved. That's what you were going to say. The man you loved." Hunter pointed to a chair at the kitchen table. "Give me five minutes and then I'll go. I'll give you your phone back. You can call 911 if you want, but I'll go. I won't come back."

Her hands went to her throat. She sucked in air. Her gaze never left his as she backed away. She slid into the chair and pointed to the clock on the kitchen table. "Five minutes starting now. It doesn't matter what you say. I'm calling 911 and I'm calling my attorney. I'm getting a restraining order."

Hunter allowed himself to breathe again. *God, give me the words. Please soften her heart and open her ears to hear what I have to say.*

"I can't believe you kept that painting up." He cocked his head toward a huge oil hanging on the wall behind the kitchen table. He'd caught her grandparents, gray heads close, love on their wrinkled faces, chuckling over some inside joke as they shucked corn on the cob on the front porch. One of their cats, Tinker, slept on the porch swing. The Hill Country served as their front yard. "Doesn't it remind you of me?"

"No. It reminds me of Nana and Pops." Anguish made her hoarse voice guttural. "Please, please get this over with."

"I had ten years to think about what happened, how it went down, and why someone would want Corey dead—"

"You had a fight over the co-op. You wanted to shut it down. He didn't. You couldn't understand how important it was to him, how he poured everything he had into it after our grandparents died. You'd both been drinking. You were high. He was high. It didn't have to make sense."

"I loved Corey. Do you really think I stabbed him over studio space?" No amount of time would make Delaney's willingness to believe in Hunter's guilt less hurtful. "Yes, I drank too much. Yes, we made ourselves into stupid moron zombies with pot that night. But I didn't kill him. I told him I was done. I was through cobbling together the money to pay rent on a studio when I was lucky to sell a painting every two or three months—if that. I was through eating Ramen noodles for supper every night so I could pay rent on a one-room apartment I never saw because I was either with you or at work or at the studio.

"He called me a quitter. He said I wasn't a real artist. Artists never gave up. He'd sell his clothes and his shoes at a garage sale to make enough money to buy canvas and paints."

Or worse. Hunter paced between the island and the table. He'd practiced this speech all these years, and now that he was here, he didn't know how to say it. "Do you remember a guy named Guillermo Sandoval? We called him Willy Wonka."

Because he had all the good "candy."

Delaney rubbed her forehead, her expression turned inward as if reviewing old memories. "Not the drug operation thing again. Seriously. It didn't fly in court. It won't fly now."

"Do you remember Willy?"

"Sure. He was so tall his pants were always too short. He was super skinny and talked liked he had marbles in his mouth. He hung around but he wasn't an artist. Corey said he was a friend from high school."

"That's the one. Corey did know him from high school but not because they went to school together. He bought his pot from him. Willy was from the south side. He got mixed up in drugs and gangs. His grandmother sent him to live with an aunt who had moved out by Leslie Road."

By O'Connor High School on the far-north side where Corey and Hunter went to school, in other words.

"Whatever—"

"Let me finish, please. Corey had a cash-flow problem. Willy didn't do credit. Not even for friends. Especially friends who were dabbling in speed and ecstasy and coke."

"Like Corey could afford coke. I can't believe you're still trying to blame Corey's murder on him."

She was in denial. Just like Ellie had been. Corey himself had been in denial. He insisted he could quit anytime he wanted. He simply had no desire. In his befuddled brain, drugs fueled his creativity. "Corey did coke. That means he was in close proximity to drug dealers. You didn't notice how much weight he'd lost or how little he slept? Or how erratic he'd become?"

"He was Corey. One minute he was up, the next he was down. His highs were higher than ours, his lows, lower. When I needed money for school, he gave it to me. When my car broke down, he paid to have it fixed. He drove me to campus in the meantime. When I asked him about our finances, he told me not to worry about it. He would take care of it."

"Corey made good money from his paintings. The problem was a lot of it went up his nose. The financial problems were rooted in his addiction."

"It wasn't enough to murder him, you have to tear him down too?"

"I hate this. I hate it." Truth be told, Corey didn't have a jealous bone in his body when it came to art. He'd wanted everyone at the co-op to succeed. He wanted to help. He let Hunter run a tab on his rent when he couldn't pay. That kindness added to Corey's own financial burden. "Willy said he couldn't run a tab, but Corey might be able to help in another way. He suggested Corey meet with his big boss, not the next guy up the rung but the one running their distribution on the south side."

"You want me to believe Corey went for it? Why didn't you stop him? Why didn't you talk him out of it?"

"He didn't tell me until after he'd met the guy. A Tango Orejón gangbanger. They were searching for new ways to move product for one of the Mexican cartels. Fronts for their operation. Places the DEA wouldn't suspect."

"Do you hear yourself? This is Corey we're talking about."

"He agreed to move product through the co-op. Once he met with the guy he had no choice. He knew too much to back out. I think that was Willy's intent. Suck him in and then force him in so deep he couldn't get out, even if he wanted to."

"He told you all this? He made you complicit by simply knowing."

"Exactly. He was freaking out, but he had to make good on his promises. By the time he admitted it to me, he was into them for serious money. I told him to go to the police. He was paranoid that I would do it if he didn't. I wouldn't have, but he didn't believe me. He got all worked up."

"That's when you started fighting."

"Not physically."

"How did his studio get so messed up?"

"It wasn't me. I figure he took my advice and told Willy he was out. Things went downhill from there."

"Where was Willy during the trial? Where was the evidence then?"

"My public defender was fairly worthless. I shouldn't be so harsh, I guess. Public defenders don't have the same resources available to them that the district attorney's office does. Willy had disappeared." Or his boss disappeared him. "My public defender couldn't come up with any corroborating evidence."

"So how do I know you're not making all this up?"

"I intend to find a way to prove it. Other artists at the co-op knew Willy. They bought from him. When we had parties at the co-op, drugs flowed freely, and Willy was always there. He had family, friends. I'll find someone who can give me the name of the guy Willy worked for."

"Let Detective Ramos do it. He'll have sources in the gang unit who can help track him down. And the DEA."

"Does that mean you believe me?"

"That means you have to prove it with hard evidence. Even then it doesn't mean you didn't kill my brother. You were so angry that he would put the co-op in peril by consorting with drug dealers, you killed him in a fit of rage."

"Except I didn't. I stormed out, I drove under the influence to

La Villita. Parked and went into NIOSA with every intent of buying myself more alcohol while I waited for my girlfriend to show up."

"Did you intend to tell your girlfriend about this argument, about what Corey was allegedly doing?"

Good question. One for which Hunter didn't have a clear answer. "I was messed up. I walked around still hearing the argument in my head. I hope so. I think so. We needed to work together to drag him out of that mess, get him help, get him clean."

It was impossible to tell if this was the answer Delaney had wanted. She held her body so still. Her green eyes pierced him to the core. She pointed to the clock. "Your five minutes are up."

"I know. I'm hoping you'll give me the benefit of the doubt. Let me prove myself to you. Please."

"There's no going back."

"I know. I'm not expecting you to magically or miraculously take me back like the past ten years didn't happen. I just need for your faith in man and God to be restored."

"You think you can do that all by yourself? You have a big ego if you think you still have the ability to affect me in any way that is meaningful."

"Maybe I don't, but God does."

Delaney crossed her arms and shook her head. "Eight years in prison for a crime you say you didn't commit, yet you still believe in God. How is that possible?"

"When everything else was torn away, I had nothing to cling to. I was drowning in a cesspool. I couldn't breathe. I couldn't sleep. I couldn't eat. And then the chaplain stuck his hand out and pulled me out. I clung to Jesus after that."

"Good for you."

"I hope you mean that."

"I do. You better go."

"Okay."

Hunter started for the door. Delaney followed. "I didn't see your truck out front. How did you get here?"

Hunter explained. Delaney frowned. "So how did you intend to get home?"

"Hitchhike."

"On 16 in the dark? Do you have a death wish? Call a rideshare."

"I don't have a phone or a credit card. Or cash for that matter. I used the last of my money to pay the kid who brought me out here."

Her face a study in conflicting emotions, she stared at him. "It's late. Too late to get Mel to do it."

She knew his family dynamics well. Mel was the only one he could call when he needed help. Mel and his mom, who would be asleep by now. "I'll hitchhike. It'll be fine."

"A rideshare out here would be astronomical. I can't afford it either—"

"Like I would ask you to pay."

"Just shut up and listen. You can sleep on the couch." Red blotches spread up her neck and across her cheeks. She'd always hated it when that happened and it did every time she got nervous. "There's no guest bedroom. I turned it into a workout room."

No matter how different she tried to be, at her core Delaney hadn't changed. Helping people was knitted into her DNA. Only she would offer shelter to a man she hated, a man she was certain killed her only brother.

"Are you sure—?"

"Don't get any ideas. My bedroom door will be locked." The blotches darkened and spread until her entire face turned crimson. "I'll have my stun gun and my pepper spray with me. In the morning you'll use my phone to get Mel to pick you up."

"Thanks for doing this. I know it's a big deal."

"I'm doing it because I try to be a decent human being. You did your time. It wasn't enough, but it's what the jury gave you. You get to get on with your life. Unlike Corey."

"Thank you for letting me stay. I'm so sorry about—"

"If you're hungry, help yourself to whatever's in the fridge. All I have to drink is water."

She couldn't help herself. She was the ultimate decent person. It was wrong to take advantage of her innate kindness. "In the morning, I'm gone."

She gave a curt nod. "Good night."

Just like that, the love of his life walked away, leaving Hunter standing in her kitchen. Of all the endings he'd imagined for this evening, sleeping on Delaney's couch on his first night of freedom had not been one.

She still didn't believe him. Nor did she still care for him. Hunter couldn't let the part of him that wanted to read more into it overtake common sense. Delaney hated his guts.

Just keep telling yourself that.

Still, he was here. She'd let him stay. She wasn't afraid of him. She had shown him mercy and grace—more than she thought he deserved.

Hunter went into the living room and sat on the soft, worn couch—the same couch where he'd watched dozens of old black-and-white films with her. Where they'd cuddled and kissed after Corey went to bed. Where Hunter had slept after Corey was murdered and Delaney was afraid to be alone at night.

Despite her anger, she'd let him back into her life during that horrible aftermath of Corey's murder. She had needed him. He was her best friend. Only to have her faith in him shattered when the police arrested him.

Hunter wanted that faith back. For both their sakes.

He grabbed a pillow and stuck it behind his head. He closed his eyes. The house smelled like her shampoo. Citrus. Even the pillows had her scent. Her face with that noble nose, sprinkle of freckles, full lips, and intelligent green eyes stared at him.

He rose and wandered down the hallway to what had once been a spare bedroom. It now featured a treadmill, weights, a recumbent bicycle, a punching bag, a speed bag, and a wall-mounted flat-screen TV. She'd decorated the punching bag with a big, red happy face and the words MACHO MAN. Very funny. The scent of sweaty towels and sneakers hung in the room.

It was hard to imagine the old Delaney working out. She'd been a catcher and a solid hitter—a natural athlete feared by opposing pitchers, but she wasn't into physical fitness. She played softball because it gave her a way to feel like she was part of something. She belonged somewhere. Her team served as a built-in family.

Feeling like a voyeur, he backed out and trudged to Corey's old bedroom. The door stood open. Delaney had transformed it into a workroom. What had he expected? A shrine to her dead brother? Instead, a huge oak table occupied the center of the room. On top were the tools of her trade: a sander, glass cutter, a large guillotine trimmer on a stand for cutting mats and paper, and a hodgepodge of other tools.

Did she bring home her work to occupy her hands and mind? She had never married. Did she date? Was she like him? Afraid to feel?

So many questions and no way to get answers. Delaney had closed herself up tight as a locked treasure chest. Traces of her grandparents remained, but she'd wiped away every trace of her brother. Hunter opened the closet door. Among her framing supplies nestled one box of sketch pads along with a box of sketching pencils.

He grabbed one of each and headed back to the living room. This was the one thing he knew how to do.

CHAPTER 13

What an idiot. Delaney rolled around in the bed she'd slept in since she was eight years old. She could've upgraded to Nana and Pops's master bedroom, but it never felt right. This bedroom felt safe. Until now.

What had possessed her to let her brother's convicted killer spend the night in her house? Corey used to tease her about being a Goody Two-shoes. He said she always thought the best of people.

As if it was a character flaw. That character flaw could get her killed.

Hunter didn't look like the same person. He didn't sound like the same man. His chest muscles and biceps popped under his T-shirt. His black hair, once held back in a thick and curly ponytail, had been buzzed short. His eyes, once dreamy and focused on something only he could see, were wary. An ugly scar somehow managed to give his face character. He believed in God. The chances of a guy coming out of prison a better man weren't that great. Yet, if she believed Hunter, he had.

And he looked good doing it.

He was also six two and weighed between 180 to 185. Solid muscle. If he had been her attacker at Ellie's, surely she would've known it was him. She would've felt his presence, recognized his voice, even after eight years. She had tonight. Every nerve in her body had responded to his nearness. His scent. His voice.

It wasn't him in Ellie's shop. It couldn't have been. Or her body would've betrayed her. Heart and head still did battle, even knowing what he did—or what she thought he did—ten years ago.

Delaney rose up and pounded on her pillow, then plopped back down on her side. Hunter lay on her couch in her living room. Just like he had done during those horrific days after Corey's death and even before that when he had drank too much to drive home.

In those days they couldn't keep their hands off each other. All he had to do was look at her with those delicious amber eyes and her muscles turned to water. He ran his finger over her collarbone and her heart exploded against her rib cage. She was sure any day he would ask her to marry him.

When he kissed her, she had felt it in every bone in her body.

Delaney threw off the comforter, then the sheet. She got up, padded over to the window, and opened it. She stuck her head out and let the cold, March night air dry the perspiration on her face and with it the ache for human touch. A simple hug. An affectionate kiss.

Contact. When her parents had died, she still had her grandparents. Nana and Pops made sure Delaney got plenty of TLC. Every night they came into her room to dispense good-night hugs and kisses to a little girl who missed her mommy and daddy.

Until Delaney barely remembered what they looked like. Occasionally a smell—like gingersnaps baking—would dredge up a buried memory. Her mom handing her a cookie and kissing the top of her head. Her dad kissing her mom when he thought Delaney wasn't peeking.

But they were gone.

Then Pops went out to mow the grass one day and didn't come

back. Corey had found him keeled over on the second love of his life—his John Deere riding mower.

All the stuffing went out of Nana. She said Pops should've waited for her. She couldn't wait to "get up yonder."

A few months later she had gone to bed one night and didn't get up the next day.

Poor Corey. He tried to wake her, but she, too, was gone. She'd left him in charge.

Maybe that was why Corey chose to escape with drugs. Maybe it was too much. Why hadn't Delaney seen that? Why was she so wrapped up in her own pain that she couldn't see Corey's?

She'd been too busy nursing her own wounds. Too busy seeking solace with Hunter. Hunter of the sweet kisses and warm hugs that filled her need for contact. For touch.

For a lifeline.

In those days, only the voice in her head that sounded suspiciously like Pops had kept her from breaking the promise she and the other women in her church's small group had made to honor God in their relationships. She'd hung on to her vow by the hair on her chinny chin chin.

Mostly because Hunter never had pushed. He always stopped short of crossing the line—he stopped first. He was that kind of guy at heart.

Yeah, the good, old days. The glory days.

Think about something else.

Delaney plopped on the bed but didn't lay down. Instead, she grabbed a pillow and hugged it.

Hunter's story about Guillermo Sandoval introducing Corey to his boss rang true. Corey had told Delaney he intended to save the co-op, whatever it took. He wouldn't let his tenants down. Most of them had fit the stereotype of the starving artist. Billy was a bouncer. Zach worked as a cashier at a feed store. Hunter waited tables at a Mexican restaurant on the River Walk. Good tips in the summer, so-so tips in the winter. Sandy Carter and Cam stripped. Neither bothered to tell people they were dancers. They made more in tips in one night than Delaney did in two weeks making smoothies.

Corey's determination to save the co-op even when more than half the artists were behind in their rent had made him seem noble. Not a good businessman, but bordering on Goody Two-shoes himself. *Corey, I need you now. I need to know what to do, what to believe. You were a selfish jerk to go and leave me alone.*

After ten years, she still felt his absence like a gaping hole in her chest.

He was desperate. So desperate he was willing to risk his own career and life by hooking up with a gang that had drug sales and distribution for the entire west side sewn up?

Corey would have seen himself as the rescuing hero, the superhero. The ends justified the means.

Hunter would've tried to talk him out of it. For all his laid-back, jazzy improvisational approach to life, at his core Hunter believed in basic moral truths. He had his mother's values; he simply didn't want to admit it.

Did such a man shed those values in the throes of a pot- and alcohol-induced rage long enough to stab his best friend to death?

God, is he for real?

Delaney froze. She hadn't spoken to God in almost ten years. *Oh, no You don't.* He didn't get to come traipsing back into her life because Hunter had. On the other hand, only God would know the measure of Hunter's alleged faith.

She desperately needed something besides a pillow to hang on to. Going it alone was exhausting.

Forget it.

God, I need answers.

Stop it.

She wouldn't get answers from God. She never did.

She needed to talk to someone. Cam would be asleep, Jaime by her side at this time of night. Who would be awake? Jess. He had trouble sleeping when he was in the middle of a bad custody case. She grabbed her phone and thumbed a text.

Are u awake?

Yeah. Are u ok?

Can't sleep. Hunter's here

Call 911! Get out of there!

Jess had never been a fan of Hunter, even before Corey's death.

It's fine. I'm fine

I'm on my way!

He also never stopped seeing himself as the guardian angel of the women in Corey's entourage. Like the celebrity's bodyguard.

No. Don't come. He's sleeping

Are you crazy? I'm coming

No. I just needed someone normal to talk to

What does he want?

To convince me he didn't do it

A jury of his peers said differently

I know

If he tries anything zap him with that stun gun
I will
Call me if u need me. I'm there
I know

That's why she'd texted him. To remind herself that she had friends. People she could count on. A lifeline. Jess was like that. Simple. Reliable. Comforting.

Thanks Jess
For what?
For being you
Talk to you in the morning
Sweet dreams
Hah

There would be no sleep for Delaney either. Not as long as she harbored such despair of ever having a normal relationship with a man. Because of the one lounging in her living room.

How dare he?

How could he?

Leave it alone. Let it go.

She needed to work out. That's what she did when she couldn't sleep. She punished her body until it gave in. All the frustration, loneliness, and despair flowed out through her sweat.

Delaney glanced at her sweats and T-shirt. Adequately dressed. *Deep breaths.* She slipped from her room and down the hallway to what had once been the guest bedroom.

Her friend the punching bag waited for her. It never complained or talked back. After her warm-up stretches, she donned her bright-red gloves and started with the speed bag. The need for concentration and a steady rhythm took over.

Sweat began to build immediately. Her body warmed. Her mind zeroed in on the bag.

No other thoughts.

Breathe. In and out. She didn't pretend the speed bag was Hunter's face anymore. It seemed juvenile, but her therapist had said it was a healthy substitute for the real thing.

One-two-three. Switch. One-two-three. Switch. One-two-three.

When her arm and shoulder muscles screamed for mercy, she turned to the seventy-pound punching bag.

"Okay, Macho Man, are you ready for me?" She'd painted an enormous happy face on the black bag. Macho Man was always happy to see her. "Let 'er rip."

Feet shoulder width apart, left in front of the right, knees slightly bent, weight off the heels. The stance used to seem counterintuitive, but now it felt natural, giving her body the torque it needed to throw her weight into the cross.

Left jab, right cross, jab, cross, jab, bob and weave, jab, jab, roundhouse, bob and weave, jab, jab, upper cut, dodge, parry, jab, cross.

Sweat rolled into her eyes and burned. Her muscles howled. Her vision tunneled into that face. The intruder's face had been hidden. Who was he? Why did he kill Ellie? Why hadn't he killed Delaney? Blood. Blood everywhere. Adrenaline whooshed through her.

Jab, jab, roundhouse.

Her footwork was lousy, but she'd never had boxing lessons. What she knew she garnered from watching YouTube videos and film of fights. She'd even dragged Jess and Cam to several bouts at the Alamodome. Cam spent most of the time with her hands over her eyes while Jess kept up a running commentary along the lines of "barbaric," "cavemen," and "ouch, ouch, ouch." There had been a time when she would've agreed. Her perspective had changed. Life had changed it for her. Boxing allowed two opponents to fight to the mat under a strict set of rules bound by a certain sense of honor. Much like a duel.

Boxing as a form of therapy might have saved her life.

"Laney?"

A voice penetrated the fog. She whirled, gloves high, ready to throw her weight into a punch. Her front kick landed square in Hunter's chest.

Boom, down he went.

CHAPTER 14

The solid kick felt good for a second. Then fear set in. And shame. What if she'd hurt Hunter? Delaney staggered toward the spot where he sprawled, flat on his back. Always take the high road, that was her motto. Now she'd fallen off the wagon. She was as bad as Hunter was.

"Whoa, whoa!" Hunter threw up both hands, like a stop sign that had been knocked over. "I come in peace. I heard noise . . ."

Gasping, Delaney leaned over and propped the gloves on her knees. Sweat rolled down her face. She swiped it on her sleeve. "What do you want?"

"Nothing. I . . . nothing." He rolled over and scrambled to his feet, never taking his gaze from her as if she might strike again. "I was surprised, that's all."

"Me too. You shouldn't sneak up on a person."

"You never liked boxing."

"I didn't like it because you didn't like it. The new me has her own opinions, and I understand the allure much more than I used to." Delaney sucked in air like a fish suddenly on dry land. "It's what I do when I can't sleep."

"They have pills for that."

"This seems healthier."

"I didn't do it, Laney. As God is my witness, I didn't do it. I can say that now because I'm a believer." Rubbing his chest, presumably in the spot where Delaney had nailed him, Hunter backed away until he leaned against the wall. "We switched places on that one. How weird is that?"

"What time did you get out of prison?" Delaney straightened. He might be the one who got knocked to the ground, but she was the one who felt off balance having him so close.

She turned back to the bag. *Jab, jab, jab, cross, bob and weave, jab, cross.* She stopped, stilled the bag, and tried to breathe. "Where were you this afternoon around four?"

"You think I killed Ellie?" The humor was gone, replaced by raw anger. "You knew me better than anyone else in the world. I let you into my life the way I let no one else. You *knew* me."

"You hurt me. You went there and fought with my brother. You got high. You got drunk." Delaney whirled and delivered a solid side kick to Macho Man's midsection. The bag sailed out and back. She hit it with a powerful, one-two, left-right combo. "You did all the things you promised me you wouldn't do. I sat through the entire trial. I heard the evidence. It all pointed to you."

His breathing turned as torturous as Delany's. "I hurt you? You have no idea how you hurt me. You believed I killed your brother, my best friend. Like I'm some kind of monster. I wanted to marry you. I wanted to have children with you. You bailed on me without a fight. You didn't believe in me."

"This isn't some stand-by-your-man country song." Delaney stilled the bag. Macho Man's leer taunted her. She leaned her head against it and closed her eyes. "They had evidence—enough evidence to convict. The police arrested you in this house. I couldn't let my heart stand in the way of the truth. I had to accept it. I had no choice, even if it meant losing everything. Everything."

Her dream of marriage and children with the only man she'd ever loved, gone. People thought she'd get over it. She was young. Her pastor said she'd learn to go on. Even Ellie had moved on. Not Delaney. She simply couldn't find a way to trust her heart with someone new.

She faced Hunter. "You didn't just kill my brother, you destroyed my ability to trust. You destroyed my dreams. You left me alone. I'm still alone after all these years because of what you did."

"Go to bed, Laney." His anger had dissipated, replaced by a soft tone even more damning. "You're tired. You've had a horrific day. I'm sorry I made it worse by coming here. I'll leave in the morning, like you asked." Hunter backed from the room. "The person who killed Corey is still out there, walking around free. Think about that. It should make you as angry as it does me. I promise you I will find him and make sure he pays."

Then he was gone.

He didn't tell her what to do, when to go to bed, or what to think. Delaney took a halfhearted swipe at Macho Man. Her shoulders and back ached. Her leg muscles quivered. She ripped off the gloves and laid them aside.

Enough was enough. It had nothing to do with Hunter.

Delaney trudged to the bathroom, undressed, and stood in the shower for ten minutes. The sweat washed down the drain, but it refused to let her anger and pain hitch a ride with it. The grime of her conversation with Hunter stuck to her skin. No amount of soap would remove it. Hunter's words repeated themselves in the singsong of the water rushing from the showerhead.

No escape. A few minutes later, she slid under the sheets and cupped her hands over her ears. It didn't help. A killer living life while Corey was dead. Anger didn't begin to cover it.

If it was true.

Sleep came in fits and starts. Ellie's wide, startled eyes brought Delaney awake with a gasp. No amount of water could abate the fierce ache in her throat. Finally, light peeked through the window. She got up and padded down the hallway. She slowed at the old-fashioned archway, poked her head around the corner, and peered at Hunter.

His eyes were closed. He clutched a pillow to his chest just as she had done. He looked so much younger. Like the man who'd cheered himself hoarse at her softball games. Like the man who took her body-surfing on Padre Island. Like the man who kissed her for the first time at Leon Springs Dance Hall. He'd tasted like fried pickles and barbecue sauce and smelled like spicy aftershave.

A sketch pad lay on the coffee table. Tiptoeing, she slipped close enough to grab it. His perception of her from the previous evening: wild eyed, hair mussed, bat in hand.

Drawing was Hunter's preferred form of therapy. The next one featured a detailed rendition of her kitchen with all the seedlings she would plant in her vegetable garden in the next few weeks.

Another caught her in midkick, assaulting Macho Man. Her face distorted in a fierce grimace. He'd drawn his perception of her—strong and powerful. Not anything like how she felt.

Hunter worked through problems and feelings with his art. Delaney had done the same with her dioramas. Only Hunter understood that. He never suggested she try to sell them or find a more commercial art form.

She laid the pad back where she found it and tiptoed away. It wasn't fair to stare at someone while he was sleeping. She headed to the kitchen. If she could mainline coffee she would. Instead, she fired up the coffeepot and dumped extra coffee into the filter. A double dose.

A perusal of the refrigerator revealed eggs, a jar of mild picante sauce, flour tortillas, and shredded cheddar cheese. Hunter called them gringo tacos. Delaney had learned to cook from her Norwegian grand-mother. Mexican dishes had not been in Nana's repertoire. Delaney usually skipped breakfast and saved making tacos for the weekend when she had more time.

The shop would have to wait until later in the day. While scrambling six eggs in Nana's cast-iron skillet, Delaney considered her plan of action for the day. First stop, Michael's house to peruse Ellie's boxes. Hunter intended to seek answers. So did Delaney.

Ignoring Ellie's voice in her head insisting it was sacrilegious, she stuck four tortillas in the microwave to heat them. After Ellie's house came Ellie's shop. Somebody had to clean up the mess. And at the same time Delaney could search for more clues as to what Ellie was upset about.

At some point Michael needed to decide what to do with the shop. Let the lease go? Hire someone to run it? Both were unimaginable.

"Smells like Laney's Taquería in here."

Delaney took her time turning around. Hunter stood in the door-way rubbing sleep from his eyes like he had so many times before.

Not like those times. No "morning, babe." No kiss. Definitely no kiss.

"The coffee's ready." She busied herself with grabbing oversized mugs and pulling a quart of almond milk from the refrigerator. "I don't have any fancy creamers. There's stevia on the table."

He used to like a little coffee with his sugar.

"Thanks." He came as close as the island. Delaney slid the mug to the middle. He smirked. "I promise not to touch you. I wouldn't want you to get prison cooties."

"Do you think that's funny?"

"I have to laugh. It beats crying. Nobody likes a crybaby in prison." Hunter eased onto a chair at the table. His feet were bare. He had fine black hairs on his toes. That always struck Delaney as odd. He dumped two spoons of stevia into the coffee and stirred. "So what's with all these plants?" He motioned to the wrought-iron racks that hugged the west wall of the kitchen and its four windows. "You have a Home Depot nursery in here."

"Seedlings. I'm getting ready to transplant them to my vegetable garden."

"You have a vegetable garden?" He coughed and set his mug on the table.

Her therapist had suggested it. At first Delaney had resisted the idea. She didn't have time to mess with a garden. She knew nothing about it, except that it would be hard to grow anything in rain-starved South Texas.

Once again, her therapist had been right. The smell of the dirt, the tactile feel of it in her fingers, the heat of the sun on her face, the breeze that cooled her, the orderly nature of making rows and planting seedlings—the all-encompassing tasks released her anxiety. Her stress fell away.

She laid her phone on the counter. "It's better than drinking or smoking pot."

A direct hit. But a low blow.

Hunter's chuckle had a bitter tinge. He took his time responding. "What kind of vegetables?"

She pointed to the labels and reeled off the names. Summer squash, sweet potatoes, pumpkins, cucumbers, bell peppers, broccoli, cantaloupe. "I have to rent a rototiller and prepare the soil. The growing season here is short."

"What do you do with all of it?"

He didn't have to state the obvious. She was one person. Thanks to him, she lived alone. She had no need for bushel baskets of produce.

"I give them away. I take some to the food bank and the Methodist church in Helotes for their food pantry. Give them to friends. One of these days I'll learn to can."

Once upon a time she'd dreamed of having a boatload of kids to feed.

Not anymore.

"What happened to Samson, Tinker, and Dizzy?"

Pops's blue heeler and Nana's cats, one black and the other an orange tabby.

"Seriously? They were old when Grandpa died. Dogs and cats don't live forever."

"I suppose not. You never got another dog? You loved Samson." His gaze bounced around the kitchen. "It's a big house to live in alone out here in the boonies. Animals are good company."

"Are you worried I've been lonely? That's rich."

She was a coward. That was the truth. She couldn't bear the thought of getting attached to another living creature, only to have him die. "I work long hours. It wouldn't be fair to an animal to be out here alone all the time."

"I suppose not."

Delaney turned her back on him and busied herself fixing two plates with tortillas, scrambled eggs, cheese, then zapping them in the microwave long enough to melt the cheese. She carried the plates to the table along with the jar of salsa and a spoon.

Her phone to his ear, Hunter looked up at her. Surprise bloomed on his face. He mouthed the word *thanks*.

She shrugged and went back to the counter where her plate still sat. How could she eat with Hunter sitting at her table in her kitchen? Her throat closed. She dumped the tacos into the trash and slid the plate into the dishwasher.

The conversation with Mel was a quick one. Hunter laid the phone on the table. "She's on her way." He bit into a taco. His eyes closed. "You can't imagine what it's like to eat real food after all these years. My taste buds are in shock. They may never recover."

"I don't think store-bought tortillas and salsa with scrambled eggs qualify as real food. At least Ellie wouldn't think so. She made the best salsa, and her homemade tortillas rocked."

Hunter's gaze stayed on the plate. "I can't believe she's gone."

Not gone. Murdered.

Delaney washed the skillet and set it on the drying rack. She quickly stowed the remainder of the food. "I have to go."

Hunter used the last of his tortilla to wipe salsa from his plate and popped it in his mouth. Still chewing, he picked up his plate and brought it to the dishwasher. "So go. I'll finish cleaning up and then I'll wait out front."

Delaney tried to duck past him. They were stuck between the kitchen counter and the island. They both bobbed right, then left.

"Hey, we're dancing." Hunter didn't smile. He backpedaled to the end of the island. "Ladies first."

Her face burning, Delaney dashed past him. She flew into her bedroom, grabbed her purse, and raced to the front door. It was too much. He was too much.

"Hey, Laney." He'd followed her. He held out her phone. "You might need this."

She stifled a groan and marched over to retrieve it. "Thank you."

"No, thank *you*. For breakfast and for letting me stay. I know it was the last thing you wanted." He let go, but not before his fingers brushed against hers. Unlike Corey's thin, expressive fingers, Hunter's were strong and callused. What had he been doing in prison? "You always were the nicer person."

"No need to thank me." Heat burned through Delaney. His hands were his best attribute, after his eyes. "Just don't be here when I get back."

"I won't."

"Goodbye."

"Goodbye."

Not "see you later." So much emotional baggage stuffed into that word.

Delaney whirled and careened out the door like a rabid dog chased her.

Instead of the image of an amber-eyed man who once had held her heart in those hands.

CHAPTER 15

The accusatory *thunk-thunk-thunk* of Cam's cane followed Delaney up the stairs to the third floor of Michael's house. Delaney didn't dare glance back. Cam's shock and righteous indignation shouted in the silence and the space between two old friends.

"Come on, Delaney. I may be a cripple, but I can smack the snot out of you with my cane." Cam puffed a little but not much more than Delaney. "What is wrong with you? How could you possibly let Hunter spend the night at your house?"

Delaney reached the top of the stairs and grabbed the banister pole. Despite all the time she'd spent working out, she was winded. After a sleepless night, she was exhausted and punchy.

The wide-open space smelled musty and unused. Dust tickled her nose. "He had no way to get home. He used the last of his cash to get some kid in his neighborhood to give him a ride out to the house. Even an Uber would be too expensive from where I live."

"Not your problem. He could've hitchhiked."

"On Highway 16? I abhor what he did, but I won't be responsible for his death when some yahoo doing eighty in the dark on those curves runs over him."

"You should've called the police. Detective Ramos gladly would have taken him off your hands. He could escort him right back to prison."

"The conditions of his parole don't prohibit him from talking to me."

"So why didn't he call you?"

"Because he knew I would hang up on him." Delaney let her gaze sweep the third floor. The family that owned the home prior to Michael had opened up the space, installed theater seating, soundproofing, dark window treatments, and a high-end sound system. When Ellie moved in she took over the space. Her boxes occupied the floor and many of the chairs. "These can't all be Ellie's. She had one studio, and she hardly ever used it. Do you think she cleared out some of Corey's stuff too?"

"Don't try to change the subject, sister." Cam pulled back the blackout curtains one after the other on six floor-to-ceiling windows. Sunlight flooded the vast room. Dust particles danced in the brilliant streams. Then she opened window after window. Cool morning air drifted in on a spring breeze. "He broke into your house. He physically assaulted you. He took your bat and your phone. These aren't the actions of an innocent man. He's a psycho."

"He was defending himself. I assaulted him. I came at him with a bat. He didn't act like the psycho. I did. Besides, I can handle myself."

She would never allow herself to be a victim. Nor would she be taken in by any man—especially this man—again.

But the story he told, the details—they had a ring of veracity about them that was hard to ignore. Her decision to let him spend the night on her couch had nothing to do with the way she'd felt when that first shock of recognition hit her. As though her best friend had walked back into her life after a long, painful absence. If her life was a romance novel, this would've been where her heart leaped. Unfortunately her brain refused to be ignored. It screamed danger, pulled up the drawbridge over the moat, and hunkered down behind thick fortress walls.

With only seconds to spare.

"He did his time. He's paid his debt to society. If I had opened the letters from the parole board, I would've known he was out. Instead, I stuck my head in the sand and tried to pretend I never knew him."

That I never loved him.

"That doesn't mean he gets to waltz back into your life."

"Nobody's waltzing anywhere. But his story about that Willy guy made me think." Earlier she'd filled Cam in on all the details over sinfully rich Starbucks lattes and cinnamon-raisin bagels with cream cheese. Charlene had come directly from the airport to pick up the kids, according to Cam, who said she herded them into her car still in their pajamas, promising them a Denny's breakfast. Michael, in his infinite wisdom, had gone to work to try to "clear his head."

"Corey was off the rails those last few months. Not Hunter. He could've pled self-defense, and I would've been tempted to believe him."

"What if Ellie knew about the drugs? What if she had proof that Corey was a criminal and didn't come to Hunter's rescue?" Cam sneezed into the crook of her elbow. "This dust is killing me. Maybe he's been seething and plotting his revenge for the last ten years. That's a motive for killing her."

"So he wasn't a killer in 2010, but now he is?"

"Anybody who thinks prison rehabilitates is deluding himself."

On that they agreed. Delaney surveyed the boxes. It was hard to know where to start. "Let's see if we find anything incriminating here, how about that?"

"She probably took whatever it was with her. Or she could've destroyed it." Cam balanced on her cane and used her other foot to shove a box out of the way. "Just so you know, I'm calling Detective Ramos to let him know about Hunter's visit. I'm not taking a chance on you ending up like Ellie."

"Please don't—"

"Not open to discussion."

"Going back to my earlier question, then. Why do you think Ellie kept all this stuff?"

"Initially, I think she wanted to spare you from having to deal with it. I also think it was her way of hanging on to Corey." Cam step-dragged her way past Delaney toward the boxes stacked next to a series of drop cloths draped over what Delaney assumed to be furniture from the co-op. "It's a little creepy that she moved this stuff into Michael's house after they had married. I can understand why Michael resented it. It was like she was still stuck in time. She couldn't bear to part with it."

"Which box was she digging in when she freaked?"

Cam tapped her forefinger against her lips. "We were working right here." She pointed to a series of open boxes. Their contents were strewn across the carpet. "But they're not all here. We hadn't made this much progress."

"Maybe she already sent the stuff to Goodwill."

"She was going to have them pick up everything at once."

"I can't believe she kept the ratty, old furniture from the communal kitchen and meeting space." Delaney pulled back the drop cloth to reveal a scarred fake-wood table and six worn chairs. Big box discount furniture store stuff. How many microwaved bean-and-cheese burritos had she eaten at this table? How many pieces of pepperoni pizza? "It was junk ten years ago."

"She couldn't let it go. As much as she tried to hide it from you."

The removal of more drop cloths revealed a lumpy couch, a love seat, and four beanbag chairs. "You couldn't sell this stuff at a garage sale or a flea market."

"That's what I told her. She said it had sentimental value."

Delaney had spent her share of nights curled up sleeping on the couch. Yet she had no emotional ties to it. Instead, she couldn't bring herself to touch it. As if it carried germs that would infect her with the desire to relive that season of her life.

They were simply pieces of furniture. They held no power over her. Wedged between the furniture and the wall was one more drop cloth. She leaned one knee on the couch and reached across the back to pull it off. A row of stretched canvases faced the wall. Delaney's heart thrummed. A sudden chill invaded the room. She stood and worked her way around the couch to get closer. With a shaky hand she turned the closest canvas so it faced out.

The oil featured Ellie in a white embroidered Mexican dress, her rich ethnic heritage on full display. She leaned against a red brick wall. A huge pot at her feet held a pink bougainvillea with blossoms that reached up and across the wall. Her dark hair flowed down her back, her expression was sunny, and her eyes spoke love for whoever stood beyond the frozen moment in time.

"She told me I had whatever was left of Corey's paintings." Delaney knelt in front of it. The painting had all the hallmarks of Corey's work. Realism to the point of photographic. Intense color. A sense that he had wrapped himself up in the scene and the subject. She touched the blooms. "Why would she lie? Why would she keep this hidden away?"

"It's worth money now." Frowning, Cam chewed her lower lip. "Back then she might have wanted to spare you the pain."

"This is Corey's legacy. Of course I would want his art. Each one is a piece of him." Pieces she could hold on to when memories faded and disappeared into that dark tunnel of time.

Delaney eased the canvas aside. She turned each of seven more paintings so they could be seen, side by side, along one wall.

A waitress at Mi Tierra Restaurant filled a box with *pan dulce* while a woman perused the restaurant bakery's selection of delectable pastries.

A boy and a girl snuggled on a bench, waiting for a bus at Travis Park.

Delaney, dressed in shorts, a T-shirt, and sneakers, waved a bat at home plate.

An elderly couple walked hand in hand on a tree-lined nature trail.

Two kids sat on the hood of an old Ford pickup, watching a movie under a starry sky at the Mission Drive-In.

Nana poured strawberry jam into waiting jars while her two cats, Tinker and Dizzy, watched from their perch on the kitchen windowsill.

The last one featured a shyly smiling Jess, sitting on the makeshift patio they'd created outside the co-op. He sat in a lawn chair and strummed a guitar, likely one he'd created himself. He wore a red T-shirt and jeans. His feet were bare and his blond hair touched his shoulders. His head was back, his lips turned up as if laughing at something only he could see.

Life according to Corey. He recorded ordinary scenes as if he were an outsider unable to get in. He never did these everyday things because he was far too busy recording them. He wanted this normalcy, but he couldn't figure out how to get there.

"They're beautiful," Cam whispered, "but painful somehow."

"Like taking a walk through Corey's memories." Delaney leaned against the back of the sofa and studied the paintings one by one. "It must have been so painful for Ellie to see them. Yet she couldn't let go of them. They were her memories, too, in living color. She didn't want to share with the rest of the world. The world needs to see these.

We could do a retrospective exhibit with these and ones the rest of us have."

"And sell them. You could use the money."

Cam was right. Delaney's shop was in a tourist district with high rental costs. She sold something tourists didn't need—framing. "I don't think I could sell them. At this point I'm not sure they're mine to sell. They were in Ellie's possession. I guess that means they belong to Michael now."

"He won't want them and Ellie should never have kept them. She and Corey weren't married. His property didn't become hers. You were his beneficiary. He left everything to you. These paintings belong to you."

His VW Bus still sat in the garage. After a year, she'd given his clothes to Goodwill. After two, she threw out the dried-up paints and gave his art supplies to artist friends. After three, she turned his bedroom into a room where she could practice the art of framing. At first it was a hobby, then an apprenticeship, and now her livelihood. She took his name off the household checking account. Stopped getting mail with his name on it. Stopped using him as her emergency contact.

That had been Ellie's role. Now Delaney would have to ask Cam to fill it.

Bit by bit, her brother had disappeared from her life.

The paintings could mean something or nothing at all. Delaney turned her back on them. "I can't deal with this right now. Let's go through the boxes. We can finish what Ellie started, and Jess can help us carry everything out. Michael won't want any of this."

"Take the paintings home. They need to be cleaned and framed. The longer they sit around up here, the more they'll deteriorate."

Cam was right. Delaney squatted in front of the first open box. "I will, but let's finish up here. One thing at a time."

Cam lifted another box onto the couch and rummaged through it. "What did you think of Michael's confession regarding his client?"

"It makes more sense than theorizing Ellie's death had something to do with Corey's. Now that we know, it seems wrong not to tell Detective Ramos. On the other hand, I don't want to get Michael into legal trouble."

"I think he should make a deal." Cam wiped her face, smudging dust that decorated her cheek. "Give them what they need to know to get Knox in exchange for immunity from prosecution."

"It's a dangerous proposition. If this guy really had Ellie killed, how can we be sure the police can protect Michael and the kids?"

"He can't let Knox hold their safety over his head in order to make him do Knox's accounting. That's an untenable situation. Michael needs to do the right thing."

"I agree, but it's easy for us to say that. He has to live with the consequences."

"Here's a card Corey had sent Ellie after a fight." Cam held it up. "Very mushy make-up stuff."

"I don't need to know." Delaney rolled her eyes. She'd seen enough of her brother's make-up sessions with Ellie to know what the content would be like. "It's private."

And now that both were gone, what happened to those mementos? "Throw it away. Michael doesn't need to see it. Neither do the kids."

They worked in silence for the next hour. Cam wasn't the sort who felt the need to fill every minute with words. One of her best qualities. Delaney dug her way through four boxes. Nothing of note. No smoking gun. Just the sad remnants of a time when they'd all been innocent, vulnerable, and a little crazy, and sure they would take the art world by storm.

She scooted on her knees to the next box. The flaps were open.

Loose photos filled it. Corey in shorts and no shirt washed the VW Bus. He had a hose in one hand and a beer in the other. Jess manning the grill on the deck in his parents' backyard. The pool was the main draw but also the endless supply of meat, mostly venison and elk, provided from his dad's frequent hunting trips.

Hunter . . . Ellie had kept photos of Hunter. Why would she do that? In this one he had his arm around Delaney. They both had their heads thrown back, mouths open, laughing. Jess photobombed them from one corner, a spatula in his hand. Their laughter caught, suspended in time, for as long as the photos survived.

Life hadn't been like that in a long while.

Another one of Jess spraying Hunter and Corey with a hose. No one was smiling.

Fourth of July. Their last Fourth of July celebrated together. Hunter and Corey had been arguing—about money, of course. Only this time they went too far and ended up in a fistfight that started with Hunter throwing a beer bottle and hitting Corey center mass. Brave Jess had intervened with a garden hose. It worked. Of course, then they turned on him and Jess ended up in the pool. That's the way Hunter and Corey were—like brothers from different mothers.

Unfortunately for Hunter, Ellie had told this story in all its gory details for the jury.

Who took the photos? Delaney couldn't remember. Why hadn't she seen them before? Because Ellie didn't want to take that stroll down memory lane? Delaney didn't blame her. That Fourth of July battle had been a prime example of their often-volatile relationship. It helped convict Hunter of Corey's murder.

Delaney dropped the photo. No more memories. She pulled her hand away and moved to close the flaps. A torn bit of photo caught her eye. A photo had been ripped apart.

Let it go.

She pushed the flaps back a second time and dug deeper. A dozen or more photos had been torn into small pieces and hidden under the others.

With shaking fingers she laid the pieces out, trying to make sense of them. A photo of Corey and Ellie in swimming suits, torn in five pieces. Another of them clowning for the camera on the Golightlys' deck ripped in two. Pieces. Lots of pieces.

Cam knelt next to Delaney. "Anything interesting?"

"I think I found what had upset Ellie." Delaney motioned to the pieces. "Someone tore up a bunch of these photos."

"Why would someone do that?"

Delany's phone rang, saving her from having to answer. It was Gail, who had agreed to open the store for Delaney this morning. "What's up?"

"I'm so sorry, Boss, so sorry." The normally laid-back college senior sounded harried. "When I came in this morning, the park police and a security guard were already here." A sob followed. "Someone broke in and trashed the shop."

"I'm on my way."

CHAPTER 16

A park police officer stood outside You've Been Framed, writing on an electronic tablet. Delaney explained her presence. He nodded, told her SAPD was on the way, and went back to his report.

Gail sat in a rocking chair on the porch. Her face ashen, she popped up the second she saw Delaney and scooted down the steps. "It's awful, Delaney, just awful. I'm so sorry."

"It's okay. We'll survive." Delaney folded the other woman into a hug. Gail's chunky body shook. Delaney hugged tighter. "It's not your fault, for goodness' sake."

"The park policeman told me to peek inside. He wanted to know if anything was missing." Gail's tears wet Delaney's shoulder. "Everything is destroyed. Like a tornado blew through. All your equipment. Our customers' artwork."

Like Ellie's shop.

"I have insurance. We'll be fine." After weeks of being closed and losing business. "I'm just glad no one was here when it happened."

"Just the person I need to see." Detective Ramos strode up the walkway. He'd replaced his snazzy gray suit with a navy one. He dressed well, but that didn't hide the fact that he was obviously tired. "Persons, I should say. I assume this is your employee, Gail Simpkins."

Delaney disengaged from Gail. She introduced the detective. "Gail discovered the break-in, but she wasn't here when it happened."

"I don't know anything," Gail added. "I didn't see anything."

Delaney slid her arm around the college student. "When the park police officer said SAPD, I didn't realize he was talking about a homicide detective."

"Park police had instructions to let Detective Flores or me know if anything of interest happened here at La Villita that might have a bearing on Ellie Hill's case." Detective Ramos pulled his notebook from his pocket along with the stubby pencil he seemed to favor as a writing utensil. "I still need to ask Ms. Simpkins a couple of questions. It won't take long. Why don't you have a seat on the steps?"

Gail did as she was told. Delaney sat next to her.

"I didn't see anything." Her tone anxious, Gail stared up at Detective Ramos like he might pounce on her any second. "It was over when I got here."

"I understand. What time do you normally open the shop?"

"Nine o'clock. I'm never late."

"Have you had any unusual customers lately?"

Gail hunched over. She rubbed the tattoo of a unicorn on the inside of her wrist. "Not that I can think of. Lately it's mostly been people on spring break. Out-of-towners. They come in, realize we mostly frame artwork, and leave. We have a lot of repeat customers stopping by to pick up their finished artwork. All very civilized."

"What about on the street? Anybody loitering? Somebody you think you've seen before, then you see him again the next day? Or in the parking lot?"

Delaney could anticipate the answer to that question. Gail was a typical college student. Earbuds in, listening to music. Phone in hand, texting. A camel could prance by and she might not notice.

"Not that I remember, but we have all kinds of weird people downtown." She shot a bewildered look at Delaney. "A homeless guy who talks to himself and yells at cars on the street. A lady who wears an overcoat in the summer. I remember her because she smells so bad."

"Not like that." Keeping her voice soft, Delaney squeezed Gail's shoulders. She looked twelve, not twenty. Like a kid who wanted badly to please but didn't know how. "I think Detective Ramos is talking about someone who hasn't been around before, but suddenly seems to be here a lot."

Gail held her hand over her eyes to shade them from the morning sun cresting over St. John's Lutheran Church across the street. "I can't think. Let me think." She closed her eyes and opened them. "The only thing I noticed was an old gray car parked on the meter when I came out last week. For just a second I thought it was my sister's car, but she's at Port Hood, so I knew it couldn't be hers."

Detective Ramos moved a step closer. "You saw it just the once?"

"No, twice. It's not the kind of car we see parked here. It was an old Camry. They're usually nice rentals. That's another reason why it stuck in my mind. I don't know anything about cars, but Meagan taught me to drive in her car."

Delaney ignored the twinge of every heartstring. Her grandpa had taught her to drive in the Trailblazer after forbidding Corey to do it. He said a driving instructor with only a few years of driving experience was a disaster waiting to happen. No one talked about his real fear—that he would lose his grandkids to a car accident like the one that took his daughter and son-in-law. "She's a good big sister."

"She is. I miss her." Gail wiped at her face with both hands. "I peeked in it, just out of curiosity, I guess. I couldn't help myself."

"See anything interesting?" Ramos's timbre deepened. What he really meant was anything that would help find the car. "Do you know what year it was? Was it a two-door or a four-door?"

"It had a beaded rosary hanging from the rearview mirror." Gail's forehead wrinkled in concentration. "It was a four-door, like Meagan's."

It wasn't much. There would be hundreds of old Camrys in a city where most folks earned less than the federal income guidelines for poverty. Especially downtown. People supported families on food service—industry jobs that barely paid minimum wage in hotels and restaurants that catered to tourists.

"If I get some pictures from the different years, could you pick it out?"

"Absolutely. I think."

"Thank you, Gail." He tucked the pencil behind his ear and stowed the mini notebook in his pocket. "You've been very helpful."

"Really?"

"Really." Detective Ramos produced a business card and handed it to her. "If you think of anything else, please call me."

"I promise."

"You did good." Delaney stood and cocked her head toward the street. "Now go home. Eat something. Don't you have classes this afternoon and a project due at the end of the week?"

Gail hopped up. "I can skip. I want to help you clean up."

"I doubt we'll be able to clean up anytime soon. No skipping class. You don't want to waste that expensive tuition." Delaney had been clear when she hired Gail that she didn't want the job to interfere with the woman's studies. She'd had a great boss at the smoothie shop when she was in college. She planned to pay it forward. "Go work on your project. I've got this."

Fresh tears in her eyes, Gail reluctantly tromped down the steps.

At the bottom she stopped and swiveled. "Call me if I can help. Promise?"

"Absolutely."

Detective Ramos watched Gail walk west on Nueva before he turned back to Delaney. "How well do you know her?"

"Seriously? I interviewed ten candidates for the job and hired her. She's an honor roll student, one of five kids, a talented potter, and she had experience working at Hobby Lobby and a retail store in North Star Mall. She has no criminal history, and her references called her creative, reliable, honest to a fault, good customer service skills, articulate, and kind."

"No one's perfect."

"She's vegan."

"There you go." He flashed a brief smile. "No boyfriend problems?"

"No boyfriend. She says she's taking a hiatus right now to focus on her studies and her art."

"Smart woman."

Smarter than Delaney had been at that age. She'd been wrapped up in Hunter, her first and only serious boyfriend, all through college. Look where that had led. "Wise beyond her years."

Detective Ramos pivoted toward the shop. "Shall we check out the damage?"

She nodded. The park police officer stepped aside and she followed the detective up the steps. Her breakfast bagel threatened to make a sudden reappearance. She pressed her hand to her lips and willed her stomach to behave. He opened the door and let her enter first.

Gail had been right. The intruder had inflicted maximum damage—Delaney's matting boards and frames were strewn across the floor, racks filled with art prints had been toppled, and art cards were scattered. Framed artwork was smashed and flung to the floor.

Her workbench had been overturned with her sander, matte cutter, glass cutter, and other tools of the trade on top of it. Chairs were up-ended. Nothing had been left untouched.

Someone had gone on a search-and-destroy mission in her shop.

His smooth-shaven face tight with concern, Detective Ramos's hand came out as if to take her arm. He hesitated. His hand dropped. "I'd find you a chair to sit down, but we can't touch anything just yet. I called CSU. They're on their way down. As I explained to the park police officer earlier, this isn't a run-of-the-mill break-in. I want every-thing documented."

"Me too. I'm fine." Delaney's throat threatened to close. It was never run-of-the-mill for the property owner. She swallowed. "I planned to clean up Ellie's place so Michael doesn't have to do it. I guess this will be next."

"What about her part-time employee?" Detective Ramos studied the floor for a second. "Kimberly . . . Martinez?"

"Michael planned to talk to Kimberly later today to tell her—gently, I hope—that she's been furloughed until further notice. He's not sure when or if the store will ever open again."

"I'll need to speak to her as well."

If he was trying to take her mind from the destruction around her, it wasn't working. "Michael can give you her contact information."

"Why didn't the alarm company contact you directly?"

"They call the police and then the admin office. The physical prop-erty officially belongs to the city, not me."

"Did they call you?"

"Actually Gail did."

"The shop's alarm sounded just before dawn, but park police officers saw nothing when they investigated." Detective Ramos's tone was reminiscent of a zookeeper dealing with a wild animal. "A security guard came by later and noticed the door standing open. He entered and then reported the break-in to park police."

"I don't understand. You don't break into a place like mine for money. I don't keep much cash here. I deposit three times a week, but most of my transactions are credit or debit card. There's not a lot of real value except the paintings and the jerk destroyed those."

"Can you tell if anything is missing?"

Delaney swept her gaze over the shop. "Can I move around?"

"Just be careful where you step and don't touch anything."

Delaney stepped over piles of debris that had once been merchandise and slipped behind the counter. The cash register was intact. Her laptop, printer, and credit card machine remained in plain sight. "I don't see anything missing. I'll have to sort everything out before I know for sure."

"It was a deliberate attempt to vandalize and destroy."

"I agree." Delaney made her way back through the detritus that represented her livelihood. "I just don't understand why."

Detective Ramos led the way outside. "I know this is the last thing you need right now. Let me buy you a cup of coffee at the café. You can sit down and gather your wits while we talk."

He really was a decent person with an awful job.

"My stomach can't take any more coffee right now, but an *agua fresca* would be nice."

They grabbed seats on La Villita Café's outdoor patio after getting their drinks. Delaney took a long sip of the pineapple-strawberry concoction and let the breeze cool her face. The mingled aromas of bacon frying and refried beans cooking wafted from the restaurant. The sign over the double wooden doors urged customers to EAT LOCAL EAT FRESH. US, Mexican, Republic of Texas, and Canadian flags hanging from the rafters flapped in the breeze.

She closed her eyes for a second and breathed.

Her cell phone dinged. A text from Jess.

Cam told me what happened. Are u Ok?

Cam meant well. She wanted to circle the wagons with Delaney in the middle.

I'm fine. The shop's a mess. Talking w/PD now
I'll come over
No need. I've got this
Let me help u
I'll call u later
Promise?
Promise

Delaney laid the phone down.

"Did something happen?" Detective Ramos scooted his chair across the cement and dropped his notebook on the table. He jerked his chin toward the phone. "I mean something else."

"No, just Jess wanting to know if I'm okay. Cam told him about the break-in."

"It's good that you have friends who have your back these days." Detective Ramos tugged on the pencil he'd stuck behind his ear. "Did you make someone angry recently?"

"I frame artwork and sell art on consignment. It's not exactly a controversial occupation. As I said before, that's one of the reasons I chose it."

"How long since you've been involved in removing children from their homes?"

"Five years."

Detective Ramos's thick scrawl was impossible to read upside down. He tapped his pencil on the table's wooden top. "Some people have long memories."

"Desperate parents with anger issues don't wait five years to exact their revenge." The image of a father, his face suffused with anger and hate, wielding a machete, filled her mind's eye. There was a reason why officers accompanied caseworkers on these missions. "They attack you outside the courthouse or when you arrive at their homes to remove their children from their care."

"No cameras inside the shop?"

"No, only outside."

"I'll check them out with the office." He jabbed his pencil toward the ceiling. The offices were located on the second floor above the café. "The guy had to have been recorded."

Delaney intended to accompany him on his trip, whether he liked it or not. "Ellie was murdered in her shop next door yesterday. Mine was destroyed today. It doesn't seem likely that it's a coincidence."

"Except that this breach occurred while you weren't here. The offender didn't break in with the intent to do physical harm." Detective Ramos drew a circle around something he'd written in the notebook. Delaney stretched her neck and leaned forward. The detective's hand curled around the top of the notebook. "I understand Hunter Nash paid you a visit last night."

Cam was as good as her word.

"He did."

"You should've called 911. Did he threaten you?"

"I threatened him. With a baseball bat, a stun gun, and pepper spray."

"You know he fits the description of your assailant and Ellie Hill's killer in terms of height and weight."

"So does Michael. My gut tells me I would've known if it was either of them. I didn't recognize the voice. The way they move would've seemed familiar."

Detective Ramos didn't seem convinced. "What did Nash want?"

"To convince me Corey did something really stupid that resulted in his murder."

"Which would be?"

Delaney ran through Hunter's story.

"It's the same story he tried to tell at the trial, but the prosecutor shot him down—rightfully so. There was no evidence of this collaboration with Tango Orejón. Do you think he's telling the truth?"

If only she had an answer for that question. Some small part of her wanted it to be true. Hope wanted to gain a foothold in her heart again. *Don't be stupid*. "I can't fully refute it." There, she'd admitted it. "This guy Willy did hang around the co-op a lot. Everything about him said gang member. The tats, the baggy pants, the attitude. I thought I saw a gun stuck in the back of his pants once. Corey told me I worried too much. On the other hand, I had no idea Corey did other drugs besides pot. Either he hid it well or I was just clueless."

"THC, alcohol, and Xanax were identified in his tox screen."

"I know, but he had a prescription for the Xanax. He'd smoked pot for as long as I could remember."

"It sounds like Corey and Willy were from two different worlds. Why would Sandoval hook up with a White guy artist? The gangs are racially segregated, for the most part."

"Which would make the co-op a perfect front for Tango Orejón's drug operation, wouldn't it?"

Detective Ramos nodded, but he ran one hand through black hair long enough to touch his collar. His smile was begrudging. "You've given this some thought."

"Along the lines of what I could've done differently, yes. My brother had been up to his eyeballs in drugs, not only using but facilitating their distribution. I didn't see it. Or refused to see it. I thought he just needed a little counseling. I didn't want him using drugs to numb the pain. I wanted him to get help. I tried to get him to talk to my pastor."

"That sounds like something a caring sister would do. You tried. That counts for something."

"I should've tried to get him into rehab. I was deluded to think a pastor could help him."

"You've lost your faith, then?"

"What does this have to do with the investigation?"

"To my way of thinking it's more important than the investigation."

"If you start spouting Scripture, I'm leaving."

"Understood. Nash swore to you your brother had a drug problem. He needed money to support it. He got in bed with a drug dealer in order to make that money."

"Corey was an artist who loved what he did. I could see him selling his soul to buy art supplies and keep the co-op open, but not because he wanted to buy more drugs. Why are we talking about a ten-year-old murder right now instead of the murder of Ellie Hill?"

"I'm not convinced they aren't somehow related." Detective Ramos wadded up his receipt and tossed it into the coffee cup. "But you're right. The investigation of your friend's murder takes priority. Have you thought of anything new that will help?"

Delaney studied the pink-and-green caladiums flourishing in a pot next to one of the columns that supported the second-floor balcony. Should she tell him about Michael's client? As much as she wanted to, Michael needed to do it. She met the detective's unnerving gaze. "Michael has some theories. Maybe you should talk to him."

"I plan to. I was surprised to learn he went to work today."

"He needed to work for a few hours. He still needs to make a living."

"You don't?"

"I do, but I was . . ." She was rooting through boxes in Ellie's house to see if she could ascertain what made her friend so upset. "Is it possible the killer didn't just make a mess? That maybe he was searching for something?"

"Like what?"

"I don't know. When can I get back into Ellie's shop?"

"The crime scene folks are done. They've documented everything and taken anything that might possibly be evidence. It's been released as a crime scene. However, it might be better for Mr. Hill to hire someone to clean it up."

He'd suggested the same thing after Corey's death. Scrubbing away the blood of a loved one only created more scars on a person's soul. Detective Ramos scooted his chair back and stood. "Are you sure there's nothing else you want to tell me?"

"Nothing."

"I'm good at reading people. Keep that in mind."

"Duly noted."

"I plan to have a word with Nash. He won't be bothering you again."

"It's not necessary. I can take care of myself. Hunter knows that now."

Detective Ramos closed his notebook and stuck it in his pocket. "I need to see those digital recordings. If you ever change your mind about that other thing we were talking about, I'm available or I can steer you to someone you might feel more comfortable with. Right now, you should go home."

"I have a therapist." She stood and headed for the stairs that led to the second floor.

He quickly overtook and passed her. He glanced back. "Are you following me?"

"No. I need to talk to the admin folks myself. I'd also like to see those recordings. I saw the man who killed Ellie. I might be able to tell if it's the same man. It seems to me that would be helpful to you."

"Fine. Then you go home."

"Then I'm going to record the mess in my shop for insurance purposes. I need to call my customers and let them know I'll be unable to fulfill their jobs as originally scheduled." Their artwork or photographs were likely damaged. Thankfully she paid big bucks for hefty insurance. "I need to know how quickly I can clean up and get back to work. Like Michael, I have to make a living."

Detective Ramos's scowl deepened. "We're not going to have a problem, are we?"

"I'm not. What about you?"

"I'll tell you the same thing I plan to tell Nash. He has a parole officer to worry about. You have a killer who told you to stay out of it. So stay out of it."

"Yes, sir."

Detective Ramos didn't need to know she had her fingers crossed behind her back.

A few minutes later they were standing side by side reviewing the recordings. The city had hired an outside firm to provide on-site security in the historic district. The guy on duty gladly queued up the recordings from both incidents for Delaney. She was the shop owner after all. Detective Ramos's presence didn't hurt, of course.

The camera that hung from the roof's eave outside the back entrance was well positioned. The motion-sensor security lighting helped as well. The intruder was around six feet tall, weighed around 175 or 180 pounds. He wore black sweats, a long-sleeved black T-shirt, and black sneakers. The same thick black mesh stocking covered his face.

"It's the same guy." Delaney straightened. The contents of her stomach did a cha-cha-cha. Her head throbbed. "He knows where the camera is too. Even with his face covered, he's keeping his back to it. Where were your people when this was going on?"

"It's not people. It's one guy. He walks the entire district." The security company employee raised both hands in surrender. "It's not like we have someone sitting here watching the cameras. If we do see something, we call park police. That's what the contract provides."

Minimal coverage, minimal cost.

Good enough for government work.

Delaney kept those thoughts to herself. Detective Ramos seemed lost in thought. She waited a few seconds. "Well?"

"Well, nothing." He shrugged and proceeded to stick his notebook in his jacket pocket. "I'll need those recordings. The originals. Dump them in Dropbox, please."

"What next?"

Another shrug. The guy's beefy shoulders were getting a workout. "I have places to go, people to see. You mentioned the same."

"You'll let me know if you find out anything?"

"It doesn't work that way and you know it."

CHAPTER 17

"Are you following me?"

Ignoring the barely veiled hostility in Nash's challenge, Andy tossed his car keys in the air and let them land on his outstretched palm. He took his time straightening from his spot leaning against his car and strolled over to the other man's pickup truck parked in front of the Joyous Faith Community Center deep in San Antonio's west side gang country. "No. I called your house. Your mother told me you were on your way here."

"My first day of freedom and you show up at my house. My first day of work and you're the welcoming committee. Come on, Detective, I need this job." Nash glanced at the weary-looking building with its eighties facade marred by multiple coats of gray paint covering graffiti. "I want this job. I'll be good at it. Don't mess that up."

"What kind of job starts this late in the day?"

"The kind that involves kids who come to the center after school lets out. It's spring break, but the classes are always late in the day."

"I'll walk you in."

"I'd rather you didn't."

"I don't want you to be late." Andy maneuvered around a clutch of teenage girls in hoodies and skinny jeans who were ogling his metallic gray Challenger and giggling. "It being your first day and all."

Nash turned his back on Andy. He pulled a duffel bag and a backpack from the truck's passenger seat. "What do you want?"

"I got a call from Camille Sanchez this morning. She's very concerned about her friend Delaney Broward. She says you entered Ms. Broward's house without permission. I told her I couldn't believe you would be that stupid, but she said you were. Then I saw Ms. Broward herself, and she confirmed this incomprehensible piece of information."

"Did she also tell you why I was there?"

"To expound on your old cockamamie story about gangbanger drug dealers killing Corey because he got cold feet about letting them use the co-op as a storage and distribution point for their wares."

"It's not a story. That's what we fought about."

"So why didn't your attorney put this guy on the stand during your trial?"

"We couldn't find him. Probably because he didn't want to be found. Or his boss didn't want him found. Corey was alive when I left. I've had years to think about it, and it's the only thing that makes sense. I had no proof and my attorney wouldn't let me testify. Even he didn't believe me."

Ignoring Nash's scowl, Andy leaned against the truck and let the March sun warm his face. Many men went to their graves proclaiming their innocence. "I encouraged Ms. Broward to get a restraining order. Jess Golightly can help her with that. If you show up at her house again, your parole officer will hear about it."

"I know you don't believe me, but I'm trying to help her."

No, Nash wanted back in her good graces. He wanted to pick up where he'd left off. Fat chance. "Helping her would've been walking away from a fight with her brother."

"Which is exactly what I did." Nash dropped his bags in the middle of the sidewalk and turned to face Andy. "I'm going to prove I didn't kill Corey. If Ellie's murder is related to his death, I'll prove that too."

Big mistake. "I strongly urge you to leave it alone."

"I can't. I have to prove to Laney that I didn't do it."

Sometimes love was like that. It refused to die. Especially when a guy spent years in prison with nothing else to think about. "I get that."

"No, you don't." Nash moved until he stood directly in front of Andy. His voice was low, hoarse. The muscle in his jaw worked. "She didn't just lose her brother; she lost the man she loved. But even worse, she lost her faith. She lost everything important to her."

Andy straightened. The reason for Nash's careless disregard for the consequences of digging into Corey's murder became abundantly clear. In his shoes, any caring person would want to do the same. Andy had tried himself. "You think you can restore her faith? Only God can do that."

"I can't be responsible for her living in this world without faith." Nash's mouth twisted in a painful grimace. "I wouldn't wish that on my worst enemy. Faith is the only thing that kept me alive in Dominguez. So even if she never believes in me again, she has to believe in God. For that to happen I have to prove to her I didn't destroy her life."

"God is working in her life. Her salvation doesn't depend on you. She needs to have faith even if you did kill her brother."

"Easy for you to say." Nash glanced at his phone and groaned. "I have to go. Investigate a gangbanger named Guillermo Sandoval. Goes by Willy. Pull his string and the whole thing will unravel."

"What gang?"

"What do you mean?"

"Corey went to school on the north side. How did their paths cross? What gang crossed over those territories?"

"Willy's grandmother sent him to live with his aunt. He went to O'Connor High School briefly. But he was already neck deep in Tango Orejón. Moving him to the north side didn't matter. And if you think there's no gang activity out there, consider how much tagging there is in some of those neighborhoods. By the time we started the co-op, which is on the south side, Willy was back at the housing project."

"Gangs are everywhere, but they're territorial and most often are segregated." Andy didn't need a lesson in gang activity or geography. He lived it every day. "It doesn't make sense that they would engage with a White guy like Corey."

"A gang member sold to that White guy. They had a relationship. He decided to capitalize on it. Somebody higher up in the hierarchy thought it was a good idea. It's not like they asked Corey to join the gang. They just used him."

A portly man dressed in army-green cargo shorts, a white polo shirt, and white sneakers with matching ankle socks pushed through the double glass doors and strode toward them. His potbelly proceeded him by a step. "There you are, Hunter. I was getting worried."

Nash lowered his head and closed his eyes. His long breath was audible over the noise of a passing car. He turned. "Hey, Pastor James. I was just on my way in."

Pastor James kept right on coming. He had *veteran* written all over him from the VFW ball cap to the U.S. Marine Corps tattoo on his forearm to the wary expression in his faded topaz eyes. "Your mom called the office. She said you were headed this way, but she was concerned you might get waylaid."

The combination of mother and middle school teacher made Mrs. Nash a formidable opponent. Did her meddling in his business get on Nash's nerves or did he consider himself blessed to have a mother who cared? Too many didn't.

"I'm fine. This is Detective Ramos. I told you about him. He stopped by with a couple more questions."

"Sure he did." Pastor James cocked his head toward the door. "I have a dozen teenagers chomping at the bit to meet you. The arts and crafts room is set up for you. All the supplies you asked for are there. Detective, you're welcome to come in to observe if you like. Unless you have investigating to do somewhere else."

A not-so-gentle hint. Pastor James was okay. He took his role as mentor seriously. Andy eased away from the truck. "I have more stops to make in a homicide investigation. I'll be seeing you, Hunter."

Relief evident in his face, Hunter grabbed his bags and headed for the doors. Pastor James lingered. He dug around in his pockets and came up with a business card. "This is the name of the attorney who'll represent Hunter in any legal matters that may come up in the future."

"How well do you know Hunter?"

"I visited him at Dominguez once a month for six years as part of my church's Kairos Prison Ministry. The chaplain there is a friend of mine. We took turns working with him."

"So you think his *I-found-Jesus* thing is for real?"

Pastor James's round face filled with disapproval. "That's not for me to judge. Or you. Only God knows what's in Hunter's heart."

"I agree. I'm praying his faith is genuine. And that he has admitted his sin to God and repented."

"You're a Christian, then."

"I am."

"Good. That means you value truth more than being right. I

believe Hunter when he says he's innocent of the crime for which he was sent to prison."

"I wish I were less of a cynic, but every criminal I've ever helped put away has insisted he didn't do it."

"I would imagine so. Have you ever had one come out of prison intent on proving it?"

It was rare. By that time most had moved on—usually to other new crimes.

When Andy didn't respond, Pastor James tipped his ball cap, revealing a shiny brown pate. "I thought not. I just hope you're not refusing to consider the possibility because you don't want to investigate and find out you'd sent the wrong person to jail while the real killer escaped punishment. Am I right that there's no statute of limitations on murder?"

"You are correct." The blurred picture of that possibility slowly slipped into sharp focus. Andy started toward his car. "It was nice meeting you."

"I'll pray for you, Detective."

It sounded more like a threat than a promise.

CHAPTER 18

"Be yourself. They can see right through a poser." Hunter repeated Pastor James's words in his head like a mantra. Ignoring his sweaty armpits and shaking hands, he trudged into the community center arts and craft room with a smile firmly affixed to his face. His gut still rocked from his encounter with Ramos, but these kids deserved Hunter's undivided attention.

A dozen teenagers sat at tables arranged in a horseshoe. Their expressions ranged from baleful to bored to doubtful. They needed him and Hunter needed them. Together, they would focus on art and staying out of jail or prison or trouble in general.

After group introductions, he ran through a quick bio and then explained the curriculum he'd worked up during his last week behind bars. Mostly hands-on art activities. Fun stuff to get them warmed up with pencil, ink, charcoal, finger painting. Then papier-mâché. *Papel picado*. Then watercolor and acrylics. If Pastor James could get more art supplies donated. So far, a downtown art store had been more than generous. His new students would get art appreciation and history from better teachers later in their careers—if they were really serious about art. First order of business: doing art for the sheer joy of it. "Any questions?"

"How'd you get that scar?" A skinny girl with a pimply face and a Slytherin House tattoo on her forearm posed the question. Her name tag read *Krystal*. "It's wicked."

"I meant any questions about the class."

"Were you really in prison?" A kid named Elvis pulled his black hoodie up around his face and jerked his chin toward Hunter. "What'd you do? Steal art supplies?"

Snorts of laughter and titters greeted the questions.

"I did time for killing my best friend."

"That's some serious s—"

"You know Pastor James's rule." Hunter pointed to the list of rules posted on the wall in fancy black calligraphy.

NO CUSSING. NO KISSING. NO FIGHTING. NO GUNS. NO SMOKING. NO DRINKING.

Below it was a second sign.

WHAT IS ALLOWED: FUN. FRIENDSHIP. LAUGHTER. DANCING. LEARNING. DAYDREAMING. CREATING. READING. WRITING. GROWING.

Why the list of prohibited activities would interest teenagers more was simply a product of human nature. "As I was saying, I did time for killing my best friend . . . only I didn't."

"Right." Elvis leaned back in his chair. He tapped his pencil on the table's scarred laminate. "Said anyone who ever went to jail."

"I hear you've spent some time in juvie. What'd you do?"

"Beat up my sister's baby daddy. Cracked his jaw in two places." Elvis pumped his fist and high-fived the rotund guy sitting next to him. "It's nothing worse than he done to her."

They all had those stories. The goal here, according to Pastor James, was to help them channel the anger, hurt, and pain into their art. Hunter pulled his latest sketches from the leather portfolio he'd unearthed in his closet this morning. He clothespinned them to the wooden easels Pastor James had provided.

"I've only been out a few days. I don't really want to talk about it." He smoothed the sheet of drawing paper. The sketch featured a melee in the prison recreation room. In the center two men grappled on the floor while those around them cheered, their faces filled with furious joy at what they seemed to perceive as entertainment. "What about you, Elvis, you want to talk about it?"

Elvis shook his head. "Not really."

"So draw something."

"Like what?" Dawn sat closest to the door. She wore braces that made her look younger than the other teens in the room, but her almond eyes were hard. The crook in her nose suggested it had been broken at some point. "I thought you was gonna show us how."

They were here because Pastor James knew something about them—their family lives, their interests, issues at school. All of them had talent currently being wasted. "I'm thinking y'all will show me how."

More suspicious stares. After a few seconds, a girl named Mercedes pulled a sketchbook from her backpack. She had sleek black hair that fell to her waist, russet eyes, and thick dark eyebrows that stopped just short of meeting in the middle. She was dressed entirely in black. Even her fingernails had been painted a deep ebony. Her expression doleful, she bent over her pad and went to work.

Some of the others followed suit. Elvis wiggled in his chair. He leaned back, then forward.

Hunter shuffled his notes. "You don't want to sketch?"

"Naw. I'm not feeling it today." Elvis leaned over and tried to see what his buddy was drawing. "Got a crick in my neck."

The bulldozer of a guy in the next chair glared at him. "Back off, homie."

"I'm not your homie."

"Easy, guys." Striving for a nonchalance he didn't feel, Hunter pulled a stack of sketch pads along with several boxes of high-quality sketch pencils from a shelf behind the desk. "Pastor James said we could use these if we wanted."

Elvis eyed the supplies. "How much?"

"Free. They were donated."

"You sure?"

"I'm sure." He held out a sketch pad.

Elvis snatched it, then grabbed a pencil. "Thanks, man."

"Don't thank me, thank Pastor James." Hunter waved a pad in the air. "Anybody else?"

Two of the other students raised their hands. Next time he would know to make the offer first. The last thing he wanted to do was embarrass a kid who didn't have the funds to buy his or her own art supplies.

Live and learn.

Hunter's phone chirped like a cricket. He jumped. Elvis chortled.

Hunter could count on the fingers of one hand the number of people who had his new number. He wasn't in a big hurry to reconnect with some people. Besides, it was probably the first of many spam calls.

Nope. It was Mel.

"Keep drawing, y'all." He grabbed the phone and stepped into the hallway to answer. "I'm teaching—"

"Listen, someone broke into Delaney's shop overnight and trashed it."

"Ramos was just here. He never mentioned——"

"Of course he didn't. It's not his job to share. My friend in Dispatch said a security guard discovered it this morning and called park police. Ramos probably came from La Villita to see you. What did he want?"

"To warn me to stay away from her."

"Good advice."

"It wasn't advice. He was throwing his weight around." Hunter peeked into the activity room. The quiet was almost unnerving. They were engrossed in their work. "He recommended she get a restraining order."

"Do you think she will?"

The sound of Delaney's punches pummeling Macho Man filled Hunter's head. As did the image of Delaney handing him a plate bearing two tacos made by her own hand. The way their fingers brushed when he handed her the phone. The way she filled out her jeans and the blue cotton blouse that deepened the green in her eyes. He'd been hanging on to those memories all day. "I hope not."

Mel's groan hurt Hunter's ear. "This isn't about solving the murder, is it?"

"Sure it is."

"You need to let her go."

"Easy for you to say. Thanks for letting me know about the break-in. If you hear anything else——"

"I will. Be careful. Be safe."

What Mel really meant was "guard your heart." His heart hadn't been his for years. "I gotta go."

For three hours Hunter concentrated on building bridges with his new students. Pastor James was right. They had talent. Raw talent.

Elvis and Dawn showed more promise than Hunter ever had. Once that would've hurt. Now it just gave him hope for them and for a world that could be made better by their art.

Finally, Hunter turned them loose early with an invitation to return the next day with a sketch of something important to them from their homes. Amazingly, they agreed to come back.

He hadn't flopped. He stuffed his portfolio into the truck and headed for downtown. As usual parking was nonexistent. He ended up on Cesar Chavez Boulevard and hiked on Alamo Street to La Villita. The trek gave him a chance to practice his new speech. Delaney had had time to think about his theory. To embrace it. They could figure out this puzzle together. Ellie's murder, the break-in, Corey's murder—they all had to be related.

Stepping onto Villita Street was like slipping into a time warp. The last time he'd been on this brick thoroughfare, he'd been drunk and stoned at NIOSA while Corey lay dead on the floor of his studio. The police had taken him into custody in the French Quarter section in the middle of The Banjo Brown Band's set. They'd made him throw away his shrimp étouffée.

Nothing had changed. Everything had changed. Delaney owned a shop called You've Been Framed. No irony there. No salt in his wound. No past stuck in his throat. He trudged north on Villita Street, hung a left on King Philip Walk. The shop was at the corner of King Philip and Nueva Street.

Hunter heaved a big breath. His stomach rocked. He hadn't eaten since those gringo tacos at Delaney's house. Gritting his teeth, he bounded up the steps and tugged on the door.

It didn't budge.

She wouldn't leave. Not with her shop a mess. Delaney was a neat freak. Corey's penchant for chaos drove her to the other extreme. She wanted an orderly life. She needed a port in the storm. She always would.

"Where are you, Delaney?"

"You always did talk to yourself." Delaney stood on the sidewalk. She had that fight-or-flight look she'd had the night before. "What are you doing here?"

"Waiting for you."

She had her phone in her hand. She lifted it toward her ear.

"No, no, don't do that, please. I heard your shop got broken into. It's all related, you have to see that."

"How, how is it related?" Her tone plaintive, she raised both hands in the air. "And how did you find out? Did Detective Ramos tell you?"

"Are you kidding? He came to warn me to stay away from you, but he never said a word."

"He warned you to stay away, yet here you are."

"Here I am."

"You don't get it, do you?"

"No, *you* don't get it." Hunter slammed down the steps. Careful to stay out of her space, he stopped short. "No matter what happens between us, I have to do this. I'm not backing off."

"What do you want from me?"

Her heart. Her trust. Her hand in marriage. Hunter shoved those thoughts aside. "I want to see where Ellie died. I want you to walk me through it. I know it's a lot to ask, but studying the crime scene is the first step in solving a crime."

He'd read a lot of textbooks in prison. One day he might even go back to college.

Her gaze reminded him of the kids in his class. Every bit as assessing, as distrusting, as calculating. He held his breath. Delaney ducked her head and took off for King Philip's Way. "You want to see, be my guest. It makes no sense to me. I don't know who could possibly make sense of it. Unless you suddenly sprouted a Mensa IQ and got a degree in criminal justice."

Bitter didn't suit her. Hunter kept that thought to himself. He followed her to the squat hut next door. Delaney didn't bother to make conversation. She opened the white picket fence gate and pushed it open. "Detective Ramos says they're done with the crime scene. I'm not sure what Michael plans to do with it."

"How bad was the damage to your shop?"

"Someone destroyed my tools of the trade. He wrecked my workbench. Every bit of my inventory of cards, posters, postcards, and art supplies destroyed." Her hands fisted. "The worse part was seeing what he did to my customers' artwork. I'm dreading calling them."

"I'm sorry. Will insurance cover it?"

"They're sending out a claims adjuster. I have to put together a list of everything—customer projects, equipment, tools, furniture. It'll take time."

"What about the shop itself?" Maybe if he kept her talking, she wouldn't dwell on the space they were about to enter. "Is that on you or the city?"

"The manager was extraordinarily nice, all things considered. It's a nightmare for the city, too, dealing with what happened to Ellie here in the middle of a tourist attraction and another break-in a day later. I have to clear the debris first. They'll assess for structural damage, clean the floor, the restroom, and the walls. Make repairs and paint. In the meantime I'm not earning a cent."

"Will insurance pay for lost income?"

"I don't know."

"I can help you clean up."

She shook her head. "Please don't do that."

"Do what?"

"Act like nothing happened."

"I'm not. I need to figure out what happened to Ellie. Somehow it's related to Corey's death. It's the only way I can make things right with you."

"Do what you have to do, but there's no way you can make things right with me. Not ever."

CHAPTER 19

Talk about losing her mind. Delaney huffed as she inserted her key into the lock at Mother Earth Oils & Candles. What was she thinking? Letting Hunter into Ellie's shop. Letting him into her life. She gave him an inch at the house the previous evening and now he wanted forty miles. Quelling the urge to tell Hunter exactly that, she opened the door and flipped the light switch. A whiff of mingled scents hit her in the face. Despite the desire to retreat, she moved forward so Hunter could step inside. "Shut the door and lock it."

No one would catch them unaware. Not again.

The carnage hadn't magically disappeared. At this rate she would never eat again. Slowly, reluctance burrowing deep into her core, Delaney slogged through the mess. She edged around the spatters of now-dried rusty-brown blood and the bigger puddle where her best friend had died.

Keep moving. Keep moving.

Her feet refused to move. Hunter brushed past her. His face registered shock, pain, grief, anger—all the same emotions that buffeted Delaney when she contemplated the last few minutes of her best friend's life.

"It's so wrong. She went through so much." Hunter smacked his fist into his open palm. "To have it end this way is so hard to understand."

"That's my point exactly. You say you went to prison for something you didn't do. Corey was murdered. Ellie was murdered. How can you say God is good with a straight face?"

"God didn't do this."

"No, but He let it happen." Delaney's stomach roiled. She put her hand to her mouth. *Don't vomit. Don't vomit.* "I'm sorry I brought it up. What do you want to know?"

"What about her laptop?"

"The killer took it. He also took her wedding ring. Police would've thought it was a robbery if he hadn't said what he did to me. He messed up. It doesn't make sense."

"Were her business records on the laptop?"

"She was all about being environmentally responsible. Paper free. As little toner as possible. But I'm sure she backed them up on the Cloud. She was smart too. Michael will figure out how to access them when he's ready."

"Mommy Earth with a healthy dose of techie."

"Exactly."

"Maybe if we start putting stuff back where it belongs, you'll be able to see if anything is missing."

It beat standing around staring at each other like lost souls.

Delaney forced herself to start on one side while Hunter took the other. They righted display racks, chairs, and tables. That made it easier to return merchandise to its proper resting places. When—if—Michael decided to reopen, the shop would need a deep cleaning and fresh staging.

Delaney swept up broken glass, smashed candles, fliers, and tiny bottles of essential oils, while Hunter held the dustpan. He set the heavy-duty trash bags on the porch. They would take them to the Dumpsters at the end.

What once had been fresh, clean, and comforting scents combined for a stench that made Delaney's nose burn and her head ache. And still, nothing jumped out at her.

"What about this filing cabinet?"

Delaney followed Hunter's finger pointing at a three-drawer filing cabinet wedged between the counter that held the cash register and the back wall of the shop. "She kept tax receipts and inventory, stuff like that, in there."

"It's worth checking out."

It felt like sticking her nose where it didn't belong. As if Ellie would care. Even when she was alive, she wouldn't have cared. Hunter pulled the cabinet out into the open space. Delaney settled cross-legged in front of it. She handed a stack of files to Hunter and kept a stack for herself. He was so close she could see the tiny scar in the middle of his cheek. A neighbor dog had bit him. An ER doctor had done a decent job. Five stitches along his jawline and three in the middle. They hardly showed—unless a person knew they were there.

Focus.

For a free spirit Ellie had a keen sense of organization. One folder held all the lease information. Another contained all her tax receipts that year. Vendor invoices. Merchandise catalogs.

"I wonder what this is." Hunter held up a manilla envelope addressed to Ellie. It had no return address.

Delaney craned her neck from side to side. The pain didn't subside. "Probably just another catalog. She collected them."

Hunter opened the envelope and pulled out the content. A stack of yellowed newspaper clippings—all the coverage of the trial. Nothing sinister there. His Adam's apple bobbed. He dropped them like they burned his fingers.

"I clipped them too. I don't know why."

"It almost seems like a form of punishment." Hunter's voice dropped to a pained whisper. "Do you ever read them?"

"Never. But when I went through Nana's things after she had died, I found the article about Mom and Dad's accident. And a copy of the obituaries. The funeral program. People keep things like that as mementos, I suppose."

"Huh, what's this?" Hunter pulled a second envelope hidden among a bunch of essential oils catalogs.

Photos. Eight by tens. Black-and-white. Hunter dropped them faceup on the floor one by one. Some were taken at a distance in a parking lot. The building behind it appeared to be a strip mall with vacant or yet-to-be-occupied stores. Ellie stood beside her car talking to a man who sat in his vehicle. Her body language was tense, her expression fierce. One hand was up, finger pointed at the car's occupant. Classic give-'em-grief Ellie. It was impossible to say who the man was. Only that it wasn't Michael. The man had hair.

Delaney took her time. She used a tissue to pick up each of the four photos and examine them. In the third one Ellie leaned forward, her hand on the car door frame. In the last one she leaned into the car, her back to the camera. Her body obscured what she was doing, but the possibilities crowded, all wanting the front of the line. Like kissing the occupant of the car. Why else get that close?

The second set of photos were taken in front of a hotel. A valet handed keys to Ellie standing by the driver's-side door of her SUV. No sign of who might be with her. "That's the Hyatt Regency downtown." Delaney pointed to the emblem on the concierge's podium near the automatic sliding-glass doors. "It's on Losoya Street. I went to a conference there once, and you had to park in a garage across the street if you didn't use valet parking."

"Is anything written on the back?" Hunter kept his hands on his hips. If anyone knew better than to touch what might be evidence in a murder, it was a man convicted of it. "Something handy like a date or location or caption?"

His sardonic tone matched the retort that died on Delaney's lips. She checked, then shook her head. No hint of when or where they were taken. Or by whom. "No, but what about the envelope?"

Hunter turned it over. No return address, of course, but it did have a postmark from here in San Antonio. "They were mailed to her a week before her murder."

"Blackmail?"

"It's possible."

"A busy hotel on the River Walk with tons of valet parking attendants—no way anyone would remember her or who she was with. We're not law enforcement. We can't check her credit card statements to see if she paid for a room. Or subpoena hotel records to see if a room was reserved in her name." Delaney chewed on her thumbnail. "Besides, the other person—assuming there is another person—could've reserved and paid."

If Michael had already found them, he would assume the worst. And it would also give him a motive for murder.

Why didn't Ellie confide in Delaney? They were best friends. They'd held each other together at Corey's funeral, through the trial, and in the days afterward when people expected them to go on with life as if nothing had happened. Delaney had been Ellie's maid of honor. She'd even worn that awful hippie gown and stood barefoot on the white sand on a Riviera Maya beach for Ellie's destination wedding.

"None of this makes sense. Why didn't she tell me?" Delaney

gripped her hands together so hard her fingers hurt. Pain pounded in her temples. Her stomach flopped. "Why didn't she go to the police?"

"Because whatever she was doing, she didn't want her husband to know, at least that would be my guess."

"This is crazy. She loved Michael. She wouldn't cheat on him."

"What about the other photos?" Hunter used a tissue to pick up the photo of the gray car in the strip mall parking lot. "Do you recognize the car?"

It looked like a four-door sedan of some kind. A Toyota Camry, maybe. Gray. "No."

"Too bad the shots are too tight to show the license plate."

Only on TV detective shows did that happen. "Gail told Detective Ramos and me she saw an old gray Camry parked outside the shop a few times this past week. She noticed because her sister has a car like it."

"That can't be a coincidence. Any idea where it was taken?"

"San Antonio has a strip mall on every street in town." Delaney couldn't contain a groan. "Either one under construction or one that is only half full. That's par for the course around here."

Hunter spread the photos out and picked up what appeared to be the first in the sequence of shots. It had the widest angle. He pointed to the sign over a store door and then held it out. "Can you read that?"

Delaney took it. Squinting—as if that would help—she brought the picture closer. "Does that say . . . Torres Family . . . Mexican Restaurant? There's a neon sign in the window. I think it's for Modelo Cerveza."

"That narrows it down considerably." Hunter took the photo back and employed the same squint technique. He tugged his phone from his back pocket. "I'll search the location."

"None of this may be what it seems like." Jumping to conclusions was too easy and not what a good investigator did. Delaney perused all four photographs. "Michael has some unsavory clients, or at least one unsavory client."

She shared the high points of Michael's confession the previous evening. Hunter listened without interruption. Even when she finished he said nothing. Instead he stared, forehead furrowed, at the photographs. Delaney waited. She counted to ten. Still nothing. "Any theories?"

"Maybe his client had someone follow her. Maybe with the intent to scare her." Hunter ran his fingers along the ridge of the scar on his jawline. He shook his head. "Instead, he found out she was doing something she shouldn't be and used the photos to force them or her to do something illegal."

"She kept the photos. She hid them in her shop. If this involved Michael, then why do that?"

"We need to visit this location."

"Why? And we?"

"Maybe where they met with tell us something." Hunter used the same tissue to slide the photos back into the envelope, along with the clippings. "It's a place to start."

"Shouldn't we give them to the police?"

"We will. As soon as we've checked out the location." Hunter unfolded his long legs and stood with more grace than should be possible. "I don't trust them. I don't have any reason to believe they won't try to pin this on the wrong person—like me."

"You were in prison."

"They'll say I had an accomplice or I hired someone. Or a member of my family did it to get even for putting me in prison."

"Seriously, you sound paranoid."

"I spent a whole lot of years that I can't get back—my youth, as it were—in prison for a crime I didn't commit. You bet your behind I'm paranoid." Despite the fury running through his words, Hunter didn't raise his voice. The old Hunter would've been cursing and shouting in his righteous indignation. "Especially when Ramos keeps coming around to interrogate me and try to intimidate me."

"I get it." The sudden urge to comfort him assailed Delaney. Her hand on his back. A hug. A touch. Startled, she scooted back on her hands and knees. "That's fine. I'll keep the evidence. I'll check out the location—"

"We'll check it out. Ellie's dead. We're talking about a killer. You're not going anywhere alone."

"I'm not going anywhere with you."

"You're sitting here in Ellie's shop. With me. Alone."

Having him here, flesh and blood, with the same deep voice, the same warm eyes, the same guy scent, made it almost impossible to believe Hunter was a killer. A convicted killer.

Or an innocent man wrongly convicted.

"I can't believe I'm saying this."

"Saying what?" Hunter's fierce gaze pinned Delaney to the wall. "What are you saying, Laney?"

"We go together, but it's strictly professional. Nothing personal."

"I'll take it." He cleared his throat and held out his hand. "Tomorrow, for breakfast. How's that sound?"

Delaney eyed his long fingers. The same fingers that once had brushed her hair from her face. The same fingers that had tickled her until she laughed so hard she cried.

His hand dropped, but his gaze held hers. Neither of them moved or spoke.

Her phone dinged, breaking the silence.

She glanced at the text. "It's Cam, wanting me to know Michael has hired a company to clean up Ellie's shop. Not to worry about it. I guess I should've checked first."

"I think you needed to do it. It gave you a sense of control over the situation."

"Thank you, but I already have a shrink."

"Good."

"What's that supposed to mean?"

"Nothing. I'm glad you have someone to talk to. A neutral third party helps. I have Pastor James. He helps me keep my head on straight."

"It's late. I need to go home." Despite her best efforts, Delaney looked toward the bloodstained rug. Ellie loved that rug. She called it whimsical. Delaney had suggested quirky was more accurate. Like Ellie. They'd traded jabs as they rolled it out on the floor and stood back to admire their handiwork.

"Come on, let's go." Hunter nodded toward the door. "I'll walk you to your car."

She got to her feet. "There's no need."

"There is and you know it. Don't be so stubborn." With a sigh Hunter strode to the door. His expression somber, he held it open for her. "I'm so sorry," he whispered. "I know how much you loved her."

Unable to speak, Delaney slipped past him and into the dark night where he wouldn't be able to see her face.

He might see himself as her protector, but all she could see was another heartbreak waiting to happen.

CHAPTER 20

Time was not on their side. Twenty-four hours had passed since Ellie Hill's death. Andy shoved his chair back and plopped down in front of his desk in the PD Homicide Unit. It had been a ridiculously long day and the night might be just as long. He'd called Pilar to tell her not to wait on supper for him. His loss, she said. Peanut chicken curry and refried rice. She would keep it warm for him. Because she was nice like that.

Ignoring the rumbling of his stomach, he grabbed the Corey Broward murder book and opened it to photos of the crime scene.

He hadn't been wrong. Nor had the prosecutor. Or the jury.

Hunter Nash killed Corey Broward. End of story.

Nash at least nominally fit the description of Ellie Hill's killer and Delaney Broward's assailant. She was right about Michael Hill fitting it as well.

Whether she should've recognized either of them in the brief adrenaline-slash-fear minutes in which she fought for her life remained open to debate.

So why did Andy have that irritating itch between his shoulder blades and pain between his eyes like a drill set on high?

Flores's hunt-and-peck typing stopped. "Why so glum?"

"Too many questions, not enough answers." Andy had let Nash get in his head. He didn't have time to reinvestigate a case signed, sealed, and delivered with a guilty verdict. "The Broward case keeps sticking itself into the Hill case."

He brought Flores up to date on his interview of Nash, the break-in at Delaney Broward's shop, and Gail Simpkins's sighting of a gray Camry—which might or might not have something to do with their case. "If Broward had been in the middle of jumping into bed with drug dealers, we would've seen it. Everyone conceded he had money problems, but no one shared this tidbit about drugs."

"You didn't see anything interesting in Broward's phone records?"

"As I recall there were some calls to and from an untraceable burner phone, but we were never able to run them down. We had fewer resources to work with ten years ago."

"What about Nash's records?"

"All his calls were to Delaney, Corey, his other co-op buddies, and family. Nothing suspicious. This was a fight that got out of hand, a crime of passion, in a sense. He picked up a utility knife and killed his best friend."

Nash's fingerprints were all over the studio. The defense noted that the fingerprints of several other co-op members, including Delaney Broward and Ellie Cruz, were found in the room as well.

The jury didn't care. They convicted Nash.

Flores hopped up and pulled a dry-erase board over to a spot centered and parallel between their two facing desks. "I reviewed the murder book. The case against Nash was circumstantial at best."

"Enough that the DA was willing to take it to court. Enough that the jury convicted."

"Nash would've been covered with blood. What happened to the bloody clothes? He said he went directly from the co-op to NIOSA."

"Obviously he didn't." Murderers lied. Andy relaxed his fists and spread his fingers across the desk. Flores meant no disrespect. "He cleaned up, changed, and disposed of the clothes."

"All the while under the influence of drugs and alcohol."

"Yes."

"I'm surprised he didn't appeal." Flores made a *tsk-tsk* sound like a peeved schoolteacher. "He could've argued ineffective assistance of counsel."

"He did. The court upheld his conviction."

"There you go. If the two homicides are connected, solving Ellie Hill's murder will likely reveal that. We need to prioritize the new investigation. If it reveals new information about Corey Broward's murder, we'll follow where that information leads." Flores wrote Ellie's name on the board in his thick block print. At the other end he added Corey Broward's name. "If the wrong guy got convicted, a murderer has been walking around free for the last ten years. Hurt ego aside, I imagine that doesn't sit well with you."

A guy could count on Flores to speak his mind. The drill-bit pain stopped spinning into Andy's skull. "I hate being wrong. I don't think I'm wrong. But I own up when I make a mistake. I'm all in."

"Excellent. I just came from Mrs. Hill's autopsy."

"And?"

"The assailant inflicted three stab wounds in the abdominal area. The most damaging one penetrated her left abdomen at the level of her navel. It was about two inches long, running at a forty-five-degree angle. This thrust lacerated her liver, causing internal hemorrhaging. Abrasions on the edges of the wounds indicate the perpetrator thrust the weapon in to its hilt. She bled to death."

Andy took a moment to digest his temporary partner's succinct summary. Then he returned to the murder book he and Pilar had amassed in the 2010 Broward case. He flipped through the pages, searching for the autopsy report. "The Broward murder was different. There were multiple wounds. It was a stabbing frenzy. The coroner described it as a crime of passion by someone who stabbed indiscriminately. Broward had defensive wounds on his hands and forearms. He saw the guy coming and fought back. Any speculation on the type of knife used on Ellie Hill?"

"You know how they loathe to speculate." Flores slapped a photo of Ellie Hill's wound on the board under the one taken of her on the shop floor. "He did say it likely had a five- to five-and-a-half-inch blade. It had one sharp edge. It was a clean thrust, no twisting. If he had to guess, a hunting knife. Fixed blade."

Five and a half inches kept it within the legal limit for carrying in Texas. Andy found the murder book page he sought. "The knife in Corey Broward's case was left at the scene. It was a utility knife used for opening boxes and cutting canvas. Six-inch blade." Andy didn't need to view the photos of the victim. His first case remained fixed in his mind's eye. "A dozen stab wounds to the abdominal area, six of them deep, the rest superficial. Consistent with a frenzied attack. Did Ellie Hill have defensive wounds?"

"No. It's likely the assailant overpowered her and stabbed her before she had a chance to throw her hands up. Ms. Broward said he was a big guy."

"Corey Broward had several incised wounds on the palms of his hands and fingers, some deep enough to contact bone, some superficial." Andy double-checked the autopsy report. Yep, he had it right. "Nothing under his fingernails except paint."

"Still, he saw it coming and fought back."

"Which fits with the scenario presented by the prosecution that two friends got into a drunken brawl over money."

"By the way, we found a joint that had been lit at some point in Mrs. Hill's purse along with a bottle of Xanax prescribed by her doctor." Flores took off his glasses, wiped them on his shirt, and returned them to his nose. He stared at the board as if seeing it anew. "It'll be a week to ten days before we get back the tox screen, but I'm betting one or both will show up. Maybe there aren't any defense wounds because she was too stoned to defend herself."

Delaney Broward hadn't mentioned her friend's drug use. Because she didn't know? Or because she was in denial just as she had been with her brother? Andy made a mental note to ask her. If drug use played a role in both murders, that might be a thread tying them together. "Anything else?"

"ME says she was likely standing when stabbed. The attacker was taller. He held the knife, sharp side up, and thrust upward."

"In other words, he knew what he was doing. Unlike Broward's killer, who held the knife sharp side down and thrust downward repeatedly."

"Different method of attack." Flores struck a pose like an attorney in front of a jury. "Which leads us to speculate what? Different perpetrator or a perpetrator who has upped his game in the last ten years."

"If they're related, why now? Why ten years later?"

"What's changed?" Flores threw the question back at Andy like an opponent on a squash court. "Who benefits?"

"Ellie Cruz married Michael Hill."

"In a nutshell. She inherits two stepkids and an ex-wife who isn't happy with custody arrangements."

"So what about Hill's ex-wife?"

"She was on a flight from Newark to Charlotte at the time." Flores wrote Charlene Hill's name on the board. "They'd only been divorced a year when Hill remarried. That had to hurt. He wanted the divorce because he said she was an absentee mother. It was bitter. Both wanted full custody of the two kids. But the judge gave the dad primary custody with a generous visitation schedule for the mom. She wanted her parents to be primary caregivers in her absence."

"Obviously he knew what she did for a living when he married her." If anybody understood the difficulty balancing career and home life, Andy did. He was blessed that Pilar gave up homicide in favor of a desk job in cyberterrorism. They couldn't both be on the street for the girls' sakes. "I could see why she might harbor ill will for her replacement. She could've hired someone to take out the woman who was usurping her role as mother."

"We can try to get warrants for her bank and phone records. I don't know if a judge will sign off on one at this point. But if she paid out a large sum of money to someone, we should be able to track it. I'm also wondering if the transition was rockier than Michael and Ellie had thought it would be. How many of her old friends were still hanging around when she became the wife of a stodgy accountant?"

"Ellie Hill remained friends with her dead boyfriend's sister. She was still friends with some of the co-op crowd. Camille Sanchez and Jess Golightly in particular." Andy flipped past the crime scene photos. They were engraved on his memories, along with the ones of Delaney's tear-streaked face. She had kept wiping her nose with her sleeve until someone came up with tissues. "In 2010 we interviewed the whole group. They were like a dysfunctional family. They ate, drank, and slept together. Although I don't know how much sleep was involved. Michael changes the dynamic.

"As far as the other co-op members, some of them complained Corey Broward was a terrible manager and dissed the co-op, but they didn't have any motive for killing him."

Flores had written Corey Broward's name on the board. Now he listed all of the persons of interest under it. "You didn't spend a lot of time on these folks after you began to piece together the timeline and the reports of friction between Nash and Broward."

"It all pointed to him. His fingerprints were all over the place. His truck was in the parking lot. He admitted to being there and to having an argument with Broward that night." Andy didn't mind Flores's insinuation that tunnel vision might have caused them to go after the wrong man. They'd scrupulously vetted all the co-op members. It had been a labor-intensive investigation with dozens of interviews. "Eyewitnesses saw him enter the co-op that afternoon. Ellie Cruz, now Hill, testified that they argued all the time."

"His public defender said they argued like brothers do. I can attest to that kind of arguing. It's one of the reasons I didn't want kids." Flores tapped Nash's name on the board with the marker. "The public defender also argued that Nash was in Broward's studio all the time. Naturally his fingerprints were all over the room as well as the communal kitchen and meeting room. Nash had claimed Broward had been alive when he left that day."

"The jury didn't believe him."

Flores started a new column with Ellie Hill's name at the top. "Once again we've got Delaney Broward, who found both victims—"

"She has no motive—"

"In both instances she was found with the victims. Her fingerprints aren't on the utility knife, but they are in the room. She had a close relationship with her brother, but she didn't deny arguing with him." Flores underlined Delaney's name. "She didn't approve of his drug use. She was afraid they were going to lose the co-op."

"She wasn't invested in the co-op." Flores hadn't seen her that day with the dead man in her arms. Andy had. "She was studying to be a social worker."

"Still a wannabe artist to this day. Hence the switch from social work, after investing in a master's degree, to an art frame shop."

"So what's her motive to kill her best friend ten years after the death of her brother?"

"She married an accountant instead of pining forever for Broward?" Flores grinned. He picked up his coffee mug and took a sip. It was good to have his fresh insight on the case. Even if hindsight was twenty-twenty. "We have to interview all these folks again. Just because she says they're best friends doesn't mean there weren't underlying currents."

"Moving on. Nash could be good for this one." Andy ignored the return of the drill bit whining as it dug deeper into his skull. "He left Dominguez with plenty of time. Took that walk to the lake at the right time."

"Why?"

"Not that killers need a *why*, but revenge. Ellie testified against him."

"Wouldn't Ms. Broward have recognized him?"

"She didn't know he was out of prison." Andy was reaching and he knew it. Nash had been Delaney's boyfriend for six years. They probably would've married. How could she not recognize his voice or his eyes or the way he moved? "She wasn't expecting it to be someone she knew. He wore a stocking. It's possible she wouldn't recognize him."

"Possible but not probable."

Flores was right. Andy went at it from another direction. "He could've had a buddy from Dominguez take care of it. Prison is a one-stop shop for crimes."

"A little more likely. I still don't know why he'd wait until now to do her." Flores wrote *contract killing* next to Nash's name. "I'll take a look at cell mates, visitors, phone calls."

They were grasping at straws, but they had to start somewhere. "What did you find out about the husband?"

"Michael Hill. No priors. A couple of speeding tickets. We should interview neighbors, see what their thoughts are. There's a better chance of getting a warrant for his financials. It's always the husband. On the other hand they're practically newlyweds. Why marry her just to kill her? I'm still waiting for Ellie's phone records and financials. The shop owners all liked her. They said she brought treats for everyone and gave out samples freely. Always attended tenant-association meetings. I'll talk to the kids' teachers. It's amazing what kids tell their teachers and what they hear them say to other kids."

The phone on Andy's desk rang. The officer at the information desk in the lobby said he had a visitor demanding to see him immediately. Michael Hill.

Odd how things worked out.

CHAPTER 21

Five minutes later Ellie Hill's husband sat across the table from Andy and Flores in a PD interview room. His eyes were bloodshot and surrounded by dark circles. He reeked of BO and his rumpled gray suit and long-sleeved dress shirt appeared slept in. The fact that he'd shown up without an attorney suggested he wasn't thinking straight. The first words out of his mouth confirmed that suspicion.

"I'm responsible for my wife's death." Tears welled in his dark-brown eyes. He swiped at his face with his sleeve. "She's dead because of me."

Andy exchanged glances with Flores. The other man's thick black eyebrows lifted slightly. He pushed a box of tissues toward Hill. "When we spoke earlier you said you were at work all day. You said your staff could corroborate your whereabouts. Are you changing your story?"

"No, it wasn't a story. I was at work. I didn't stab her. I might as well have, but I didn't. It's all my fault."

His mangled sobs filled the small room. Andy studied the notebook he'd laid on the table. In the ten years he'd worked as a homicide detective, he heard hundreds of stories, listened to heart-wrenching sobs, offered water, coffee and/or tissues to hundreds of people. He steeled his heart.

Focus on the facts.

That didn't mean he felt no sympathy or empathy. He simply couldn't let it get in the way of his goal—justice for the victim.

"Just to be on the safe side, we should read you your rights, Mr. Hill." Andy didn't give the man time to object. He pulled the card from his pocket and launched into the Miranda spiel. If they were about to wrap up this murder, he wanted it to stand up in court. "Do you understand these rights as I have read them to you?"

"I do." Another ragged sob. Hill rubbed his neck and cleared his throat. "I didn't . . . I don't . . . it wasn't . . ."

"Take your time, Mr. Hill." None of the excitement Flores had to be feeling bled into his soft tone. "When you're ready, tell us why you came here. Tell us why you're responsible for your wife's death."

"I'll get you some water." Andy rose and moved toward the door. Sometimes it helped to give the interviewee space. Plus Flores had a way with people and years of experience nudging them toward confession. "Or would you rather have coffee?"

"Water," Hill croaked. "Please."

A polite killer.

Andy stepped out of the room and into the adjoining one where he could see and hear the interview. Hill blew his nose and grabbed another tissue. "You have to promise me you'll protect my children. I don't care about me, but my kids are innocent." Hill's voice went hoarse. He rubbed trembling hands over his slick shaved scalp. "He said he'd hurt my family and he did. I can't take a chance on my kids."

"We'll do everything we can to help." His tone assuring, Flores leaned forward in his chair. "Who threatened you?"

"My client. I took on a client who gave me a great deal of work. He really needed to hire a full-time accountant. I told him that. He said he didn't want the hassle. I should've said no. All I saw were dollar signs. He told me he ran a trucking company. A big one."

"Who is your client?"

"Gerard Knox."

If there was an illicit way of making a buck in San Antonio, Gerard Knox had his thumb in it. Eight-liner video slot machines, private gambling clubs, money laundering, prostitution, and human trafficking.

Shaking his head, Flores leaned back in his chair. He whistled. "You didn't know his reputation?"

"I'm an accountant. I don't move in the same world you do. He presented himself as a businessman in need of accounting services. No red flags popped."

"So what happened?"

"He doled out work to me slowly at first. He insisted on dealing with me directly. Not my staff. I had no problem with that. I didn't see any issues with the trucking company. Everything seemed like it was on the up-and-up." Hill's left shoe tapped incessantly on the floor. Any second he might combust. "As time went on I realized a whole lot more money came out than could possibly be made with the trucks he had on the road. Then he added a chain of dry cleaners. A string of low-end rent-by-the-hour motels. Same thing. Lots of revenue. Big numbers. What kind of businessman diversifies that way? Why not invest revenue in the stock market? Develop a portfolio?"

Bingo.

"Money laundering." Flores drew the same conclusion.

"That was my suspicion. I was afraid to say anything to anybody. Instead, I just told Knox I had taken on more work than my firm could handle. I needed to let go of a few clients. I could recommend a larger firm that would be better suited to handle his myriad business interests. He chuckled. His administrative assistant even chuckled.

"Knox recommended I hire another accountant to take care of my other clients. He even said he'd increase his fees. I shouldn't worry. He'd take care of me. 'I always take care of the people who work for me. One way or the other.' That's a direct quote. The man had all the trappings of a legitimate businessman. Nice office. Professional demeanor. No gold chains and garish suits."

People watched too many movies about the Mafia.

Andy hustled to the break room, grabbed two bottled waters, and strode back to the interview room where he set one bottle in front of Hill. The man grabbed it, twisted off the lid, and sucked down half of it like a man who saw desert as far as he could see.

Andy handed the other one to Flores, who nodded his thanks. "Mr. Hill was threatened by Gerard Knox."

"Okay." Summoning a suitably shocked expression, Andy sank into the chair next to his partner. "What did he say?"

"He asked me how my wife's business was doing. He said his wife had a thing for essential oils and she liked to take baths with candles all over their master bedroom's en suite. He said he might send one of his guys down to buy her a gift at Ellie's shop."

Borderline creepy but not necessarily a threat. "Was that it?"

"I never told him Ellie had a shop. I never even told him her name."

"Okay. That would be creepy." Not necessarily a threat but questionable. "What else?"

"It was lunchtime. He claimed to be on his way out so he walked me to my car. He's very genial. Gregarious. He said he thought our kids were close to the same age. He was trying to find a good preschool for his daughter." Hill cleared his throat and took another swallow of water. Sweat beaded on his forehead, even though the AC cooled the room nicely. "He posed a question: 'Do you feel like your son, Jacob, is safe at the Montessori school he attends?' I never told him Jacob's name, let alone the school he attends."

"How did you respond?"

"I said yes. He said I shouldn't be too sure of that. Father's sins are often visited upon his children. He smiled and asked me if I got his drift. I said I did. He patted me on the shoulder like I was a good boy. I assured him I would never tell anyone about his business. I would be like his accountant priest. He said, 'I know you won't. You're a good guy.'"

"You agreed to stay on, to do what he asked. What makes you think he had Ellie killed?"

"It was his way of showing me he meant business. Who else could've done it? My wife had no enemies. Everyone liked her. I know people always say that when their loved ones die, but in Ellie's case, it was true. She took on the Mother Earth persona and made it her own."

Flores cocked his head toward the door.

Andy nodded. "Sit tight, Mr. Hill, we'll get back to you."

"Get back to me? Am I in trouble?"

"Just try to remain calm. We'll be back."

Andy followed Flores into the hall. "Thoughts?"

"It's worth exploring, but there are some pieces that don't fit." His eyes half closed, Flores leaned against the wall as if he might doze off. His persona. While his brain revved at ninety miles an hour. "One, the guy tore the place apart. What was he searching for? Two, he told Ms. Broward to stay out of it or she was next. How does that fit with Hill's story? And why didn't he tell us this when we had interviewed him the first time? He had to know time is critical in any homicide investigation."

Andy nodded. "All very good points."

"We still have to confirm his alibi with his employees. I think we have enough now for a warrant for his financials. I could see a murder-for-hire situation here as well. Why, I don't know. But he could be trying to throw suspicion on Knox in order to keep himself off the hot seat. We can work both angles in tandem, Knox and this Willy Wonka character. Take your pick, keep me posted, and we'll reconvene tomorrow."

"Good deal."

Flores's cell phone rang before he had a chance to open the interview room door. A few monosyllabic responses and he hung up. "A guy who says he's Hill's attorney is downstairs. He wants to see his client forthwith."

Out of curiosity Andy followed Flores into the interview room. Hill cradled his head in his hands. "I think my kids need protective custody."

Flores nodded. "We can talk about it. Your attorney is on his way up."

"I don't have an attorney, at least not a criminal one."

"So you didn't call him?"

"I don't even know who he is."

The door opened and Jess Golightly strode into the room.

"You shouldn't be asking my client questions without his attorney present. You know that, detectives."

In his ill-fitting suit with sweat stains on the pits, Golightly was the epitome of a personal injury lawyer chasing an ambulance. Andy didn't have any business questioning Hill's choice of lawyers, but Golightly wasn't a criminal attorney. "I don't know how you caught wind of his presence here at HQ, but he came to us. He's not under arrest. And he didn't invoke."

"Then we'll be on our way."

"Wait, wait!" Hill slapped both hands on the table. "I can't go out there. I need protection. My kids need protection."

Golightly's mouth dropped open.

Andy caught Flores's gaze. "They're all yours."

Flores's expression said "Lucky me."

CHAPTER 22

Despite being stuck in a half-vacant strip mall, Torres Family Mexican Restaurant did decent business for breakfast. A dozen cars crowded the parking spaces in front of the building, overlapping into parking for a closed hair salon and three vacant properties. Two families hustled inside while Delaney waited for Hunter to arrive. The aroma of carne guisada, green pepper and onions grilling, and freshly made tortillas floated in the air. Scents that reminded Delaney of Ellie. Which reminded her of the shop and that dried bloodstain where she'd found her best friend a day and half ago.

"Are you okay?" The manilla envelope in one hand, Hunter approached from his pickup truck. That same pickup truck in which he'd picked her up for their first date. Where they'd necked before she hopped from the truck and ran inside to escape the sensation that she was in too deep, too fast, too far with this man. "Perfectly fine."

He jerked his head toward the restaurant. "Shall we go in?"

"Did you realize this place is only a block from the co-op?"

"Yes. I could see the warehouse on Google Maps." He shrugged. "Is that significant?"

"I don't know. It seems like it should be. Ellie hasn't been to the co-op since she had all Corey's stuff packed up and moved to her parents' house." Delaney stared in the direction of the co-op. The nondescript flat-roofed building painted army green loomed large in her vision despite being a dot in the distance. "This restaurant wasn't here back then, but somehow its proximity to the co-op seems important."

"Ellie's been here. That's all we know for sure."

"She's been in the parking lot."

"Let's see if anyone inside remembers her." Hunter held the door for Delaney. His sardonic grin said he knew this made her uncomfortable but didn't care. "I wouldn't mind grabbing a plate of huevos rancheros while I'm here."

Sitting down to eat with Hunter was not on Delaney's calendar. "I'm not hungry."

"It'll be easier to get information if we're customers."

Without acknowledging he was right, Delaney picked a table in the middle of the cramped dining area rather than the green Naugahyde booths that ringed the room. It featured the obligatory red plastic table-cloth, a white candle in a red glass holder, and a variety of condiments.

A waitress swooped down on them the second Delaney's behind hit the chair. She slapped down a basket of tortilla chips on the table, a bowl of red salsa, two oversized menus, silverware wrapped in white napkins, and two large, red plastic glasses of ice water. "I'm Araceli. Call me Sally. I'll be your waitress. Do you need time to look at the menu?" Snapping her gum, she smiled brightly. "Or are you ready to order?" She stuck the tray under one arm, grabbed her pen from behind her ear, and stood poised to write.

"I'll have the huevos rancheros with flour tortillas and a Dr Pepper." Hunter returned the menu. "Could I get a side of queso to go with the chips?"

"Good choice, muchacho." Sally's long black hair was caught back in a ponytail, but curly tendrils ringed her plump face with its smooth mocha skin. Her smile blossomed as she wrote down the order. "The cook's specialty."

Did she say that about every dish ordered by her customers? Delaney forced her gaze to the menu. Her stomach rocked. She grabbed the manilla envelope and pulled out a photo. "We were wondering if you'd seen this woman here in the restaurant."

Sally's finely shaped eyebrows rose. She frowned. "Señora, do you know how many customers we get in a day, a week, or a month?" She gave the photo a cursory glance and started to hand it back. Hunter intercepted it. "When are you talking about? Like today or last month?"

Hunter's sneaker connected with Delaney's shin. His expression growled at her without making a sound. She lifted her chin and plowed forward. "Any time. She might have been with a man. Could you please take a look?"

"She's our friend and she died recently." Hunter held out the photo. "We're trying to figure out what happened to her. We could really use your help."

"For you, hombre, I'll try." She studied the photo for a full thirty seconds. Her forehead wrinkled. She tapped a red-painted nail on it. "I'm sorry, I don't recognize your amiga."

"That's okay. Thank you for looking—"

"I'll take it back to the waitstaff station." She laid it on her tray. "Are you ordering, señorita, or just watching your amigo eat?"

"I'll have an egg-and-bacon taco and a cup of coffee."

Sally didn't seem impressed. She whirled and trotted toward the kitchen.

"You used to have more patience." Hunter snatched a chip, dipped it in the salsa, and consumed it with obvious satisfaction. "And you actually ate food."

"I used to be a lot more naive." She used to have more faith in humanity. More faith, period. "Apparently I was too young at eight to understand about my parents dying and what that said about the world. My maternal grandparents stepped in and they were such good people, I didn't feel the full effect of my parents' absence. When every person you care about gets erased from your life, you get the message loud and clear."

His expression somber, Hunter laid his chip on his napkin instead of dipping it. "What message is that?"

"Don't be so quick to risk your heart."

"We've all experienced heartache and loss." He broke the chip into four pieces with his fingernail. "In this world there will be trouble. But He has overcome the world."

"Does that comfort you?" Hoping to swallow the lump in her throat, Delaney took a long drink of water. "Because it seems to me He could spare us a lot of that heartache and loss. He chooses not to. What kind of God does that make Him?"

"One who knows how important it is for our faith to be honed. For us to grow in our faith."

"Who are you and what have you done with the Hunter I used to know?"

"I left him in prison."

"I can't take much more loss." Delaney tore the paper from her straw. She never used straws, but it gave her something to do with her hands. "I'm so over it."

"I'm praying for you."

"Stop. Please. You can't imagine how fake that sounds coming from you."

"It's not fake. It's as real as the pain you feel every time you think of Ellie. Or Corey."

Delaney's phone dinged. A text saved her from answering.

Are u ok?

Jess. Cam must've told him what had happened.

I'm fine
Did Cam tell you about Michael?
What happened to Michael?
**The idiot tried to turn himself in last night. I had to
rescue him. he's a mess**
I'll go to the house after this
After what? Are u with Hunter? Tell me you're not

"Somebody's persistent."

Delaney put her phone down. Hunter drew circles in the condensation on his water glass. She met his gaze straight on. "Jess. Michael
tried to turn himself in to the police last night. He feels responsible for
Ellie's death. Jess went to the PD and brought him home."

"Maybe he is responsible. Maybe we're headed down a rabbit hole."

"We have to follow every lead, right?"

"Right."

Delaney's phone dinged again. Jess *wasn't* giving in. "He's worried
about me."

"He has no reason to be."

"He forgets I can take care of myself."

I'm filing an RO. U don't have to put up with this
No worries. We're in public. At a restaurant. I'll text u
later
**At least tell me what restaurant so I know where to
start looking for u if u disappear**

Don't be melodramatic. I'm at Torres Family Mexican
   Restaurant

It didn't hurt to have her location on the record.

What are u doing there?
Eating
Laney!
Talk to u later

She laid the phone facedown on the table. "Sorry. Like you said, he's persistent."

"Sally said y'all are asking about Señora Ellie." A waiter in the usual black slacks, white shirt, and black apron approached the table. His name tag identified him as Antonio. He held up the photo. "She ordered eggs ranchera with refried beans, corn tortillas, and a side order of pico de gallo. She drank like four cups of coffee with half-and-half."

"How long ago was this?" Hunter sat forward in his chair. "Was she alone?"

"The guy ordered migas, refried beans, flour tortillas, and coffee."

"How do you remember all this?" Delaney took the photo and slid it back into the envelope. "How long ago did they come in?"

"A few weeks. I remember all my regulars."

"They were regulars?"

"Once every few weeks. Wednesdays for breakfast. The lady said she didn't dare come more often. She was watching her waist." The waiter grinned and made a motion with both hands as if outlining a woman's shape. "So was I. Hers was just fine."

Wednesdays. Ellie said she had a breakfast meeting of her SBA

Women Entrepreneurs group every other Wednesday. "What did the man look like?"

The waiter shrugged. "I'm not looking at him. Only her. She did the talking. She also paid. Why I look at him?"

"You don't remember anything about him?" Hunter jumped in. "Was he White, Latino, Black?"

"He ordered migas, refried beans, flour tortillas, and coffee. I remember that."

"Did you happen to hear what they talked about?" Delaney shot Hunter a warning glare. They had more than they did before. "Did they seem friendly or did they argue?"

"Both."

The waitress returned with their food. "Shake a leg, Tony. Table number three is getting antsy. And number four got flour tortillas. They wanted corn."

"Gotta go." He patted his tray. "I don't get tips talking. I get tips working."

"Anything else you can tell us?"

"He was more into her than she was into him."

"How could you tell?"

"Whenever he tried to hold her hand, she picked up her phone and started texting."

"Thanks for your help."

"No *problema*. If you see her, tell her I've got a pot of coffee on for her."

"Tony, seriously." Sally slid Hunter's plate onto the table, added the bowl of queso, and turned to the waiter. "*El jefe* has his beady eyes on you."

"Oops, that's the boss."

Antonio saluted and trotted away.

Delaney waited until Sally set her food down, asked Hunter if he needed anything else, and rushed to another table where a patron had dumped her coffee on the floor. "Ellie was having an affair, or she was seeing two different men and married one of them."

"Or having secret meetings with someone who was interested in having an affair." Hunter pulled a tortilla from the covered basket, slathered it with butter, and rolled it up. "It sounded one-sided to me."

"We need to know who it was." Delaney tore a piece from her tortilla. It was warm and soft, like the ones Ellie's mom made. Delaney's throat closed, and she laid it on her plate. Never in a billion years would she have believed it. Not Ellie. "We told each other everything. All she talked about was Michael and the kids. If there was someone else at any point, she would've told me."

"Which leads me to believe it was something else. But that's not to say that someone else didn't jump to the same conclusion. Someone was watching them." Hunter dug into refried beans mixed with eggs and ranchera sauce like a man who hadn't eaten real food in years. He chewed and swallowed. "Someone took photos. Someone sent those photos to her. Maybe it was Michael. Maybe he hired a private detective to snoop. Maybe he thought something was going on."

"Do we ask him?"

Ranchera music, the clank of dishes, and the murmur of other patrons filled the space while he chewed.

Patience, have patience.

Hunter shook his head. "I don't think so. If he did have her followed and knew about these regular trysts—"

"Meetings."

"Meetings. You'd think he might be a suspect." Hunter wiped his mouth and took a swig of DP. "I'm not buying that scenario. What if this guy is tied to what happened to Corey? What if Ellie knew what was going on back then? She was Corey's girlfriend. She kept the books."

"So why wait until now to kill her?"

"All we have are more questions." He polished off the last of his tortilla and reached for another one.

"Hunter?"

His expression turned sheepish. "I told you. I've been desperate for real food. It's like I can't get enough."

"Do you want my taco?"

"You have to eat something."

She gestured to her plate. "Help yourself."

"Don't mind if I do." He slid her small plate in his direction. "How would you feel about stopping by the warehouse?"

"I have to get back."

"Because Jess says so? I don't remember him being in charge of himself, much less anyone else."

"He's freaking out that I'm within a hundred yards of you. He's all set to file a restraining order for me."

"I'm no threat." Hunter tossed his napkin onto his empty plate. "I think you know that."

It didn't matter what Jess thought. If Ellie's murder was in any way related to Corey's, she needed to know. Working with Hunter allowed her to know what he was up to and what he was thinking. "I'm not going to the warehouse. I saw the crime scene. We both sat through all the testimony regarding what was found there. Besides, it's not the co-op anymore. Everything's gone. Some company uses it for storage and a distribution point. What's next?"

"What do you mean, what's next?"

"You want to find out who really killed Corey. If you really are innocent, so do I." Delaney slid the envelope into her backpack. "What's next?"

"We confront Michael about the photos. See what he knows."

"The man is a basket case. I'm worried about the kids."

"He went to the police. He told them what he'd done." His expression thoughtful, Hunter demolished her taco. At this rate he would regain the weight he'd lost in prison. Not necessarily a bad thing. He took another swig of DP. "Mm-mm, I've missed Dr Pepper. Nectar of the gods. Michael's actions might be considered rational. Either way, it allows the police to follow through. It may give them something to nail Gerard Knox for his illicit activities, even if those don't include murder."

"But you think they're going down a rabbit hole."

"I do."

"Shouldn't we give them the photos? Let them pursue that rabbit hole too?"

"It's our rabbit hole. We can handle more than one."

We? There was no *we.* "I'll confront Michael with the photos tonight. With Cam and Jess."

"If you want. Find out from him what the police are doing. See what Jess knows. In fact, talk to everyone in the old gang. See if they knew about Ellie's clandestine activities."

He couldn't talk to them himself. Any theories he espoused would be subject to disbelief. She wouldn't lie to her friends about his involvement either. "I'm telling them the truth. About why I'm asking."

"That's your call. They'll try to talk you out of it."

"They'll probably be right." She had to do it. For Corey's sake. Not Hunter's. "Again, what's next?"

"I told Pastor James I'd come into work early today to help teach an art class to the seniors. Then I have the kids. Tomorrow, I plan to track down Willy."

Willy Wonka. "I want in on that."

"What?"

She raised an eyebrow. "Did I stutter?"

"I'll pick you up in the morning—"

"I'll meet you wherever you're going."

"I don't want you driving around in that neighborhood. It's no place to get lost."

Another man stuck in the past. "You don't have any say in what I do now. Besides, as I told Jess, I can take care of myself."

"Okay, logistically it's simpler to go in one vehicle. It's less threatening to the people we're going to see."

"Then pick me up at the shop."

"Deal." He reached for the ticket.

Delaney swiped it first. "It's on me."

"Why?"

Good question. Because she wouldn't allow him to pretend this was a date. Because he had shown up at her door almost penniless the night before. Because she was a business owner with a house and an SUV that had been given to her free of debt. "You just got out of jail. You don't have two nickels to rub together."

"My mom fronted me an advance on my first paycheck." Hunter held out his hand, palm up. "Your shop is trashed. I suspect your source of income just dried up for a while."

Delaney handed over the bill. "Fair enough. We go Dutch."

"Just like old times."

Nothing like old times. "Don't make me regret this."

Emotion flitted across Hunter's face. He could never play poker. "I was about to say the same thing."

CHAPTER 23

Regardless of what Delaney said, Hunter needed to walk through the warehouse that had once been the co-op. He needed to confront the ghosts that surely flitted from room to room, reliving that awful day that provided the punctuation for what was *The End* of Hunter's youth.

He had dropped Delaney off at her car on Cesar Chavez Boulevard and headed to the warehouse. She agreed to go with him to find Willy. She'd been almost cordial when she hopped from the truck, turned, and leaned in the passenger window to say goodbye. Her expression was part exasperation and part resignation. "See you tomorrow."

Those three words held so much promise. Even if they both needed bulletproof vests and mile-high wading boots to traverse the cesspools where they might find Willy.

Hunter pulled into the warehouse lot, parked, and turned off the ignition. The sign read WILEY PAPER GOODS MANUFACTURING AND DISTRIBUTION. He rolled his shoulders, cranked his head side to side, and got out. No time to waste. His stomach cramped. He wasn't used to stuffing himself full of Mexican food. That wasn't the problem. He had a cast-iron stomach when it came to jalapeños, onions, and garlic.

Corey had died here.

Maybe they'd be closed.

The double glass doors swung open easily. A guy in a tan uniform stretched tight over a basketball-shaped belly propped up on toothpick legs looked up from a clipboard. His forehead furrowed under patches of gray and white frizz that passed for hair. "Sorry, sir. We're not open to the public. This is a distribution center."

"I figured as much. But there's something I need to do."

The man didn't seem convinced. "What can I do for you?"

What could he do for Hunter? Give him a do-over? A mulligan? Allow him to change twenty minutes of his life ten years ago? Or simply excise those moments? Maybe Hunter didn't come to the co-op at all. Or he came and saw Corey was in a funk so he offered to bring him a Whataburger and a milkshake instead of drinking another beer and lighting up a joint with him. "I used to have a studio here. I just wanted to visit for old time's sake."

"There's nothing of that artsy-fartsy stuff left." The man scratched his gray whiskers with his pen. His grin revealed a gap the width of a jumbo eraser between his two front teeth. "All we got are loads of toilet paper, napkins, and paper towels."

"I know it's been years, but I have sort of a sentimental attachment to this place."

Not that the interior appeared anything like it did before. A counter ran perpendicular to the foyer on one side. They'd set up an office with desks, filing cabinets, and a table with chairs behind it. Long rows of metal shelving that reached to the building's exposed ductwork hanging below a tin roof extended for as far as the eye could see. The employee, whose embroidered name tag read TODD WORTHINGTON, had stacks of paper towels on a front-end loader ready to roll.

"Where was your studio?" Worthington said the word *studio* like it was dirty. Like a boudoir or lair. "Front or back?"

"Northwest corner by the back entrance."

Adjacent to Corey's bigger, airier studio that featured one of the few windows in the building.

Worthington pulled a pair of glasses from his shirt pocket and set them on his nose. Squinting, he perused Hunter as a scientist would a bug under a microscope. "I've seen you before." He wiggled his fat forefinger in Hunter's direction. "Your picture was in the paper. You killed that other artiste, the one who ran the joint."

Maybe because the murder happened during Fiesta. And maybe because Hunter was taken into custody at NIOSA and maybe because they were artists who had sold their work at Fiesta events, the media had picked up on the murder and, later, the trial. *"Artist kills best friend, heads to NIOSA to party"* had been one headline. *"Artist murders girl-friend's brother, parties at NIOSA"* was another. The ladies of the San Antonio Conservation Society must've been devastated to see their annual fund-raiser linked to a crime that didn't even occur on the grounds of the vastly popular event.

The media squeezed every drop of bloody sensationalism from the trial. They weren't allowed to shoot video of the jury, but the judge allowed them to shoot inside the courtroom. And photos of Hunter, Ellie, and Delaney trudging into the courthouse—separately, of course—had appeared in the local newspaper.

"I didn't kill him."

"That's what they all say." Worthington jerked his head toward the hall. "They also say criminals always return to the scene of the crime."

"Can I look or not?"

Worthington stuffed himself onto the front-end loader's seat. "Sure, but I have to escort you."

The front-end loader hummed. Hunter followed Worthington down the long main aisle. The squeak of Hunter's sneakers on the cement floor was the only other sound. For some reason it unnerved him. "Where is everybody?"

"We close at five. I stayed late to finish stocking a load that's going out first thing in the a.m."

"No security?"

"Sure. I imagine he's on the loading dock smoking a cigarette and wishing he'd gone to college."

Any minute they would arrive at their destination. What did Hunter expect to see? Or do? His heart sped up, and his stomach did a loop-de-loop. His chest tightened.

This is stupid. There's nothing here. This is a flight of fancy.

Most of the walls that had created the smaller studios had been removed, but the two largest ones, which included the break room and Corey's studio, were still there. Hunter's adjacent studio with the walls he painted a pale yellow meant to remind him of sunshine was long gone. The walls in the break room had been painted a gunmetal gray. Industrial-style furniture crowded the space, along with a refrigerator, stove, and microwave. What had once been Corey's studio now functioned as a conference room with a long fake-wood table and a dozen padded folding chairs.

It didn't matter. Dr Pepper, salsa, and green sauce burned in Hunter's gut. His kingdom for a Tums. He breathed through his nose and wiped his damp palms on his jeans.

"Told you. It's nothing like before."

"Can I have a minute?"

"Sure, sure. Just don't swipe anything. I'm responsible for the product."

Like Hunter was going to shove twelve-packs of toilet paper under his T-shirt. "No worries. I'm a convicted murderer, not a thief."

"Good one." Worthington cackled. He slid from the front-end

loader and lumbered into the bowels of the rows across from the break room. "I'll be back to check on you. Make it snappy."

Hunter almost went after him. *I've changed my mind.*

"No, you haven't. You're just chicken." Corey's taunting voice echoed against the walls behind him, taking Hunter back to that day, that moment when everything changed.

Hunter turned. The walls were summer sky blue again. That's what Corey had called it. Delaney called it powder blue or baby blue.

"I'm not chicken."

"Go on, leave like you did that night."

A whiff of the earthy green odor of pot trailed through the air, mixing with turpentine and stale beer. A Lady Gaga song blared. Too loud. Hunter's head hurt. He needed a drink. Hair of the dog. Corey was always good for that.

Corey had his back to the door. He'd stripped down to his ripped jeans. A brush in one hand and a bottle of Lone Star in the other, he leaned into his work like he might plant a kiss on the canvas.

"I thought you were going to the house."

"I'm in the zone, man." Corey sucked the last of the beer from the bottle and tossed it in a nearby trash can. His eyes were red and ringed by purplish-black circles. "I had an itch I had to scratch. You know how it is."

"I do." Hunter grabbed a beer from the cooler sitting on top of a folding table in the corner. One long swallow and his throat felt better. So did his headache. "The girls will be ragging on us any minute."

"I know. I'm a jerk. I just need to paint. We have bills to pay."

Rows of unframed paintings still on stretcher bars crowded one wall. Corey was nothing if not prolific. He never lacked for inspiration. He chose to paint rather than take care of the more mundane tasks that turned art into a business.

Hunter edged closer. His friend's latest piece featured an explosion of color: Ellie's sisters, her mother, and grandmother in Mexican dresses, making tamales. A *tamalada*. Corey didn't shy away from cultural and ethnic differences. He celebrated family in all its forms. As if he sought what he'd never had.

"Nice."

"It's crapola." Corey wasn't being humble. He had little sense of his own talent. He didn't seem to care. Something drove him to paint and it wasn't acclaim or ego.

"You need to get these paintings ready for an exhibit." Hunter perused the finished pieces. A skateboarder in the middle of a busy street. An older couple hiking a trail. A couple snuggling on a park bench. Gorgeous colors. Confident strokes. Like peeking into someone's life as they passed by. Vignettes. Hunter had never been jealous of Corey's talent, only protective. "You wouldn't be so strapped for cash."

"Look who's talking."

"I could paint until the cows come home and I'd never produce anything this good." Hunter touched a painting of a child in a diaper running toward his smiling mother, who held out both hands as if to say, "Come on, you can do it." First steps? Both looked as if they could step off the canvas, reach each other, and embrace. "You know it and I know it."

Hunter's technique was good. His composition might even be called excellent. But that something-something was missing, that spark, that thing some might simply call creative talent—but it was more nebulous than that—was missing. "You could sell these in a snap. Let Ellie set up something with the Blue Star."

"Stop worrying about my finances and start worrying about yours." Corey laid down the brush. He had red and black paint on his hands and his jeans. His ribs stuck out on his skinny chest. He padded to the cooler and pulled out another beer. It dripped with icy water and condensation. He didn't seem to notice. "You wanna talk money? How about the three months of back rent you owe the co-op."

"I'm working on it."

"No, you're headed to NIOSA to spend money on Delaney. Not that she doesn't deserve a night out. But how much are the tickets now? Twelve bucks a piece? And then the food tickets and the drink tickets. Adds up fast, doesn't it?"

Corey didn't need to know Hunter and Delaney usually cobbled together the money to pay for their dates—or combined event calendars for freebies. Delaney never expected Hunter to pay. NIOSA was expensive. It was also a tradition and a treat. "So why are you on your high horse tonight? Any reason in particular?"

"You started it." Corey tugged a bag of pot from the tattered backpack on the floor next to the table. He sank onto a beanbag and extracted a package of rolling papers from the bag. His expression somber, he creased the paper, shook out a fat row of the crushed green leaves, lifted it to his lips, and licked the paper. He smoothed the edges together and held the joint out. "Don't say I never gave you anything. Spark it up for me, will you?"

Delaney's pleading voice boomed in Hunter's brain. *"Pot makes you stupid. Plus it's against the law. You drink too much beer, but at least it's legal. Why do you have to get stoned too? If you stop, maybe Corey will too. You're both frying your brain. Drugs don't make you a better artist, they just make you think you are."*

All true. She wasn't a nag; she was like the good angel sitting on his shoulder. So who was the bad angel on the other one? His absentee dad? His overbearing brother? Hunter's own self-destructive tendencies?

He took Corey's offering and lit it. The sweet smell enveloped him. He closed his eyes and welcomed it. Pot smelled like it wanted to be his friend. The first hit burned all the way down. Fighting the urge to cough, he held the smoke in for as long as he could, then handed the joint back. *Sorry, Laney. I need this.* "I promise I'll get caught up."

"Don't worry about it." Corey grabbed the joint and unfolded his long legs to stand. "I've got you covered."

Hunter might not be the most talented guy in the co-op, but he was an inaugural member and he always paid his debts. For the co-op to survive everyone had to pull their weight. "What do you mean? How?"

"I made a deal with Willy Wonka."

Icy dread slunk into the room. "What kind of deal did you make with a guy who sells you dope?"

"The kind that will keep the co-op afloat for years to come." Corey held the joint like a cigarette in one hand and lifted the beer bottle to his lips with the other. He swallowed and took another drag from the joint. A two-fisted high. "The nice thing is we don't really have to do anything. We're not at risk. They'll use the co-op as a distribution point. All we have to do is stay out of the way and keep our mouths shut."

"We? And who is they?"

Corey grinned and handed Hunter the joint. "Take it easy, bro. Everything is copacetic. I know what I'm doing."

Hunter couldn't let it go to waste, could he? Another nice hit. Maybe the knots in his shoulders and neck muscles would loosen. Maybe he'd be able to paint again.

No such luck. Instead, anger revved through Hunter. His gut clenched. The headache returned with a vengeance. "Are you nuts? Seriously?" He couldn't seem to control the volume of his voice. He flicked the joint at Corey. It smacked him in the leg and plummeted to the floor. "You made a deal with the devil without asking the rest of us?"

"What's wrong with you, dude?" Corey snagged the joint with his thumb and forefinger. "This is expensive stuff."

"Answer my question."

"You don't need to know the details. In fact, it's better if you don't know." Corey took a hit. He turned up the music. A Drake song pounded the room and shook the walls. He grabbed a roach clip from an ashtray filled with them and attached the remnant to it. "My name is on the lease. If we crash and burn, it's on me."

"If the DEA raids this place, we all go down," Hunter shouted. Corey shook his head and pointed at his ears. Passive-aggressive, that was a good name for him. Hunter turned the music down. "When is this happening?"

"It's a done deal. The head honcho toured the facilities, as it were, last week." Corey brushed past Hunter. He turned up the volume. "They're working out the logistics as we speak. They've already invested in the co-op. Like silent partners. That's what we're calling it. Silent partners."

"Will you stop?" Anger boiling over, Hunter hit the Off button. Silence boomed. "Don't do this. Call it off."

"I can't. You don't back out on these guys. Once you're in, you're in." Corey's smile twisted. "Anyway, I don't have a choice. I used the money to pay back property taxes on the homestead. I paid off my debt to Willy and replenished my stash."

"You bought drugs with the money?"

"It's not like I have savings. I cleaned out my account to pay the spring semester tuition, fees, and books not covered by Delaney's scholarship. Do you think her checks from the smoothie place cover utilities and groceries?" Fury infused every word. Corey finished off the joint and dropped the clip on the table. He elbowed Hunter hard. "Stop messing with my tunes, jerk."

"Stop being an idiot." Hunter elbowed him back. "Don't do this to Laney."

"I'm not being an idiot. I'm taking care of Laney."

Corey shoved Hunter. He stumbled into the table. The ice chest crashed to the floor. Paintings skittered sideways. The easel collapsed, taking with it the still-wet painting in progress. Corey howled, "Now look at what you did."

"Me? That's the least of your problems." His vision blurred and streaked with red, Hunter lowered his head. He charged Corey. Their bodies collided. Corey went down with an *oof* that sounded like a balloon deflating.

A flurry of obscenities filled the air. "Get out, get out, get out before I break your neck." Corey, flat on his back on the beanbag, flopped like a fish on dry land. "Get out now!"

"Tell me this. Does Ellie know?" Hunter backed toward the door. "Is she down with being an accomplice to possession with intent to distribute?"

"It was Ellie's idea."

Ellie would never. She hated drugs even more than Laney did, if that were possible. "You're a liar."

Corey met that statement with another string of obscenities.

Hunter bolted from the studio. He found himself back in the warehouse hallway surrounded by rows of toilet paper and paper towels. He leaned over, clamped his hands on his knees, and sucked in air. The details were so vivid, so real, so eviscerating. His last words to his best friend had been, "You're a liar."

"What's up, dude? You're a little green around the gills."

At the sound of Worthington's concerned voice, Hunter straightened and used his sleeve to wipe cold sweat from his face. "Something I ate, I guess."

"Sure. Or the past tastes like roadkill."

Worthington was smarter than he seemed. Hunter started down the hallway. He needed out now. "Thanks for letting me look around."

"I didn't want to be next on your hit list." Worthington's voice held enough humor to make it clear he was joking. Even if it was a bad joke. "I have to show you out."

"Fine. Whatever." Hunter's pace bordered on running by the time he hit the doors. Outside, the sky opened up and the rain came. Eyes closed, Hunter stood in the middle of the parking lot and raised his face to the deluge. In seconds he was soaked. He didn't care. In prison he sometimes got a whiff of the scent of rain in the rec yard, but he was never allowed to experience it. Next to the perfume that rose from freshly cut grass, it was one of his favorite scents.

Rain washed the earth clean. It could wash away the hurt, the pain, the filth of his life.

"God, I'm sorry. I'm so sorry." He swallowed back tears. "I'm sorry for the wasted years. I'm sorry for not being a better friend to Corey. I'm sorry for being so stupid. Thank You for the rain. Thank You for letting me survive prison. Thank You for my freedom. Thank You."

Thunder boomed. He opened his eyes in time to see lightning crackle across the sky. He wiped rain and tears from his face and sloshed through puddles to his truck. Shivering, he slid onto the seat and tugged the door shut.

Ellie knew. It was her idea.

Did she really know, or did Corey lie? Or did Hunter make that up? Why hadn't he remembered that before?

He pulled out his phone to text Delaney. His thumb hovered over the screen. She'd just lost her best friend. Did he really want to besmirch her memory? That's what he was doing with Corey, wasn't it?

He tossed the phone on the seat and started the truck. Delaney wanted the truth. So did he. Together, they would find it. But not today.

CHAPTER 24

Just because Hunter had to get to work immediately, didn't mean Delaney did. She should, but she didn't. Instead, she'd waited until he drove away from La Villita, trotted to her SUV, and made a beeline for Michael's house. She needed to know what Michael knew about the photos of Ellie. Hunter would not be welcome—especially if Jess was still there.

After paying quick lip service to pleasantries, she laid two photos from each location on the slick mahogany table in front of Michael.

"What's this?" His shaking fingers brushed against the first one. Shoving it back in her direction, he squinted and raised his head to frown at her. "Where did you get these?"

"Do you know whose car this is? Have you seen these photos before?"

"Where *did* you get them?" Jess, who sat next to him, dragged one of the photos closer. He pulled down reading glasses from atop his head and peered more closely at the one of Ellie shaking her finger at the unidentifiable man in the car. "When were these taken and where did you get them?"

"In a filing cabinet in Ellie's office. Hidden in a bunch of catalogs. The postmark on the envelope was a week before Ellie's murder."

Michael wrapped his hands around his BEST DAD EVER coffee mug. His dark-brown eyes had sunk into his skull in the last two days. His suit was rumpled and he smelled of BO, coffee, and faintly of whiskey. "You said you'd go through Ellie's stuff upstairs. You didn't say anything about the shop."

"We—I was trying to help. To clean up. It occurred to me that Ellie's attacker might have been searching for something and I interrupted him." Delaney tapped the photo. "Maybe he was searching for this. Or maybe he was planting them. I don't know. They could be incriminating, or maybe they're completely innocent. I know this is hurtful, but I have to ask. Is it possible Ellie was having an affair?"

"You tell me!" Michael slammed his fist on the table. His mug shook and coffee sloshed, soaking the paper napkin under it. "Ellie told you everything. When she had good news to share, she called you first. Before me. If she was sorry she married me, she would've come to you for advice. If she was cheating she would tell you."

Delaney jerked back. "Ellie never confided in me about anything other than the fact that she loved you and the kids. She loved her shop and her life."

"I can't believe she would cheat on me. This is about something else. I'd lay odds that something had to do with Gerard Knox." Michael flipped both photos over so they lay facedown. "He probably had her followed. Maybe his guy threatened her to get to me. Maybe he blackmailed her. With Knox anything is possible."

It sounded so far-fetched. A newlywed essential oils shop owner and an accountant living an ordinary life, suddenly immersed in San Antonio's criminal element. Sure Ellie had smoked pot, but that didn't mean she was enmeshed in the city's dark underbelly. Where did she buy her pot? Had she tangled with the wrong dealer?

Delaney forced herself to soften her tone. Michael had lost the woman he loved. He couldn't be expected to think straight. "What did you tell the police?"

"Too much." Jess folded his arms across his chest. Distaste pinched his pudgy features. "I arrived just in time to save him from himself. I don't know what you were thinking, going to the police without representation. You're smarter than that."

"I was thinking I didn't do enough to protect my wife." Michael's mouth twisted in anger. "I have to do better with my kids."

"Let's all calm down. Michael needs to eat something. Knowing you, Delaney, so do you." Cam hobbled across the room, pushing a cart that held a tray loaded with a platter of fresh fruit, granola, yogurt, sandwiches, and coffee. Michael was her first stop. She set a plate filled with food in front of him. "We're all on the same side. Michael's been through hell. We need to find a way to help him."

"Stop talking about me like I'm not here." Michael dropped a napkin over the plate. "What I really need is some Dewar's on ice."

"Wrong. It's not even lunchtime. What you need is to stay sober for your kids." Delaney accepted a plate from Cam and selected a few pieces of fruit and a container of yogurt. She needed to counteract all the coffee in her system. What she really wanted was a long run and a session with Macho Man. She needed to work up a sweat. She needed to wear herself out so she could sleep. "They need you to show them how to grieve in a healthy way."

"They're still with their mother. I think she's preparing to mount a campaign for full custody."

"So you'll deal with that. Jess will help. Eat something, take a shower, and take a nap. You need to give your body and your mind a rest."

It was easy to give advice to someone else. Hard to take her own advice. Delaney dipped a fresh strawberry in yogurt and forced herself to eat it. "Hunter was with me when we found the photos."

"Are you nuts?" Jess's solicitous smile disappeared, replaced with a horrified grimace. "What is going on between you two? He killed your brother. He spends not enough time in prison, and you welcome him back with open arms?"

"He's determined to prove that he's innocent and find the real killer. I did not welcome him back with open arms. I want to find Ellie's killer. So does he. At least this way I can keep an eye on him."

"I have to agree with Jess." Cam's expression matched her concerned tone, soft and nonthreatening, as though she was dealing with a volatile person. "You're setting yourself up to be hurt again. I'm worried for you."

"Don't be. Once again, hear me loud and clear. I can take care of myself." How many times did she have to say this? They were her friends. They'd seen her efforts to hone her body and live her life as a self-sufficient, independent woman. Yet they still questioned.

But they were off topic. Maybe because Michael wanted it that way. "A waiter at the restaurant where these photos were taken said Ellie came in on Wednesday mornings twice a month. She and a man ate breakfast together. This doesn't sound like something Gerard Knox or his employees would do. And why didn't she tell anyone? Why go to this hole-in-the-wall restaurant and lie about it? In the other photos she's coming out of a downtown hotel. Do you know of any reason she would be at that hotel?"

"We just got married." Michael let his head sink into his hands. "We were talking about having a baby of our own."

No one spoke for several seconds. What could a person say to such anguish? Such loss and grief? People liked to say it would be okay, but it wouldn't. Delaney could attest to the years it took to climb that mountain, sliding down and starting over just when a person thought she'd made it over the hump.

"I'm sorry, so sorry." Cam rose and enveloped Michael in a hug. She always knew what to do. What to say. The simplest, most direct thing. "We all are. Why don't you take a shower and get some rest? You'll feel a little better. We'll talk about this later."

Cam helped Michael to his feet and put her arm around his waist. Frowning, she looked back at Delaney. "You should turn those photos over to the police. You should've done that immediately."

"We—I will. I just wanted a chance to talk to Michael first." And she'd let Hunter sway her. "Michael, what's the best way to get in touch with Knox?"

"No, no, don't do that." He halted and turned to face her. "Are you nuts? Stay away from him. He's toxic. Dangerous."

"Michael's right. Stop playing detective with Hunter. You'll get hurt. Think of the rest of us. We've lost so much already." Jess's fair skin turned a deep red. He pulled his phone from his suit pocket and glanced at the time. "I have court this afternoon. Michael, do not talk to the police again without me, please. If they come around, call me and wait until I arrive to answer questions. Promise me."

"I promise." Michael resumed his shambling gait toward the stairs. "Stay away from Knox, Delaney."

"Try to rest."

He paused at the bottom of the elegant staircase that wound its way up to a second-floor landing. "That's not an answer."

Didn't he burn to know who had killed his wife? That wasn't fair. "I stood aside when Corey died. I lost everything. It's possible the police got the wrong man. I can't let that happen again."

A harrumph from Jess was the only response. It was followed by the slam of the front door. His opinion mattered, but the truth about what had happened ten years ago and what had happened two days ago mattered more.

CHAPTER 25

Hunter pulled into the Good Samaritan Community Center on Saltillo Street and parked in the shade of a live oak with roots that had broken through the sidewalk that rimmed the asphalt. The morning sun hid behind gray clouds that hung low, making for a dreary backdrop. He kept his gaze on the massive tree. It didn't do any good. Delaney's nearness flooded him. It knocked him off balance. Her scent tantalized him. She smelled like soap and citrus and woman. Sometimes at night he'd awoken on his prison bunk convinced he could smell her. It was enough to drive him crazy.

Dressed in black jeans, a red peasant blouse, and purple Converse sneakers, hair loose down her back, she looked as good as she smelled. *Keep it light. Don't get your hopes up. Keep it simple, stupid.* Being close to her was enough.

He would keep telling himself that.

She'd been silence wrapped in barbed wire since he picked her up at the Presa Street parking lot. His inquiries about how the rest of the previous day had gone for her had been answered with monosyllabic responses. "This is it."

"I figured as much." She slid her sunglasses—was she wearing them to hide her expression from him?—into her purse. "Why here?"

"Pastor James knows the guy who runs this place. He says it's an oasis in the middle of some of the roughest gang territory in the city."

Delaney opened her mouth. Hunter's cell phone rang. He held up his hand. "It's my mom."

She shrugged and went back to scrolling through something on her phone.

It was weird to be reconnected to the world after ten years. To be able to talk on the phone anytime he wanted. Even if the list of people he could call these days was short. "Hey, Ma."

"Hey, son. You left early this morning. Thanks for leaving me a note with your new number."

"Thanks for fronting me the money. I set up a payment plan. I'll pay you back with my first paycheck."

"No worries. I have ulterior motives. Now I can talk to you any time I want." She chuckled, the sound sweet in his ears. "You'll be sick of hearing my voice."

"Never."

"I thought you didn't have to be at work until this afternoon."

"I had some errands to run."

"Be careful."

As if she knew where he was. "I will be. I promise."

"There's a ton of leftovers in the fridge. When you get home tonight, help yourself."

Another strange new reality. He lived with his mother. "See you later."

He hung up. The mundane, the ordinary, the normal. He would never take it for granted again. Being able to move about freely. He could take a shower whenever he wanted. Eat when and what he wanted. Wear whatever he wanted. Talk to his mom whenever he wanted.

He could talk to whomever he wanted—almost. He couldn't

consort with known felons. He didn't intend to consort with them. Just bring a killer to justice. Which started with finding Willy Sandoval. "You ready?"

Delaney nodded. "What does your mom think about you trying to find Corey's real killer?"

Hunter searched for any trace of sarcasm on her face and found none. "She doesn't know."

"She's such a good person. I always liked her."

"She never gave up on me." Hunter stuck the phone in his pocket and opened his door. "She never stopped believing in me."

"I guess moms are like that."

Unlike girlfriends. Grateful he hadn't said it aloud, Hunter slid from the seat. "Let's do this."

Given the noise level in the center, a person might think a Spurs game was in full swing. Instead, a pack of preschoolers played a rousing game of musical chairs. In another room a group of mothers did aerobics to a Taylor Swift song in front of full-length mirrors. Seniors huddled in front of computers while an instructor used a pointer to illustrate something on a large screen. Hunter had to yell to be heard. A custodian pointed toward an office with windows that gave the director of youth and teen services a clear view of the lobby.

Santiago Martinez filled up the small office, barely leaving room for two visitors. He'd fit right in playing in the Dallas Cowboys' defensive line. A tattoo sleeve covered one arm. The other arm featured older, cruder tattoos of the gang variety. He squeezed a second chair into his office from the lobby area and encouraged them to take a seat. "Jimmy left me a message saying you'd be coming by, but he didn't say what it was about. What can I do for y'all?" Despite an all-business tone, he smiled. "I've got a hoard of teenagers coming my way in about ten minutes. I promised them a spring break dance party in the gym."

"We're trying to find a guy named Guillermo Sandoval. Goes by Willy."

Martinez's smile faded. "Are you cops?"

"No."

"Warrant servers?"

"Nope."

"Angry husband or wife?"

"No, absolutely not."

"People come to the Good Samaritan for a hundred different reasons. Legal advice. Tutoring. Help getting out of gangs." Martinez had the voice and the smell of a pack-a-day smoker. Two of his front teeth were likely fake. His nose had been broken—probably more than once. But his tone was polite and even. "They need help finding jobs. Some come just to have fun on neutral ground where they can feel safe. We work hard to keep it that way."

"We understand."

"I don't think you do. We're not in the business of giving out information about people who come to us for safety."

"I'm not trying to cause any trouble. I was wrongly convicted of a murder that occurred ten years ago. I just got out of prison—"

"So you're seeking payback. Some justice."

"Not the way you mean. I want my life back, and the only way to get it back is to prove I didn't commit the crime. People I care about need to know I didn't do it." Hunter ran through the bare essentials of the story. "Willy can help me prove my innocence. He can help me find the person who killed Corey Broward so he's not still walking around a free man while my best friend's ashes are floating on the waves in the Gulf of Mexico."

Martinez's gaze swiveled toward Delaney. "What's your stake in all this?"

"Corey Broward was my brother."

"So you think this guy is telling the truth, that he didn't do it?"

"I don't know what to believe. But I want to know. Two days ago my best friend was murdered in her shop. She was Corey's girlfriend." Delaney sideswiped Hunter with a steely glare. "Hunter thinks the two are related. I intend to find out if he's right. I intend to find out who killed Ellie and make sure he—or she—pays."

Martinez leaned back in his chair and steepled stubby fingers. "You're telling me you want to find Willy, but not because you think *he* did it."

"I don't think he did. He didn't have the gumption. He was a pot-head." Hunter jumped back in. "He liked to sample his own wares. But he can connect me to the people who did do it."

Martinez picked up a folder from his desk, then laid it back down. "Willy can't connect you to anybody."

"So you do know him. Why can't he help us?"

"Willy's dead."

A band tightened around Hunter's chest. The urge to kick something came and went. He wasn't that guy anymore. Maybe he wasn't supposed to solve this murder. Maybe he was supposed to move on and accept the role he'd played in Corey's death. He'd enabled Corey's drug use. He'd left him at the co-op that night. If he'd stayed, maybe Corey would still be alive.

Or they'd both be dead. Sour bile rose in Hunter's throat. Too much coffee, not enough sleep. He rubbed his eyes. A dead end. The one name he had. He'd hung on to that name for all these years. For nothing.

Delaney's hand brushed Hunter's arm. He glanced her direction. Empathy softened the fine sun lines around her eyes. For a second the old Laney stared from her emerald-green eyes. Then she was gone and the new Delaney, leather-tough, dropped her hand.

"I'm sorry. I know that's not what you were hoping for." Martinez splayed his fingers across the folders. "I didn't really know him. He got busted with a bunch of other gang members for possession with intent to distribute narcotics and firearms charges. It was a big joint operation. Meth disguised as ecstasy. Drugs dressed up like Easter candy. The worst kind of drug trafficking. He got sent up to the federal penitentiary. When he got out, he graduated to the big time. He hooked up with the Tango Orejón. He got capped at Cassiano Homes last year."

Delaney stood. "Thank you for your time, Mr. Martinez."

"You're welcome. I wish you the best in your search for justice."

Hunter had misjudged the sloth-like pothead. Willy had enough gumption to get himself killed. Tango Orejón controlled a big slice of drug sales in San Antonio. Executions, drug sales, racketeering, and extortion replaced drive-bys, car theft, graffiti, and vandalism. Anyone who'd spent time in prison knew enough to either join or stay as far away from them as possible. "Wait a minute. How do you know all this? You said you didn't know him."

"I know his brother Eloy. He's a friend. He works in a gang outreach program we operate here at the center."

"Can we talk to him?"

"That's up to him."

"Maybe if you make the introduction, he'll consider it."

Martinez leaned back in his chair and stared at the ceiling. The brown pleather chair groaned under his weight A tattoo of a snake curled around his neck. He cranked his head from side to side. His neck popped. "I'll text him. But I'm not vouching for you. I'm just telling him you want to talk to him and that you knew his brother."

Hunter cocked his head toward Delaney's empty chair. She was so anxious to leave behind this line of questioning. She sank back into the chair.

"I appreciate it." Hunter had a toe in the door. "Thank you."

"Don't thank me yet."

Martinez texted like Hunter's nieces and nephews did. With both thumbs moving at a rapid-fire pace. Hunter's old phone didn't have text messaging. The new one did, but he hadn't graduated from hunt-and-peck yet.

While they waited for Eloy to reply, Martinez gave them a run-down of Eloy's role at the center. He and two other former gang members with master's degrees in social work held weekly war councils with gang leaders from the area's three housing projects. The object was to mediate differences. That might even include actual physical fights. "One on one though. The conflict is isolated to the two guys with a problem. It's actually cut back on drive-bys."

Interesting strategy. "How did Sandoval get out of gangs? I thought once you were in, there was no going back."

"His gang disbanded. I know it's hard to believe, but it actually happened. They were in their thirties, they had kids, they wanted them to be safe, so they just stopped. They said no more."

Like a small miracle.

Martinez's phone chirped. He picked it up. His expression didn't change. He thumbed a return text. "He's at Cassiano Homes on South Laredo Street. He's in front of the first building. You could walk over, but I suggest you drive. We don't see a lot of white folks around here. Unless they're cops."

Hunter expressed their thanks again. He held the door for Delaney, who said nothing. Together they hiked out to his truck. Keys in hand, he paused in front of it. "Are you good with this?"

"Why wouldn't I be?" She tugged her door open. "I planned to see this through to the bitter end. Don't you?"

"You think it's a wild-goose chase, don't you?"

"Let's just say I'm trying to keep an open mind."

"That's not nothing."

Delaney smiled for the first time since encountering Hunter in her house. It took him by surprise. His heart couldn't defend itself against such a simple, straightforward assault. In the old days, she'd never seemed aware of its effect on him. Nor did she now. "You should let me drive. I had clients in this neighborhood."

No wonder she smiled. No one drove his truck except Hunter. "I don't think so."

Much had changed but not her smile. Or his truck. He could work with that. Maybe she could too.

CHAPTER 26

Cassiano Homes was a quick six-block drive from the community center. It blended in with the south-side neighborhood of mostly working-class Latino families. Clothes hung from makeshift clothes-lines. Toddlers waddled around postage stamp–sized front yards while their mothers sat on the steps gabbing. Stray dogs sniffed at trash cans.

The San Antonio Housing Authority had worked hard to upgrade the housing projects on San Antonio's west, south, and east sides, but they still looked like the projects. Except for some huge murals painted on the sides of the two-story buildings. Hunter slowed down. They were the work of graffiti artists—talented artists. One told the story of a boy who'd been shot when he tried to quit a gang. An elderly woman wept by his coffin. Others depicted Aztec gods and modern-day heroes. Hunter's students could've painted them.

"I think that's him." Delaney pointed at a man standing on the corner of Laredo and Loma Vista. He lit a cigarette and leaned against a VIA bus stop sign. The guy could've been Willy, only older. Same skinny body and big head. Same round face. He wore a brilliant white T-shirt and faded jeans. A tattoo sleeve covered one arm. A thick swatch of white beat a path across his jet-black hair.

Hunter pulled over and rolled down his window. "Eloy Sandoval?"

"You Hunter?"

"I am."

Sandoval sucked on the cigarette. He leaned over and peered past Hunter to Delaney. "And you are?"

"A friend." Her expression hard, Delaney stared back. "An interested party, you could say."

Sandoval cocked his head toward the apartments. "Pull in. I told some of the kids I'd show up for a basketball game about now."

Hunter did as he was told. They left the truck in the housing complex's parking lot. The three of them walked toward the court where the sound of a ball smacking asphalt and a stream of cussing suggested the game had begun without Sandoval.

"Saint said you knew my brother back in the day." Sandoval tossed the cigarette butt on the asphalt and ground it out with the heel of his dirty white sneaker. "Why are you asking about him now?"

No getting-to-know-you dance. "Willy was my best friend's dealer ten years ago. I think he hooked him up with someone higher up the ladder in his gang. I need to know who that someone was."

"You think you can just sashay into our turf and start asking questions?" Sandoval snorted. "You got some guts, *wey*. How do I know you're not PD or DEA?"

"If you're on the right side of the law, what do you care?" Delaney stepped in before Hunter could respond. "Your brother is dead. Nothing you say can hurt him. Did they get the guy who murdered him?"

Another snort followed by an obscenity. "No. Not that they tried very hard. Willy was a gangbanger with a rap sheet a mile long. They figured good riddance. The cops didn't notice he was a human being. He had a wife and three kids."

"I get that." Delaney's tone softened. "Willy was friends with my brother Corey. Corey was murdered. I know how it feels."

"Saint says Nash here did time for it. The cops got your brother's murderer? Or do you think he did the time but not the crime?"

"I don't know. If Hunter was wrongly convicted, then he's right. A killer has been walking around free for ten years while my brother's ashes are floating in the Gulf."

Hunter could relate. It didn't matter how long it had been since Corey's murder. It still hurt. "Corey needed money. He said Willy hooked him up with his boss. They were arranging to use our art co-op as a drug distribution point. It was a repurposed warehouse on the edge of downtown. I tried to convince Corey to back out. It's possible he tried and maybe it got him killed. I'd like to see the person responsible pay."

He was responsible for urging Corey to change his mind. If he hadn't, he might still be alive.

"This Corey was a White boy? Tango Orejón doesn't admit White boys."

"That's what made the co-op the perfect front."

Sandoval's grizzled features melted into a smile. He and Willy shared genes, no doubt about it. Only the older brother was worn by time and loss. "Sure, big gringo like you did some time, you think you're tough, tough enough to take on Tango Orejón."

"Eloy! *¿Qué pasa?*"

The boys on the court had noticed their arrival. The ball sailed in Sandoval's direction. He caught it and sent a bounce pass to a kid who wore jeans so baggy they sagged around his legs, showing off a pair of blue plaid boxer shorts. How did he run like that?

"Be with you in a sec, *compa*."

Shouts dissing his decision greeted his words, but the boys shot toward the other end of the court where the shortest—and fastest—kid hit a basket from three-point range.

"I'm not messing with Tango Orejón. I'm talking ten years ago." Hunter sought words that would convince Sandoval to trust him. His mission did sound insane, even to Hunter. "Before he did time. Willy was dealing pot, ludes, coke, ecstasy—your basic one-stop shop."

"Tango Orejón. Same game."

"Why didn't he join Latin Kings with you?"

"He always went his own way. Then he went to live with our *tía* in Helotes. I was smarter. I wasn't stupid enough to get caught. *Abuela* thought I was her good boy." He shook his head. "Poor thing. She deserved better. She died before Willy did, *gracias a Díos.*"

"Did you try to find whoever did it?"

"I wanted to. Then my wife marched me into my kids' bedroom and told me to take a good look at *nuestros tres angelitos dormidos.* She asked me if I wanted to be around to watch them grow up." He grabbed the lock-wire fencing that surrounded the basketball court. His fingers curled around it like a prisoner's around bars. "Willy drew the short straw. He never had a chance. I want better for my kids. That means being around, being a father to them, teaching them right from wrong, protecting them."

Not an argument with which Hunter could take issue. His own father hadn't been around. His example had been to cut and run when the going got rough. Mom had done her best, but Hunter had been a selfish, self-absorbed kid determined to push every button.

Yet she still loved him. "You have your priorities straight. I don't have any kids." At the rate Hunter was going, he would never have them. "Let me take this on."

"How do you know Willy didn't kill your friend?"

"We don't. I thought of him as harmless. I guess I underestimated him. Does it matter? He's gone. If he did it, then he's where he should be."

Sandoval didn't blink at this harsh assessment. "Before Willy went away, he used to come to Abuela's house with a *vato* who tried to get me to join up with them. He wore Tango Orejón colors."

"Is he still around?"

"He just got out after doing time in the federal pen for conspiracy to distribute."

Otherwise he'd probably be dead too. "Name?"

"They call him *El Tiburón*."

"The Shark."

"You speak the language, compadre?"

"Mostly just the cuss words and high school Spanish. Your brother taught me some words though."

Like *mota*. Pot. And words that couldn't be repeated in mixed company.

Sandoval chuckled. "That's my brother."

Shouts from the basketball court drew his attention. *"Aye, chihuahua."*

Sandoval dashed toward a knot of players that surrounded two kids, the bigger one punching the smaller one in the head. "Hey, hey, stop it." Followed by Spanish too rapid-fire for Hunter to follow.

The older kid, his face sweaty and filled with rage and disgust, talked a mile a minute, gesticulating with both hands.

The younger kid, shoulders hunched, head down, trudged from the court.

Sandoval grabbed the ball and threw a hard pass to Hunter. "I gotta do this."

Hunter bounced it once and took his shot. The ball hit the backboard and slipped through the net. "That was brutal."

Delaney snagged the rebound and tossed it back to Sandoval. "You let him get away with that?"

"The kid made a pass at his little sister. She's ten."

Sandoval sent a bounce pass to the older kid. He nodded and took off for the other end of the court, his opponents in pursuit. Sandoval had no trouble keeping up.

Delaney trotted down the out-of-bounds line in pursuit. "Where do we find El Tiburón?"

"Do you know where the Maldonado family's boxing gym is on Zarzamora Street?" Sandoval dribbled, shot past a much shorter defender, and headed to the basket, still talking.

"I do." Hunter stayed on the sidelines with Delaney. The Maldonado family had produced some of San Antonio's biggest boxing legends before drugs, alcohol, and the inevitable life of crime that follows caused them to crater into oblivion. "Is it still open?"

"A distant cousin bought it and took it over after Louis crashed and burned."

"Does El Tiberón work there, or is he a boxer?" Delaney's hands fisted. What was she thinking?

"Both."

Hunter tried to picture himself walking into a gym and asking for The Shark. "Does he have a real name?"

"You mean like the one his mama gave him?" Sandoval stopped and tossed an easy two-pointer from the paint. He had a definite height advantage. "I'm sure he does. They all do, but he didn't share it with the grapevine."

"El Tiburón it is."

"Take your gloves."

Hunter glanced at Delaney. Her expression held grim determination. The image of her all-out assault on Macho Man punching bag surfaced. What she lacked in form, she made up for with anger-fueled strength. Hunter had watched boxing a few times when his dad had been in town. He and Curtis loved it. They said anyone who didn't was a wuss. Hunter didn't want to be a wuss so he joined in. In hindsight, he saw a sensitive kid who needed to be loved by his dad, who would've done anything for his approval.

That kid could've used a few boxing lessons before he went to prison.

He shut the door on painful memories and thanked Eloy. "We'd better go."

Delaney nodded and took off. They walked across the grass toward the parking lot without speaking. She seemed to be deep in thought, and Hunter didn't mind. Sandoval had given them plenty to think about.

Traffic had picked up on the street where he'd parked his truck. It was lunchtime. He needed to drop Delaney off and get to the center. He vacillated between being excited to see what the kids had drawn for their second assignment—a portrait of someone they cared about—and nervous about whether they would even show up.

A dark-blue Thunderbird, its engine rumbling, slowed as it passed the park. The passenger-side window came down. A dark form rested a long, black weapon on the door frame.

Gun blasts fractured the air.

CHAPTER 27

Bullets whizzed by Delaney. They whistled and then pinged against tree trunks, benches, and water fountains in a bizarre, drunken musical number. Delaney embraced grass and dirt. She flinched with each new sound. Hunter's weight crushed her. Gravel bit into her cheek. Pain surged through her nose. Her tongue hurt where she'd bit it after Hunter knocked her to the ground.

Time did a weird one-step-forward, two-steps-back warp.

She tried to raise her head.

"Stay down." Hunter's voice boomed in her ear. He was close. Too close. "Don't move."

"Let me up." Her voice squeaked. Her lungs couldn't expand. She couldn't breathe. "Get off me."

She needed to see. She needed to understand. Someone was shooting at them.

They wanted to kill her. Or Hunter.

What about the kids on the basketball court? *God, no.*

Why did she still turn to Him when the chips were down?

Because no one else was omnipotent, omnipresent, and omniscient. The three *O*s. Nana had taught her that. *Do Your thing, God.*

Please. The please was an afterthought.

Tires squealed. The *rat-a-tat-tat* of automatic gunfire ceased.

Only the sound of their ragged breathing remained. No dogs barked. No kids yelled. Time stood and dusted itself off.

Minutes began to tick by and disappear into the past once again.

Still, Hunter didn't move. Was he hurt? *God, don't let him be hurt. I just got him back.*

No, no, no. Adrenaline raged through Delaney. He was so not back. "Are you okay?"

Hunter's arms tightened around her. "Yeah, you?"

"Yeah."

His scent of aftershave and soap lingered in her nose. His embrace protected her, surrounded her, saved her.

God, don't do this to me. Please. "Get off me."

Gasping for air, Hunter rolled over with a grunt. He pulled himself upright on one elbow. "Are you sure you're okay?"

"Yeah. You?"

"Freaked out, but the only pain I feel is where you elbowed me in the ribs."

You're not gone from my life all over again. Thank You, God.

It was too much. Too much to fathom. Hunter and God back in her life at the same time. What did that mean?

Nothing. She couldn't allow it to mean something. As soon as she did, Hunter would do something stupid and she'd be alone all over again. *Fraidy-cat, fraidy-cat.* Her heart taunted her. Her mind shook its finger at her. *Don't be stupid, girl. You know better.*

Hunter lay flat on his back and patted his chest with both hands. "At least I think am."

Delaney scrambled to her knees. She gave him a once-over. "I don't see any blood." *Thank you, Jesus.* She staggered to her feet. "Did you get a license plate? Did you see the guy?"

"Are you kidding? I was on the ground with my eyes closed in two seconds flat." Hunter stood as well. "It happened so fast—"

"What about the kids?" Delaney whirled and shoved past him. She ran toward the court. "Eloy? Eloy!"

"Nobody's hurt." Eloy rose from behind one of the concrete benches that lined the court. The boys popped up in twos and threes. They had grins plastered on their faces. "These little *vatos* know what to do. It's not like they haven't experienced a drive-by before." He turned to the boys. "*No les vayan, hombrecitos.* The police will want to talk to you."

"Aww, *n'ombre.*" The short one with the sharp three-point jump shot protested. "I don't want to talk to no *policía.*"

"Did you do something wrong?"

"N'ombre."

"Then you got nothing to worry about. Shoot some hoops."

Still grumbling, the boy did as he was told. The others followed suit.

Brushing dried leaves and dirt from his jeans, Eloy strolled across the court toward Delaney and Hunter. "I called 911. You two okay? You got blood on your face, *chica.*"

Delaney touched her lip. Between the clanging of the blood pulsing through her head and her strangled breathing, she could barely hear him. Or feel anything. Her fingers came away bloody.

"Let me see." Hunter took her arm and forced her to stop. His expression stony, he looked her over. "You've got a fat lip and a bloody nose. Sorry about that. I took you down hard."

"Don't apologize." Delaney tugged free of his grip. This was no time to go soft. "It's better than being shot."

"You're welcome."

"Excuse me?"

"I kind of saved your life." He managed to look pleased with himself while trying to be suitably modest. "He was aiming for you."

"How do you know that? How do you know they weren't gunning for Eloy or one of the kids on the court?" *"Stay out of it or you're next."* Ellie's killer had warned her. "We don't know yet who the target was."

Sirens blared in the distance. The sound always made Delaney shudder. Whether it was coming for her or someone else. They came for her far too often.

"You two lovebirds need to stop bickering and start figuring out who you made mad."

"We're not lovebirds." The adrenaline that had been subsiding surged again. Delaney edged away from Hunter. "But you're right. Who knew we were going to be here? No one. We didn't know until we talked to Santiago."

"It wasn't Santiago. He doesn't have a horse in this race. Who knew you were headed to the Good Samaritan?"

"Friends. People I trust." Delaney's legs wanted to fold. A wave of dizziness engulfed her. She eased onto a bench at the closest picnic table. "Michael Hill, my friend's husband; my friends, Cam and Jess. Jess is a lawyer. None of them would've done this."

Eloy lit a cigarette. His hands were steady. He held out the pack. Delaney shook her head. Hunter took one. *Seriously?* He'd survived a shooting so he thought it was a good idea to kill himself with nicotine? "You don't smoke."

"And you don't box."

"Are you sure you two aren't a thing?" Eloy took a long pull on his cigarette. "Somebody wasn't happy you were talking to me about Willy. Figure out who that was and you'll find your killer."

Hunter's face reddened. "We're not—"

"I'm gonna check on my boys."

Eloy strolled away, leaving Delaney with Hunter looming over her. He kept glancing at her, but he said nothing. It was better that way. Delving into the whirlwind of emotions caused by going through a life-threatening situation together would serve no purpose.

None whatsoever.

So why did she feel so incredibly relieved and thankful that Hunter hadn't been hurt?

He was a human being. It would be callous not to feel relieved.

The screaming sirens didn't help. The closer they came the more her fight-or-flight instinct kicked in. She stood. Sat down. Stood and walked around the table twice, three times.

"It's okay. We're okay." Hunter touched her arm. His fingers were warm and surprisingly steady. Maybe prison had given him defense mechanisms for times of danger. "The police are on their way."

The fire trucks arrived first, then the ambulance, and the cops. Patrol called Homicide/Attempted Homicide after Hunter explained their connection to Ellie's murder. Time slowed to a trickle. His phone to one ear, his hand over the other, Hunter talked to his boss. His second day of work and he had to call in. Delaney felt for him. It was okay to feel empathy for him.

Wasn't it? It didn't mean anything.

A paramedic cleaned her lip and gave her an ice pack for her nose. She turned down his recommendation that she be transported to the hospital. "I have a big nose. It got in the way. It'll be fine."

She and Hunter took turns telling a patrol officer what had happened. He told them to sit tight. As if they had a choice.

A metallic gray Challenger pulled up to the curb behind the marked police unit. Detectives Ramos and Flores emerged. They didn't appear happy. Detective Flores headed for the patrol officers while Detective Ramos made a beeline for Delaney and Hunter.

"Tell me you're back with CPS and that's why you're at Cassiano Homes." Detective Ramos bulldozed past the pleasantries. "Tell me you didn't come here together."

His scowl bounced to Hunter. "Tell me you didn't ignore my strong recommendation that you stay away from Ms. Broward."

"That's not your call, Detective." Delaney planted herself next to Hunter, a move that surely surprised her as much as it must've Hunter. "What we're doing is none of your business."

"If you're investigating Ellie Hill's murder, then make no mistake about it, it is my business." Detective Ramos pulled his notebook from his suit pocket. "Officer Marconi says you were here talking to a Good Samaritan Community Center employee when the shooting occurred. Why?"

"You keep addressing Delaney." Hunter crossed his arms and stuck out his chin. "It's on me, not her. It was my idea. I told you I planned to prove my innocence. Whether Corey's death is related to Ellie's remains to be seen. There's no law against us being here, is there?"

"If you interfere in a police investigation, yes."

"That's bogus and you know it." Hunter barked a humorless laugh. "You have no intention of following up on my story about Guillermo Sandoval. You closed the books on Corey's murder. You let a killer roam free for the last ten years."

"As a matter of fact, we're pursuing all avenues to determine if Mrs. Hill's murder is related to Corey Broward's." Detective Ramos jabbed his pencil in the air for punctuation. "However, Mr. Hill has offered up some information that bears investigating and has nothing to do with Corey's death."

"Which means what for Corey's murder? Nothing, right? It falls to the wayside."

Hunter's belligerent tone wasn't helping. He was worked up. It had to be a delayed reaction. The Hunter she knew didn't talk to authority figures like that. She touched his arm and tried to telegraph her concern. He shook off her hand.

"Nothing has been discarded." Surprisingly, the detective's tone turned placating. "Let's start over. Take a seat at the picnic table and run through what happened."

Ten minutes later, Detective Ramos slapped his notebook closed. "I suggest you heed this warning and lay low until we find the perpetrator who killed Mrs. Hill and just tried to kill you."

"Maybe he was after Hunter."

"Mrs. Hill's killer told you to stay out of it. You obviously haven't done that and he knows it."

"How? How does he know it?"

"Maybe he's following you."

"Why?"

"The question of the day. I plan to find out."

Detective Flores approached, notebook in hand. He squeezed onto the bench next to Ramos. "Were you two here earlier when Mr. Sandoval broke up a fight?"

Delaney nodded. "We were. Why?"

"Describe what happened."

Hunter went first. Delaney filled in the gaps. "Why?"

"It's possible the shooting was retaliation, that's why. Mr. Santos pointed out that no one knew you were going to be in the park, except the community center staff member. We'll follow up with him."

"So you think this attempted murder had nothing to do with us?" Hunter rolled his eyes like a teenage boy. "Come on, guys, seriously?"

"Mrs. Hill was killed with a knife. So was Corey Broward."

Detective Flores shrugged. "Then he decides to take you out with an automatic weapon in broad daylight in a city park? It doesn't track."

Detective Ramos leaned closer, his scent of Polo and authority wafting over Delaney. "What my partner is saying is leave the investigating to us."

"So what have you learned so far in your investigation?" Hunter slid the question in with a deft touch. "If you don't mind my asking."

"I do mind." Detective Ramos's tight smile held only a smidgen of humor. "But be assured we are pursuing every lead. That includes Mr. Hill's clients, Mrs. Hill's friends, and even family."

Delaney smoothed her backpack purse with a still-trembling hand. "What if Ellie knew something about Corey's death—something that got her killed?"

"Ten years later? Why now?"

"We found some photos—"

"Laney!" His tone mutinous, Hunter slapped his hands on the table. "I thought we—"

"Agreed to pass the photos on to the authorities." To do the right thing, whether he liked it or not. "We found some photos in Ellie's office that show her talking to a man in a car in a strip mall."

Detective Ramos's face turned stony. "When? When did you find them?"

"Yesterday."

"And you failed to turn them over?"

Delaney pulled the envelope from her purse and slid it across the picnic table. "We're turning them over now."

Shaking his head, Detective Ramos took a disposable glove from his coat pocket, donned it, and picked up the envelope with two fingers. "Did it occur to you that the envelope and its contents might have fingerprints on them?"

"It did, actually. We were careful." Delaney soldiered on. "They were hidden in the back of her filing cabinet. The postmark is a week before her murder. They have to be relevant to her death."

She proceeded to share with the detectives everything they'd learned from the waiter and Michael's reaction to the photos—which had been grief and fear. "He didn't know about the breakfasts. He'd never seen the photos."

"Or so he said. Did it occur to you that it would be better for us to do those interviews rather than following in your footsteps?" Detective Flores's eyes could cut stone. A muscle twitched in his jaw. "You've given both parties a heads-up. Time to get their stories straight."

"They don't know any more than what they told us. It could be an affair, but Michael wants to see it as something Knox initiated to scare Ellie into doing something she didn't want to do." Delaney hastened to mollify him. Maybe he was right, but Michael was much more likely to speak freely to Delaney than to the detectives. He'd tried that and Jess had shut him down—rightly so. "Maybe Knox told her he would do something to Michael or the kids if she told him."

Detective Ramos tugged at his tie, loosening it. "Why hide the photos in her shop?"

"Keeping the evidence that she was being coerced or blackmailed or extorted or whatever it was the perpetrator was doing. She wanted to be able to prove she was under duress."

"All supposition. You don't have a lick of evidence."

"Just a gut feeling." Delaney slid from the bench. She was done talking. She needed to tend to her shop and deliver bad news to her customers. "It's your job to prove it. Your job to get evidence. So do your job."

Detective Ramos stood and loomed over her. "Stay out of our way and we will."

Delaney whirled and stalked toward the parking lot. She glanced back at Hunter. "Are you coming?"

He scrambled to his feet. "Yes, ma'am."

"Delaney."

Reluctantly, she pivoted. Detective Ramos's expression had softened. "Do you think Ellie Hill was having an affair?"

She stuck her hands in her pockets and studied the grass stains on the knees of her jeans. "The truth? I don't know."

"The truth is always a good place to start."

Sometimes a person had to dig deep for it, through layers of friendship, grief, sweet memories, and the sheer desire to slough off anything that would hurt. To the aching, bruised, incontrovertible truth.

CHAPTER 28

"Why did you tell them about the photos?"

After going ten rounds with Detectives Ramos and Flores, Delaney wasn't in the mood to argue with Hunter. She craned her head from side to side and rolled her shoulders. Her nose throbbed and her head ached. Her heart didn't feel much better. "He has way more resources, experience, and time to determine their origin than we do." She stared out the passenger window. "And because it was the right thing to do."

With a snort Hunter pulled into traffic. "You could've told me about your conversation with Michael."

"This way I didn't have to repeat myself."

"You don't trust me."

"Michael and Jess don't trust you. I'm reserving judgment."

That shut him up. It revealed a miniscule shift in her attitude toward him. One she shouldn't have admitted. The next few miles were driven in silence.

"I'll drop you at your car so you can go home and get cleaned up." Hunter swerved to avoid a mobile raspa vendor who apparently thought he owned the road. "Or did you want me to go through a drive-through first? You didn't get lunch."

"I'm not hungry, but if you need to eat, feel free." She leaned her head against the door frame and closed her eyes for a few seconds. Blood pulsed in her ears. "I'm not going home. We still have to find El Tiburón, and I want to talk to Gerard Knox."

"You heard what Ramos said."

Delaney raised her head and drilled Hunter with a stare. "Aren't you standing down?"

"No."

"Detective Ramos can get you sent back to prison on the pretense of parole violations. Don't let his compassionate air fool you. He'd do it in a heartbeat." If Hunter really didn't kill Corey—and the jury was still out on that—Delaney didn't want him to spend one more day in prison.

She opened her purse and pulled out a packet of wipes. "I, on the other hand, am an upstanding citizen and business owner. If I want to talk to other business owners, I have the freedom to do so."

"I'm not giving up."

"I'm not talking about giving up. I'm saying, let me take it from here." She wiped her face and hands, then tried to clean her shirt. The dirt smeared. She gave up. "Hang back. Enjoy your freedom."

"Not happening." His scowl could've fried an egg. "I'm headed to the Maldonado Family Gym. Are you coming or not?"

"Fine. Next stop, Maldonado Family Gym."

The gym had been the recent recipient of a new coat of white paint. A bright red-lettered sign indicated it was now called STEP IT UP BOXING GYM. A couple of elderly muscle cars were parked in the cramped lot adjacent to the building.

Inside, the desultory spin of several large metal ceiling fans threw the smell of sweat and dirty gym clothes in Delaney's face. Not unlike PE in high school, one of her favorite classes. She excelled at most sports, but her job kept her from participating in anything but softball.

Corey refused to let her give it up—something for which she would forever be grateful. Over the years her teams gave her a place where she belonged and built-in friends during some of the worst times of her life.

Boxing was different. She didn't have to depend on anyone. No teamwork. No trust required. "I've thought about getting a sparring partner, but I've never felt good enough."

"You looked really good the other night." Hunter smiled. "Lethal, actually."

That smile.

Down, girl.

She surveyed the facility. Two big rings, a dozen heavy bags spread along one wall, speed bags on the other side. An area with weights and other workout equipment. Two women sparred in the bigger ring. A man, presumably a coach, yelled encouragement in a gravelly smoker's voice. A guy pounded a bag to Delaney's right, while a woman drilled a speed bag to her left. Fight posters, including several that featured Maldonado family champions, provided the only attempt at décor.

No one glanced their way. Time to find out who was in charge. "There's an office in the back." Delaney pointed to a glass enclosure beyond the rings. "A good place to start."

The man in the office didn't bother to change positions when Delaney stuck her head in and asked for a moment of his time. He remained tilted precariously on the back legs of a chair behind a gun-metal gray desk and identified himself as Joe Taylor. He was not the elderly, grizzled boxing gym manager of the movies. Instead Taylor was ripped, from his thick pecs to his oversized biceps and six-pack abs. His gray hair cut military style was at odds with his baby face.

"I'm thinking about doing some training." Instinct said a straight-on approach wouldn't work in this situation. Delaney glanced at Hunter. He wouldn't like where this was going, but with any luck, he'd follow her lead. "Any chance I could find a sparring partner here?"

"We don't do boxing lessons. We don't do boxing as exercise. No Tae Bo classes." Disdain ran rampant through Taylor's words. "We train boxers for amateur and professional boxing. That means you have to pay your dues to the American Boxing Association."

Shelling out money at this stage didn't seem wise. Delaney adopted what she hoped was an eager expression. "How about a trial run before I decide?"

Taylor let his chair bang onto the floor. His gray eyebrows rose and fell. "Are you sure you didn't already do ten rounds? What happened to your face?"

"I ran into a door."

"That uncoordinated, huh?" He cackled. "Have you ever been in the ring?"

"No, but I have spent a lot of time with the heavy bag and the speed bag."

"It's your funeral. I'll introduce you to Letty." Taylor stood and edged around his desk toward the door. "She's always around."

"You don't want to do this." Hunter stepped back, allowing Delaney to go first. "If Letty is a regular, she'll make mincemeat out of you."

"Maybe." That was a distinct possibility. Heat burned Delaney's cheeks. Her armpits were wet. She sucked in air and forced a grin. "I may get my clock cleaned, but it'll be worth it. I think."

"A little fear is healthy," Pops had told her when she asked him about his service in Vietnam for a school project. *"Fear keeps you from doing stupid things. The trick is not to freeze. Stay calm. Don't lose sight of your objective. Let adrenaline do its job."*

Thanks, Pops. Delaney sped up to match Taylor's bowlegged stride.

"I heard you have a coach that trains boxers here by the name of El Tiburón."

Taylor halted in front of the big ring. His glance turned appraising. "Where did you hear that?"

"I was asking around for a trainer and his name came up."

"Who gave you his name?"

"It just came up."

"Maybe you should try the city's gym over on Martin Street."

"I like yours."

"Letty!" Taylor waved over a short, muscle-bound woman clad in black leggings and a green tank top over a purple sports bra. Her short brown locks curled tight across her forehead. She double tapped the heavy bag and loped in their direction. The manager pointed at Delaney. "She wants to spar."

Letty's grin widened. At least two of her teeth were fake. An angry red scar sliced through her left eyebrow. "Are you sure, *chica*?"

"No, but I've always wanted to box." Delaney rolled her shoulders. She bounced on the balls of her feet. "I figure I need to give it a shot before I'm too old."

"Honey, you're already too old." Letty cocked her head toward the ring. "But I don't mind proving it."

Taylor kindly helped Delaney with wraps and a borrowed pair of gloves.

"You sure you want to do this?" Hunter whispered as he spread the ropes so Delaney could climb in the ring. "It's not necessary. We'll get the information—"

"I'm doing it. Wish me luck."

"I don't believe in luck."

"Then pray."

"Done."

Delaney strode into the center of the ring. It seemed a lot bigger from the inside looking out. Her heart pounded like a sledgehammer. Heat and cold took turns blowing through her. She shivered.

Letty grinned. "You ready?"

Feet shoulder width apart, one in front of the other. Knees slightly bent, weight off your heels. Gloves up protecting your face, elbows pointed toward your knees. "Ready."

She began to circle, gaze fixed on Letty's left glove. The boxer was right-handed. The jab would come first, followed by a cross thrown as she rotated her hips and shoulders to generate more speed that would produce more power.

If her tutorial boxers knew their stuff.

Here it comes, here it comes.

Indeed. The first time Delaney managed to dodge with a quick— and totally instinctual bob—knees bent, behind sticking out. Before she had time to recover, Letty jabbed and threw another cross. This time Delaney blocked the cross with her left forearm. The impact shook her body all the way to her toes.

Strangely, it didn't hurt.

The rest of the world disappeared. Her vision tunneled. Letty's gloves loomed huge and black.

Taylor's voice penetrated from a great distance. "Don't just stand there, Broward, move your feet. Do something."

"Bob and weave, Laney, bob and weave." Hunter sounded scared.

At the next jab Delaney managed to parry. Letty's cross bounced away. Delaney got off a decent hook. Letty blocked it and came back with an uppercut that hit Delaney in the chin. She staggered back.

"Don't let your arms drop after a punch, protect your face." Taylor's squeaky voice got higher when he was perturbed. "Pick up your feet, Broward. Move around."

Delaney recovered and danced away from Letty. The other woman advanced steadily. Her roundhouse caught Delaney in the ear.

A second later Delaney exploded with a series of jabs, crosses, and a solid roundhouse.

"See, not so bad." Hunter's voice floated in the air. "Keep it up, Laney."

"You're flopping all over the place, Broward." If Taylor agreed with Hunter, it didn't show in his running commentary. "Tighten up those punches, protect yourself. Move your feet, come on, move."

Delaney circled. She tried another uppercut and a roundhouse. Letty deflected both and came back in time to land a solid punch to Delaney's midsection. Gloves flailing, she stumbled back. Letty kept coming. She drilled Delaney with a second solid punch to the midsection. Another to her chin.

Delaney went down, flat on her back, on the canvas.

Still moving, light on her feet, Letty leaned over Delaney's prostrate body. "You okay?"

She didn't even have the decency to breathe hard. Or break a sweat.

"I'm fine," Delaney gasped the words. Her solar plexus was on fire. She couldn't suck in a breath. Her face hurt, her gut hurt, her body hurt. Delaney scrapped up a smile. "That was fun."

In a bizarre, kill-or-be-killed way.

His face red, eyes bulging, Hunter loomed over her. "Fun? She could've killed you."

"Your footwork is sloppy. You're trying to powerhouse your opponent to the moon, and you leave yourself wide open on every punch." Wearing a self-satisfied grin, Taylor held out his hand. Delaney took it and he pulled her to her feet. "Otherwise, not bad for a newbie."

High praise. A sudden wave of dizziness blew through Delaney.

She breathed through it. Adrenaline's fade to black. "Thanks for the feedback."

She tapped gloves with Letty. "Thanks for not killing me."

"My pleasure." Still grinning, Letty hopped from the ring and strolled away.

Delaney turned to Taylor. "Good enough to ask The Shark to train me?"

"Not in this lifetime." Taylor's snort could've been a laugh. "His boxers include a welterweight and a heavyweight champion. He only coaches one woman and she just floored you in less than ninety seconds."

Delaney studied Letty's retreating back. "Thanks, Joe. We'll catch up with you later."

"What are you doing now?" Hunter handled the ropes so Delaney could exit the ring. "Enough is enough. Let's get out of here."

"We don't have what we came for." Delaney caught up with Letty at a speed bag. "I hear your coach is El Tiburón."

"Joe has a big mouth." Letty's steady, circular motion, *one-two-three, switch, one-two-three, switch*, never wavered. "And what's it to you?"

"I thought maybe you could put me in touch with him. I'd like to ask him to train me."

"You don't go to Rick. He sees you fight. He comes to you." Letty chuckled. "And honey, you ain't got what he wants. Not to mention you're older than dirt."

"Maybe I could convince him."

Letty stilled the bag. She gave Delaney a once-over. "You're not a boxer, but you are his type. If you're that hot to meet him, I could introduce you as potential girlfriend material." Her gaze encompassed Hunter. "If you're not already taken."

Hunter's face turned a peculiar shade of purple. "I don't think that's a good—"

"Perfect." Ignoring Hunter's huff, Delaney dug a card from her purse. "My cell number is on this."

Holding up her gloved hands, Letty nodded at a nearby duffel bag. "Stick it in my bag."

"Thanks." Delaney did as she was told. "And thanks for the session earlier. I know what I need to work on. Everything."

"Conditioning is important too. Run. Jump rope. Work the bag. Get a regular sparring partner."

"Got it."

As soon as they were out the door, Hunter lit into her. "What were you thinking?"

"I was thinking you don't walk into a place like that and ask to talk to a drug kingpin."

"So you get in the ring with a professional boxer?"

"It really was fun." *Fun* wasn't the right word. It didn't even come close. "There's something about using every muscle in your body to keep from getting obliterated that gets the endorphins flowing. Total fight-or-flight reaction. Adrenaline through the roof."

"I've never seen this side of you."

"You've been gone a long time. A lot has changed." She patted the truck's hood as she walked around it. "Most of it good. It's better than living in the past."

"I'm not living in the past. I'm trying to put it to rest."

"I'm a different person than I was when we were together." Delaney sucked in crisp spring air. The sky seemed bluer than it had before the sparring match. Hunter looked good. Only the truck's solid structure between them kept her from throwing her arms around his waist and kissing him. *It's the adrenaline. Just the adrenaline.* "I don't need a man to survive."

"I never thought you did." His expression bemused, Hunter fumbled his keys, dropped them, disappeared for a second, then reappeared. "I'm just saying you look good from where I stand."

"Good."

"So what now?" He unlocked the truck and opened the door.

"We wait to see if this shark guy takes the bait."

"And in the meantime?"

"I think I'm finally hungry." The revelation startled Delaney. She went with it. "I think I'd like a steak. On me."

CHAPTER 29

"I think yesterday's drive-by is unrelated." Andy threw the thought out for Flores's benefit as his partner started his car in preparation for driving them to Charlene Capstone-Hill's house. "The drive-by shooting didn't fit. Their killer preferred knives."

"You think it was a gang thing?" Flores always found Andy's wavelength.

"I think we should ask the Gang Task Force to check it out for us. Eloy Sandoval said a couple of those boys got into a fight on the court half an hour before the drive-by. He sent one of them packing."

"It's possible, but it's also possible Nash's contention that Corey was killed because he tried to back out of a deal with Tango Orejón has some bit of truth in it. They wouldn't want that kind of attention.

"On the other hand, Ellie Hill's killer told Ms. Broward to stay out of it." Flores pulled from the HQ parking garage and grabbed the ramp to IH-10 W. "She obviously hasn't. Maybe it was a warning."

"It's possible, but the more I think about it, the more it doesn't fit."

It wouldn't hurt to explore all possibilities. Andy made the call to a task force detective with whom he'd gone to the academy while Flores maneuvered in rush-hour traffic to the exit that led to 281 and headed north.

First stop of the day: Charlene Capstone-Hill.

Michael Hill had gone from one extreme to the other in his choice of wives. Capstone-Hill, a tall, willowy woman, could've walked off a New York catwalk. Dressed in a pink silk blouse and navy capris that showed off an hourglass figure, she waved them into her home without questioning their presence at her door on a beautiful morning. She guided Andy and Flores into her living room where she offered cranberry-oatmeal muffins and fresh smoothies as if they were invited guests.

At Pilar's insistence Andy had eaten a bowl of granola and Greek yogurt with blueberries for breakfast. Gone were the bachelor days of breakfast tacos of chorizo and eggs. He declined the offer while Flores asked if coffee might be an option. It was.

"Nice digs." Flores waited until Capstone-Hill left the room to make the observation. "If you like a southwest vibe."

Andy didn't. He left the interior decorating to Pilar, and she preferred something she called country living. As long as it meant she lived with him, he was happy.

Hill's ex-wife lived in a northeast-side subdivision with cookie-cutter houses built by a developer most interested in stretching construction dollars with a bare minimum of amenities. Andy settled onto a soft leather sectional while Flores grabbed one of two wingback chairs. Photos on the fireplace mantel featured the two kids and no one else. A southwest art print adorned the wall over it. Nothing more. No fuss, no muss.

"We haven't seen her ex's place yet. It's in Monte Vista. You can imagine what that'll be like." Another go-round with Hill was on their list for the day, but Andy wanted to gather ammunition first. "He must be doing well to afford that neighborhood."

Monte Vista was an affluent neighborhood with homes designed by famous architects dating back to the late 1800s when cattle and oil barons had lived there. Andy might have a photographic memory, but when it came to architecture and history, he was picky about what he chose to remember.

Capstone-Hill returned with the coffee on a silver tray a few minutes later. "Now how can I help two of San Antonio's finest?" She eased onto the other wingback and crossed her ankles in a demure pose. "I assume this is about my ex-husband's wife."

"It is." Andy dove in. "I notice you're still using Hill's name, as in Capstone-Hill?"

"As much as I'd love to ditch the jerk's name, I want to have the same last name as the kids, so I compromised. Call me Charlene, please."

"How long were you married to Michael Hill?"

"Twelve years. Twelve long years." She took a sip of her smoothie and sighed. "Don't get me wrong. We had good years. Very good years. But Michael insisted we had to have kids. All our friends did. I finally caved to the pressure. We had Jacob. But that wasn't enough. We had to have two. So along came Skye."

"You didn't want kids?" Flores perked up. Andy's temporary partner had taken plenty of guff from his family when he and his wife chose not to produce offspring. "It's not that unusual in this day and age."

"Don't get me wrong. I love my kids dearly." She tilted her head, showing off a long, elegant neck, and patted her chignon with fingers that ended in shiny pink nails. The sound of children laughing floated into the room from somewhere in the interior. "You hear that? Who doesn't love it? Kids are fun. They're sweet. They're also a full-time job. I have one of those. Michael wasn't going to give up his career for them. He's also a tightwad. He waffled when I asked him about a live-in nanny. I needed concessions. He refused to budge. He wanted me to quit flying. I refused. When I suggested my parents move in with us, he went through the roof."

"Who asked for the divorce?"

"What do these questions have to do with Ellie Cruz's death?"

That she didn't use Ellie's married name wasn't lost on Andy. He stepped into the fray. "We're trying to understand the dynamics of their marriage."

"Is he a suspect? I mean, they always say on the TV shows that the spouse is the number-one suspect in a murder." Her smile morphed into a smirk. "Followed, of course, by any ex-spouses, boyfriends, girl-friends, etc."

"At this point we haven't eliminated anyone."

"So you're checking me out?"

"To be frank, yes."

"Michael asked for the divorce, but it was mutual. I knew the writing was on the wall. I wasn't maternal enough, womanly enough, for him. I wasn't getting any younger. I never figured Michael for the type to turn in his wife for a younger model, but I figured wrong." Her hands, devoid of rings and wrinkles, spread in a what-can-I-say gesture. "We were very young and just starting in our careers when we married. We grew up and grew apart—at least he did."

She didn't appear that old. She didn't have an ounce of fat on her. Her muscles were toned, her skin tight. The blonde color of her hair seemed natural enough, but Andy wasn't a particularly good judge of such things. Pilar had dark-brown hair that started to streak with silver soon after she turned thirty. "Are you telling us there's no hard feelings?"

"Not until he tried to get full custody and his attorney suggested to the judge that I was an absentee mother, that the children needed more stability than I could offer."

The sound of laughter turned to a shriek and then crying.

Capstone-Hill didn't seem to notice.

His dark eyes perturbed, Flores shifted in his chair. "Did you need to see about that?"

After another sip of her smoothie, she shook her head. "No, my mother is with them. They love her more than me, which is fine. Better than them loving Michael's new wife more and calling her mommy."

So there were hard feelings. Enough to kill Ellie Hill? "So you didn't think highly of the new Mrs. Hill?"

"The Mother Earth thing got old. Michael was infatuated, but I couldn't for the life of me see it. She acted like a woman suffering from arrested development. I was biding my time to take him back to court once I had evidence that she smoked pot. She was also the girlfriend of an artist who was murdered. Who's to say she didn't kill him?"

"The man who killed her boyfriend was convicted and sent to prison."

"Maybe she was an accomplice. Maybe she paid him to do it. Sometimes the police are sloppy. They get their guy and don't dig any deeper."

She had no problem speaking ill of the dead—or the police. "How did you know about the pot and the murdered boyfriend?"

"Truth? I hired a private investigator after Michael decided to marry her so soon after the divorce."

Jackpot. "What did you learn?"

"She floated around like a spirit fairy because she smoked pot every chance she got. She bought it from some old friend who works as a nightclub bouncer. Just what I need, a stoned woman taking care of my kids. I was all ready to contact my attorney when she was murdered."

"What else did your PI discover about the new Mrs. Hill?"

"She wasn't as innocent as she pretended to be." Capstone-Hill's nose wrinkled in obvious distaste. "The PI got photos of her meeting a man at a restaurant on the south side. More than once. Mother Earth was cheating on her new husband."

Bingo. "Do you have those photos?"

"I do." She rose and left the room.

A few seconds later she returned and laid an envelope on the glass table in front of Andy. Flores stood and maneuvered to peer over his shoulder. The photos were identical to those Delaney had discovered in Ellie's shop. "Mrs. Hill possessed copies of these same photos. How do you suppose that happened?"

Capstone-Hill's full lips curled into a frown. "I have no idea. I planned to spring them on Michael at the custody hearing. I liked the element of surprise."

"Are you sure you didn't engage in a spot of blackmail to try to get her to encourage her husband to give you custody?"

"Of course not."

It would be impossible to prove otherwise with the victim of the alleged blackmail now dead. "What about the private investigator? Could he have engaged in some extracurricular blackmail?"

"He didn't strike me as that sleezy. He's a retired police officer. You might know him." She pulled a business card from the folder and handed it to Andy. "His rates were astronomical, but he came through and I didn't feel like he padded his hours."

Andy studied the card. Phil Tremaine. The name didn't ring a bell. Andy handed it to Flores who glanced at it, shook his head, and returned it. "Was he able to identify the man in the car?"

"He said the car's license plate number came back to a woman named Leah Pritchard. He was supposed to let me know where that took him. It's been a week or more since I heard from him."

"May I keep the card?"

"Surely. I have his information."

Andy stood. "Thank you for your time."

"Y'all must think I'm a coldhearted person, but Michael made sure my children spent more time with a virtual stranger than they did with their own mother. That tends to leave a mark."

"It's not our job to pass judgment." Their job was to find a killer. If Capstone-Hill hired a private investigator, what was to say she didn't also hire someone to take out the woman usurping her rightful place as mother to her children? "Why do you suppose Ellie Cruz married your ex-husband if she was involved with someone else?"

"Money, I suppose. Michael's done well with his firm. I understand he's taken on some big clients in the last year." She glanced at her smart watch. "I really need to pack or I'll be late to the airport."

Surprise flitted across Flores's face. "You don't need to stick around to make sure the kids aren't traumatized by what's happened and that they're safe?"

"I still have to pay my bills. Michael has primary custody so I don't get child support from him." Capstone-Hill moved toward the hallway. "The swine—Michael, not the judge—acted like it was only fair since I make what he called *good money* as a flight attendant."

She paused. Her mouth opened, then closed. Her expression clouded. "What do you mean? Safe?"

Hill hadn't shared his concerns about the children's safety with his ex-wife. Andy exchanged glances with Flores. His expression said, "Be my guest."

"Maybe you should sit back down."

"What's going on?" She wavered, glanced at her watch again, then sat on the edge of the couch. "I don't have much time."

"Your husband thinks one of his clients might have killed Mrs. Hill.

He's afraid he may send someone after him and/or the kids to make a point. He didn't tell you about this?"

"No. No. He didn't." Her face a molten red, the woman's voice rose a full octave. "No wonder he agreed to let the kids stay with me, even knowing I had to work. What is wrong with that man?"

Other than he seemed distraught over the death of his new wife, full of guilt and self-loathing, and fearful for his own life? Other than being a suspect in her murder? "We're working to determine if his fears are based in reality. But we thought you should be aware of his concerns."

"I'll have my parents take them to their cabin in Cloudcroft until this is straightened out." She rose a second time and strode toward the door. "Now you really do need to go."

She stopped, hand on the door, seeming to compose herself. "Of course, thank you for sharing that information with me. You're far more decent than Michael."

"If something should come of Mr. Hill's concerns, we'll inform you."

Capstone-Hill opened the door. Flores went out first. Andy had to ask one more question. "If you disliked Ellie so much, why not tell Michael straight out about the pot or the cheating? He might've divorced her. Problem solved."

"He divorces her and the custody agreement remains status quo. I needed to be able to take my findings to the judge." Capstone-Hill sniffed and wrinkled her nose again. "Of course, if it turns out he killed her, they'll end up with me anyway."

"Do you think he's capable of murder?"

"Isn't everyone, under the right circumstances?"

She was a smart woman. "So what are you going to do now?"

"Ask for a hearing to determine Michael's fitness as a parent, given the death of his new spouse and the environment the children have been living in. They're traumatized. There's a chance he might even be a murderer."

Or framed as a murderer by an ex-wife who would stoop to whatever means necessary to make her ex-husband pay and keep him from seeing his children.

"We'll be in touch."

Capstone-Hill's elaborate shrug matched her cool expression. "I have no doubt. I'll be back in town in three days."

Flores waited until Capstone-Hill closed the door to explode. Just barely. "People never cease to amaze me. I've seen some pretty self-absorbed people in my life, but man, she takes the prize. I pity those kids. At least Michael Hill is concerned."

Being judgmental wasn't acceptable either, but Andy couldn't help but agree with Flores. Hill and his wife both wanted the kids—so the other couldn't have them. "A tug-of-war with two young children as the rope." *God, help them.*

"I say we add getting that warrant for her financials and phone records to our to-do list today."

"You betcha."

CHAPTER 30

Could Michael Hill know about his new wife's extracurricular activity? Perhaps he'd seen the photos that were sent to his wife and kept quiet until the moment he deemed right for exacting his revenge. Andy mulled that scenario while Flores manhandled the unmarked PD vehicle into traffic and headed south to Hill's home north of San Antonio's downtown district.

The sun's glare forced Andy to lower the sun visor. It didn't help. He slid on his Ray-Bans and leaned his head against the headrest. Robert Cray's "Smoking Gun" provided food for thought. They could use one of those in this case—or more fittingly a smoking knife.

"Hill went shopping for a new wife after the first one refused to fit in his mold." Flores had a habit of reading Andy's mind. "Then he finds out wife number two is just as independent minded and she's already cheating on him."

"That's a good theory. It needs evidence to give it legs to stand on."

"Maybe the PI has something we can work with. Change of plan?"

"Sounds good."

"Read me the address on the card and I'll get us there."

The private investigator had an office near the Bexar County Courthouse. The Craftsman-style house had been converted into law offices, but a sign on the door led them to Suite 100 where the words PHILLIP TREMAINE JR. INVESTIGATIVE AGENCY had been stenciled onto the door's opaque window.

"Very noir-ish." Flores grinned as he grabbed the doorknob. "I feel like I should be a dame in a tight-fitting skirt clutching a purse and a hankie."

Andy rolled his eyes and let his temporary partner go first. "If he has a feisty receptionist and smells like whiskey, I want my money for my ticket back."

Tremaine had no receptionist, even though he looked more like an attorney in his expensive navy suit and silk tie. A recumbent bike took up one corner of the spacious office that featured a large picture window overlooking the Main Avenue traffic. "I'm always happy to help my brothers in blue." Tremaine flipped a letter opener through his fingers like a drum majorette handling a baton. "What can I do for you?"

Andy took a seat on a soft-as-velvet leather chair and ran through the preliminaries. "Ms. Capstone-Hill shared with us that she hired you to follow the new Mrs. Hill. There's no issue with client confidentiality. She sent us to you."

Tremaine dropped the letter opener and rolled in his chair from his desk to a filing cabinet against the opposite wall. "Charlene Capstone-Hill. A lovely lady with a viper's tongue."

An apt description.

He pulled a folder from the first drawer and rolled back to his desk in a nifty, energy-efficient slide. "I showed her a series of photos—"

"Yes, we've seen your photos—twice." Flores, who'd chosen to remain standing near the picture window, didn't hide his impatience. "What we're trying to figure out is how they came to be in our victim's

242

possession. The prevalent theory is that someone was blackmailing her with them."

"Ellie Hill had copies of the photos?" Frowning, Tremaine scratched at his trendy five o'clock shadow. He shrugged. "She didn't get them from me. The problem with your theory is that the blackmailer wouldn't have killed his or her source of income. Why would she have kept the photos?"

"So how did she get the photos?"

"I have no idea. I never approached the woman—per Charlene's instructions." Now Tremaine had shifted to a full-out scowl. His right leg did a jig, his foot tapping on the carpet. "Nor did I share the photos with anyone except my client."

So why did he show all the signs of a man searching for an escape hatch? Andy leaned forward and held Tremaine's gaze. Sometimes it helped to switch topics and work his way in through a back door. "What can you tell me about the man she had these Wednesday morning breakfasts with?"

"Stocky build. Average height. White. Blond hair. Too far away to get eye color."

"How old?"

"From a distance it's hard to say. I couldn't see his face. Could've been twenties, could've been thirties. His hair wasn't gray, so not too old."

So vague. "You didn't try to see his face, to identify him?"

"When I drove up he was already in the car, getting ready to leave." The foot tapped harder. "I barely got the photos you've seen. He drove away and I never saw him again."

"A witness at the restaurant described him as being more into her than she was into him. Does that strike you as accurate?"

"Again, I didn't enter the restaurant. My instructions were to follow her, document where she went, and take pictures." Tremaine closed the folder with a definitive snap. "Ms. Capstone-Hill didn't want her ex-husband to know she'd hired me. I was not to be seen under any circumstances. Any slipup and I was toast. I don't like your insinuations. I'm trying to help you because I used to be you."

"What about the photos at the hotel?"

"They're self-explanatory."

"I don't see a gray Camry or any sign of the man from the restaurant."

"I waited around for a while. He never came out."

"Maybe you bugged out before he left."

"Like I said, I don't like your insinuations."

"We appreciate your cooperation, Phil." Andy summoned a placating tone. "When did you retire and start your agency?"

"Three years ago. I did my twenty on the streets too. No cushy desk jobs."

Which explained why Andy hadn't run into him before. He made a mental note to check into the investigator's personnel record. "You're still relatively young."

"I work at it. I run. I stay in shape." He flexed his biceps as if Andy could see his muscles through a long-sleeved white dress shirt. "I refuse to be a walking cliché. I don't even like donuts."

"I'm with you there." Andy glanced at Flores. "I'm more of a lean red meat guy myself."

His nod was almost imperceptible. Andy had primed the pump. "What about the car? What can you tell us about it?"

"Gray four-door Toyota Camry. Several years old. It had seen better days."

Delaney Broward's employee had seen a gray Camry parked outside La Villita in the days prior to Mrs. Hill's murder and the break-in.

"The plates aren't visible in the photos. Were you able to get the number before he drove off?"

"I did."

"Did you run them?"

"PIs can't run plates." Tremaine's lazy smile boasted that he knew he'd avoided a trap. "I run an aboveboard, legit business. You guys need to stop reading so many crime novels."

"Ms. Capstone-Hill said you traced the car back to a woman named Leah Pritchard."

"So I still have friends in SAPD." Tremaine's bravado leaked away. "Whose names shall remain confidential."

"We don't care about that." Flores chose a more conciliatory tone. "We're trying to apprehend a killer."

Tremaine reopened the folder. He perused the contents for a second. "Leah Pritchard. White. Eighty-two. Widowed. Enjoying life in an assisted living community. According to her Facebook profile."

Everyone had a social media profile these days. Everyone except Andy. And probably Flores. "Children? A son who could be using her car?"

"I don't know. I sent a friend request. She never responded. Which isn't surprising. A lot of women have become more savvy about their online presence and their safety. I can't see her posts. She doesn't make them public."

He leaned back in his chair and stared at the ceiling, as if seeking wisdom from on high. "I did a search of Bexar County properties. She owns a house on West Malone Avenue. I'm betting she has family members living there."

"But you didn't check it out?"

"When I read in the paper that Ellie Hill had been murdered, I figured Charlene would no longer need my services. I picked up a couple of other cases so I've been busy elsewhere." Tremaine's phone dinged as if on cue. He picked it up, scrolled through a text, frowned, and laid it aside. "If that's all, I've got other business to tend to."

Andy studied the PI's expression. Somewhere between impatience and studied indifference. "Just a few more questions. Do you think she's capable of hiring someone to kill her husband's new wife?"

"If she did, she didn't share that information with me."

"That's not an answer."

"She reminds me of the Evil Queen in *Snow White*. She wants to be the fairest of all and she's willing to have Snow White killed to maintain her title."

"I don't think I'll be reading that fairy tale to my daughters." Andy stood and moved toward the door in tandem with Flores. "Thank you for your time. If you learn anything else, we'd appreciate a call."

Tremaine trailed after them. "Do you really think Charlene had her competition knocked off?"

"We're investigating all avenues and leads."

"Come on, guys, don't give me the standard line. I'm one of you."

"Used to be one of us. I thought you were through with your case." Andy held out his hand. "I would've thought you'd be in a hurry to bill your client."

Tremaine shook, but his expression was that of a man trying to learn to tap dance. "Charlene called me about twenty minutes before you showed up. Just to give me a heads-up. She said to email her the invoice."

"So you told her about Leah Pritchard's whereabouts?"

"It's not like she'll put a hit out on a little old lady."

Andy wasn't so sure of that.

At the car Flores dug the keys from his pocket and tossed them to Andy. "Your turn to drive. So, what do you think of our friendly brother-in-blue-turned-PI?"

"He said all the right things." Andy caught the keys but didn't move to get in the car. Something about Tremaine didn't set right with him. "But his body language told a different story. He knows more than he's telling us."

"Not only that, he's lying about something."

"But what, exactly?"

Flores growled, brushed by Andy, and tugged open the passenger-side door. "What's really eating at me is, how did Mrs. Hill end up with those photos? It had to be him. The ex-wife still had her copy."

"A spot of blackmail by our friendly PI?"

"He's right about one thing, why would he kill her? You can't blackmail a dead woman."

"So maybe he tried to blackmail her and the secret lover didn't want her telling anyone."

Flores smacked the hood of the car and then folded his long body into it. "With Mrs. Hill dead, the only way to know is to find the killer. Then maybe we can nail Tremaine too. Are you getting in or what?"

Andy bit back an irritated retort. Flores was right. He jogged around the car and got in. "We keep following the bread crumbs. Next up, a visit with Ms. Pritchard."

"I can't help but notice that we're only a few blocks from Rosario's."

The rumbling of Andy's stomach ratcheted up a notch. Rosario's served his favorite tacos de carnitas. He glanced at his phone. "It is lunchtime. It's probably lunchtime at the nursing home too."

"Do you think our intrepid PI is headed out there?"

Chuckling, Andy yanked open the car door. "I don't think his chair rolls that far."

"Rosario's, here we come."

Chips and pico de gallo and a side of chile con queso. What Pilar didn't know wouldn't hurt her.

CHAPTER 31

Leah Pritchard might reside in an assisted living community just south of downtown San Antonio, but she needed no assistance in expressing her opinion. Andy had opened his mouth several times in an attempt to slow the flow before he and Flores even entered her tiny unit. To no avail.

When they arrived shortly after a quick lunch, Mrs. Pritchard had surveyed their badges, harrumphed loudly, and allowed them in her apartment only after they carefully wiped their feet on her welcome rug—three times. Then she proceeded to rant about the criminal elements allowed free reign in her city by the likes of policemen like the two sitting in her living room.

Andy nodded, nodded again, and finally broke in. "Ma'am . . . ma'am. Ma'am!"

"Don't ma'am me." She shook a finger gnarled with arthritis at Andy. "You come in here asking me about a car I haven't driven in five years, not telling me what it's all about. You wave your badges around like that gives you the right to interrogate an old woman who hasn't had a valid driver's license in years. I may live in an old folks' home, but I still pay property taxes. I pay your salaries."

"Of course you do, Mrs. Pritchard." His heartburn—thanks to

Rosario's pico de gallo—flamed higher, but they were getting nowhere fast and they did indeed have work to do on the taxpayers' dime. "If you'll calm down—"

"Don't tell me to calm down. How dare you—"

"Zip it up." Flores made a zipping motion with his index finger and thumb. "My partner will explain why we're asking about the car."

She opened her mouth. Flores zipped his lips a second time. She glowered, but her mouth closed.

"The car is in some photos taken of a woman who was murdered last week." Andy squelched the desire to pinch his nose. The sweet, cloying scent of potpourri fought with a peculiar odor he associated with his grandmother's feet when his mother used to clip her toenails. "We're trying to trace the occupant seen with the woman."

"Who was this woman?"

"Her name was Ellie Hill. Ellie Cruz before she had married."

Mrs. Pritchard tapped her teeth with a yellowed fingernail for a few seconds. "I don't know her."

"You haven't driven the car in five years. I take it you gave it to someone. Who would that be?"

"I have several leeches in my family. My son likes to mooch off me. He lives in my house with his wife, who works a lot more than he does, I'm sorry to say." Mrs. Pritchard smoothed her green pantsuit's polyester fabric, even though it wouldn't dare wrinkle. "It was his idea for me to move in here. Very convenient for him. But they have one of those fancy SUVs. They don't need an old car like mine."

"Who else then? Does he have children who might drive it?"

"My family visits me once in a blue moon." Mrs. Pritchard popped up from her glider rocker and waddled in fuzzy pink bedroom slippers across the tiny living room to the counter that separated it from a galley kitchen. She snatched a tissue from a box decorated with a pink crocheted cover. "There was talk about giving it to my grandson. He's what they call learning disabled. He tries, but he's not very bright and people are always taking advantage of him. The school counselor once told my son that Vince has poor impulse control. I call it poor parenting. A swift kick in the seat of the pants would've cured him of some of his bad habits."

"It would be helpful to have their names."

She availed herself of the tissue with a big honking snort and tossed it in a wastebasket at her feet. "They didn't have anything to do with this woman's death."

"How do you know that?"

"Art doesn't have the gumption and poor Vince doesn't have the brains."

Was that a recommendation? "Are both your son and grandson happily married?"

"Art's been married to his second wife for twenty-five years. Cancer took the first one. All he does is complain, but the woman is a saint. How she puts up with him, I'll never know. Vince is Art's youngest of five. He's one of those guys who's always looked for love in the wrong places. He divorced once and the current wife wants a divorce. She's trying to keep him from seeing his kids. Vince may not be all that bright, but he's a good daddy from what I've been told."

"You think he has the car."

"Maybe."

The sound of a cricket squeaking emanated from the phone lying on the counter. Mrs. Pritchard grabbed it. "A text from my friend Nadine. You'll have to go. Unless you're good at canasta. Canasta, pinochle, or bridge. It's game day in the community center." She scooped up an oversized purse and swept past them. "Run along, run along."

Like they were pesky children in her way.

"Where does Vince live?"

"How do I know? Ask his father." She had the door open. "Out, out, out."

Out they went.

"Thank you for your time." Flores's tone was dry. "You've been so helpful."

Waving with both hands and still wearing her bedroom slippers, Mrs. Pritchard trotted down a sidewalk lined with esperanza, Pride of Barbados, and fire bushes. "Too-da-loo."

"We're two for two on women who are pieces of work today." Chuckling, Flores removed his glasses and wiped them with a cloth he'd extracted from his pocket. "Do you want to check out the son or the grandson next?"

Andy glanced at his phone. "It's after two. I want to talk to Hill again today, and we need to get back to HQ to fill out the warrant paperwork. Let's save the Pritchard men for later. It may be a rabbit hole anyway."

"Not if one of them fits the description of the man Tremaine saw with Ellie."

"If you can call that a description. Her son would be too old. Vince Pritchard, maybe."

"True. If we have time after we talk to Hill, we'll head that way. Otherwise, we can do it in the morning."

Flores's phone played a B. B. King tune. "Give me a minute. I'll catch up with you."

Andy headed for the car. A few minutes later Flores slid into the driver's seat. "My mom's running a fever. I need to head over to the rehab center. Sorry about that."

"No worries. Family first." Andy was blessed to have two healthy parents. Flores's dad was in a memory unit at an assisted living center, while his mother, who recently fell and broke her hip, had been moved to a rehab facility. "Just drop me at my SUV. I'll take it from here and we can regroup tomorrow."

"It really stinks seeing them like this." Flores hunched over the wheel and started the engine. "If my mind goes first, take me out and shoot me, will you? If my body gives out but my mind is trapped in my body, same thing."

"How about I pray instead?"

Flores grunted. He wasn't much of a praying man. "Whatever turns your crank," he muttered.

CHAPTER 32

If looks could kill, Delaney would be as dead as an armadillo in the middle of IH-10 in West Texas. Delaney refused to slink into Michael's living room despite Detective Ramos's eviscerating glower when she opened the door to allow him entry. Unlike Detective Ramos, she'd been invited. Cam had left to teach a class, but Jess was here. Fortunately. A third interview might mean Michael had moved up the suspect list.

The reason for Michael's invitation had become apparent immediately. He wanted to know what Delaney knew about the police investigation into Ellie's murder. Which wasn't much. Now they would hear what Detective Ramos was willing to share. Which wouldn't be much, no doubt.

"Have you figured out who was shooting at us yesterday?" She slid the question in while they were still in the hallway that led to the living room where Michael had sat slack-mouthed, staring into space since she arrived an hour earlier. "Do you think it was related to Ellie's murder?"

After all, the assailant had told Delaney to stay out of it. The question became how he knew she would be in the park adjacent to Cassiano Homes. She hadn't even known it until that morning.

"We're exploring a few scenarios." Detective Ramos shot Delaney a cranky glare. "No wonder your nose is such a mess. You're in worse shape than you were yesterday."

"It's big. It gets in the way a lot."

He didn't need to know about her foray into professional boxing.

"You're blessed to have survived. I hope you learned a lesson."

Blessed to have survived the boxing too. Again, none of his business.

"I learned that we're getting close to something that unnerved the killer." Delaney had left Hunter with that thought when he dropped her off at her shop the previous day. They hadn't talked about that moment on the ground, bullets flying, when his body had covered hers. Or the seconds afterward when his arms cradled her. Her muscles had turned to water—surely from fear, not desire.

She had spent most of the night reliving those moments, seared into her brain, full of longing. "You're not following up on Hunter's drug distribution theory, so we decided to do it ourselves."

"Number one, you have no idea what we've followed up on." Detective Ramos stopped to stare at an enormous framed photo of Michael and Ellie on their wedding day, the Gulf of Mexico behind them, Skye and Jacob building a sand castle in the distance. "Number two, you have no business doing anything with a convicted murderer."

"We're on to a completely different scenario and it's promising." He moved closer and squinted at some detail in the foreground. "It has nothing to do with drugs. It's much more personal than that. It leaves your brother's murder in the past where it belongs and focuses on what happened to Mrs. Hill and why."

Fine. Delaney moved straight ahead to the arched door that opened into the living room. "Michael, the detective is here to talk to you."

Jess looked up from the files he was examining. "You've already talked to my client twice. What could you possibly need to know now?"

"Let the man do his job, Jess." Michael moved to the grand piano in the corner where he sat on the bench. He fingered the keys, playing a few melancholy notes. "It'll be over a lot sooner."

"Fine, but don't answer any questions unless I say so." Jess set aside the files. He transferred from the couch to a wingback chair closer to the piano. "You're the husband of the victim. Unless he's here to update you on any progress they've made in the case, he has no business bothering you at a time like this."

"You know better. The husband's always a suspect." Michael kept playing. The melody became clear. One of Chopin's nocturnes.

Delaney's knowledge of classical music wouldn't fill a notebook page, but Ellie liked to show off what she'd learned from her spouse whenever Michael had played while she and Delaney huddled on the couch chatting. She said Michael played well. Delaney took her word for it.

At the moment his music mourned a deep loss. "If you're going to arrest me, Detective, now's the time to do it. The kids are with their mother. I'm not doing anything in particular today."

"Why would we arrest you?" Detective Ramos eased onto the matching wingback chair, which allowed him to face the piano and the pianist. "Are you confessing to something?"

"I'm guilty of putting my wife in danger. I'm guilty of not protecting her." His head down, Michael leaned into the piece as his fingers stroked the keys. "I'm guilty of working for a hoodlum disguised as a businessman."

"That's a beautiful piece you're playing." Ramos relaxed in the chair. His hands rested in his lap. For once his omnipresent notebook remained stowed away. "Frédéric Chopin is one of my wife's favorite composers."

"Does she play?"

"She does." Detective Ramos closed his eyes. "Not as much right now, with two little girls and another on the way. But when she does it's magic. She's planning to teach our girls to play."

"I tried teaching Jacob. He hated it. Skye can play Chopsticks and 'Twinkle, Twinkle, Little Star.'"

"That's a start." Detective Ramos opened a manilla envelope and pulled out several photos—those very same photos of Ellie and the unnamed man. He laid them out on the coffee table. "I need you to look at these photos and tell me what you think they mean."

Michael kept playing. "They don't mean what you think they mean."

"Which is?"

"Ellie wasn't cheating on me."

"How do you know?"

"She told me she'd once cheated on a boyfriend and it had terrible consequences, ones she found it hard to live with. She told me she'd never do it again."

"Which boyfriend?" Delaney's determination to be a fly on the wall flew out the window. Ellie had boyfriends before Corey and a few after, though none serious until Michael. "What consequences?"

"She didn't say and I didn't ask." Michael's playing didn't falter. The famous piece, called a nocturne because it spoke of contemplation and repose brought on by nighttime, was short, but he simply repeated it. "Why would I want to know the sordid details of her past? I certainly didn't need to know she'd cheated on Corey or whoever it was."

"You think it was Corey?"

"Ms. Broward, do you mind?" Detective Ramos's glare singed Delaney's eyebrows. "I'll ask the questions. If you can't be quiet, you should leave the room."

"Can you two stop bickering long enough to focus on finding the monster who murdered my wife?" Michael smashed his hands on the keys. The discordant notes injured the air after such a beautiful piece of music. He slid around on the bench so he faced the detective. "Let's get this over with, shall we? What do you want to know? Did I kill my wife? No. Do I know who did? I told you. Gerard Knox. Am I responsible? Yes. Now let me ask you a question. When will my wife's body be released so I can give her a proper burial?"

"We plan to interview Mr. Knox." Detective Ramos sat forward, propping his elbows on his knees and clasping his hands. "The medical examiner's office will call you when her body is ready to be released. It shouldn't be much longer."

"What do you want to know?"

Detective Ramos slid the photos out from under the tray. He rearranged them so they told a story—a story no one who knew Ellie could believe. Or wanted to believe. "Do you recognize the car in these photos?"

"I do not."

"Did you know your wife regularly had breakfast with a man at a south-side restaurant?"

"Don't answer that, Michael." Jess rose and went to stand next to the piano, as if guarding his client. "Whether you know is neither here nor there."

"I did not." Michael lowered his head and stared at the Oriental rug under his feet. "She told me she had SBA committee meetings. She said it helped her keep up-to-date on business practices."

"Did you know your wife smoked pot?"

"Don't answer that." Jess shook his head, his expression fierce. "Listen to your attorney."

"She never did it in front of me, but sometimes I got a whiff of it on her clothes." Michael plowed onward. "Sometimes her breath smelled like an overdose of peppermint. I knew she was covering it up. I didn't care if she smoked as long as she didn't do it around the kids or when she was supposed to be taking care of them."

Even though it was illegal. Even though drug use had contributed to Corey's demise.

Delaney clasped her hands in front of her. Her fingernails dug into her skin. What had Ellie been thinking? Did it make her feel closer to Corey? Surely it made her miss him more.

"If you knew, why didn't you stop her?" So what if Detective Ramos had told her to be quiet. Her best friend was dead. Drugs could have played a role. Hunter might be right. "I'm sorry, Detective, but drugs have caused nothing but heartache for Ellie and me. I can't imagine why she would take up such a horrible habit again."

"It's not a bad question." Ramos finally pulled the ubiquitous notebook from his pocket. The stubby pencil followed. "It's illegal and it meant she was consorting with a dealer to get her stash. That's always dangerous."

"My biggest mistake in my first marriage, hindsight being twenty-twenty, was to try to marry a woman thinking I could change her. I loved Ellie for who she was. Free-spirited, smart, funny, quirky, whimsical." Michael's shoulders hunched. He closed his eyes. He rubbed his temples. "So she smoked pot and reeked of patchouli and liked to listen to Bob Dylan on scratchy 45 rpm records. I loved her."

"Did you know your ex-wife hired a private detective to investigate your new wife?"

A string of expletives met that question.

"I take it the answer is no."

The question opened up a whole new can of investigative worms. The private investigator, along with the former Mrs. Hill, could know who the driver of the car was. They might know just how far this relationship went. "Why did she do it? What did she find out?"

"Delaney!" Detective Ramos shot her the evil eye. "Do not speak."

"Whatever happened to the First Amendment?"

"Hush."

Michael shot up from the piano bench. He paced to the fireplace and back. "Charlene is a vindictive b—"

"We get the idea." Detective Ramos adopted the softened tone one would use with a volatile suspect about to blow. "She told us she hired him because she wanted a better custody arrangement, not because she disliked your new wife or that you had married again."

"I'm sure she did her best to cast herself as the aggrieved victim. She likely forgot to mention how often she leaves the kids with her parents while she flies all over the country, gone days and nights at a time."

Jess stepped into his client's path. "Please sit down. And try to stop talking. Please."

Amazingly, Michael took his advice and returned to the piano bench. Jess faced Detective Ramos like an attorney delivering a closing argument in front of a jury box. "Michael has spoken often about his ex-wife's desire to get full custody even though her job is not conducive to full-time parenthood. She wants the children because she didn't want my client and his new wife to have them. Especially Ellie. And now that's not a problem anymore. Which sounds like motive to me."

"Except she was going to ask the judge for full custody after presenting the evidence that Ellie was promiscuous and using illicit drugs—possibly around impressionable children." Detective Ramos consulted his notebook, as if he needed help remembering. He probably recalled Corey's shoe size. "With Mrs. Hill's murder, she's pivoting to your client not providing a safe environment for them and the fact that he is a person of interest in his dead wife's murder."

"Promiscuous? Charlene of all people would stoop that low. Ask her about the layovers in Atlanta and a certain pilot." Michael scrubbed both hands over his bald head and emitted a low growl. "She should be a person of interest—more than that, a suspect. She resented Ellie. She hated her."

"Believe me, we're looking at everyone in your wife's circle of acquaintances. Do you know who sold her the pot?"

"No. But it has to be someone from the co-op."

Likely Billy. He made no secret of the fact that he supplemented his income by selling small quantities of pot.

Delaney kept her mouth shut. Billy had nothing to do with Ellie's death. He had no reason to kill her. Like everyone else, he was half in love with her.

Fortunately, Detective Ramos moved on without pressing the issue. "Do you know a woman named Leah Pritchard or a man named Art Pritchard and/or his son Vince Pritchard?"

Delaney bit her lip to keep a flood of new questions from escaping. The Pritchards must have landed on the private investigator's radar. How and why?

"The names don't ring any bells."

"Are you sure?" Detective Ramos leaned forward. "You didn't pay the Pritchard men to kill your wife after you'd found out she was cheating on you? Did the PI Phil Tremaine contact you and offer the information for a price? Did you decide to put a stop to your ex-wife's plan by getting rid of your new wife?"

"No. No, I'm not a killer—"

"That's enough." Jess moved so he stood next to Michael. "Unless you're arresting Michael, and we all know you don't have any evidence that would give you probable cause to do that, we're done here. I'm sure Delaney will be happy to escort you out."

"My partner is busy getting a warrant for your financials, Mr. Hill. If we see any large sums of money paid out to the Pritchards—or anyone else—I'll be back."

"Have at it." Michael muscled his way around Jess. "I have nothing to hide. I didn't kill Ellie. I loved her. She wasn't cheating. She wouldn't do that to me."

How many spouses cheated and admitted it before they got caught? Not many. Ellie confided everything in Delaney. At least she thought her friend had. How could they know each other all these years and not confide something so heart-shattering? Why marry Michael if she intended to cheat? Delaney shoved her questions aside and stood. "I'll show him to the door."

"You do that. And don't let him back in unless he has a warrant." Michael's voice rose. "They can take their theories and their speculation and shove them where the sun don't shine."

The rise and fall of Jess's calming voice followed Delaney into the hall. She picked up speed. The sooner Detective Ramos left the better. "Michael's under a lot of stress right now."

"It's understandable. Losing a spouse is a terrible thing." Detective Ramos sounded truly sympathetic. His steps slowed as he reached the front door. "But that doesn't mean he didn't do it. If there's anything I've learned in this line of work, people can be so angry, they kill their loved one and then they're racked with guilt and despair and sadness, which eventually is their undoing."

The same theory he'd applied to Hunter.

"I'm sure it happens all the time." Delaney opened the door. "But not in this case. Ellie was happily married. She waited years to find the right man. Michael was that man. I don't care what Phil Tremaine said or saw or thinks he saw, Ellie wasn't cheating."

"You may be right. We'll know, one way or another, soon."

"The Pritchards. What do they have to do with Ellie's death?"

"That remains to be seen."

A bell dinged from the depths of his suit. Detective Ramos extracted his phone from his pocket and studied it. His finely sculpted features turned to stone. "I have to go back to HQ. The chief wants a briefing because the city manager wants a briefing."

Which meant the mayor wanted a briefing. Not because it was Ellie. Because it happened at a popular tourist attraction. City coffers would be affected. So typical of politicians. They didn't care that Ellie was a taxpaying citizen, an entrepreneur who served those tourists with her shop, a wife, daughter, sister, and would-be mother. And a friend. "Please. Purely on the face of it, what made you ask about the Pritchards?"

"The car in the photo is registered to Leah Pritchard. The men are her son and grandson."

That was something. A crumb. Put enough crumbs together and the trail would lead them to the killer. "Thank you."

"Have a good evening. Stay home. Stay safe."

"I will." Delaney stuck one hand behind her back and crossed her fingers. Childish, but somehow it allowed her to feel like she hadn't lied. Of course she knew she had. It didn't feel good. There was no excuse for it.

She closed the door, leaned against it, and dug her phone from her pocket. "I can't believe I'm doing this."

What are you doing?

After a few seconds, Hunter responded: **At work**

Do the names Leah, Art, or Vince Pritchard mean anything to you?

No. Who are they?

Detective just interviewed Michael again

And?

Leah Pritchard owns the car in the photos

We need to talk to them

Agreed. I'll try to find an address for them

I'll ask Mel

Excellent idea

Talk soon

How easily they fell into sync. No. No syncing.

"What are you doing?" Jess strode down the hallway. "You didn't come back, and I wanted to make sure Ramos left."

"I was just checking my email." Delaney shoved her phone in her pocket. Another lie. Not her finest hour. Jess wouldn't be happy that she was sharing information with Hunter. Or talking to him at all. "Detective Ramos is gone. Let's hope he's done harassing Michael and starts focusing on finding the actual killer."

"He was a bulldog during the investigation of Corey's murder. Now he has ten more years of experience." Jess pivoted and headed back to the living room. "He won't give up until he has the killer in custody. But I'll make sure he stays off Michael's back."

Delaney followed. Michael was back at the piano, playing another dirge-like melody. "I hope so. The kids need Michael. I can't believe their mother hired a PI to investigate Ellie."

"Me neither. But I guess we shouldn't be surprised. The stuff I see in family law and you saw as a social worker, nothing should surprise us."

"You're right. That's why I got out. Do you ever think about quitting law and doing something else?"

"Even if I wanted to, I couldn't. I'm still paying off student loans." Jess dropped onto the couch. He picked up his legal pad and a pen, already preparing to go back to work. "Besides, I like helping people during difficult times in their lives. Everyone has them. No family is perfect. I'm always going to have business, that's for sure. Are you ever sorry you left social work?"

"No. And I'm still paying my student loans too." Delaney settled onto the couch next to him. "I guess I'm not as tough as you are."

"Don't you believe it." Jess put his arm around her and squeezed. "You're as tough as they come. You're my hero."

"Thanks." He was always so sweet. "You know, a good woman needs to snap you up. You're a catch."

"Ha, ha." His fair skin reddened. He turned his back on her and picked up another fat folder. "I'm definitely not. But you are. That's why you need to stay away from Hunter."

"I'm not . . . we're just . . . we want to find out who killed Ellie."

"And exonerate Hunter. You're tilting at windmills. Hunter is a killer and you're letting him manipulate you."

"I'm not. Nobody manipulates me." Anger burned through Delaney. How had they gone from complimenting each other to this in two seconds? "Not anymore. I resent you suggesting that he can. That anyone can."

"Sorry. I'm sorry. You're right." Jess held up both hands like stop signs. "I just worry about you, that's all. Don't be mad at me. Friends?"

Their friendship, forged in the fire of two murders, would withstand much more than a small spat. "I'm not mad at you. I'm just tired and I still have work to do."

Work that involved finding a killer and making him pay.

CHAPTER 33

In this age of indiscriminate sharing on social media, the Pritchards had done a good job of keeping their contact information private. With an irritated sigh Delaney shut her laptop. Nothing on any social media platform that hinted at where they lived. How dare they? She snorted and sipped the cold dregs of her coffee.

With any luck Mel would be willing to call in a favor and save the day. What was it like to have two sisters and a brother and a mother and aunts and uncles and nieces and nephews?

"Stop. No feeling sorry for yourself. Work." Unable to face the mess at the shop, she'd come home with a promise to herself that she would work on framing Corey's paintings instead. "Stop procrastinating."

And stop talking aloud to yourself.

Delaney changed into sweats and a UTSA Roadrunners T-shirt. She lugged the eight paintings she and Cam had found in Ellie's third-floor stash into her workroom. Finally. She'd left them and the box that held the old photos and photo albums in the Trailblazer for three days for reasons she refused to examine.

Fortified with an energy drink and a bowl of homemade cranberry-dark-chocolate-almond granola, she stood in the middle of the room and stared at the impromptu retrospective of her brother's work. The paintings represented his perspective of the lives other people had. Uncomplicated. Full of relationships. Full of love.

Unlike his own? Did he paint what he lacked? What he saw others having that he did not?

Or did she read into the broad strokes of color, light, and dark her own much-sought-after desires?

No thinking, just working.

Starting with the painting of Nana pouring strawberry jam into waiting jars while her two cats watched from their perch on the kitchen windowsill. Nana wore her usual placid expression when working in the kitchen. Perspiration gave her wrinkled face a soft shine over her faded cotton apron.

So much for avoiding that stroll down memory lane. Delaney inhaled as if she could reel in that remembered scent of strawberries and dab it on her neck like sweet perfume. "Oh, Nana, I miss you. I miss Tinker and Dizzy too."

The longing hit her in the gut. She fought the urge to double over. It had her talking aloud to herself again.

No thinking. Just working.

She opened Spotify on her phone and found her favorite playlist featuring Lady Gaga, Adele, Katy Perry, and Billie Eilish. Strong female vocalists who made their own way.

Music helped clear her mind.

She sorted through sheets of mat board, searching for the right shade of antique linen that would play host to the multitude of colors in the painting. An antique bronze fillet would offer a nice contrast to the linen. An understated oak frame would provide a country feel. She had more choices at the shop, but her stash here at the house yielded a pleasing combination.

Delaney went to work sizing and cutting the mat board. It was exacting work that required her total concentration. Perfect for a night like this one. *Measure twice, cut once.*

That done, she straightened and rubbed her neck. Next up: measuring and cutting the frame itself. More exacting work. She studied the row of paintings along the wall waiting patiently, biding their time for her attention and affection, the way art often did. Her gaze went to the one on the far end.

Ellie's image captured when she was at her most beautiful. Smiling, her dark hair flowing, her feet bare. Her eyes spoke of her love for the man who stood outside the image, painting her because that was his language of love.

What did Corey see when he painted that scene? Delaney dropped the mat cutter and moved toward it. Neither of them had any way of knowing what the future held. Ellie was frozen in time. A good, sweet, lovely time. If they had known what was coming, would they have held on to it longer, laughed harder, loved more deeply? Did Corey know something she didn't? Did he want to capture that moment, knowing few such perfect moments would follow?

Hindsight was twenty-twenty, even with paintings.

Delaney knelt and pulled the box of photos closer. It couldn't be any worse than pulling a bandage from a wound that had never healed. The first handful of photos revealed Hunter with his arm around Corey's neck. They both had goofy grins on their faces and beer bottles in their hands. Another featured Cam and Ellie clad in bikinis eating ice cream cones on the back steps of Jess's parents' house. The sunlight streamed down on their beautiful faces.

Sorry, you guys. Not tonight. I can't do this tonight.

She dropped them back into the box. One day she would have the guts to go through them.

Bang, bang, bang.

Delaney started, fell back on her behind, and shrieked.

"Like a girl," Corey would've said.

The banging at her front door continued. "Coming!"

Heart pounding, she raced from the room, grabbed her stun gun from the table by the front door, and peered through the peephole.

Hunter. Delaney jerked the door open. "What are you doing here?"

"You stopped answering my texts."

Because she was done talking. Done thinking. "You couldn't take a hint?"

"Can I come in?"

Delaney stood back. "After you." He brushed past her, smelling of paint and turpentine. Another cologne all its own. "I'm framing."

Hunter followed her into the workshop. He halted. "Wow."

"Yeah. Wow." Delaney hadn't told him about the find. "Ellie had them with all the stuff she'd saved from the co-op and Corey's studio."

He squatted in front of the same painting that had captured Delaney a few minutes earlier. "These are some of his best. I can't believe she kept them to herself all these years. She had no right to do that. These should have been yours. They should've been in a showing so the public could see them. This is . . . Jess is so . . ."

"Exactly."

Hunter leaned back on his haunches and surveyed the others. "This one of Ellie is so her. She really was beautiful. He had a way of bringing it out in her . . ." His shoulders hunched. The sentence trailed away.

"Would you like some granola?" Delaney grabbed her ruler and busied herself measuring the fillet. "There's water or energy drinks."

Hunter scooted around so he faced her. "Don't do that."

"What?"

"Play hostess to hide your emotion."

He stood, his back to those beautiful paintings that were like memories for both of them. "When those bullets were flying, all I could think of was you. I had to keep you safe. I couldn't let you be hurt any more. I needed time to prove myself to you."

Dangerous territory. How did she tiptoe through this emotional landmine field? "I don't want to do this. Not now."

"I do. I lost a decade of my life. I don't have time to waste. I need to figure out who killed Corey and Ellie so I don't waste another decade."

"I need to know too." He wasn't the only one who'd lost a precious chunk of time. "I'm trying. I'm trying to find a way." A way to trust. A way to feel again. The muscles were rusty. They didn't want to work. "You don't have any right to make demands on me."

Hunter took a step toward her, then another. His dark eyes captured her. He raised one hand and touched her face. His thumb outlined her jawline, her cheek, and her chin. "Tell me you don't feel anything for me anymore. Can you honestly tell me that?"

Heat warmed Delaney's neck and seeped into her bones. Her heart pumped. Her pulse jumped. She swallowed. "I don't know what I feel."

"Yes, you do."

He moved closer. He cupped her face in both warm, solid hands. "You're all about people's feelings. Tell me what *you* feel."

"Confused," she whispered. "Terrified and confused. How can I feel this way after what happened? What I thought happened? What I thought you did?"

"Because you knew in your heart—you know in your heart—I could never do something like that. It wasn't in me then and it's not in me now."

Delaney didn't dare move. She didn't want to move. She wanted to stay where she was, those warm, callused hands touching her, forever.

What are you doing? Are you crazy? Move away.

Her feet didn't move. They were planted like an old live oak tree with roots dug deep into the rocky Hill Country soil.

Hunter's gaze went to her lips. His head inclined.

Breathless, Delaney closed her eyes and waited.

Nothing happened.

She opened them.

Hunter shook his head. His hands dropped. He stumbled back until space widened between them. "I'm sorry. I'm so sorry. I got ahead of myself."

"Ahead of-of yourself?" Embarrassment scorched Delaney's cheeks. "You've been ahead of yourself since you broke into my house. Why stop now?"

"I have to find Corey's killer. That's the only way I can prove to you I didn't do it. I don't want that doubt festering in you, hanging over us. You'll never truly trust me until the true killer is behind bars."

Delaney whirled and marched behind the workbench. "So the name Pritchard doesn't mean anything to you?"

"No." Hunter eased back onto a straight-back chair that occupied space next to her frame display. "Has Ramos interviewed any of them?"

"Leah Pritchard, she actually owns the car, but she's in assisted living. It's either her son or grandson. I'm betting on the grandson. He'd be closer to Ellie's age."

"We need to find him."

"I did an internet search. Nothing came up. Nothing on social media. I thought everyone was on social media." Delaney kept up accounts on several platforms in order to market her business, but she shied away from anything personal. Even then sleazy creepers latched on to her profiles and tried to friend her. "Did Mel get an address?"

"I haven't heard back from her yet. I'll follow up." He leaned over, elbows on his knees, and picked at paint on his index finger. "I went to the warehouse."

"And?"

"It was hard. I won't lie." He met Delaney's gaze. His dark eyes were full of pain. "I remembered some things. Things I'd rather forget, I suppose, but one piece stands out. I don't know if I blocked it out or it just got lost in the drugs and alcohol. Ellie knew."

"Knew what?"

"About the plan to jump in bed with a bunch of gangbangers. According to Corey, it was her idea."

"I don't believe that. She never said a word about it." Delaney picked up the mat board, laid it back down. He was nuts. He was making this up. "If that's true, why didn't she say something during the trial?"

"Because it would make her complicit in a criminal enterprise and in part responsible for his death?" Hunter ran his hands through his hair. "I don't know. Because she knew it would destroy your friendship?"

Maybe. Would she let Hunter go to prison for a murder he might not have committed? Would she do that to Delaney? *Ellie, how I wish you were here so I could talk to you, so you could help me understand.* "It doesn't make any sense. None of it does. Why did she keep these paintings? Why didn't she tell me she had them? Why hide them?"

"It seems like Ellie had a ton of secrets. She hid stuff from you, from Michael, from everyone. Corey's death messed her up. It messed us all up."

"Are we never going to be whole again?"

"With enough prayer and patience and love, yes."

He had so much more faith than she did. How was that possible? "I hope you're right."

"I worry about the kids in my class. How many of them are in gangs or doing drugs. They're surrounded by both. How can they resist if people like Corey couldn't?"

"They have your pastor friend and you and the community center to help them. They're the lucky ones—"

"It's not luck. It's a God-thing. He put Pastor James there. He planted Pastor James in my life. I'd like to think He planted me in their lives too."

"I suppose you think He planted you in my life."

"Honestly? I don't know. You were good with your faith until Corey died and I went to prison. They say trials are a way of honing our faith. I keep thinking mine has been plenty honed by now." His laugh brittle, he stared at the paint on his hands as if trying to figure out how it got there. "Instead of honing your faith, loss and tragedy caused you to lose yours."

"Maybe that means it was weak to start with." Delaney selected a piece of precut antiglare glass and moved it to her workbench. Anything to keep her hands busy. Framing a painting in these circumstances was a big no-no. She'd end up cutting something wrong and wasting materials. Or worse, damage the painting. "I went to church because Nana and Pops did. When they were gone, I stopped, even though I still thought I believed. Then Corey . . ."

"Then you felt as if you'd lost everything."

"I had lost everything."

"Except God. He was always there. He never leaves us."

"I spent five years being a social worker. I saw children who'd been starved, beaten, and murdered by people who were supposed to love them. God didn't lift a finger to help them."

"He did. He put you in their lives."

"I wasn't enough. Children died on my watch."

"God didn't kill them."

"He let it happen."

"God gave people free will. We live in a broken world—"

"I don't need the broken-world speech. I live in that world. So do you. You spent eight years in prison for something you say you didn't do. How can you still defend Him?"

"I survived. Only by the grace of God. You have no idea." He stopped. His Adam's apple bobbed. "You have no idea. But because of that experience, I have Pastor James in my life now. I have direction. I know how I want to use my art. I know what's important. I've stopped drinking. I came out the other side a better person."

"Most people would be bitter."

"I'm getting another chance to be the person God calls me to be. I'm blessed."

How could he say that? He said it without a trace of sarcasm or anger or artifice. He believed it. Faith looked good on him. It didn't try to push other people around. It softened his features and gave them a kindness that had been missing before.

He stood and approached the workbench. Delaney averted her gaze. She couldn't share in his shiny faith and beautiful hope. She picked up the ruler. Her hands shook. She put it down. "I'm glad for you."

"God knows what you been through, Laney. He understands. He's there for you too."

"You need to go now. I'm tired."

"Okay." His voice lowered to a whisper. "It's been a long day. You need your rest. What about tomorrow?"

"What about it?"

"The Pritchards."

Nothing—not even her crazy mixed-up feelings for this man— could stand in the way of finding out who killed Ellie. "We're not waiting for Detective Ramos to track them down, are we?"

"I'll call Mel. If she can get us an address before I have to be at work, I'll text you. We'll work out something from there."

The way he said it, the way he looked at her, the way his hands fisted, said so much more. He would meet her where she was.

For now that would have to be enough. For him. And for her.

CHAPTER 34

The call came through not long after Andy settled on the faux hard-wood floor between Becca, three, in her Moana costume, and Gina, five, in her Belle costume. They loved dress-up and they loved it when Daddy joined in. They thought he made a great Maui or a perfect beast—depending on which daughter had the upper hand in the day's make-believe playtime.

For Andy playtime provided the perfect way to decompress after a day investigating the vicious murder of a young woman. He'd love to ignore the ringing and simply bask in the unconditional love of his daughters. But he couldn't. "I'll be right back."

"Aww, Daddy."

Acutely aware of their disappointed faces, Andy crawled over to the couch and leaned against it. Even when he was working a case, he tried to be home every night for supper and bedtime. Sometimes it worked. Sometimes it didn't.

The caller had a deep, cultured voice. Like a National Public Radio DJ.

"Gerard Knox here. I received your message regarding an inter-view. I'm not sure what you think I can tell you. I never met Michael

Hill's wife. I know of her, but I don't know her. I certainly don't know anything about her tragic death."

"Be that as it may, I'd like to speak with you in person. Just covering all my bases."

"I'm available now if you'd like to come by my office."

"I'm at home for supper with my family. Could we do this first thing in the morning?"

"I'm headed to Austin for a business meeting in the morning, then to Las Vegas for a short holiday. We could get together upon my return if you prefer."

Andy glanced at the clock on the built-in bookcases that took up one living room wall. "How long will you be in the office?"

"Another hour, hour and a half, tops."

"Give me thirty minutes." That would give him time to pick up Flores and make it downtown. "I'm on my way."

"As you wish."

Andy disconnected and called Flores. Voice mail kicked in. His temporary partner had mentioned stopping by to visit his mother at the rehab center before heading home. Andy left a message, hung up, and studied his two girls. They'd gone back to serving each other plastic plates piled high with imaginary donuts, cookies, and brownies, laid out on a purple plastic table with four matching chairs.

"Sorry, *chiquitas bonitas*, I have to go."

"Awww, Daddy!"

They ran to him—Gina arriving first thanks to her longer legs while Becca struggled to disentangle from the costume wrapped around her shorter legs. "You can't go, Maui. You haven't eaten yet."

She was right about that. Pilar was making his favorite—chiles rellenos. Inhaling their scent of baby shampoo and animal crackers, he planted kisses on his daughters' heads. "Save a chocolate donut for me, please. I need to talk to Mommy before I go."

Becca wrapped her thin arms around his neck and laid a fat, slobbery kiss on his cheek. "It's your turn to read the bedtime stories."

"I'll do two turns to make up for it."

He scrambled to his feet, both girls clinging to his jean-clad legs, and clomped into the kitchen where the aroma of blackened Anaheim chiles scented the air. His mouth watered. What a guy did for his job. "Mommy, I have a present for you—two presents for you."

Her face flushed from the oven's heat, Pilar turned and set a cookie sheet lined with foil on waiting pot holders on the quartz island countertop. "Just what I needed, two little girls to help me eat all the chile rellenos."

Pregnancy suited his wife more each time. At thirty-eight weeks and counting, she moved like a river parade float—slow and majestic. Her face filled out, making her cheeks plump, her dimples deep. Her baby bump was more of a watermelon. Her shiny, dark-brown hair hung in a ponytail down her back. Her deep-brown eyes studied Andy as she shucked off oven gloves. "So what's up?"

"I have to go out."

"Now?"

"Sorry, babe."

"Is it the Hill case?"

While Pilar liked cyberterrorism, she missed homicide. She'd been the one to sacrifice career aspirations in order to have family. She didn't complain, but sometimes she looked wistful. Like now. "Did you get something on Nash?"

The fact that she'd been intimately involved in putting Nash away made standing on the sideline even harder for her. She loved being a homicide detective. Thankfully she loved being a mommy more.

"Nope. This is related to the Hill case." Andy tickled daughter number one until she let go of his leg. Daughter number two followed suit seconds later. He raised his voice to be heard over their peals of laughter and pleas for more. "Gerard Knox claims tonight is the only time he has available for an interview."

"I'll keep a plate warm for you." Pilar padded barefoot around the island and kissed him hard on the lips. Her expression somber, she pushed away. "Are you picking up Flores on your way?"

"I left him a voice mail. I'll text him in a minute. He may still be with his mother at the rehab place. He has his hands full."

Pilar frowned. "So wait until the morning."

"Knox is headed to Vegas in the morning." Andy tucked one long bang behind her ear and kissed her cheek. "I promise to be back by bedtime, *mi amor.*"

"As long as you're locked and loaded."

"Always."

She plucked a pink plastic barrette from his hair and laid it on the counter. "It doesn't really go with your ensemble."

"Are you sure?" He patted his hair and pretended to preen. "Would purple be better?"

He didn't bother to change back into his suit. Knox would just have to deal with him in his evening attire of jeans and a polo shirt. He retrieved his weapon from his gun safe and added a Windbreaker to make it less noticeable.

More kisses for the two squirts on the floor and Andy made it out to his car five minutes later. His text to Flores went unanswered. By the time he arrived at Knox's office building, pink and purple streaks across the sky heralded another beautiful sunset.

He pushed the after-hours button and waited. A behemoth of a man dressed in black from head to foot appeared at the double glass-plated doors. Without a word he ushered Andy to an elevator and up five floors. Attempts at conversation like, "How 'bout them Spurs" and "How long have you worked for Mr. Knox?" were met with raised eyebrows. Maybe he didn't speak English.

When the elevator doors opened, the big talker led Andy through a carpeted hallway lined with offices to one at the far end. A man Andy presumed to be Knox was ensconced behind a desk so big as to be ostentatious. He held a pipe that filled the air with a fragrant cherry scent in one hand and a heavy crystal glass containing an amber liquid in the other.

He didn't stand or offer his hand.

It felt like a bad reboot of *The Sopranos*.

After introducing himself, Andy settled into a chair designed for a much smaller person and dove in. "You employed Michael Hill."

"Employ." Knox held up his glass. "Would you like Dewar's on ice, a bottle of sparkling water, coffee? Harry makes a great espresso."

Andy declined. The behemoth disappeared without a sound. "I'm under the impression that Mr. Hill would like to sever the relationship."

Knox puffed on the pipe, the smoke curling around his head. He could've been an Ivy League college professor. "That's news to me."

"Did you resort to threats to make sure Mr. Hill stayed on as your accountant?"

"I'm a businessman, Detective, not a thug."

Sometimes it was hard to tell the difference. "Had you ever met Mrs. Hill?"

"Never had the pleasure. Such a tragedy. A newlywed at that. I've expressed my condolences to Michael and assured him that I can live without his services for a few weeks."

"Did you send one of your . . . associates to speak with Mrs. Hill?"

Andy tugged several of the photos from the manilla envelope he'd brought along with him and spread them across the desk. "Have you seen these before?"

To Knox's credit, he set aside his drink and took the time to study Andy's offering. He picked each one up and laid it down. "I take it this is Mrs. Hill."

"It is."

"No, I haven't seen these before." Knox stoked his pipe with a silver lighter. The smoke drifted toward Andy, forcing him to sit back. Knox didn't seem to notice—or care. "They're quite illuminating, are they not? What makes you think I would've seen them?"

"Just asking questions, following leads where they may take me." Andy coughed into the crook of his elbow. "You don't recognize the car?"

"Could be an older Corolla, maybe. I'm not much of a car buff. One of the perks of being the boss is that someone drives me around."

"It's a Toyota Camry. You're sure you don't know who it is? You didn't have someone follow Mrs. Hill?"

"I assure you I have better things to spend money on than tailing Mrs. Hill, no matter how attractive she might have been."

Knox had seen Ellie or photos of her. He thought she was attractive. She had been once, before someone stabbed the life out of her. "The theory has been floated that perhaps Mrs. Hill was engaged in an affair and/or she was being blackmailed."

"Neither of which is my concern."

"Why do you suppose Michael Hill is so intent on leaving your employ?"

"That would be a question for Michael, but I will say he is a very high-strung man. Not what one usually sees in an accountant. He also seems to have a rather unhealthy imagination."

"Do you make it a habit of pressuring people to remain in your employment?"

"I make it a habit to pay them well and show them how much I appreciate their work." Knox laid the pipe in a Texas-shaped glass ashtray big enough for five such pipes. He leaned back and tented his fingers. "I let them know I'm a family man and I take interest in their families. My companies are family centered."

A very nice sentiment used to dress up Knox's thinly veiled threats. "Where were you Tuesday, late afternoon?"

"At home. I felt a little under the weather that day."

"Can someone confirm that?"

"I was alone. My wife had a spin class followed by a massage. Of course, my driver can confirm he dropped me off there."

"You never drive yourself anywhere?"

"Occasionally. I have a Jaguar and a Mercedes. I like to take them out for spins on occasion. What's the point of having nice cars if you never drive them?"

Andy wouldn't know. A driver would confirm whatever his employer asked him to confirm. But Knox wasn't the kind of man who got his hands dirty. His employees would handle the dirty work. Like Mr. Tall and Silent. He loosely fit Delaney Broward's description of her assailant.

"What business are you in?"

"Businesses. I have a diverse portfolio that includes a trucking company that hauls imports to various parts of the country. I own a chain of dry cleaning stores. Recently I invested in a string of convenience stores."

All of this matched up with Michael's description of his boss's business assets.

A tap on the door halted his litany. "Come."

The manservant-slash-bodyguard appeared.

"Ah, my ride is here. My wife gets irritated if I'm late for dinner. I don't know why. She never actually eats any of the food our chef prepares. She might gain an ounce."

No point in mentioning that he was missing his own supper in order to interview Knox at the time of his choosing. "What if Mr. Hill came across something in your financials that caused him concern?"

"Then he should share those concerns with the bookkeepers for my companies. That's his job." Knox jabbed his stubby index finger in the air. "The work he does for me is confidential. Like a priest and his parishioner."

"I didn't mean to imply that Mr. Hill spoke out of turn. I'm simply contemplating what would make him so anxious to step away from what must be a very lucrative relationship."

"I told you. He has an overdeveloped imagination. I went over the accounts with him personally. He was satisfied with my review and feedback."

Knox should play a few hands of poker while in Las Vegas.

"Do you know Mr. Hill's first wife, Charlene Capstone-Hill?"

"I haven't had the pleasure."

"A PI named Phil Tremaine?"

"I have in-house security that takes care of my needs in that realm."

"Does the name Leah Pritchard mean anything to you?"

Harry the behemoth gently cleared his throat.

"Yes, yes, patience, my friend." Knox drained the last of his scotch. He stood and reached for a suit jacket hanging from a rack behind his desk. Harry the behemoth helped him slide into it. Finally, Knox turned back to Andy. "That name is unfamiliar to me. I'm sorry I can't be more helpful. If you speak with Michael, let him know I'll be checking back with him soon. I'd like to attend the service. You don't happen to know if it's been scheduled?"

"Mrs. Hill's body hasn't been released by the coroner yet, but it should be shortly. As far as I know the services are still pending."

"It was nice to make your acquaintance, Detective Ramos. Harry will see you out."

How the silent mountain could stride down the hall without making a sound—not a creaky joint or a squeaky sole to be heard—baffled Andy. At the glass double doors, he saluted his escort and offered his best friendly smile. "Nice talking with you."

Harry's mouth might have moved a millimeter, but Andy couldn't be sure. The doors closed behind him with utter efficiency.

The world took all kinds. Knox didn't have a solid alibi. Nor did he lift a finger on his own. Every interview led to another name on the list. Knox's driver. Household help. Anyone who could say whether he'd taken the Jag or the Mercedes out for a spin. Did Harry do his dirty work for him? Or his security detail?

Homicide investigations involved the long game. Doing the legwork. Building a picture and then standing back to see how all the pieces fit together. Enjoying the dusky night air, Andy ambled toward his SUV. His phone dinged. Flores had finally responded to his text.

Sorry. Mom's fever spiked. Stayed to talk to night nurse.
Headed your direction

Andy walked and thumbed a response. He could do two things at once.

No worries. Done w/Knox. I'll fill you in tomorrow.
Prayers yr Mom feels better

On Main Ave. There in 5 minutes

Flores was a stubborn cuss. Andy slowed to a stop next to the Traverse. He'd done a nice job parallel parking it, if he did say so himself.

Go . . .

A hard body slammed into Andy from behind, knocking him against the SUV. The phone sailed into the dusk. Adrenaline blasted through him with a heady boost of energy. He thrust back from the vehicle with both hands.

His assailant rammed him a second time, smashing Andy's face against the passenger window. Pain ripped through him. Blood flowed from his nose.

Pilar. Becca. Gina. Baby to be named.

Why hadn't they given her a name yet? Because they couldn't agree.

They still had time.

The assailant wrapped an arm around Andy's neck and squeezed. More pain, this time in his back. Sheer, unadulterated anger raced through him like an out-of-control car. He jabbed his attacker with both elbows. The grip loosened.

Andy reached for his gun. His hand closed around the Sig Sauer. Another glancing pain, this time to his right arm. He clung to the weapon and kicked back, catching his attacker in the groin.

A grunt, a low groan, and sudden release.

Staggering, Andy turned. The assailant, dressed in black, hunched over, stumbled back. He still held the hunting knife in one gloved hand.

Blood ran down Andy's arm onto his hand and fingers, making the gun slick and his hold on it precarious. He gritted his teeth and raised his weapon. The assailant took off.

Andy fired two shots and raced after him. A block right, a block left. His attacker knew the neighborhood better. Plus Andy was bleeding like a stuck pig. He lost him.

A block left, a block right. With every step back to his car, Andy left a trail of blood drops. Gasping for air, legs weak, he halted. He bent over and put his free hand on his knee. The phone. He had to get the phone. Three long breaths, in and out, in and out. He dropped to his knees and scoured the ground for the phone.

God, please, the phone.

There. He grabbed it. *Thank You, Jesus.*

He jabbed Flores's number. His partner picked up on the first ring. "I'm around the corner."

"Change of plan. I think a visit to the ER is in order."

Cusswords flowed. "Where are you?"

Andy described his location. Flores hung up. A minute later he came around the corner doing at least sixty, slid his Charger to a halt cattywampus, and burst from the car. "What happened?"

"Apparently somebody didn't like me talking to Knox."

More cussing. "I'm calling an ambulance."

"Don't you dare. Just give me a ride. Seriously."

"Get in. Just do me a favor, don't bleed all over my upholstery."

"You're all heart." Andy sank onto the seat, grateful to be off his feet. The adrenaline faded, leaving behind rubbery legs and a sick feeling in the pit of his stomach. "I just need a quick pit stop to stitch me up, and then we can go find the jerk who did it."

Find him and throw his carcass in jail—after he spilled his guts on who ordered the attack.

CHAPTER 35

"It's irreplaceable."

"I know and I'm deeply, deeply sorry for your loss."

Delaney held out a much depleted box of tissues to her customer. The woman, who had been sitting on the shop's porch when Delaney arrived at eight fifteen, cradled her ripped vintage gouache on paper by Amado Peña like a baby in both arms. She ignored the offering, instead wiping her nose on her Baja hoodie's sleeve like a toddler. She wore her white hair in long braids that reached her waist, adding to the image. "This is a vintage painting from his Mestizos series. *Patrones de la Portadora.* I paid forty-five hundred dollars for it."

"I know, I know." Delaney kept her voice soothing. She set the tissues within reach and added the information to the growing list for her insurance adjuster. He was due any minute. "My insurance should cover the loss—"

"It's not about the money."

Any true art lover would understand, agree, empathize, and sympathize. Unfortunately, that was all Delaney could do at this point. "At least with the insurance settlement, you can consider another one of his paintings."

Peña, an artist of Mexican-Yaqui descent, brought to life the Pascua-Yaqui culture in what was now Arizona and New Mexico. Fortunately he was prolific.

"I can't believe you didn't have better security," the woman wailed. "Two break-ins in two days. What is wrong with the city? They care more about potholes than art."

Again, Delaney empathized. But in fairness, the city of San Antonio did the best it could with limited resources. If this woman was like most taxpayers, she wanted lots of services, including police and fire at the drop of a 911 call, but she didn't want her taxes to rise. "I can try to salvage something, put the pieces back together. In a way it would be a new piece of art that tells a different story. It could represent the way indigenous tribes have been treated by interlopers over the centuries through the rips and tears."

The woman's face brightened. "That's a beautiful thought. Can you still claim it on your insurance?"

"Absolutely. And no charge for the framing."

"It won't be the same, but it's something." The woman gently laid the painting on the counter. She slung the braids over her shoulder. "But I'm almost afraid to leave it here. The police haven't caught the ogre who did this, have they? What if he comes back?"

"I understand your concern. The police are working hard to track down the perpetrator. And SAPD has beefed up patrols." And, for the first time in her life, Delaney was considering buying a gun. But the woman didn't need to know that. "I plan to do some work from home while I get the store back in shape. I'll take your painting home. How does that sound?"

"I don't know—"

The bell over the door dinged, drowning out the woman's response. One of the tiniest men Delaney had ever seen entered, followed closely by two much larger hulks. He definitely wasn't the insurance adjuster. He stood half a foot shorter than Delaney and was so thin and androgynous he could have been a female model. He wore a sleeveless tank top, faded jeans, a tweed newsboy hat, and aviator sunglasses. The tank top allowed him to show off an elaborate tattoo of a shark that swam up his right arm from his wrist to his shoulder. The shark had a bloody stump of a leg in its mouth.

Be that as it may, the Shark was a minnow.

"I'll be right with you."

"No worries." El Tiburón had a soft, almost monotone, voice. "I'll wait."

Focusing on the woman in front of her, Delaney slid the pieces of the painting into a flat, brown paper bag. "I promise to guard it with my life."

The customer didn't need to know this might actually come into play.

"Fine. How soon will you get to it?"

Delaney surveyed the ruins that had once been her shop, the stack of notes representing the other destroyed paintings and mementos entrusted to her, and the man who stood perusing the rack of notecards featuring famous paintings she'd pulled up right upon arriving earlier that morning. "As soon as humanly possible."

"Don't let it out of your sight."

"Yes, ma'am."

"Don't ma'am me." The woman gathered up her Guatemalan Mayan print bag, slung it over her bony shoulder, and flounced from the shop on scuffed all-terrain Crocs.

How should Delaney address her new visitor? Mr. Shark? Letty had referred to him as Rick. Dare she?

"Rick Tellez at your service." He solved her dilemma with this simple, surprisingly elegant introduction. Tellez removed his glasses and handed them to one of the hulks who moved in lockstep with him as he approached the counter. "I heard you're looking for me, Corey Broward's little sister."

His gaze seemed to encompass her in one fluid motion. His lips were cherry red and his teeth brilliantly white. He reminded her of puzzles someone had mixed together and tried to make the pieces fit by shoving them together by brute force. *Stop staring.* "So you know who I am."

"I know you're not interested in boxing."

"Actually I am."

"Letty said you took a beatdown like a good sport. But I suspect you really want to kick butt and take names, not get in the ring for money. Naw, your gig is more like a 'We Are the World' thing."

"How would you know? You don't know me."

"Your brother liked to talk about you."

To a drug dealer? Delaney picked up her backpack and laid it on the counter between them. It held her stun gun and pepper spray. She slid her hand into her front pocket and wrapped her fingers around her phone. "That was a long time ago. People change."

Unless they died. Then they were suspended in time, forever young, forever naive.

Forever loved.

"Water under the bridge." His tongue flicked over his lips. *El Serpiente* might've been more apropos. "Which begs the question, why come searching for me now? Or at all? You don't look like the kind of chica who has trouble getting a date. I promise you I'm not your type."

On closer inspection Tellez had deepening lines around his pale-brown eyes. The salt-and-pepper stubble on his chin and the gray wisps of hair peeking from under his cap suggested he was older than he seemed at first. And harder.

Delaney held his gaze. "I want to know if you or your . . . associates know what happened the night my brother was murdered."

He laughed.

Heat burned through Delaney. Sweat dampened her palms and her pits. "I assure you I don't find anything about my brother's death funny."

"They got the guy who did it."

"He says no. He has another theory."

Tellez rubbed a smudge on the glass countertop, his expression contemplative. "You can tell him his theory is wishful thinking. Your brother came highly recommended by my . . . associate Willy Sandoval. We were about to enter into a mutually beneficial business arrangement. Ask yourself what did my business have to gain by removing your brother from the equation?"

"Hunter tried to convince Corey not to get the co-op involved in . . . your business."

"He failed, *mi amiga*."

"What would happen if Corey changed his mind and tried to back out?"

"Once you're in, you're in."

"What if Corey told you he changed his mind?"

Tellez lifted his hat and let it settle on thinning gray hair slicked back without a part. "That night we spoke via phone. He said he was all in."

That night . . . the night he died. Could she believe Tellez? He was protecting his own interests by insisting Corey hadn't changed his mind. "Why did you come here? The police never even knew about Corey's plan. Only Hunter—"

"I came to tell you that it's not smart to poke a sleeping bear." Tellez's tongue flicked out. "Nobody spreads lies about El Tiburón. I'm a legit businessman. I got world champion boxers. I got a wife and five kids and a *sancha* on the side. I don't need somebody stirring up trouble over some White boy dead ten years. Tell your boyfriend I'm asking nicely this time due to my respect for your brother. Next time, it won't be so nice. For you or him."

Maybe he'd already tried to make his point—with a drive-by shooting in broad daylight. Delaney kept her mouth shut. Better not to poke a sleeping bear.

Tellez reached across the counter and touched her bruised face. His fingers were cold. Definitely more snake than shark. She suppressed a shudder. "Hunter's not my boyfriend." Her protest sounded weak in her own ears. She swallowed hard. "So who do you think killed Corey?"

"You have a one-track mind."

"He was my brother. Didn't it at least make you angry that your plan to . . . collaborate with him was destroyed by his murder?"

"Ay, chica, you're so sweet it makes my teeth hurt. So we can't do business with Corey Broward. We find somebody else. There's a world of possibilities in San Antonio." Tellez shook his head, feigning a sadness he obviously didn't feel. "Ask yourself who stood to gain something with him out of the picture."

The door opened and slammed against the wall. Swinging wildly, the bell dinged and fell to the floor. Hunter dashed into the store. "Laney? Laney! Did you hear? Detective Ramos . . ."

He slid to a stop. Not that Delaney blamed him. Both hulks had big guns pointed at him.

CHAPTER 36

Thank You, God, for keeping me from wetting my pants.

Hunter put both hands in the air. It had a familiar feel, one he didn't like and had hoped never to feel again. "Guys, what's going on here?"

"You must be Hunter. I'm Rick Tellez. I was just chatting with your friend here." The tiny man with a shark tattooed up one arm floated a lazy smile in Delaney's direction. "Vatos, put the guns away. I've got to get back to the gym. We'll let Laney explain."

Amazingly, the two mountainous men, both of whom could've won Mr. Universe contests while Tellez was an undersized pipsqueak, complied.

"You're El Tiburón?" Hunter kept his surprise out of his voice—just barely. "I have a lot of questions—"

"We're done here." Tellez strolled past Hunter, leaving the smell of old lady lotion in his wake. "*Vaya con Díos, mi amigo.*"

His bodyguards closed rank around him. All Hunter could do was watch him go.

"What was that all about?" He turned back to Delaney. Red spots burned on her cheeks against skin that had gone white. Hunter closed the gap between them in two long strides. "Are you all right? He didn't touch you, did he?"

"Lock the door, please. We don't need any more visitors."

Hunter whipped around and sped to the door, despite the fact that his own legs didn't feel all that steady. Once he was back at the counter, he asked the question again. "Spill it, please."

Delaney stumbled out from the counter and sank onto a stool next to her overturned workbench. "When you came through the door, you were saying something about Detective Ramos. What was it?"

Only having two 9mms pointed at him could make Hunter forget such a horrendous piece of news. "Someone attacked him, stabbed him last night outside Gerard Knox's place of business." He cleared his throat, studied his dirty sneakers for a millisecond, then leveled his gaze at her. "He'll live, but he's being kept overnight for observation according to the news reports."

Delaney shook her head. Her beautiful green eyes were filled with pain. "I guess you would say by the grace of God, he survived."

"And I'd be right. He has a wife and two kids and a baby on the way."

"I know. I met his wife. She was the first detective to talk to me when Corey died. She was so kind to me. Do they have any leads?"

"Not that the police spokesman shared." Hunter knelt and slid his arms around Delaney and pulled her tight against his chest. *Please, God, let her allow me to comfort her.*

She lowered her head and relaxed. He breathed. "I tried to call Detective Flores. They put me through to his extension, but I got his voice mail. They wouldn't give me his cell phone number. We don't know what Ramos was following up on. The Pritchard thing or the drug connection."

"Except that the drug connection was just in my shop, and he says he had nothing to do with it." Delaney eased back and raised her face so she was eye to eye with Hunter. "Rick Tellez says Corey decided to stick with his plan even after you two fought. He says he had no reason to kill Corey."

"He's lying." Hunter sat back on his haunches. The same sense of life spiraling out of control rushed at him. "I don't believe him. Who else would have done it?"

"I don't know. I have no doubt that Tellez is psychotic. He could've killed Corey without giving it a second thought, but he says he didn't. We can't prove he did."

It was Hunter's turn to hang his head. Their investigation was floundering. And they were no closer to figuring out either murder than they were three days earlier.

The feel of Delaney's fingers brushing against his hair forced Hunter to look up. Her eyes brimmed with empathy and something else. Fear. Of him? Of her own feelings? She withdrew her hand. He grasped hold of it and hung on. "Please. Don't back away."

"I can't. I can't be hurt again," she whispered. "I can't trust you. Or anybody."

"You can. I never betrayed you, Laney." He stared at her long, thin fingers, then gave in to the urge and kissed each one. "I never stopped caring about you."

The words plummeted into the space between them like a gauntlet thrown down. The air crackled. Evenings spent swaying to music only they could hear on her nana's front porch washed over him. The feel of her silky hair under his hands, the softness of her lips, the warmth of her breath, her scent of citrus—she surrounded him.

"Please don't." She tugged her hand free. "Let's stick to business."

Time snapped back and they once again squared off in the ruins of her shop and their lives.

"Okay. Whatever you say." *Don't pressure her. Give her time. Be there for her.* Was God a celestial adviser for the lovelorn? Or did He simply guide His children according to His plan?

Hunter dug up a smile to assure her. "I don't blame you for feeling the way you do. Let's figure this out and then go from there."

"No promises."

"Understood." Hunter offered his hand. She took it. They shook. He eased to his feet and helped her do the same. "What else did Tellez say?"

"He said I should think about who had the most to gain by Corey's death."

"Who would?" Hunter stifled the urge to groan. He certainly hadn't gained anything from Corey's death. It had been about loss—loss of a friend, loss of his girlfriend, loss of the co-op and his art, and ultimately, loss of his freedom. "Everyone loved him."

"Maybe we just thought everyone did because we did." Delaney strode around the counter. "Just like we thought everyone loved Ellie."

Fine. Hunter forced his fists to relax. He stepped up to the counter that separated them. "Ramos upset somebody he interviewed. Doesn't seem like it would be Leah Pritchard."

"Maybe she called her son to tell him the detectives came around. Where was Detective Ramos when he was attacked?"

"The news report said it occurred on Broadway in front of Knox Affiliated Services."

"Gerard Knox. Michael's client." Delaney ran her thumb across a paper sack lying between them. The corner of a painting peeked from the top. "The one Michael thinks could've killed Ellie to get back at him."

"Knox wouldn't try to take out Ramos in front of his own office building."

"No. I don't imagine he would." Delaney rubbed a spot between her eyes. They were clouded with frustration. "So where does that leave us?"

"Maybe Ramos poked his nose too close to El Tiburón." Hunter stuffed his hands in his jean pockets. They wanted to smooth away the pain on her face. She'd made it clear that wasn't allowed. "Maybe we are on the right track."

"Do you honestly think Rick Tellez is stupid enough to have one of his guys try to murder an SAPD homicide detective? He knows the Feds are watching his every move as it is. He hasn't survived all these years by inviting the entire SAPD to rain down hellfire on him."

"Then what?"

"No word from your sister on where the Pritchards live?"

"No, she had to take Trina to Urgent Care. She fell and broke her wrist."

"Ouch. Let me know."

Banging on the door startled them both.

"My insurance adjuster. I totally forgot about him."

Hunter strode to the door. A man in a USAA polo waved from the porch. After letting him in, Hunter glanced at his phone. He needed to go to work. As much as he wanted to retrace Detective Ramos's steps, he still had to make a living. He signaled to Delaney that he was leaving.

She nodded and waved. "Be careful out there."

If the killer was getting rid of people trying to discover his identity, one or both of them could be next.

"You too."

CHAPTER 37

"How do you want to approach this?"

Hunter's question contained the most words he'd uttered since picking Delaney up from her shop an hour after texting her to say his sister had come through with an address for Art Pritchard. Monosyllabic best described his conversational style this morning. Whatever he'd been thinking and feeling the previous day was now carefully tucked away behind a stony facade during the drive to Art Pritchard's house.

Contemplating her answer, Delaney stared at the dilapidated one-story house painted a mousy tan with a tiny front yard behind a chain-link fence. A concrete driveway took up most of the lot that faced West Malone, a narrow one-way street with No Parking signs posted on every block. An ancient minivan with a rusting body and a white cargo truck with the words Pritchard and Son AC Repair painted on the side shared the driveway. The gray Camry wasn't in evidence. "We could tell him we're trying to locate friends of Ellie's to invite them to her memorial service."

"Most people just put an announcement in the paper or let the funeral home take care of it."

"What would you suggest?"

"We're investigating Ellie's death and we think his son might be able to help us figure out where she'd been and what she'd been doing leading up to her death."

"The truth. That's a novel approach."

He opened his door. "I've found it works well and it makes it easier to keep your story straight."

No one came to the door at first. Hunter pounded harder the second time. And the third.

Finally the heavy tan drapes on the front window lifted. A man the shape of a tree stump—if tree stumps were hairy—peered out at them. The curtain dropped. The door opened. "What do you want?"

"Art Pritchard?"

"Who's asking?"

"We're friends of Ellie Hill's. We're trying to track down your son, Vince Pritchard."

Pritchard tugged a dirty handkerchief from the pocket of his gray-and-white-striped overalls. He wiped his nose, all the while staring first at Hunter and then at Delaney. "I don't think so."

Delaney craned her neck to peek beyond the man's hairy shoulders exposed by his wife-beater undershirt. The living room held a sagging couch, a recliner, and a large flat-screen TV. Shelves on one wall were filled with knickknacks and photos in cheap frames. "What makes you say that?"

"My son works with me in my AC business. He's not the brightest tool in the toolbox, but he can help me out. He's with me every day and when he's not he's with his kids."

"Could we come in and talk to you for a minute?" Delaney gave him her most ingratiating smile—the one she used when she went to talk to a CPS client for the first time. "We really need to get in touch with Vince."

Pritchard's fat lips protruded, like a pouting child. They matched eyes that bulged behind lenses covered with fingerprints and grease smudges. "Who are you again?"

Delaney introduced herself and Hunter. "We think your son knew Ellie. She died recently. Under mysterious circumstances. We're trying to talk to everyone who saw her in the last few months. Retracing her steps, as it were."

Pritchard blew his nose again. He stared at the handkerchief's contents like a seer studying tea leaves. Finally, he took a long step back. "I got a job at ten so you best be quick about it."

What would it be like to have an AC repairman of Pritchard's ilk show up at the door? People had to be desperate to let him in their houses. Glad Hunter followed behind her, Delaney squeezed by Pritchard and traipsed into the living room. Her sneakers sank into the plush brown carpet. Cigarette smoke hung in the air. The sofa was covered with *People* magazines and old copies of the *Express-News*. A Big Red and a plate of Oreos next to the recliner suggested that was where Pritchard had been sitting.

Uncertain, Delaney paused in the middle of the room. Pritchard lumbered to the recliner and sat down. The chair groaned under his weight.

Hunter picked up the magazines and stacked them on the floor. "Have a seat." As if it was his home.

Instead, Delaney went to the shelves to examine the photos. An old wedding photo. Too old to be Art Pritchard. Maybe his mother and father? Photos that had to be Art as a kid with two others who might be siblings.

Another wedding photo. Art Pritchard, this time in a pale-blue tux with a frilly shirt. His bride was half his size.

"Is your son helping you with the job you have at ten?" Delaney continued to browse the photos as she posed the question. "Will he come here, or is he meeting you at the job?"

"I dunno. I've tried to call him twice this morning, but he ain't answering."

"Is that like him?" Delaney picked up a photo of Pritchard holding a baby in his arms. His grin said proud papa. "You said he stays here sometimes."

"It ain't like him. He's stays here when his old lady throws him out. My old lady doesn't like it much, but he's my son."

"She's not his mother."

"None of your business, is it? She's my second wife. The other one died of cancer when Vince was a kid."

"I'm sorry for your loss." Delaney moved down the row. Between a Precious Moments figurine of a mother and a ceramic angel stood a framed photo of Art with a man who could've been a twin but was much younger. They sat at a picnic table, half a dozen beer bottles between them. "That must have been so hard for both of you."

"It was a long time ago." His chair squeaked. Rustling told her he was getting restless.

She turned with the eight-by-ten photo in her hand. "Is this your son?"

He lifted the bottle of Big Red to his lips, chugged half of it, and set it back down. "That's him. I thought you said you knew him."

"Our friend Ellie knew him." Delaney studied the photo. Vince was a big man, built like a massive tree trunk, while his father was more of a tree stump. He had scraggly blond hair, blue eyes, and the same bulldog face. In the photo he wore a green jumpsuit that had *AC Repair* embroidered on the pocket. "Did he go to O'Connor High School?"

"He started at Burbank, but like I said, he ain't none too bright. Managed to get his GED though. Some lady from the special ed department tutored him. They was gonna get him a job, but I said no, he could just as well work with me."

Delaney surveyed the remaining shelves. Surely the Pritchards had photos of Vince with his wife and the grandkids. What grandparents didn't? There. On the end. Behind more Precious Moments trinkets. Vince with a slender, dark-haired woman, again half the man's size. He held a baby wrapped in a blanket. She had a little girl on her hip and held a small boy's hand. They were smiling.

Delaney set the photo back on the shelf. "Does your son drive a gray Toyota Camry?"

Pritchard grimaced. "What does my mother's car got to do with anything?"

"Someone driving a car like it met with Ellie at a restaurant on Wednesday mornings for the last few months."

"With a man like my son, anything is possible. The counselor said Vince is a pleaser. He wants to please, he wants to fit in, so he lets people push him around." Pritchard guffawed. "He tends to hop into bed with any woman who's nice to him. He and his wife have had some knock-down, drag-out fights. He's had to go to court a couple of times for domestic violence. CPS threatened to take his kids. Total bull. His wife gives as good as she gets."

It made no sense. How could Ellie's and Pritchard's paths have crossed? Where? Why? This man had a history of domestic violence. Family court. Maybe Jess could help her delve into Vince's past. Somehow Vince had connected with Ellie.

Or someone in his car had. They couldn't be sure Vince was the man in the car in those photos. The possibility that Pritchard had been carrying on an affair that included breakfast at Torres Family Mexican Restaurant was so far-fetched as to be ludicrous. "Could we get Vince's address and telephone number from you?"

"I don't give out his contact information to strangers. I'm not stupid."

"We only want to talk to him."

"Give me your number and I'll pass it on to him. If he wants to talk to you, he'll call you."

Better than nothing. Delany wrote her cell phone number on her business card and handed it to Pritchard. "It's really important that we reach him."

Pritchard examined the card. His lips pursed, he dropped it on the coffee table. "It's up to my boy. I stopped telling him what to do a long time ago. He don't listen anyway."

"I don't think . . ." Hunter must've read something in Delaney's face. He let the sentence go and stood. "Yes, thanks. We'll get out of your hair. You've got that appointment. You probably need to get ready."

"Don't get up. We'll show ourselves out." Delaney headed to the door.

A few seconds later Hunter followed. He closed the screen door behind him and stomped down the steps. "What was that all about? We hadn't found out a thing—"

"It doesn't make sense. There's no possible connection between Vince and Ellie." Delaney's stomach churned. *Hold it together. Just hold it together.* "They live in different worlds. It's a dead end. Unless Jess can help me dig into Pritchard's criminal record. He was charged with domestic violence. He had to appear in family court. That's Jess's wheelhouse. He's eager to help."

Resignation written across his face, Hunter tossed his truck keys from one hand to the other. "It's a long shot, but it's the only one we've got. I'm sure Jess will be delighted to see an old friend."

CHAPTER 38

Delight didn't begin to cover it. Hunter didn't rush to fill the awkward silence that blossomed when Jess realized Hunter had followed Delaney into the attorney's office. The welcoming smile slid away, replaced with a neutral expression as Jess shoved his chair back and stood behind his desk.

The last time their paths had crossed was when the bailiffs led Hunter, secured in handcuffs, from the courtroom moments after the judge had pronounced his sentence. Jess stood toward the back, one arm around Ellie, the other around Delaney. They'd watched him go like spectators observing a Christian being fed to the lions. With an air of celebratory satisfaction.

Hunter's sense that he should've waited in the truck had been correct. Jess didn't believe in his innocence then and he didn't believe in it now.

"Are you okay?" Jess trotted around his desk and greeted Delaney with a bear hug. "I saw what happened to Detective Ramos. Have they caught the guy who attacked him?"

"Not that I know of." Delaney broke free of the embrace. She swiveled and cocked her head as if to encourage Hunter to enter the circle. "I'm just so thankful it wasn't more serious. He could've been killed."

He could've ended up dead like Ellie and Corey.

"Yep. So what's going on? On the phone you said you needed me to do some research for you. About what?"

Delaney ran through their encounter with Art Pritchard and the information he'd shared about his son. "He spent time in family court on domestic violence charges. CPS was involved."

His forehead wrinkled, Jess leaned against his desk and crossed his arms. "You think because I do family law, I might know the guy? Thousands of cases go through family court every year. This is San Antonio, the beer-drinking capital of the world. The more people drink, the more they fight. Saturday night fiestas turn into shoot-outs in the backyard. It's practically a form of entertainment here."

"Can you just see what you can find out? The gray Camry in the photos belongs to the Pritchards. This son has been driving it. We need to figure out what the connection is between them. His father wouldn't give us his contact information. Maybe you can get it."

"You should stay out of this, Delaney. Let the police do their job." Jess ran one hand through his short blond hair. "It's not safe for you to stick your nose into the investigation. Look what happened to Detective Ramos. He carries a gun and he knows how to use it. The killer still got to him."

Jess's gaze bounced to Hunter. Thinly veiled anger simmered in his eyes. "You used to care about her. I guess you don't care enough now to make sure she doesn't do something stupid like try to find a killer."

"I do care. Of course I care." The words stung. Jess was right, but he seemed to have forgotten that Delaney had always been her own person. "But I'm not in charge of Laney. She makes her own decisions. You know how obstinate she is. At least I'm along to protect—"

"I'm not obstinate. I'm tenacious." Delaney stuck both hands on her hips. "And I don't need protection. I'm allowing Hunter to tag along because he claims he didn't kill Corey. If he didn't, I want to know who did. I also want to know if the two deaths are connected."

"Of course he killed Corey." Jess stomped back around his desk and threw his pen down next to the remnants of a greasy hamburger and french fries congealing in a puddle of ketchup. "I'll never understand the hold he has on you."

"He doesn't have a hold on me." Delaney turned her back on Hunter. She put both hands on Jess's desk and leaned in. "No one does. I just want the truth. I need the truth. Don't you?"

"The truth is your old boyfriend is a murderer. He killed your brother."

"What if he didn't?"

"You're delusional if you believe him."

"I don't know what to believe. It's been so long since I could trust anyone, I'm tired, Jess."

"You can trust me."

"Hey, guys, I'm still in the room, you know." Hunter crossed his arms and spread his feet in his most take-charge stance. Jess could take his doubts and stick them up his nose. Only Laney mattered. "I don't care what you think of me, Jess. I don't have to prove anything to you. I'm going to prove to you, Laney, that you can trust me. You've always been able to trust me. That will never change."

Jess snorted. "Whatever. Get out of my office. I'll look into Pritchard and get back to you, Delaney."

"With pleasure." Not waiting to see if Delaney followed, Hunter stomped from the office. The woman seated at the reception desk looked up, then away, as if she saw something she didn't like in his expression.

How did they manage to revert to their old patterns of interacting so quickly? Like they had time traveled to the days when they hung out together twenty-four seven. A bunch of semi-adults who'd graduated from college but hadn't quite graduated to life.

"Whatever." Hunter shoved through the door with Jess's name stenciled on it. He let it slam so hard the window reverberated.

All grown up.

CHAPTER 39

"Now what?"

"Do you want to talk about what just happened in there?" Delaney ignored Hunter's surly tone. She turned down the volume on the classic rock station he'd jacked up as soon as he started the truck. "Or do you just want to wallow in your little boy pique?"

"Jess never liked me."

"You were convicted of killing my brother. He has every right to feel the way he does. And he's a good friend. He wants to protect me."

"I know. You're right. I'm glad he's a good friend." Hunter smoothed his hands across the wheel. "I'm glad he hung in there with you and Ellie when you needed him. It's just hard when I know I didn't do it. I wish he would give me some grace."

"That's a lot to ask. You were never very nice to him." Delaney flipped through a mental scrapbook of all the memories—good and bad. "You guys picked at him. You teased him. You made him feel like an outsider."

"We did not."

She arched an eyebrow. "Really?"

"Okay, maybe some, but he made it so easy."

"You guys ganged up on him. Remember that time on the Fourth of July when you and Corey got into a fight? A shoving match? He sprayed you down with a hose to get you to stop. What did you do? You turned on him. You shoved him into the pool."

"It was all in good fun." Hunter wiggled like a kid in the principal's office. "Besides, he was such a little puppy dog, always begging for approval. Especially from you and Ellie. Why didn't he ever get his own girlfriend?"

"This is ten years ago we're talking about." Delaney sorted through more memories. Jess had dates. Hadn't he? If he did, he never brought them around. "Maybe he was a late bloomer."

"He's never gotten married. Does he have a girlfriend now? A significant other?"

If he did, he hadn't introduced her to Delaney and Ellie. Or even mentioned her. "He doesn't have the best social skills. Maybe he has a hard time meeting women. Plus he works all the time. His clients are often abused women, children caught in custody battles, and couples who use each other as punching bags. It doesn't exactly showcase marital bliss."

"So he has lots of excuses."

Like Delaney did. Her dates had been limited to ones set up by Ellie or Cam. Most could be assembled in one category: disaster. Not that she planned to share that history with Hunter. "I'm just saying, cut him some slack."

"I'd consider it if he'd do the same for me."

"Drop me off at the shop. The insurance adjustor is done, but it'll take at least ten business days to get my check. I can start cleaning up in the meantime. I'll follow up later with Jess to see what he's found out about Vince Pritchard."

"Don't do anything without me. I'll be off at nine."

"I'll text you."

What happened next would depend on what Jess uncovered about Pritchard. Jess and Hunter couldn't work together, that was obvious. Jess had only agreed to help her because he couldn't say no to her. Hunter might upset that balance and right now, Delaney needed all the help she could get.

Could old patterns never be broken? Was that why she had allowed Hunter back into her life? She had changed. He had changed. Both for the better. Yet he and Jess immediately reverted to their immature, posturing juvenile alter egos.

Why did Jess bring out the worst in Hunter? And vice versa?

On Nueva Street Hunter pulled in next to a miraculously open meter and put the truck in Park. He leaned against his door. "I'm sorry about the scene with Jess."

"I don't get it. I really don't."

"I know you don't. There was a lot going on back in the day that you didn't know about. Undercurrents. Stupid male ego stuff. Stuff that happens when friends spend too much time together."

"Between you and Jess?"

"I always felt like he had a thing for you."

"You're kidding." Delaney chuckled. The closest she'd come to laughing since finding Ellie's lifeless body. She rolled her window down and let the March breeze cool her burning cheeks. "That's ridiculous. He treated me like a little sister."

"He followed you around like a puppy dog."

"He was nice. He *is* nice. A nice guy. A good friend."

"Okay, so I read too much into it."

"Not to mention it was ten years ago, for Pete's sake."

"There's no statute of limitation on jealousy."

"Regardless of how Jess might or might not have felt, it wasn't a two-way street." Delaney shoved open her door and hopped down from the truck. She turned and stuck her head through the window. Hunter was jealous. Of Jess. Did the fact that she took a tiny bit of pleasure in that make her small? Or human? "Surely you knew that. Know that."

"You spent a lot of time together. Jess helped you study for exams. He helped you work on your hitting. You hung out with him at the co-op when you worked on your pieces and he worked on his guitars."

"Wow, you've actually given this some thought." His sketch of those days took on life, bringing with it a flood of nostalgia and longing. Things had seemed so simple. They worked, they ate, they played. Sure, they bickered, snarled, and fought, but they were like family. The family she never had and desperately needed.

Delaney shook her head. "Ellie was always there. Those two finished each other's sentences. When we decided on movies, they always voted me down. Same with music. We all hung out together when you were working. When you came around, I came running."

Hunter's grin held a touch of the sardonic. "I miss those days."

Maybe they were both painting sentimental pictures of the so-called good old days when they debated whether to pay the rent or the water bill. Pooled their coins to buy dollar tacos when money ran out at the same time as the groceries. "Do you really? Wouldn't you rather have a relationship with an independent woman who has the confidence she can take care of herself?"

"Are we going to have that relationship?" The grin died, replaced with a bashful—no, hopeful—expression. "You and me?"

"I don't know yet. We'll see."

"My mom used to say 'we'll see' when the answer was no."

"I'm not your mother."

"I'm aware. And thankful." He glanced in his rearview mirror, down at his side mirror, and back at her. "Don't do anything without me. It's one thing to be independent. It's another to be stupid."

Delaney withdrew from the window. "Nor are you my keeper or my father or the corner cop."

"No, but I love you."

With that proclamation Hunter pulled into traffic and left her standing there.

They'd thrown those words around back in the day, but they were different then. Young, passionate, volatile. Now caution ruled the day. The need to know who they could trust. Hunter might be there, but Delaney remained on the cliff, unsure whether to jump.

God help me.

CHAPTER 40

I found Vince Pritchard

Jess's text arrived just as Delaney pulled her key from the shop's door. She'd spent six solid hours cleaning. Cleaning and not thinking about Hunter's declaration just before he'd driven away. Every time it tried to sneak into her mind, she grabbed the broom or the mop and swatted it away.

She fumbled her purse, dropped her keys, and plopped onto the steps. She was exhausted, which was fine, good in fact. She took a deep breath, steadied her fingers, and responded.

That was fast. Where? How? Should we call the police?
Not yet. As far as I can tell he hasn't done anything
  wrong. He doesn't want to talk to me about Ellie
  though. He says he'll talk to you
Why?
Because you were Ellie's friend
So were you

I'm an attorney. He's been to family court. He's not a fan
of attorneys

Where?

An unfamiliar address popped up on her screen.

Where is this?
He and his wife split. He stays with a friend when he
gets tired of his dad's insults and nagging

Delaney glanced at the time on her phone. Seven o'clock. Hunter wouldn't be off work for two more hours. She swiped off the text screen and punched Favorites to call Jess. He picked up on the first ring. "Are you on your way?"

"How did you find him?"

"He and his wife are battling over custody of their three kids. I talked to his attorney. He owed me a favor and gave me the guy's contact info. Without breaking attorney-client confidentiality, he did manage to convey that the guy isn't too bright, and he may have some anger management issues, but he's not a murderer." Jess sounded proud of himself. "Do you want to talk to him or not?"

"Definitely. He's at this address right now?"

"We both are. He just got here from work. He's changing his clothes. What's your hesitation?"

"Hunter wants to be in on this. He doesn't get off work until nine."

A soft sigh wafted over the airwaves. "It's your call, Delaney. You asked me to find the guy and I did. If you need Hunter, call him." He paused for a beat. Another sigh. "I don't know if I can get Pritchard to stay around. He's supposed to go to his dad's from here. He just stopped by to shower and change. Apparently Dad feeds him. And he has cable. If Pritchard does that, he won't be talking to either of us. You met his dad so you know what I mean."

Jess tried so hard to please. Why hadn't a woman snapped him up? "We can bring Hunter up to speed after we talk—"

"You can bring him up to speed. Leave me out of it. I can't stomach the guy. He killed your brother."

The closest Jess had ever come to standing up for himself. "Fair enough. I'll send him a text later. It'll take me about twenty minutes to get there."

"I'll order a pizza. That'll keep Vince happy."

"You're a good friend."

"For you, anything."

What could she say to that? "I'm on my way."

By the time Delaney fought her way from downtown in I-35 traffic to the address Jess had given her, the sun had dipped down to the horizon. It had taken longer than she expected to find the pothole-laden, one-lane road on San Antonio's far east side where Jess said Pritchard was staying. Delaney's app led her to a mobile home park—or what was left of one.

The entryway sign read JENKINS MOBILE HOME PARK. Someone had spray-painted a row of *X*s over the words. Underneath the vandal had written with a flourish: *Jenkins Graveyard: Where mobile homes come to die.*

Most of the trailers appeared abandoned with their windows boarded up, covered with graffiti, and plastered with red spray-painted NO TRESPASSING signs. Several had been flattened into heaps of metal, insulation, and Sheetrock. At least three lots offered the remnants of blackened, burnt carcasses.

Delaney slowed for a skinny black dog who halted in the middle of the road to bark at her car before it meandered away. She slowed some more, studying the rows of trailers, trying to locate lot numbers. There: 2102. The gray Camry was parked nose out next to a mobile home that had all its windows and door intact. The outer walls, possibly a pale-green color, were dark with mold. Overgrown weeds choked the base of the mobile home. Someone had cut through them to make a path from the strip of gravel parking to the cinder blocks that served as steps.

Jess's maroon Rogue sat half on, half off the road, blocking the Camry's egress.

Smart man.

She pulled in behind the Rogue.

I'm here

Come on in

A second later Jess poked his head out the door and waved.

Delaney returned the wave. The door closed. She grabbed her phone, turned off the GPS app, and paused.

"Don't do anything without me. It's one thing to be independent. It's another to be stupid."

With a groan she rested her purse in her lap and thumbed a text to Hunter, including the address. He probably wouldn't see the text until after he finished up with the kids. But she'd done her duty.

I'll text you after we talk to Pritchard, let you know if
anything worthwhile comes out of it

Feeling better, Delaney stuck her phone in the backpack's front pocket and headed for the mobile home.

Jess had said come on in, but that didn't seem right. She knocked instead. The door opened a sliver.

314

"It's me."

The door swung wide. Delaney stepped onto green shag carpet in what served as a combination living room to her left. The smell of fried eggs, cigarette smoke, and cat urine hung in the air. Someone had left a half-eaten bowl of soggy cereal on a coffee table next to an overflowing glass ashtray. A small TV hung from the wall across from a sagging couch. A WWF fight raged on the screen.

"I saw the Camry out there." Delaney hesitated. The furniture had a greasy lived-in look. The faded yellow, black, and tan plaid couch and matching chair pillows still held the shape of someone's behind, like memory foam on steroids. "Where is he?"

Jess moved away from the door. "Have a seat."

"What about the friend who owns it?"

"Apparently he took off with his girlfriend to the coast for spring break. He lives in a dump, but he has cash for the beach." Jess's words held no judgment. He dealt with all kinds in his line of work. "They're probably camping on the beach or sleeping in his car."

"Where's Pritchard?"

"Have a seat. The couch is semiclean. The pizza hasn't come yet. I don't think they like to deliver out here. They probably get stiffed a lot."

Delaney eased onto the couch. Jess took a seat across from her. "Did you have trouble finding it?"

"Why aren't you answering my question?"

"Pritchard's in the shower. He'll be out in a few minutes."

"He knew I was on my way and he decided to take a shower?"

"I told you, he's not very bright. It's not his fault."

Not very bright, but he did HVAC work with his father, was married, and had three children. "Did you get any more out of him?"

"Not much. He said he didn't really know Ellie." Jess picked up the remote and muted the TV. "Apparently he did some HVAC repair at Michael's once."

"How did he explain his car being in the photos at the restaurant?"

Jess stood. He moved onto the couch next to Delaney, sitting sideways so he was facing her. "We didn't get that far."

Quiet settled between them.

Too quiet. "I don't hear any water running."

"What do you mean?"

"I mean I've been in mobile homes before and in the old ones, like this one, the walls are paper thin. I don't hear water running."

"Maybe he's finished." Jess's hand caressed the couch pillow between them. Perspiration dampened his face. Mustard stained the pocket of his dress shirt. "He's probably getting dressed."

"What's going on? You're being weird."

"Me, weird?"

Something shiny and silver flicked through the air. It took two seconds for it to register. Two seconds too long. A knife blade, long and lean. Delaney moved, but Jess's fingers wrapped around her hair and jerked her head back. The knife's tip pricked her neck, just above her collarbone.

Adrenaline tore through her like a lit gas line. The room shrank—the entire world shrank until only Jess, the knife, and Delaney remained.

This is Jess. This is Jess. The nice guy. One of the few constants in her life for the last ten years.

She wrangled her breath under control. *Soft, easy, slow.* "Jess, what are you doing?"

"I'm so sorry." His voice cracked. "I wanted things to turn out differently."

CHAPTER 41

Fear bit its fangs in deep. Delaney gritted her teeth. *Don't move. Don't move.* Fear wanted her to freeze. Adrenaline demanded she strike out in every direction. If she did, the knife would plunge into her neck.

Jess's quick breaths warmed the chilled skin of her cheek. He eased closer. "I'm sorry, really I am, but you give me no choice. None of you did. Let go of your purse, please."

This is Jess. Sweet Jess. S'mores and hot cocoa Jess. "I don't understand. Why are you doing this?"

"Let go or you'll end up like Ellie." Despite his apologetic tone Jess tugged her hair hard. He ran the tip of the knife down her throat. "I don't want to do that to you. I really don't."

God, no, please no. Disbelief warred with fury. Delaney willed her body to remain motionless. Vomit rose in her throat. "You killed Ellie?"

The words came out in a wisp.

"No. Vince did that."

"Because you told him to?"

"Yes." The single syllable hung in the air—mournful, supplicating, sad. "I could never hurt Ellie."

But you did.

The words stuck in Delaney's throat. The knife's edge caressed her throat. Fear sucked her mouth dry. Dare she swallow?

She drew in air through her nose, but her lungs ached with the inability to breathe. "Why? Why? Why would Vince Pritchard kill for you?"

"I'm his attorney. His wife is divorcing him. He's an adulterer and a drunk, but she's worse. I told him I'd get him custody of his kids—if he does exactly what I tell him to do. If he didn't I'd send his wife a recording of our conversation regarding his transgressions. Those kids are the only good thing to ever happen to him and he knows it."

"Why didn't he report you to the bar association or the police?"

"The man's got the IQ of a sheep."

"So you used a developmentally disabled client to get to Ellie? Why? She loved you."

The knife pierced skin again. Delaney swallowed a gasp.

"No she didn't. She used me and tossed me aside like a coat that didn't fit anymore." Jess lifted the knife a fraction of an inch. The pressure ceased. His hand shook. "She found a new coat, one she liked better. The truth is Ellie loved herself. She was a narcissist. She played with people's feelings. She hung out with me as a friend of last resort. I kept trying to take it to the next level, but she never did. We went to the movies. Spurs games. She'd call me when she was lonely. You know how often I watched movies with her on Friday nights."

"I was there plenty of times. That's what friends do." In his head Jess had blown up friendship into something it wasn't and would never be. Did Ellie realize she was playing with fire? "It sounds like you wanted something from her she couldn't give you."

"I always thought we'd finally be together—right up until she introduced Michael to us."

Jess still had that same puppy-dog look in his eyes he'd had since Delaney met him fourteen years earlier. The same rumpled lived-in body. Yet he was holding a knife to her neck.

"I'm not stupid—even if everyone treats me like I'm a simpleton-oaf-second-cousin-third-wheel. Give me the stun gun."

"I've never treated you with anything but respect. I count you as a friend."

"You condescended to me." He spoke tenderly, as if responsible for her sins. "You can admit it. You felt sorry for me."

"I never did."

"Poor Jess can't get a date. Poor Jess always apologizing. Poor Jess isn't really an artist."

"I never said any of those things." Delaney dug deep for a calm kindness she didn't feel. "Where's Vince now?"

Jess gently applied pressure, forcing her to lean back against the couch. "Don't move, my friend. I don't want to turn you into thin-sliced turkey."

Lips puckered in concentration, he used his free hand to rip her purse from her arms. He transferred her phone to his pocket. "Where's the stun gun?"

"In my car. I figured with you here, I didn't need it." The gun, stuck in her waistband, bit into her back just below the waist. *Always be prepared*. She'd learned her lesson from the struggle with Ellie's killer. "I texted Hunter. He knows where I am. He'll come for me after he gets off work."

"Good. That's exactly what I want him to do. We'll have a cozy little evening together, just the three of us. Where's the pepper spray?"

All those years had Jess simply been feigning friendship? All those barbecues in his backyard. Midnight runs for Whataburgers. The lazy afternoons in his parents' pool debating life's greatest philosophical

319

questions. Baby Ruth or Butterfinger? Who eats black jelly beans? What's in Spam? Star Trek or Star Wars?

"Delaney? It doesn't do any good to stall."

"I'm not stalling."

"You don't need to lie to me. I know you think of me as one of the girls."

"I do not. I never have."

The canister of pepper spray, tucked in her back pocket, pressed against her behind.

Jess let go of her hair, but the knife stayed within inches of her neck. He dumped the contents of her backpack purse on the coffee table. Mints, feminine hygiene products, a tiny mirror, her wallet, her Leatherman multitool, tissues, a wealth of ordinary stuff scattered.

Delaney's hands fisted. Jess had fifty pounds and five inches on her, but he *was* soft. His idea of exercise involved jogging to his car for a drive to Bill Miller Bar-B-Que followed by a drive-through Blizzard from Dairy Queen.

"Hmmm, messy like your mind." After pocketing the Leatherman, he swept ink pens, Tylenol, Tums, and old grocery lists onto the dirty carpet. "Where's the gun?"

"I told you."

A stranger stared at her through Jess's red-rimmed blue eyes. "Good." He swiveled toward the hallway. "Vince, come out here, there's someone I want you to meet."

The Vince Pritchard from the photos had lost weight. His AC repair uniform hung on his tree-trunk physique. He ducked his head and hunched his shoulders. "Good to meet you, ma'am."

Like it was a social gathering and they were about to make chitchat over drinks.

"My buddy Vince is in the doghouse. Isn't that right, Vince?"

Vince's hangdog expression deepened. He shuffled his feet. "Yeah."

"Tell Delaney what you did."

"I tried to kill the detective." The big man's voice was surprisingly soft. "I thought Jess would be happy about it."

Jess tutted like a parent disappointed in his child. "Vince gets an F in following directions. Not only did he do something without my say-so, without asking me first, he thought I would be pleased. Can you fathom that? Pleased that he tried to kill a homicide detective. He is clueless as to the harm he could have done to me if he'd been successful in his reckless act of violence against a police officer."

The harm he'd done to Jess? Detective Ramos could be dead, Pilar Ramos a pregnant widow who would have had to raise three children alone. Somewhere along the line Jess had lost all perspective. Worse, he'd lost his humanity. His moral compass no longer pointed true north. Delaney's only hope now was to seek to resurrect the old Jess—the one whose heart made him choose family law.

That or stun, pepper spray, and knock this Jess unconscious.

Please God, help me reach him before Hunter gets here. Before anyone else gets hurt.

"I want to understand. I really do." Delaney forced herself to relax—or to appear relaxed. "Explain it to me, Vince. What made you think Jess would want you to kill the detective?"

Vince's face screwed up like thinking hurt. "I don't know. I just did—"

"Don't ask him to give you a logical explanation. He did it because he doesn't think things through. Have a seat, Vince, over there in the recliner." Jess nudged Delaney onto the couch. He pulled a slip-tie from his pocket and held it out. "Do me a favor and slip these on, please. That way I don't have to stay so on top of you. I'm sure it's making you uncomfortable."

Not good. So much for her wait for a moment of opportunity. Adrenaline did a number on her blood pressure. Black crept in on her peripheral vision. "No."

"Please."

A polite—to the point of obsequiousness—killer. Delaney had no experience with murderers or psychosis, but Jess had cracked. "You're not going to kill me."

"No, but all I have to do is say the word and Vince will. Isn't that right, Pritchard? You're like my personal hit man."

A sheepish grin crept onto Vince's face. "Personal hit man. I like that." The grin faded. "But I don't like killing women. My grandma says to be nice to women."

"So says the man who cheats on his wife over and over again."

"She cheated first." Vince's voice took on a whining tone. "You know that's true."

"Stop, please stop." Delaney fought the urge to clap her hands over her ears. "Jess, you don't have the guts to do it yourself so you make another man do it for you. What kind of man does that make you? I bet you don't have the guts to kill me yourself."

Hand-to-hand combat was preferable to being tied up.

Jess's face went white. A muscle twinged in his jaw. "Put the slip-ties on or when Hunter shows up, I'll give you a demonstration of what I can do. I'll fillet him like a fish in front of you."

"Hunter would pound you into sausage."

"Only if he knows what's coming. I have the advantage here because he thinks I'm nothing. A big nothing."

Delaney couldn't take that chance. Hunter had spent years in prison defending himself from hard-core killers. She'd take him over Jess even with the disadvantage of surprise. But Jess *and* Vince?

She did as she was told. Once her hands were inside the loops, Jess

322

jerked the ties tight. She rested her hands in her lap and contemplated the room. The clock on the wall over Jess's head read seven forty-five. An hour and fifteen minutes until Hunter left work. If traffic had subsided he could be here in thirty minutes.

One hour and forty-five minutes to figure out how to defuse the situation or warn him.

"Thank you." Jess eased onto the coffee table. He patted her knee. "Ellie wasn't who you thought she was. Neither was Corey, I'm sorry to say."

"There's a lot of that going around."

"Ha. Ha." Jess's attempt at a smile fell short. "Ellie complained all the time about Corey. She thought he was cheating on her. Turns out she was right."

"No. No. He adored Ellie."

"I know you don't want to believe it. You hero-worshiped your big brother, I get that. But he did. He had a fling with a waitress from that bar he liked on the River Walk. Howl at the Moon. Amber Dillon. That was her name."

"Why are you telling me this?"

"Ellie found out. She was beside herself."

"Why didn't she tell me? I was her best friend."

"And Corey was your brother. There were a lot of things she didn't tell you. She told me instead. We were close—closer than any of you realized."

"What are you saying?"

"I'm saying . . . after she found out what Corey had done, she came into my studio one night. That's how the whole thing started—"

"You're making this up." Delaney steadied her voice. Not possible. Not her best friend cheating on her brother with her other best friend. The co-op that had started out as a beautiful way of supporting each other had turned into an incestuous cesspool right under Delaney's nose. "Stop, just stop. You're lying."

"Not about this. Listen or don't listen. It didn't start out that way. We were drinking. She was dancing. She wanted me to dance with her. She needed comfort. I gave her comfort. She knew I loved her. She knew I would never do to her what Corey had done."

"Jess."

He ducked his head and wiped at his face with his sleeve. "Corey wasn't a nice person. He wasn't a good friend. And he sure wasn't a good boyfriend."

Bile burned in the back of Delaney's throat. The truth had been there in front of her the entire time, taunting her. After everything that had happened to her, she still saw only the good in people. "Corey saw you two together, didn't he?"

"Yes. He found out a few days before Fiesta started. Ellie told me. She said we couldn't be together anymore. That it was over. In fact she said it had never started. Not really, that's what she said. Then she kissed me on the cheek and told me I would find someone to love who would love me back, but it couldn't be her. She loved Corey. She said we would always be friends."

The friend speech. Delaney cringed inwardly. The blithe words of a woman who had no understanding of her impact on men. Ellie the beautiful siren in hippy clothes. *Oh, Ellie, what did you do?*

Jess grabbed a tissue from Delaney's packet and swiped at his nose.

"She broke your heart. I'm so sorry. But you didn't leave. You stayed around. Why?"

"Because I loved her."

"And you thought after that night . . . you thought Ellie would see that and be with you instead."

He raised his head. His eyes were full of tears. He nodded. "She told me she couldn't. That she cared about me. She said she never wanted to lose my friendship. But once Corey died, she stopped coming around . . . late at night."

All those years of hoping, of waiting, only to have Ellie fall in love with Michael and talk about him nonstop. Marry him.

"I loved her. Your brother didn't." For the first time, Jess's voice rose. "He told me it was no big deal. He said he and Ellie were soul mates. They would never leave each other. I was just a dalliance. Who uses the word *dalliance*? A snotty artist full of himself, that's who."

A searing moment of certain illumination rocked Delaney. Her chest hurt. Her bones ached. She clinched her hands and forced herself to whisper, "You killed him and let Hunter take the fall."

"I didn't plan it that way, but the planets aligned, I suppose. I overheard the argument. I saw Hunter leave. The opportunity presented itself. It only seemed right." Jess's face brightened. He tapped her cheek with the knife. "Hunter went to prison, and I got Ellie and you both to myself. It was a beautiful win-win. I got away with murder and I got the prize."

"You came with me to tell Ellie." *Don't vomit, don't vomit.* He had hugged Ellie. He made hot tea for them. He held her hand with the hand that killed Corey. "You would've been covered with blood."

"Like everyone else I kept clothes in my studio. I washed up, changed, and hid the clothes until I could burn them—in my parents' fire pit in their backyard."

He said it with such pride, like he wanted her to admire his prowess at avoiding detection.

Swallow. Breathe. "If you loved Ellie, how could you have her killed?"

"She was going to betray me." Disappointment fought with anger, etching misery onto Jess's face. "She came to me when that PI rat

Tremaine tried to blackmail her. I told her I'd help, if she would agree to see me . . . spend time with me. If not, I'd turn the photos over to Michael myself."

"So you became the blackmailer."

"She didn't go for it. She decided to come clean with Michael and let the chips fall where they may."

"Why trash my shop? What purpose did demolishing my livelihood serve?"

"I was hoping you'd have second thoughts about investigating Ellie's death like you're a cop. Unfortunately, you never know when to quit. It was your fault the photos were still in her shop. Vince was supposed to get the photos so the trail wouldn't lead back to him."

Delaney fought to keep her voice calm. Her body jerked. She had no control over it. "Back to you, you mean. But Tremaine knew."

"The PI rat was next on the list." Jess sighed. "He should be dead. And that snotty ex. Both of them."

"You can't kill everyone who crosses you."

Jess's misery slid away, leaving behind a cruel smile. A stranger beamed at Delaney. "But I can sure try."

CHAPTER 42

A phone dinged.

Delaney jumped. The spell broken, she dove away from Jess toward the space between the couch and the table. Hampered by the ties, she crawled in the undulating fashion of a caterpillar toward the door. "Let me go, let me go. Get away from me! You killed my brother. You destroyed my life!"

The coffee table crashed onto its side. Jess's weight bore down on her. Pain ripped through her spine and back muscles. Her face smashed into the carpet. The stench of cat urine, cigarettes, and mold enveloped her aching nose.

She bucked. His weight crushed her.

Jess wrapped his arm around her neck in a tight grip and pulled her back until he had her upright on her knees. "You were better off without Dumb and Dumber." His voice was hoarse in her ear, his breathing labored. "You had me. You can't see that, can you? You just can't see it."

Delaney gasped for air. None came. Stars sparkled in the deep, dark purple in her periphery. "Let . . . me . . . go . . ."

The grip eased. "Looky, looky, what do we have here?" Jess waved

327

the pepper spray in her face. "In the car. You said you never lied to me."

God, please not the stun gun too.

Jess patted her backside. His hand slid under her shirt, his warm, sweaty fingers touched her bare skin. "Here we go. You think you're so smart, so sneaky." He chuckled. "It's okay. Now we have more weapons to work with. Not that Vince needs much more than a knife. Mr. Convict might have prison cred, but we have the upper hand."

His face creased with worry, Vince loomed over them. Jess waved him away. "We're fine. Have a seat. I'll let you know when I'm ready for you to take over."

Ready for Vince to kill her.

Jess remained true to form. He couldn't kill Ellie. Delaney was right. He didn't have the guts to kill her either.

The phone dinged again.

"I bet that's your buddy. What's your code? No, let me guess: 0314."

She was that predictable. Corey's birthday.

Delaney coughed and heaved a breath. *Think. Think.* Her skin crawled. The hands that touched her now had taken a knife and stabbed Corey to death. And then held her hand at his funeral. And again at Hunter's trial. The same hands made popcorn for movie night. Planted Pride of Barbados and esperanza in front of her house. Made cutout cookies at Ellie's house on Christmas Eve. Played the guitar and sang old John Mellencamp songs. Taught Jacob to catch a baseball. Read *Llama Llama Red Pajama* to Skye.

He went on living as if he'd done nothing to change the trajectory of Ellie's and Delaney's lives. Or Hunter's life.

Ten years of Hunter's life. Gone. Marriage. Kids. Life milestones. All missed.

"Oh, good, Hunter wants to know what you found out. Do you still want him to come? Of course you do."

She closed her eyes. *God, please, don't let Hunter be hurt. Put Your bubble of protection around him. And me, please.*

She leaned against the couch and focused on not vomiting.

"Don't move."

She hunched, hands clutched under her. *Just wait. Just wait. You'll get yours.* "Why would I still be here? It wouldn't take this long to interview Vince."

"I'm telling him we're waiting on Detective Ramos. We're sitting on Vince as a witness until he arrives. Ramos thinks Vince is a person of interest. Vince wants a deal. He won't tell all until he gets one in writing."

It might work.

Hunter, don't fall for it. Please, God, don't let him fall for it.

CHAPTER 43

How far out is Flores? Is he coming lights & sirens?
He's picking up Detective Ramos from the hospital.
He's being released

Not good. Hunter shoved his duffel bag across the seat and climbed into his truck. Irritated at his big thumbs, Hunter managed to hunt and peck another text.

Was Ramos mad you stuck your nose in again?
No

Delaney must not want to text in front of the guy. Or maybe Jess was breathing down her neck.

U OK? On my way

No response. Worry burrowed between Hunter's shoulder blades. Delaney could handle herself. He had seen her in action. But Jess. The guy had a spaghetti noodle for a spine. Delaney and Ellie insisted on defending him, but he was always such a wuss.

At least he had been ten years ago. Today in his office he'd seemed more take-charge. Like he'd graduated from spaghetti noodle to uncooked lasagna noodle. With a grim chuckle at his lame similes—or were they metaphors—Hunter slammed his door, started the truck, and pulled from the lot. Even so, Jess probably wanted to make a deal for this Pritchard guy. The lawyer in him would take over.

Hunter had no reason to trust attorneys in general, but Delaney liked Jess. So had Ellie. So Hunter would do the same. Everyone deserved another chance. Besides, Jess was convinced Hunter had killed Corey. Until Hunter proved otherwise, Jess had a right to be wary and distant.

His phone dinged. Finally an answer from Delaney.

I'm fine

Which was good, because finding the trailer park wasn't easy. After two missed turns and a heightened—but squashed—desire to thoroughly cuss the designers of San Antonio's convoluted, congested highway system, Hunter made it to the far-east-side neighborhood.

The lack of streetlights made it hard to avoid potholes. The Ram's suspension shimmied and groaned. Hunter swerved to avoid a pack of dogs that trotted across the alleged road. "You could've warned me, Laney," he muttered.

Finally his headlights landed on a Trailblazer with Laney's RECYCLE—FOR YOUR CHILDREN'S SAKE bumper sticker. She'd parked behind a maroon Rogue. No cop cars—marked or otherwise. The gray Camry took up most of the small driveway. A naked bulb hung over the mobile home's concrete-block steps, but it didn't throw much light on the situation.

Text? No reason. They knew he was coming. Leaving his truck on a dark, narrow road in this graffiti-decorated trailer park gave Hunter heartburn, but Flores surely was right behind him.

Hunter locked the truck, said a silent prayer, and tromped up the steps to the door where he knocked lightly.

"Door's open."

Seriously? Any Tom, Dick, or Harry could be at Pritchard's door. Why would the guy allow Laney to invite someone in? The hair on the back of his neck prickling, Hunter tugged the door open a sliver.

The interior was dark except for flickering lights as though the TV might be on. Watching TV while they waited for the cops to show up? "What's going on, Laney?"

"Mr. Pritchard is getting antsy, Nash." Jess, his voice full of concern, answered. "Come in and close the door. You didn't happen to see Detective Flores as you drove in?"

"No, I didn't, but it's pitch black out there." Hunter stepped inside. The warm, stifling air smelled of stale beer, cigarette smoke, and cat pee. "It's not much lighter in here."

"We're watching home movies. You should join us."

Hunter's eyes adjusted to the darkness. Jess and Delaney sat side by side on the couch. He had his arm around her—or so it seemed. "What the . . ." He started forward.

"Hunter, don't."

The anger mixed with fear in Delaney's voice brought him to a dead stop.

The light from the TV flickered.

The knife was big and its blade firmly pressed against Delaney's neck. Cold dread followed by an anger of a ferocity that Hunter had never experienced before—even when the jury foreperson read the guilty verdict—seared through him. This kind of anger, if bottled, could be sold as an explosive on the black market.

"You need to let her go. Right. Now."

"Big man talking. I think, for once, I have the upper hand. So to speak." Jess actually laughed. The knife's edge moved, forcing Laney to arch her neck with a sudden intake of air. "I don't want to hurt her. Her life is actually in your hands at the moment."

Delaney made a tiny sound, like a muffled cough. Jess tutted. "My hand is getting tired, and it's getting shaky. I may have to hand it over to my friend Vince. Vince, say hello to our visitor. This is Hunter Nash."

A big man who matched the photos at the Pritchard house sat in a recliner, big hands limp in his lap, his head down. When he raised it, he didn't quite make eye contact with Hunter. Instead, his gaze landed somewhere to Hunter's left. "Hey, it's nice to meet you."

"So, Nash, have a seat."

The survival instinct that had served Hunter so well in prison reemerged. An animal that knew how to stop breathing at the right moment, to stand stock-still, to speak in monosyllables, to watch and wait, to dissemble whenever and however necessary to stay alive.

"You're in charge, Jess. Whatever you want."

"Good boy. I bet you never thought those words would ever come out of your mouth. I sure didn't. What I want is for you to have a seat." Jess flourished the knife toward a chair that had been placed next to the couch so that the person seated in it would be able to see the TV. "Please."

Hunter sat.

"Now toss your phone over here. Gently."

Hunter did as he was told without taking his gaze from the man who held Laney's life in his hands. "What would be nice is if you would put the knife down, let go of Laney, and we could talk about what's going on here."

"Laney, honey, would you rewind the DVD, please, and turn the sound back on? I'd like Nash to see it too."

"We've watched it four times—"

"But Nash hasn't seen it, and I never get tired of watching it."

Delaney fumbled with a TV remote in her lap. Her hands were restrained with flex-cuffs. Proof Jess knew she posed a real threat to him.

"Isn't she beautiful?"

Hunter jerked his gaze from Laney to the TV. A smiling Ellie filled the screen. The camera zoomed out, revealing that she wore a coral beaded flapper dress. Her long hair—now blonde instead of the brunette he'd known—flowed down her back. Baby coral roses had been woven into her locks. She carried a matching bouquet. A little girl trotted in front of her, flinging rose petals onto the beach between rows of white wooden folding chairs. Both were barefoot.

The camera panned to the chairs. Women in skimpy sundresses and men in guayabera shirts and white linen pants filled them. Everyone was smiling.

Another pan. An arch decorated with more roses and matching ribbons that fluttered in the breeze came into view, along with a shot of Laney in a less fancy dress in the same color as Ellie's. She, too, was smiling. A young boy in a white shirt and pants stood between her and a priest and another man Hunter didn't recognize.

Ellie's wedding. On repeat. Why? "Ellie was as pretty as ever. I liked her natural hair color though. I'm surprised she changed it. She was always into being natural." Hunter kept his tone conversational. "I can't believe she's gone."

"Me neither." Jess heaved an enormous sigh. "The wedding was so beautiful. Her parents flew us out to Riviera Maya in Mexico. Did you know that? Me and Laney were the only ones from the old co-op gang invited. Cam said her feelings weren't hurt, but I could tell, she was hurt. Funny, isn't it? Not funny, ha-ha. Ellie lived in her own little world. She never thought about how she hurt other people."

Now they were getting somewhere. Where exactly? "Did she hurt you?"

"Pause it, Laney. Right there. On Michael."

Laney complied. The somber man stood about a foot taller than Laney and the priest. The sun reflected on his shiny bald head.

"That's Michael. Her husband. Handsome man, right? Total opposite from Corey. She told me that's what she was going for. She talked to me about him all the time. 'Michael is so handsome, isn't he?' 'Michael has a huge clientele.'" Jess did a fair job of mimicking Ellie's high voice. "'Michael makes good money as an accountant.' 'Michael is buying me a Mercedes SUV to cart the kids around in.' 'Michael's taking us to Maui this summer.' 'Michael thinks I'm a better mother to his kids than his ex.' You never met him, did you?"

"No, never got the chance. What with prison and all."

Another choked cough from Delaney. Jess tutted again. "Easy, my friend. He'll figure it out, sooner or later."

"Figure what out?" Hunter frowned.

"Jess killed Corey and framed you," Delaney bit out the words through gritted teeth. "He had Ellie killed because she married Michael instead of him. You spent eight years in prison for a crime he committed."

CHAPTER 44

The barely tethered anger threatened to burst from its restraints. Hunter gripped the chair's arms with both hands. His heart thrashed in his chest, trying to rip its way out so it could throttle the man on the couch.

Ten years of his life, gone. Ten years of Laney's life. No marriage. No children. No waking up side by side in the morning. *God, help me. Help me. How does a person forgive that?*

Hunter dug deep for a semblance of calm. "Corey could be such a jerk sometimes. Of course, so could I. We were so full of ourselves in those days. It must feel good to have the upper hand now. I'm betting you didn't mean to do it, did you?"

"No. You could say it was an accident, I guess." Jess's gaze remained on the TV screen. A strange reverence softened his words. "Afterward, I felt good. I admit it. I felt like I'd done something. I stood up for myself for the first time. I stood up for Ellie. It felt good."

"You're sick." Laney rocked away from him. "You need help. Let go of me. Let us get you some help. Can't you see what you're doing here is sick? It's wrong."

"Stop struggling, girl." Jess hauled her back against his chest. "Next you'll give me that two-wrongs-don't-make-a-right speech. I have no regrets about Corey."

"And Ellie? What about Ellie?"

"Start the video."

"Why? Why do you want to watch her marry another man?"

"Start it."

The video played. Ellie faced Michael. Each recited vows they'd written. The little flower girl giggled and played in the sand at their feet. The ring bearer tried to reel her in. Laughter off camera reflected the audience's delight. A smiling Laney picked up the toddler and settled her on her hip. The boy dusted sand from the pillow and resumed his duties.

The all-important words "I do" were uttered.

"You may kiss the bride," the priest intoned.

The kiss lasted forever. Hoots and hollers could be heard.

"Hurrah for the new couple." Jess hooted. "Congratulations, Ellie. You married a man you hardly knew for security and comfort and a house in the Monte Vista neighborhood. So you could drive an SUV and take vacations to Aspen and Maui."

Laney didn't argue with him. Hunter couldn't.

The screen went black. Then bloomed again with smiling faces of guests seated at tables covered with white tablecloths. Round bowl vases filled with coral roses graced each table. The camera panned to a buffet of seafoods, salads, and tropical fruits.

Jess offered a play-by-play. "There's Mrs. Cruz. And there's Michael's father and mother, Robert and Vicki Hill. They were so ill at ease. Ellie said her parents had to pay the Hills' way. She didn't care. She wanted to get married on the beach, like a hippy, but it had to be on a beautiful Mexican beach. It had to be a destination wedding. She didn't see the irony in that.

"And the kids, aren't they cute, dancing together to moldy oldies? Who picked the music?

"Whoa, there's Delaney, isn't she a looker, Nash? I told her she was way more beautiful than the bride, but she blushingly denied it.

"And there's the happy couple gliding across the dance floor, their first dance as husband and wife. Too bad Michael had two left feet and Ellie was blitzed.

"The champagne was delicious. I imbibed, but not your friend Delaney. She was a good girl."

"Talk about blitzed. I'm surprised you remember that night." Laney's tone held barely tapped down sarcasm. "You were weaving all over the place before the first toast."

"And you spent most of the evening staring out at the ocean like you'd lost your best friend."

"I had."

"You're as bad as Ellie. You had me. But no, you took me for granted."

Delaney snorted. "Turns out that's a good thing, isn't it?"

"I was there for you every time you needed it."

"Because you killed my brother and framed my best friend for it."

"I didn't frame anyone. The police kindly did it for me."

Her best friend.

A lump the size of Fort Worth lodged in Hunter's throat. His fingers dug into the chair's padding. *Help me help her, God. Please.*

The camera revealed Jess swaying with the little girl in his arms to a Chicago song on the dance floor crowded with clearly drunk guests. Suddenly Jess lurched toward the stage. The camera followed. Child still in his arms, he leaned over a potted dahlia.

The screen went black.

"I guess the wedding videographer figured Ellie wouldn't want video of me blowing chunks."

"So you were in love with Ellie. That's why you killed Corey—for her." Hunter fumbled the pieces, trying to get them to fit together in a picture that made sense. Or a picture that made sense to an insane person. Logic didn't apply, did it? "If you loved her, why kill her?"

"I didn't. Vince did. Isn't that right, Vince?"

Vince nodded obligingly.

"Why?"

"Laney will explain. If she has time."

Ominous words. They were running out of time. "Why take on Michael as a client? He married the woman you allegedly loved. Why kill her and not him?"

"Michael didn't do anything wrong." For the first time Jess faltered. A tiny crack in his confident facade. "He didn't know. About her past. He didn't know . . . about me. A lie of omission on Ellie's part. She claimed her past didn't matter. That she wanted a fresh start. She'd already started cutting me from her life. She made me meet her at a restaurant where no one would know us for breakfast. Then she said we had to stop. But she had no qualms about coming to me to help her with the PI and his blackmail attempt.

"When I tried to get her to keep seeing me, she threatened to come clean and show Michael the photos herself. The PI was so inept he didn't even get a clear shot of me, but she was willing to tell her husband the truth. She was sure he loved her so much he would forgive her. There would be no more illicit, clandestine meetings. That's what she called eating Mexican food while I watched."

"You could frame me for a murder you had committed, but not a guy you hardly know?"

"You deserved it."

No hesitation there. Hunter squeezed his hands into fists. The desire to smash Jess's face to a bloody pulp blurred his vision and sent his blood pressure into the stratosphere. *Don't do it, don't move. Think of Laney. He's got Laney.*

Forgive me, God. I'm not an animal. I'm not one of those guys in prison. My faith is more than skin deep. Help me. Help us.

Jess grimaced. "I know what you're thinking. You'd love to pound me into a piece of bloody meat. Not today, my friend."

"Not at all. I'm working on forgiving you. You're supposed to forgive people their transgressions, no matter how hard it is, just like God forgives ours. I'm trying to walk in your shoes. I understand your frustration. Me and Corey should've been nicer to you. We were jerks. I'm sorry."

"A day late and a dollar short, as the saying goes." Jess's jaw worked. "Turn the TV off. Enough waltzing down memory lane."

Agreed. Hunter fingered the scar along his jaw. His time in prison had taught him that any time a person got into a fight with a knife wielder—or homemade sharp object—both would come away with cuts. He had scars on the outside of both his arms from trying to defend himself from the slashing shank. Another one on his left hand just below his pinkie finger.

Despite the stifling warm air in the trailer, a chill ran through him. Jess was out of shape and had no experience with fighting. Vince was another story. He was big and he'd killed once and tried a second time. Only the fact that Detective Ramos had a gun had saved his life.

"Now what?"

"Now we get on with it. You can help by turning on the light. The switch is on the wall by the TV." Jess stood, dragging Laney up with him. "Slow and easy. Think about what's at stake if you decide to do something stupid."

"You got it. No worries. The last thing I want is for someone to get hurt. We can all walk away from this."

Jess snorted but said nothing.

Hunter turned on the light. The trailer's living room had been trashed. A coffee table lay on its side. Laney's purse and its contents were strewn across the ugly green shag carpet. An upended ashtray crowned a heap of cigarette stubs and ashes. He sideswiped a glance at the kitchenette. Someone had stacked dirty dishes on the counter next to a pile of unopened mail. Out of the corner of his eye, he registered empty cat food and water bowls next to a skinny patio table for two on a greasy black-and-white-checkered linoleum.

No magic bullet presented itself that would allow them to escape this bizarre nightmare. Had he endured an undeserved prison sentence only to watch the woman he loved be killed? To die himself?

Nope. He would play the cards he'd been dealt. "What's the plan?"

"Time for you and Laney to play house. I think you two need a nice fire. You could make s'mores and drink hot chocolate. Laney likes that. Don't you, Laney?"

Her green eyes were huge, her skin chalky white, except for her nose. It was red and bruised. Her nod was almost imperceptible. Droplets of blood stained her lilac shirt. "I used to dream of playing house with Hunter," she whispered. "You took that dream away from me."

"Now I'm giving it back. The two of you deserve each other."

Why didn't that sound like a good thing?

"See those zip-ties on the floor?"

Hunter nodded. "I do."

"Grab one and put it on. Nice and tight—but not so tight as to be uncomfortable."

Nice of him to worry about Hunter's comfort. Jess's choice for flex-cuffs were a step above regular zip-tie cuffs, but not police quality. He probably thought such a purchase would draw suspicion.

Hunter slid the flex-cuffs on and used his teeth to tighten it. The fact that Jess practiced family law and not criminal law also worked in Laney and Hunter's favor. He didn't know criminals the way Hunter did. He hadn't spent hour upon hour listening to other convicts tell war stories about the times they'd eluded or escaped law enforcement. "Why use a knife instead of a gun? You don't have to get as close to your victim. You have more room to move around."

"With Corey it was a weapon of opportunity. The utility knife was there. With Ellie, I knew Vince couldn't be trusted with a gun. He'd probably shoot himself in the foot. Or shoot and miss her. We didn't have time for lessons. Besides, I'm a pacifist. I spent too much time on hunting trips with my dad, forced to shoot innocent deer, dove, quail, and turkeys. I swore I'd never shoot a living thing again."

Seriously?

Laney hacked in a half-laugh, half-cough.

"Don't laugh." Jess's lips drooped into a hurt frown. He still managed that puppy-dog persona that always irritated Hunter. "Also, I'm not stupid. I know buying a gun leaves a much bigger paper trail. The handy-dandy hunting knife doesn't—not in Texas anyway. I'll pop it back in my dad's hunting stuff when I stop by to check on him and Mom in the morning. Dad hasn't gone hunting in seven years—not since he hurt his back. Yet he won't let her get rid of all the paraphernalia."

"You've thought of everything." Hunter shook his head.

"You always underestimated me. One day I had an epiphany."

"What's that?"

"All clichés have their roots firmly entrenched in an eternal truth."

"Which in this case is?"

"Nice guys finish last."

CHAPTER 45

No Mr. Nice Guy peered out from behind Jess's doughy face. Delaney breathed through her mouth. His body odor had turned sour. The smell made her stomach roil. His hold loosened. Her legs threatened to collapse under her.

"Don't faint on me, friend." He whipped the knife from her neck to her lower back. The point pricked her skin above her waistline. "Vince. Get over here. Finish zip tying Nash for me."

"Does it help you to call him Nash instead of Hunter?" Delaney edged toward Hunter. His dark eyes were full of concern and encouragement. The farther she moved from Jess, the more elbow room she had. The more space Hunter had to maneuver. Zip tying his legs together wouldn't help their cause. "Does it make it easier for you to kill him? What about me? Why not call me Broward?"

Vince complied. He knelt in front of Hunter and began to pick at the laces.

"Don't bother untying them." Impatience tinged Jess's voice. His nerves were beginning to fray. Making him more likely to do something irrational—more irrational. "Just pull them off. Hurry up."

Vince's shoulders hunched. "His shoes are too tight for that."

"Sorry about that. They're new." Hunter leaned forward, hands tucked in his lap. "My mom bought them for me. She's so happy I'm home."

"If you're trying to make Vince feel sorry for you, it won't work. He's more concerned with pleasing me."

Vince tugged hard. The first shoe flew off. He fell back.

"Get up, you doofus."

His face brick red, Vince again did as he was told.

"Careful, I'm ticklish." Hunter managed to sound chipper. "Sorry if my feet stink. It's warm in here."

Vince wiped at his forehead with his sleeve. Despite the trailer's AC, he was sweating. "My feet always stink."

"Enough chitchat, boys. Finish the job."

"Tight, but not too tight." Jess gave Vince an air high five with his free hand. "Now get him situated on the couch. Side by side, lovebirds."

Jess nodded toward Delaney. "Now, Ms. Broward."

This time when Vince knelt, he kept his gaze on Delaney. His eyes seemed to be expressing apology. He fumbled with her shoes. Once they were off, he stroked her feet. His mouth trembled. He didn't tighten the zip ties the way he'd done with Hunter. "Sorry about this," he whispered. "I really am." He stood.

"Good job." Jess did the air high-five thing again. Vince didn't respond. In fact, he didn't seem to notice. His gaze remained on Delaney.

"Okay. Go get the gas cans from the back."

Vince didn't move.

"What's the problem?" Jess growled.

"They seem like nice people. Do we have to hurt them?"

"We are nice people, Vince." Trying to keep fear from her voice, Delaney locked gazes with Vince as if they were the only two people in the room. "We've never hurt anyone. Ellie was a nice person too.

She had a husband and two stepkids. Don't add to your guilt. Call 911. Please."

"Shut up." Jess stepped into the line of sight between Delaney and Pritchard. "Just shut up. Vince, get in there and get those gas cans. Now. If you want to keep seeing your kids, you'll do what I tell you to do."

"I'm going. Right now. I'm sorry, Jess." Vince stumbled over the upside-down ashtray, righted himself, and disappeared down the hallway. "I'm sorry, I'm sorry."

Jess trotted around the peninsula that separated the kitchen from the living room. A minute later he was back, a long, lean fireplace lighter in one hand.

Gas cans. The warm air turned cold against Delaney's skin. She struggled with the zip ties. They tightened. *Just breathe, breathe, think.* "What are you doing?"

"I thought I'd make a fire so you two can make those s'mores."

"Jess."

"You can thank me later. Oh, wait, no you can't." He chortled at his own joke. "Sit tight."

"You don't think somebody will notice and call the fire department?"

"Didn't you see the half dozen lots with burned trailers on them? It's a regular form of recreation around here." Jess swiveled toward the hallway. "What's taking that dimwit so long? Vince, get out here! People are too afraid to talk to the police, but everyone knows it's arson. No one does anything about it. That's according to Vince, and he should know. What is his problem? It was a simple task. Bring out the gas cans. Vince!"

No response. "Good help is hard to find." Jess trotted toward the back hallway and disappeared from sight.

Delaney fought to stand. "I'd rather be stabbed than burned to a crisp."

In what universe would she ever have thought she'd be uttering those words?

Hunter wobbled to his feet. "Do what I do."

He raised his arms over his head, then slammed his hands down on his chest. The ties snapped. Gasping, he leaned over. "Man that hurts."

Delaney followed his example. Nothing happened.

"Harder, as hard as you can."

The smell of smoke mingled with the stringent odor of gas. White and black plumes furled and unfurled as they escaped from the hallway. She had no intention of burning to death. Or letting anything happen to Hunter.

Delaney summoned all the fury of the past three hours. She raised her arms high and slammed them down on her chest. The plastic snapped. The skin rubbed raw stung like a son of a gun. "Ouch, ouch, ouch."

"Sorry, but it's worth it."

How did he know that would work? Now wasn't the time to ask.

Hunter dug in his pants pocket and produced a pocketknife. In thirty seconds flat he cut Delaney's legs free. He plopped on the couch and cut his own ties.

Delaney scooped up the glass ashtray. Solid, heavy. The best she could do.

Vince came first. Perspiration soaked his face and collar. His features were contorted with fear and uncertainty. Jess followed. Fire whooshed down the hall behind them, framing him in flickering yellow-and-orange flames and black smoke. Humming, Jess splashed more gas left and right. "Vince got cold feet about the plan. I told him they'd warm up when we get the fire going. He now understands we can't do the stabbing thing again. Our cop friends might start thinking they have a serial killer on their hands. Varying the MO will make it harder for the police to figure out. Right, Vince?"

Vince nodded but his chin quivered. He held the knife now. He caressed the blade as if it gave him comfort. "You're always right, Jess. But I have the knife in case the fire don't work."

"It will, I promise."

Finally Jess stopped talking. He'd caught sight of their new freedom. Smirking, he shook his head. "Too late, lovebirds."

He lifted the gas can high and allowed its contents to flow freely. His left hand held a fireplace lighter. The flame flicked on. He pointed it toward them.

An enormous orange ball of fur tore from under the couch, hissing and shrieking. It raced between Delaney and Hunter, straight at Jess.

He dropped the lighter. Delaney launched the ashtray like a Frisbee at him.

A direct hit in the forehead. Jess fell back. His head hit the entertainment center with a sickening smack. He sank to the floor, not moving.

"Jess!" Vince's features twisted in horror. "What did you do to him?" He started toward the couch. Hunter launched himself over it and hit the other man full force.

The fire didn't seem to notice or care that two men grappled in its midst. Vince was bigger and heavier, but Hunter was stronger and faster. His survival instinct was honed by eight years in prison. He knocked Vince to the floor. The other man landed with an *oof*. He swung the knife in the air, each time the blade precariously close to Hunter's gut.

Hunter scrambled away. Vince rolled over and came up on his

knees, the knife still between them. Hunter punched hard, but Vince's grip on the knife didn't lessen.

Vince jabbed and parried with the knife. A grunt from Hunter said he'd made contact. So did the blood running down his arm.

Delaney searched the room for a weapon. She vaulted over the coffee table and fell to her knees next to Jess. The pepper spray. It was in his pants pocket. Delaney dug it out, dropped it, then snatched it up again.

Flames shot up like geysers, feeding on the carpet, the pillows, and curtains. Vince was on top of Hunter. He held the knife in midair, poised to strike. Hunter bucked but to no avail.

Delaney took aim and sprayed Vince in the eyes. He screamed. The knife flailed. His free hand clawed at his face.

Hunter shoved up from the floor. Delaney landed a solid right hook to Vince's face.

The big man wavered for a second and then went down. The heat from the flames burned Delaney's cheeks. She sidestepped and made it to the coffee table and Jess's pile of zip ties. She tossed them to Hunter. He got them on Vince. "Let's get out of here. This place is done for."

"We can't leave Jess." The smoke scorching her lungs, Delaney pulled her T-shirt up around her mouth and nose. Sparks singed her face and arms. "I'll drag him out."

"I'll be back." Hunter got Vince up and shoved him toward the door. "Walk, walk, move. Don't you get it? Do you want to burn to death?"

Vince muttered something about being better off dead, but he moved.

Delaney latched on under Jess's armpits and tried to drag him toward the door. He was dead weight. The line *no pun intended* ran circles in her head.

Then Hunter was back. Together they dragged him across the living room. Delaney shoved the door open wider. Hunter manhandled Jess's dead weight across the threshold. "Come on, get out of there."

"The cat. Where's the cat?"

"We'll leave the door open."

"No." Delaney shot into the kitchen.

The oversized feline hunkered down under the sink. His tail had bloomed into a huge ball. He hissed and yowled.

"Come on, sweetie, come on. We have to go."

"Delaney, get out, now!"

The cat launched himself past her in a flying leap. He landed lightly and dashed toward the door.

Thank You, God.

No more fatalities. No more innocent lives.

CHAPTER 46

"Is he dead?"

Still clutching the knife, Delaney staggered down the steps and dropped to her knees next to Hunter, who bent over Jess's inert body. His face glistening with tears, Vince knelt next to Jess. "You killed him. You killed Jess."

"No worries, Pritchard, your psychopath is still breathing. His pulse is strong." Hunter drew his fingers away from Jess's neck. "He's just knocked out. He'll come to with a bad headache. He may need a couple of stitches."

Relief blossomed. No matter how monstrous the real Jess turned out to be, Delaney didn't want his death on her hands. Or anyone else's. "You don't sound happy about him still being alive."

No response.

Hunter stuck his hands in Jess's pockets. His search produced both their cell phones, Jess's phone, two sets of keys, and a billfold. Hunter used his own phone to call 911. His voice was cool as he asked for Fire, EMS, and police. In particular that Detectives Ramos and Flores be notified.

Finally he stuck the phone in his back pocket and glared at Vince. "He killed my best friend and her brother, Corey Broward. He had

TRUST ME

you kill Ellie. I lost a decade of my life because of him. And then he was going to kill this woman." Hunter's voice choked. "This woman whom I love."

There was that word again. *Love.*

Vince broke down and sobbed like a kid in trouble for picking a fight on the playground. "I'm sorry. I'm sorry. I'm sorry."

"I know you are, dude, but it doesn't help much. Ellie was a beautiful person. You took her life. You can never take that back. You can never be sorry enough." Hunter's hands fisted and unfisted. "Just sit tight. The police are on their way." He turned his back on Vince and folded Delaney into a hug that crushed her ribs and lungs.

Not that she was complaining.

For the first time in a decade, Delaney rested. No trying to figure it out. No standing alone, proud, on her own two feet. "I'm sorry too," she whispered into his sweaty, stinking shirt. "I'm so sorry I doubted you. I'm so sorry you lost ten years of your life. Sorry is so inadequate, but it's all I have to offer."

Hunter pushed her away. His face, wet with tears and damp with perspiration, filled with shame. "It wasn't your fault. If anything it was my fault for not seeing how Jess felt. We picked on him like schoolyard bullies. Because we could and because he never fought back. He's right. He was too nice."

"You're bleeding."

Hunter looked down. Splotches of blood decorated his white T-shirt. He pushed it up. Blood seeped from gashes on his forearm, on his wrists, another near his shoulder, and one just below his rib cage. "At least he didn't hit any vital organs."

"I'm so sorry—"

"You saved my life with that pepper spray. Don't apologize."

Jess's legs moved. He groaned.

351

"No, you don't." Hunter tossed a set of keys at Delaney. She caught them. "Open the Camry's trunk."

Delaney struggled to stand. Her legs still didn't want to cooperate. Hunter helped her and she let him. There was no weakness in needing help. None at all. Once the trunk stood open, Hunter heaved Jess into it and shut the lid.

"Just to be on the safe side. You should move your car."

Hunter told Vince to stay put. Somehow they both knew he would. He was used to obeying orders. He wanted to please. A perfect patsy for someone like Jess.

While Hunter drove the Camry a safe distance down the road, Delaney got in her Trailblazer. Her hands shook so hard she had trouble getting the key into the ignition. Her legs trembled, making it difficult to press on the accelerator. A glance in the rearview mirror revealed a stranger with a swollen, bruised nose, dried blood on it and her upper lip and thin blood smeared from cuts on her neck.

Still, euphoria billowed through her as adrenaline coursed through her veins. She was alive. Hunter was alive. Jess would survive. He and Vince Pritchard would take the punishment the justice system would mete out to them.

Not so for Ellie and Corey.

She parked and stumbled toward the fire. Hunter backed up his truck several yards, slammed it in Park, and hopped out.

People began to spill out of neighboring trailers. A skinny Black man in boxer shorts and a sleeveless T-shirt trotted toward them from the closest one, dragging a garden hose behind him. "I'll try to put it out."

"It's too late, but thanks." Hunter cocked his head toward the inferno. "Don't get too close. There may be gas lines or propane tanks in there."

The man nodded, but he tugged at the hose and kept going.

Hunter followed. He helped Vince to his feet and walked him out to the truck, then placed him in the cab. Vince didn't argue. He didn't resist. He didn't even speak.

Hunter put his arm around Delany's shoulders. Together, they leaned against the bumper and waited.

Orange and red flames blossomed across the black sky, like a beacon for the approaching fire trucks, police cars, and ambulances. Their sirens mingled in a crazy, macabre melody. The whirling lights danced and illuminated the dirt road.

"It feels like we're watching a movie." Delaney shivered. The euphoria drained up, leaving her spent, in pain, and exhausted. Nausea blew threw her. "About somebody else's life."

"We get to move on. We'll never forget what happened here or what happened ten years ago. But we'll be different people because of that. Because of what Jess did. He changed us. He changed our lives."

"Are you saying we should thank him for that?"

"No. We thank God we survived, and we try to be better people."

"I prayed you would live. That we would live."

He squeezed her shoulders. "That's a good sign."

The first responders arrived all at once, and there was no more time for talk.

That was okay. Good even. Too much had happened. Hunter was right. They were different people because of the events that had occurred in April 2010.

They weren't the same two people who'd been in love in that other life.

They might start over or it might be easier to walk away.

CHAPTER 47

Civilians. They were a worse pain than any stab wound could cause. Andy gritted his teeth and breathed through the burning ache in his side. He shoved open the passenger door to find Flores blocking his exit from the Charger.

"I can get myself out." Andy grabbed the door frame and hoisted himself to his feet. The stab wound that decorated his right side throbbed, as did more shallow slashes to his arms and wrists. Thirty stitches in all, but nothing important had been hit. *Thank You, Jesus.* "Stop babying me."

"You should be at home with Pilar." Flores had groused all the way out to the trailer park where Hunter Nash, Delaney Broward, and Jess Golightly appeared to have made mincemeat of their investigation. The trailer in question was now a smoldering pile of burnt remnants. The firefighters were still putting out hot spots. "The doctor said to take it easy."

"Just get out of way."

"Grouchy, grouchy. I'll see what the crime scene folks have."

First stop. Hunter Nash, the mostly likely suspect. He was seated in the back of a patrol car. A patrol officer stood next to the open car door, interrogating him. "I know this guy. Let me talk to him."

"He claims he and the woman are the victims of attempted murder." The officer consulted his notebook. "By a man named Jess Golightly. He also claims Golightly set the fire. And he's responsible for conspiring to murder a woman named Ellie Hill and the ten-year-old murder of Corey Broward."

Which made no sense, whatsoever. "I've got this." Andy stuck his hand on the roof of the car and leaned in. His entire body protested. "You're under arrest. Both you and your girlfriend. Have you been read your rights?"

"No, but I've already contacted Pastor James. He's getting in touch with my lawyer. He'll meet me downtown."

The voice of experience.

"You could at least hear our side of the story before you start throwing your weight around." Nash's shirt was soaked in sweat and dirty. Dried blood decorated his T-shirt. Rips in the shirt revealed bandages on his chest. More covered patches on his arms. His eyes were red rimmed. He ran his hands over his dirty face. "We solved your case for you so a thank you might be in order."

A *thank you*? "Civilians don't solve cases. They stay out of homicide investigations because they know what's good for them." Andy straightened. "Get out. I can't bend over like this."

Nash did as he was told. "Are you all right? Should you even be here? You're white as a sheet."

"You're pretty beat up yourself. Just run through what happened."

Nash spun a convoluted story that pinned everything on Jess Golightly and Vince Pritchard. He did have a way with words.

"Get back in the car."

"What?"

"Get back in the car while I talk to your accomplice."

Nash rolled his eyes but did as he was told.

The smell of smoke and burnt rubber ratcheting up his nausea, Ramos trudged over to the ambulance where Delaney sat on the bumper. She was the one who looked like minced meat. Her nose was a mess, and she had blood on her shirt. He nodded to the EMT. "Does she need to be transported?"

The EMT shrugged. "She has a broken nose and some cuts that might need stitches, but she's refusing to be transported. Same as the guy she's with."

"Not smart."

"Their choice." The EMT went back to stowing his gear.

Delaney stood. She swayed, then straightened. "I'm so glad you're okay. Is your wife okay? Any baby yet?"

"No baby yet. Thanks for asking." Not the time for small talk. "What happened here?"

"Jess did this. He killed Corey. He manipulated Vince Pritchard to kill Ellie. He tried to kill me and Hunter."

"I'd be curious to hear Golightly's version of events. Where is he?"

The patrol officer who'd been guarding Delaney took a step closer. "On his way to Northeast Baptist. Apparently Ms. Broward knocked him out with an ashtray. He woke up while EMTs were working on him. He's claiming self-defense, that Mr. Nash and Ms. Broward came after him. He says Mr. Pritchard will confirm his version of the events."

"So where's Pritchard?"

The patrol officer cocked his head toward his unit. "He's not talking. He seems to be confused. He wants to talk to his attorney, but his attorney is this Golightly fellow. Mr. Pritchard says he won't know what to do until he talks to Golightly."

Andy's head throbbed. He was so sure Hunter Nash had killed Corey Broward. Golightly, a rumpled, self-effacing artist who took care of Ellie and Delaney after Broward's murder, had never been on his radar. "We'll sort it out downtown."

"You have two witnesses to whom Jess confessed." Delaney crossed her arms over her chest. Her chin went up. "Plus I preserved the knife used in Ellie's murder and your attempted murder as well as mine. It's in the hands of a crime scene investigator now. You're welcome."

"I'll personally escort you downtown." If Andy were a betting man, he would've bet his last dollar that Nash was a murderer. But never Delaney Broward. "You can give your statement there. You might want to call an attorney."

"I know. I'm an old hand at this."

Unfortunately, she was. No one should have to go through that kind of suffering. But she still wasn't allowed to take the law into her own hands. "I need to confer with my partner. Then we'll—"

A pitiful yowl interrupted him.

"The cat!" Delaney squatted and peered under the ambulance. "Hey, there you are. You're my hero." She held out her hand. "Come on, handsome, you deserve a treat after all you've been through."

What had a stray cat been through? Stifling a groan, Andy bent over and put both hands on his knees. He couldn't see said cat. "Does somebody need to call animal control?"

"Don't you dare." Delaney patted her thigh and murmured sweet nothings. "Ignore the silly man. He's just mad because two amateurs beat him to the punch."

A huge tabby, his tail in full bloom, crept from under the ambulance. "Attaboy. Come to Laney."

Two seconds later he gracefully leaped into her arms. He was so heavy she toppled backward. She righted herself and eased to her feet.

"He is a handsome dude." Andy reached out to pet him. Ears laid back, the animal hissed. Andy jerked his hand back. "Do we need to return your buddy to his owner?"

Delaney explained how the cat had been key to getting the jump on Jess and Vince. "His owner is away, and his house is burnt to a crisp."

"I guess that means he's a hero and homeless." Andy jerked his thumb toward Flores's car. "Have a seat in the Charger. Don't say anything. Maybe Flores won't notice he has a cat in his pristine vehicle. Just don't let him pee, okay?"

For the first time Delaney smiled. "We'll see."

Andy didn't return the smile. This was far from over. A furry friend purring in her arms might be what Delaney needed to get through the ugliness still to come. However it turned out.

CHAPTER 48

Sunshine and the smell of freshly turned dirt. Doctors should offer that prescription for what ailed a person. Delaney adjusted her Texas Rangers ball cap and surveyed her work. Most of the summer squash, sweet potatoes, and pumpkins were planted in neat, marked rows in her newly tilled garden. She still had cucumbers, bell peppers, broccoli, and cantaloupe to plant. Her mouth watered at the thought of the sauteed vegetables and steamed brown rice she would make in the summer.

Her appetite had been slow to return, but color had crept into her face. The cuts had healed. The nightmares still came most nights, but her therapist said she should expect that. They would diminish with time.

That hadn't been Delaney's experience.

She straightened and rubbed her aching back muscles. The late-April sun, harbinger of an impending long, hot summer, beat down on her shoulders and neck. It felt good. Streak raised his head from his spot on the back porch where he lazed on the rug and pretended to guard the back door. So far he'd deigned to eat her food and sleep on her couch. He didn't think much of her taste in music or her boxing.

Streak's owner still hadn't shown up. A message left at the number Detective Ramos had provided had gone unanswered. The detective theorized the guy learned of his mobile home's demise and decided to stay in Corpus on whatever beach he currently chose to squat.

Which was fine with Delaney. Every country home needed a guard cat.

The next patch of garden belonged to the bell peppers. She headed to the wheelbarrow that held her flourishing plants. The last month had included multiple interviews with the police and an assistant district attorney, Ellie's funeral, as well as twice weekly sessions with her therapist. More helpful had been training with a new boxing coach at a north-side gym. Her footwork had improved. So had her confidence. She now had a sparring partner. She'd reopened her shop. Orders rolled in, keeping her too busy to brood.

Detective Ramos had come to Delaney's home personally to inform her that she and Hunter were no longer suspects. He and his partner found an entire bedroom wall in Jess's apartment plastered with photos of Ellie and Delaney. Jess's phone records revealed text messages from Ellie alternately asking for help and then begging him not to reveal "their secret." Jess made many calls to Vince Pritchard's cell phone number, including the day of Ellie's murder. When Jess couldn't maintain his innocence, he tried to blame Pritchard as "out of control" and a sociopath.

At first detectives couldn't convince Pritchard to talk. Nor could his public defender. Then he asked to see his kids. The public defender suggested he agree to tell detectives everything he knew in exchange for a visit and a plea deal so he could get out of prison in time to see them graduate from college or attend their weddings.

Pritchard jumped at the chance, and it all came tumbling out in a rambling two-hour interview. He agreed to plead guilty to Ellie's murder in exchange for a twenty-five-year sentence and no fine. A charge of attempted murder of a law enforcement officer was reduced to aggravated assault against a law enforcement officer with a ten-year sentence to be served concurrently. Still, Pritchard had to be convinced to testify against Jess.

What had Jess done to earn that kind of misguided loyalty? He'd taken advantage of a man with limited intellectual capability and his love for his children. The one role Pritchard was good at—being a dad—ultimately had led to his downfall.

On the flip side of the coin, Detective Ramos proudly shared photos of his new daughter, born on her due date, with all her fingers and toes and a full head of dark hair. The detective claimed Isabella, Bella for short, would be walking and talking in full sentences any day now. His unfettered delight was a surefire antidote for the profound lack of moral compass in the other two men.

The sound of a rumbling engine forced Delaney to abandon her contemplation of evil versus good.

Hunter pulled around the house behind the garage. She'd seen him a few times since the fire. Mostly at the DA's office and Pastor James's church. They were giving each other space. That's what she called it. Hunter called it being chicken. He had texted her now and then with just the words, **Bawk. Bawk.**

Very funny.

He slid from the truck and waved. Then he strode around the truck's bed and extracted a large box from the front seat and headed her direction.

Streak rose and stretched. After a large yawn, he trotted toward the front of the house. He didn't like men much.

"What is this?" Delaney removed her hat and wiped her forehead on her T-shirt sleeve. "I've been told to beware of people who come bearing gifts."

"You'll like this one." Hunter set the box at her feet. Scratching sounds emanated from it. The lid moved. "Go on. Open it. I promise you'll like it."

Delaney squatted and pulled back the flaps. Two bright-eyed brown puppies stared up at her. In a flash they leaped over the side of the box and proceeded to chase each other around the yard. "You didn't."

"I did. Nobody should live out in the country without dogs. Least of all you. You grew up with Nana and Pops's dogs. You know what good company they are."

They were adorable. However, puppies were a lot of work. Like taking care of babies. Delaney had a shop to run . . . They *were* cute. "You should never give people gifts that are living without asking them first. I'm told that's a rule."

The slightly bigger puppy raced up to Delaney. He nudged her with a cold, wet nose and woofed. She couldn't help herself. She knelt and petted his silky coat. He licked her hands and face.

"Puppy kisses are the best. That's Bounce. He wants you to play. He's Hop-a-long's—Hop for short—older brother. Hop's a little more reserved, but he warms up quickly."

Delaney sat back on her behind. Bounce crawled into her lap and licked her face with a vigor that felt like a good washing with a new washcloth. "Did you name them?"

"I did. They never stop moving."

"What breed are they?"

"Mutt. The lady at the shelter said they're probably a mix of beagle and some kind of cocker spaniel, maybe. They shouldn't get too big. They're three months old. Mom and her litter of six were dumped at the humane society about seven weeks ago."

Hop toddled across the yard. He stopped a few feet from Delaney and barked. He whirled in a circle, stopped, and barked again.

Hunter laughed. "He's getting impatient with his brother."

"Go on, go play." Delaney nudged Bounce toward his brother. "Your brother's calling you." Bounce went. The two nipped at each other and then raced toward the house. Streak would not be happy. "You know you'll have to share custody. I work a lot of hours."

"Perfect. I can come around in the morning and walk them since I don't go to work until after lunch."

When she wasn't home. She could deal with that. "And help potty train them."

"Yeah, sure."

"I mean it."

"I know. I have beds, bowls, and a big bag of food in the truck." He shoved his windblown black hair back from his face. He'd let it grow out since leaving prison. He looked more like the old Hunter. Except for the scar and the muscles. "I also bought some bones and chew toys in case they like to chew."

"You were awfully sure I'd say yes."

"You loved Samson."

"That was a long time ago."

"Speaking of which." He edged closer. "You know what today is?"

It was the tenth anniversary of Corey's death. The thought had driven her from bed at 4:00 a.m. into her makeshift gym, where she'd boxed until her arms could no longer lift the gloves. "I don't. I've lost track of time."

"Fiesta is in full swing. NIOSA starts tonight."

The angst mixed with longing in his voice jolted through Delaney. "Surely you don't want to go to NIOSA."

"No way. It's weird, that's all. Ten years almost to the day. It's hard to believe Corey has been gone that long. Everything has changed. We've changed." Hunter's somber gaze enveloped her whole. He blinked and the connection broke. "Your garden is big. I'm impressed. You have the right idea."

"We'll see. It always depends on how much rain we get and how fast it gets hot." Talking about gardening was far easier than facing a decade without Corey. Or the fact that his killer had walked freely, lived and breathed freely, for all those years while Hunter had been wrongly incarcerated. "Gardening in South Texas isn't easy."

"But worth it if you get fresh veggies." Hunter moved past her and knelt at the edge of the tilled earth. He scooped up a handful of dirt and let it stream through his fingers. "Did you hear that Jess plans to represent himself?"

"ADA Spinelli told me. He entered a not guilty plea. He claims Pritchard acted on his own in Ellie's death and that we lied about him admitting to killing Corey. He's a piece of work."

"His dad died last week. I wonder if he feels even one iota of guilt over the pain he's caused so many people. He probably hastened the poor man's death. He used his hunting knife."

"Jess will never take responsibility for his own actions. He blames you and Corey and me and Ellie . . . It doesn't matter as long as he spends the rest of his life in prison." Delaney picked up a bell pepper plant. "Would you like to help me with the garden?"

Hunter accepted her offering. "You'll have to show me what to do. I'm not exactly a green thumb kind of guy."

Delaney knelt next to him. He smelled of puppy, peppermint gum, and Adidas Pulse aftershave. She dug the hole and then carefully pulled the plant from its tiny container. "You just pop it in the hole and brush the dirt around it and pat it down. Done."

"When did you stop wearing glasses?"

"Hmm?"

"Your glasses. When did you stop wearing them?"

"Five years ago, when I started my apprenticeship at the shop, started working out, and boxing."

"You were making yourself into someone new."

"Sort of. I guess I did."

"Me too. Being in prison forced me to become a different person."

Hunter's exoneration had been widely publicized in the media in tandem with the sordid story of how Jess and Ellie's relationship turned sour, withered, and died. The police department's head honchos were probably holding their collective breaths, waiting for Hunter to file his civil lawsuit against the city of San Antonio.

They'd be waiting a long time. Hunter said he didn't blame Detective Ramos and his wife or the district attorney's office. Jess had been such an unlikely suspect, while Hunter and Corey had argued endlessly and in full view of the world. However circumstantial, the evidence had pointed to Hunter. A jury of his peers had convicted him.

That didn't mean Detective Ramos didn't regret that his first homicide investigation had resulted in an innocent man's incarceration. He'd offered a heartful apology to both Hunter and Delaney prefaced with the undeniable observation that no words or actions could right this wrong. He and his wife would have to live with it. Hunter's attitude of forgiveness would help.

Michael and his ex-wife were still locked in a bitter custody battle. In the meantime Delaney and Cam did their best to give Jacob and Skye "auntie time" as often as possible. Gerard Knox, perhaps out of an abundance of caution given the authorities' newfound interest in his business dealings, had decided to shop for another accountant. Michael sold Ellie's shop and remodeled the house as if that would ease the pain of her betrayal and death. Healing would take time.

"We're both older, wiser, and kinder." Delaney rested her hand in the grass a hair's breadth from Hunter's. "We grew up. Corey never had that chance."

"We have a second chance, one he didn't get." Hunter took her hand in his. "Hi, I'm Hunter Nash."

Delaney shook his hand. "Nice to meet you, Hunter. I'm Delaney Broward."

"Would you be interested in driving up to Bandera to the O.S.T. Restaurant with me one of these days?"

The O.S.T.—Old Spanish Trail Restaurant—was known for its down-home cooking and John Wayne memorabilia. "Like a date, you mean?"

"Our first date," Hunter amended. "I'll actually pay. I have a few paychecks under my belt now."

He was saving to get his own place. Delaney shook her head. "I don't mind going Dutch."

"Maybe next time."

A first date. Delaney eyed Bounce and Hop, who were engaged in a fierce wrestling match complete with deep growling and posturing. "Could we go today?"

"As soon as we plant our garden."

"Now it's *our* garden?"

"I expect to get my share of the bounty too." Hunter rose and held out his hand again. This time he helped her up. He held her there, his dark eyes a maelstrom of emotions. "At the risk of getting ahead of myself, I'm wondering if we could seal this new start with a kiss—just one, a short—"

Stretching on her tiptoes, Delaney silenced him with her lips. His arms wrapped around her waist. His lips were familiar yet entirely new. A tremor ran through her. Her heart couldn't beat fast enough to keep up. The volatile, crazy Hunter had ceased to exist, replaced by this new clean-and-sober man who was the sum of his past experiences. This Hunter kissed with a ferocity that came from years of suffering, of pain, of loss, and hurt instead of from drugs and alcohol. There was no denying this Hunter. He wanted it all, every last piece of her heart.

Nothing would keep the new Delaney from giving Hunter his heart's desire. The Pandora's box of emotions that had dogged her since that terrible day in Corey's studio closed. The lock made a satisfying *click*. She would have to deal with them, one by one, but she wouldn't be alone.

She and Hunter had each other.

Hunter leaned back and smiled. "There you are."

"Here *we* are."

Together.

ACKNOWLEDGMENTS

I feel as if I should reassure readers of my romantic suspense novels that the beloved tourist attractions in San Antonio are safe, peaceful, fun places for people to visit. The crimes described in these stories are figments of my overactive, feverish imagination. I love setting novels in a city so steeped in history and diverse cultures. It's been a joy to write these stories.

I always thank my HarperCollins Christian Publishing editor Becky Monds when I write acknowledgments, but it's never enough. With *Trust Me*, she has gone an additional extra mile (or maybe a thousand) by reading two separate versions of the book, both well over the contractual word count—a time-consuming endeavor—in order to help me decide which worked better. She helped me to get the kinks out of the plot and rev up the romance. To say her help is invaluable doesn't do her justice. As usual, line editor Julee Schwarzburg applied her finely honed skills to straighten out a thousand and one style errors. Not to mention the endless repetition of certain words. Her patience is the stuff of legends.

My love and thanks to my husband, Tim, for putting up with my crazy hours and distracted conversations. Being married to a novelist isn't easy, but he makes it look that way.

As always, I deeply appreciate my readers. Bless you for your support.

I thank God for all He has done in giving me direction and purpose. To Him be the glory.

DISCUSSION QUESTIONS

1. Delaney lost her parents in a car accident as a child, then her grandparents, and years later her brother was murdered. The man she loved was convicted of his murder. She lost her faith in God. As Christians, what should we say to those who suffer about God's plan, where God's goodness is, and what the reasons might be for their suffering?

2. Delaney knows Corey partook in pot smoking. She didn't realize he was doing other illegal drugs as well. Or she didn't want to believe it. As loved ones often do, she turned a blind eye to his downward spiral. What could she have done differently to help him? What would you have done in her shoes?

3. Delaney decides to let Hunter spend the night in her house after he'd been in prison eight years for killing her brother. Would you have allowed it? What do you think it says about Delaney's character that she makes that choice?

4. Delaney hasn't had a relationship with a man since Hunter went to prison. She's reinvented herself as a strong, self-sufficient woman, but she's closed off from relationships. She doesn't even have a dog. How would you suggest she learn to trust her heart to a man—especially if that man is Hunter—after all these years?

5. Jess felt left out and bullied by the co-op members who were supposed to be his friends. Do you think Corey, Hunter, and the other members bear some responsibility for the crimes he committed and manipulated Vince into committing? Why or why not?

6. Corey cheated on Ellie, so she cheated on him with a friend, Jess. Their poor choices led to their demise. What could they have done differently to change the terrible outcome? Is there a moral to their story? What do you learn from it?

7. Hunter was convicted of murder and spent eight years in prison for a crime he didn't commit. He grew closer to God during that time. He honed his faith and wanted to help restore Delaney's faith. How do you think you would react in a similar situation? Do you grow closer to God during difficult seasons, or are you like Delaney, who turned her back on God?

8. Detective Ramos headed the investigation that led to Hunter's wrongful conviction. An innocent man spent eight years in prison. How do you think Detective Ramos feels? How would you feel in his shoes? What would you do or say to try to mitigate the harm done? Can it be mitigated?

9. Michael Hill and his first wife divorced because she didn't want to give up her career as a flight attendant to be a full-time mother. Detective Ramos's wife chose to switch from being in the field as a homicide detective to a desk job in cyberterrorism so that their children would have one parent less likely to be in harm's way. She gave up a job she loved for her children. What do you think about the different ways in which the women in these relationships handled their roles as parents? Should women be the ones to make these sacrifices? What about the men? Are there any lessons to be learned here?

ABOUT THE AUTHOR

PHOTO BY TIM IRVIN

Kelly Irvin is a bestselling, award-winning author of nearly thirty novels and stories. A retired public relations professional, Kelly lives with her husband, Tim, in San Antonio. They have two children, three grandchildren, and two ornery cats.

Visit her online at KellyIrvin.com
Facebook: @Kelly.Irvin.Author
Twitter: @Kelly_S_Irvin
Instagram: @Kelly_irvin